To Write a Wrong

Copyright © 2012 by Eli Vlaisavljevich

All rights reserved. No part of this book may be reproduced or transmitted in any form or by any means without the written permission of the author.

ISBN-10: 1480173339
ISBN-13: 978-1480173330

ToWriteAWrong.com

Foreword: The following is the autobiography of Mr. E. Mann. Mr. E is best known as the author of numerous critically acclaimed novels including *Mom in Heaven*, *Father's Day*, and the top selling book of the last century, *Life by Choice*. The rest of you know him as a beloved author, but, to me, he will always be remembered as the best friend I no longer have. I spent my life looking up to this man. I admired his altruistic nature and tireless devotion to making the world a better place. While the world was raving about his pinnacle novel, *Dream On*, he quietly hid from the limelight to focus his time and money into his various charities. To the world, Mr. E. Mann was an inspiration. To me, he was simply my best friend. I loved this man and am saddened both by the fact that he is gone as well as the way in which he left. It is hard to lose a future with your best friend, but the true tragedy of our parting was that he was also taken from my past.

I last saw Mr. E. Mann two years prior to the publication of this book. I had driven down to meet him for lunch before he boarded a private plane in Detroit, MI. I didn't know where he was going. All I knew was that he wished to see me before he left. We had a beer and shared a few old stories. When it was time to board his plane, my friend gave me this book with the instruction that I was to be the first to read it. He told me the book's fate was now in my hands. As Mr. E boarded his plane, never to be seen again, his last words were, "Don't judge a book by its cover." I laughed as I looked down at the plain cover of what I accurately judged to be the autobiography of the colorful individual I loved. It was only after reading that I came to realize my friend's final words referred not to his book but to the main character I had misjudged for far too long. Although I have since received a few post cards, I never laid eyes on Mr. E. Mann again.

I would like to end this foreword with a forewarning. Those of you hoping to read a cheerful story about the man behind your favorite inspirational novels should immediately return this book. In the Bureau, we have files labeled "Burn After Reading," but this book is branded with a "Burn Before Reading" disclaimer for a reason. I advise all of you to close this book and move on with your lives. I spent my life struggling in a relentless pursuit of truth, and I now realize I was a man with no eyes complaining about being colorblind. I guess, in the end, I am forced to agree with my friend that sometimes the true story is not the better story. This is the true story of Mr. E. Mann. I decided to publish this book unedited because I believe it is the right thing to do. For those of you who may question my decision, I can only respond by saying that it was not easy. This book broke my heart, but I believe people have the right to know the truth no matter how wretched it may be. My motive is not to promote or glorify the views of my former friend in any way but simply to let the world know the true story behind the Mann.

Detective Derek "Derbe" Felidae
Traverse City Police Department
Federal Bureau of Investigation

TO WRITE A WRONG

Mr. E. Mann

To my enemies: May you live forever.

Table of Contents

Preface -- 5

Chapter 1: The Chicken or the Egg --- 7

Chapter 2: My Irresistible Desire to be Irresistibly Desired ---------------------- 24

Chapter 3: Mom in Heaven --- 46

Chapter 4: Father's Day --- 79

Chapter 5: Alone Together --- 94

Chapter 6: Blind Faith --- 106

Chapter 7: The Diction of Fiction --- 113

Chapter 8: Stevie Wonders -- 119

Chapter 9: Pretty Ugly --- 124

Chapter 10: The Little Injun that Could --------------------------------------- 128

Chapter 11: Life by Choice -- 135

Chapter 12: Walk like a Man -- 141

Chapter 13: The Pursuit of Purity --- 149

Chapter 14: Child Rearing -- 160

Chapter 15: The Cereal Killer --- 171

Chapter 16: Born Again --- 177

Chapter 17: Publish or Perish --- 186

Chapter 18: United We Stand --- 197

Chapter 19: Dream On --- 206

Chapter 20: To Write a Wrong -- 229

Preface: When writing his autobiography, Mark Twain so appropriately stated, "Biographies are but the clothes and buttons of the man, the biography of the man himself cannot be written." As I sit down to write my own autobiography, I am experiencing the same feeling of regret that I will be unable to share the entirety of my story with you. Any attempt to portray the true breadth of my emotional and intellectual journey would be futile. Nonetheless, the purpose of this book, my last book, is to share at least a small fraction of myself with the world and provide a few answers to questions I avoided along the way.

I have long reflected on writing my autobiography. I wondered if I should tell the entire truth as every worthwhile life includes a few skeletons in the closet. I was also unsure from what perspective I would write. The story of a person's life, ironically, turns out to be not about a single person but rather about the many different characters an individual mutates into over the course of a lifetime. In the end, I decided to write the unfiltered truth and finally explain the motivation behind my books. I know some will be disheartened by the foundation of my stories, but I caution you to remember that you can't make an omelet without breaking a few eggs. The potential of a person can never be reached, and ultimately rots away, unless you crack the shell in time. My stories are the same way. You can't resurrect a character without killing them first. The ends always justify the means. You may find that you admire some moments in my life and despise others, but I hope you will conclude that the result of my life, and the work I have left behind, has made the world a better place. I plan to leave the fate of my story in the hands of Derbe, my best friend and first reader of this book. Whether the world reads my story will be left up to you, Derbe. I grant you the power over my eternity. You have the choice to give me eternal life or let me pass quietly out of existence.

Before I begin my story, I want to thank everyone who made my life special. I had the pleasure of being part of an incredible family without whom life would have been worth living. I love you all more than you could ever comprehend. I wish I could give every one of you the gift of immortality. I am also indebted to the many friends who brought joy to my life especially my two best friends, Mike Wagner and Derbe Felidae. Additional thanks go to Derbe's colleagues at the Traverse City Police Department and FBI whose trust in me made my story possible. Finally, I want to thank the characters of my novels. Your perfection is eternal.

It is my firm belief as an author that a story is only as strong as the main character. Therefore, I fully understand this autobiography will pale in comparison to my previous books. I had the honor to write about many marvelous protagonists in my career and have been asked countless times whether these characters actually exist or are even slightly based on real people. I have always replied the same way: the characters exist as long as someone is around to read their story. Achilles was killed when he was young but is still alive today. Fiction is the one beacon shining through the storm clouds of reality.

Fiction is the lone shelter for lasting happiness in our world. As an author, I lived my life as a God creating eternal happiness out of this sorrowful reality. I transformed acute pain into chronic bliss. I am proud of what I accomplished with the supernatural gift of fiction and only hope future gods will learn from my example. The difference between my legacy and my fellow deities' is that I have never created a single life of pain. As you read my story, I urge you to keep in mind that, contrary to our own lives, my characters know only happy endings.

CHAPTER 1

The Chicken or the Egg

A happy childhood has spoiled many a promising life.

-Robertson Davies

CHAPTER 1: The Chicken or the Egg

A life is a story. This is my story. As the title of this chapter suggests, it is not always easy to pinpoint the beginning of a story, but, being a pro-abortion individual that believes life starts at the emergence of consciousness rather than conception, I will skip the initial years of my life and instead start at the beginning of my memories.

Not surprisingly, my first memory was on a hockey rink. I was three years old and had just opened my first pair of skates on Christmas morning. My parents walked me to an outdoor rink in Eveleth, Minnesota, where I would step on the ice for the first time. It was a moment I had anticipated for months, and my excitement grew with each second. I squeezed my parents' hands tightly as they guided me passively over the ice. My parents took me on one trip completely across the rink, and I crashed directly into a snow bank. I have no recollection of anything after this collision but have often wondered what motivated my parents to lead me into that pile of snow. This first memory was likely the beginning of my sadistic sense of humor and perhaps the first time my dreams hit the cold wall of reality.

The second memory of my childhood has been retold in our family for years. I was about five years old and was, once again, at an ice rink. At the time, my dad was in the process of turning me into a tough little hockey player and training me not to cry on the ice. As I skated slowly around the rink, I was knocked over by a speed skater and hurt my right arm. I immediately began to cry causing my dad to yell, "Don't cry on the ice! Do you want to be a figure skater or do you want to be a hockey player?" Fighting my tears, I whimpered back, "I-I-I-I want to be a hockey player" and grabbed my dad's hand. My dad often told the story of how upset he was as he watched me skating next to him, holding his hand with my left hand, while my right arm was curled up on my side like it had just been amputated. We continued skating for a half hour until I was no longer crying. Finally, my dad looked down and asked if my arm really hurt that bad. When I nodded in fear, we went to the locker room to check it out. My arm was so swollen that we couldn't remove my jacket and had to cut through my coat with a pocket knife. My dad was overcome with embarrassment when he heard two old ladies next to us whispering about child abuse. We went to the hospital and found out I had broken my arm in two places. I still remember my mom racing into the hospital, looking at my cast, glaring at my dad, and wrapping her arms around me. This is really the only vivid memory I have of my mom. Her cancer was discovered soon after, and she was gone within four months.

All I remember about my mom's death is that our house was filled with family. My dad had decided to bring a hospital bed home so my mom would be able to spend her last days with the people she loved. I don't even remember seeing my mom or saying goodbye. I was only five years old, and, looking back, it is basically just a blur. All that remained of my mom were a couple pictures, a sweet letter she wrote me before she died, and the stories my dad would tell. Whenever I observed people in agony after losing a parent in the subsequent years, I was always a bit envious that they had the pleasure of knowing what they had lost. I was left without any inside jokes or little reminders of my mom and always wished for even the slightest memory to connect me with this remarkable woman.

I loved listening to my dad's stories about the mom I never knew. I soon learned my mom was an absolutely perfect person. After she died, we started to refer to her as "Mom in Heaven" which is something that continued well past our childhood. To this day, my sisters and I still call her "Mom in Heaven." I always had a secret appreciation for the fact that not one person in a house full of Atheists would bring up the obvious irony of using this name. This hypocrisy was always quietly ignored. Of all the stories my dad would tell, I most loved hearing the story of how he met my mother. My dad had just returned from the war and went back to college to get another degree. A friend of my dad's asked him to give his girlfriend a ride home from the University of Minnesota to the Iron Range. When my mom walked up, my dad fell instantly in love. They talked the entire four hour drive home like they had known each other for centuries. The following week, my dad ran into her on campus and found out she had broken up with her boyfriend. My dad immediately asked her out for dinner. A week later, he asked her to marry him. A year later, they were married and spent more than twenty years happily married without a single bad day before she died. Although it took me far too long, I eventually came to realize that my idealistic perspective on women and my desire for a perfect romantic relationship could be traced back to my parents' story. There was nothing I enjoyed more as a kid than hearing about my mom and wishing I had known this flawless person.

Even though I lost my mom when I was five, I had an unquestionably enviable childhood. I was a quiet, polite kid who was consumed with playing hockey and doing well in school. These were the only things of value in my young life. All I wanted to be when I grew up was a college hockey player like my uncle Dan had been. To me, this would be reaching the pinnacle of life on earth. All my time was spent in the basement or driveway imagining I was playing in the WCHA in front of thousands of people. My entire childhood was centered on hockey. In hindsight, what I loved about the game were the friendships and memories. When I was ten, my dad even bought an old school bus to take us to tournaments around the country and throughout Canada. We replaced the bus interior with airline seats, booths for playing cards, and a huge bed in the back. I probably had more fun on that bus than anywhere else in my childhood whether it was playing knee hockey and WWF in the back or listening to the parents yell at the kids for playing Russian roulette with cap guns after the lights were turned off. I always seemed to love the hockey trips even more than I loved the hockey games.

As I mentioned, my young life revolved entirely around playing hockey and going to school. Consistently the top student in my class, I found school required only minimal effort. Because of this, I was able to devote the majority of my time to training for hockey. I was a self-motivated young man with the single minded focus of becoming the best hockey player in the world. I started lifting weights and training hours every day in hopes of someday playing for the high school team or even reaching my ultimate goal of playing college hockey. The countless hours of hard work started to pay off as I began to gain strength and improve my game. In addition to this hard work, I was fortunate to benefit from a surprising breakthrough that transformed my hockey career.

The missing link to my hockey success was right in front of me, but I simply couldn't see. Finally, fate intervened. It all started when my sister was told she needed glasses. On the way home from the optometrist, she was showing off how much better she could read the street signs. After a couple signs, it became apparent that my vision was even worse than my sister's without her glasses. The next week, I made my own trip to the eye clinic. When the doctor asked how I survived so long without telling anyone about my eyes, I informed him I never knew my vision was bad because I had never known anything else. Leaving the doctor's office with my first pair of contacts was one of the most remarkable experiences of my life. No drug in the world could recreate the incredible feeling of looking out the window on that ride home. People who have never had bad vision often laugh when I describe the experience. The two things I was most shocked to see were grass and trees. Before this day, I had never seen the individual blades of grass or the separate leaves on a tree. After finally seeing the world clearly, I was amazed at what I had been missing. Once your eyes are opened to reality, it is impossible to go back. There is no way I could function a single day without my contacts anymore. The best result, as far as I was concerned at the time, was seeing the puck on the ice. I was shocked at my first practice when I actually saw a puck on the far side of the rink. Before this point, I had to squint to barely see the puck on my stick. Ironically, the fact that I had played most of my life with terrible vision turned out to be extremely beneficial to my skill development. My hand-eye coordination and "hockey sense" were vastly improved from this experience especially once I got my contacts and could take full advantage of my years of compensating for my previous disability.

It was now the summer before I entered eighth grade, and I could see for the first time in my life. I decided to try out for the high school team even though it was rare for a freshman to make the squad let alone an eighth grader. Fortunately, my hard work paid off, and I made the team. Not only was this essential to the upward trajectory of my hockey career, but the social effects on my life were equally rewarding. My self-confidence started to blossom, and I became comfortable in my skin. Whenever I went to school events, I would get invited to hang out with the most popular seniors. When I attended volleyball games, the seniors would push someone off of the gym stage so I could sit in the seats normally reserved for upper classmen. This was quite an ego boost for a quiet kid like me. It felt awesome being the only eighth grader wearing a high school letter jacket. As trivial as these things seem today, they were immensely important as they helped me start high school on the right foot.

I had an incredible time playing high school hockey and collected a ton of awards along the way. During my sophomore year, I began to get recruited by college teams which only increased my dedication. As my skills continued to develop, I saw myself stepping ever closer to my dreams. My senior year of hockey was flawless, and I collected more awards both athletically and academically. The entire year was spent talking to scouts, taking visits to different schools, and getting ready to decide where to spend the next few years of my life. Overall, playing high school hockey was a pleasurable time that was an essential stepping stone to reaching my goals. My dream was now but a heartbeat away.

During my senior year of high school, I was offered athletic scholarships to Northern Michigan, Michigan Tech, Denver, Harvard, UMD, Boston College, and the Air Force Academy. My dad was pushing for Harvard, but, at that point in my life, I was still primarily focused on playing hockey and wanted to play in the best league in the country, the WCHA. Because Denver and UMD were offering a little less money, and no one in their right mind would go to a shithole like Northern Michigan, I decided on Michigan Tech. Everything was now set for me to live my childhood dream. Before I even arrived at Tech, I had already played hundreds of college hockey games while I was daydreaming at the local rink or on my roller blades in the driveway. I had won more championships than I could count, and it was now going to become a reality. I signed with Michigan Tech but decided to take the common detour of playing two years in the United States Hockey League before college.

I was drafted to play for the Stars in Lincoln, Nebraska, and had no idea what to expect. I had never lived away from home and was nervous about starting a new life. The first day in Lincoln, I took a tour of the rink and then met the housing family I would be living with, the Greens. After getting settled at my house, I spent the rest of my first night meeting my new teammates. The returning players had planned a huge party, and I was picked up by another newcomer, Dillon, around seven. It is ironic the first person I met was Dillon because he turned out to be one of the best friends of my life. Dillon and I got along right from the start, and, by the time we arrived at the party, we were fired up and ready to go. I had gone to a few parties in high school, but Lincoln was clearly going to be much different. The house was filled with drinks and girls. It felt like a movie. I drank more alcohol and went further with a girl in my first night in Lincoln than I had in my entire high school career. That party was just the beginning. Before this point I was a quiet, sheltered kid. Lincoln forced me to grow up fast. Every day brought a new experience whether it was signing autographs in a bar or getting free burritos at Chipotle. It was hard to believe how fabulous Lincoln was. My life had accomplished the impossible feat of being even better than I had dreamt.

My first game in Lincoln only added to my sense of awe. I have never seen a better atmosphere than the crowd at the Ice Box. We took the ice through clouds of smoke and a huge light show. When my name was called for the starting line-up, I skated under a massive star that was lowered from the rafters. I raced across the ice deafened by the noise of Thunderstruck while the crowd shook the building. When the puck dropped, my heart pumped out of my chest. The game didn't slow down for one second until the final buzzer sounded. This adrenaline-fueled blur was merely a small sample of the shock of my new situation. As the season went on, I got used to the different style of play as well as my new life off the ice. In Lincoln, we were treated like celebrities. It was exciting to get noticed by people and have swarms of girls chasing after us. At the same time, it was strange to read about my team in the Sunday paper. When we were winning, life was awesome, but, if we lost a couple games, the pressure would start to set in. The possibility of being traded was permanently tattooed in everyone's mind, and, after losing two games in December, I was forced to say goodbye to Dillon. This experience taught me a valuable lesson about the fragility of the present at a time when I was not equipped to deal with the news. Even before I became a writer, I was already becoming a critic of the author of my story. My friendship with Dillon would survive, but I hadn't yet developed the proper perspective to understand this. In my later years as an author, my broadened worldview would allow me to see the entirety of circumstances instead of being blinded by temporal myopia. However, at that moment, I was simply saddened by the loss of my friend. From that day forward, I embraced the reality of the Lincoln lifestyle and was cognizant of the uncertainty of my situation.

Other than the anxiety accompanying the persistent pressure to win, life in Lincoln was perfect. All I had to do was play hockey and have fun. My freedom during this time, along with the parties and quasi-celebrity status, made it the most pleasurable period of my young life. Even though I was beginning to hate the fact that so much of our fun depended on the scores of our games, I loved life in Lincoln and was disappointed when the year was over. After a week of debauchery following the season, I spent the entire summer training hard and counting down the days until I would return. My first year in Lincoln was a bit of a gong show, but I enjoyed every minute. It was a liberating year in which I gained invaluable perspective and had my eyes opened to a previously unknown world.

When I returned after the summer, things were even better than before. My second year in Lincoln was by far my best year of hockey. I got off to a superb start, and things only improved from there. As I continued to get points, life off the ice got even better. I would do interviews with reporters and felt like I could do nothing wrong as long as I kept scoring. I always had this feeling in my gut that it was absolutely idiotic how great I was treated for something as insignificant as hockey, but that isn't to say I didn't enjoy the attention. No one is immune to the effects of a good compliment. Praise is an addictive drug. My perspective was crippled by this positive reinforcement, and I was unable to keep myself from this emotional high. My addiction to success constantly grew, and, luckily, I continued to score points and get my fix. I made the all-star game and ended up leading the league in scoring. Lincoln was the peak of my enjoyment playing the game of hockey. Even though I thought it was comical that I was put on such a pedestal simply for success in hockey, I was completely consumed by the moment. I had accomplished everything I had hoped for when I came to Lincoln while extracting all possible pleasure out of my time in the USHL. I was now moving to college like an addict looking for his next hit. As often happens, the Lincoln high inevitably led to a hangover at Michigan Tech.

Please don't let the last comment deceive you; I loved my time at Michigan Tech. I just didn't love it for the reasons I had dreamt of. Ever since I was a young child, I imagined college hockey would be the climax of my life, and Lincoln gave me every indication that I had guessed correctly. I should have been excited for my future hockey career, but, for some reason, I could feel myself losing my passion for the game. Even during my successful last year in Lincoln, I started to hate the meaningless things that seemed to be valued as markers of success. My real strengths were my creativity and sense of humor, but I was instead known purely as a hockey player. Even though this identity came with many social benefits, I resented it more every day. The summer before I got to college, I spent significant time reading for the first time in my life. It was during this period that I scribbled part of a first draft of *Mom in Heaven* and probably unconsciously began my desire to become an author.

When I arrived at Michigan Tech, I found myself much busier than I had expected. It wasn't that the classes were hard. I breezed through the coursework with minimal effort. What actually made me busy was becoming immersed in new ideas. As a Biomedical Engineering major, I starting working in the Biomaterials Research Laboratory and completely submerged myself in the work. In my spare time, I continued reading a variety of novels and became ever more interested in philosophy. Every book I read made me regret my lack of recreational reading in previous years. I became entranced with the ideas of Mark Twain, Einstein (philosophical work even more than his physics), Thoreau, Darwin (coming from Catholic school this was a wonderful change of pace), Skinner, and many others. I also started to change my views on the world from an optimistic Deist that just enjoyed messing with other religious people to a solid Anti-theist who loved reading Hitchens and Dawkins. My mind was opened in the same way my eyes had been opened when I first got contacts and had been in utter shock at seeing the individual blades of grass. This mental awakening was just as hard to explain as my new vision back then. Looking back, I always had some amount of rebellion against religion within me. This rebellion usually came out passive aggressively when I would show up to religion class on Friday mornings during lent with a sausage McMuffin just to piss off my teacher (also because I loved McMuffins). Another example in religion class occurred when one of the girls was getting yelled at for chewing gum in church. Our teacher said she was mixing Jesus with her gum during communion and hence throwing Jesus in the trash at the end of mass. I responded by asking if it was alright for me to chew gum since I swallow my gum and that would just mean Jesus would be inside me for seven years. That was the only time I got sent to the principal's office in all of high school, but I still think it was a convincing theological argument. At one point, my body even physically rejected religion when I fainted in the middle of a Wednesday morning mass. As I passed out, my face hit the top of a pew, a book shelf, and a kneeler before I ended up in a pool of blood on the floor. I can vividly remember waking up in horror as I saw Sister Barrett's head towering over me looking ten times its normal size and pulsing along with my heartbeat. I was given fifteen stiches in my chin and a few pills to take care of the headache, but it would have been far more beneficial long-term if the doctor had addressed the problem instead of the symptoms and prescribed Atheism instead of Advil.

Religion may have been the easiest victim of enlightenment, but it was definitely not the only one. I began to question every aspect of life, society, human nature, and the cosmos. I became enthralled with the concept of consciousness and how a sense of self emerges from a collection of neuronal connections. A strict determinist in my view of people and the universe, I challenged, and eventually rejected, every notion of free will. I started to view people as nothing more than biologic machines. Although the nature of these machines changes over time, they ultimately have to act according to their wiring. My mind was absorbed in thought, and I soon began to emerge as a different person. What Lincoln did for me socially, Michigan Tech did for me intellectually. I could see no purpose in life, but only false pots of gold at the end of imaginary rainbows. I became intellectually pessimistic even though I remained emotionally optimistic for a while longer. I still had this sense that everything was going to turn out perfect, but even that slowly eroded through a couple key relationships. More than anything, I began to hate the control society had over my life. I was in my twenties and wished to be free. It didn't take long to realize I had control over very little at Michigan Tech.

By the time my freshman hockey season started, I was all settled into the college lifestyle. I spent my first year living in the dorms. My roommate, Bill, was also on the hockey team and was one of the top pro prospects in the nation. Two other freshmen, Ryan and Drew, lived across the hall. The four of us became close and had a great time together. Although we hung out with the rest of the team, the only other guy I developed a close friendship with right away was Derbe. Derbe and I got along immediately for some reason that is hard to explain. I guess our personalities just fit well. The first night I hung out with Derbe was at a team party during the second week of school. We started taking shots in the kitchen, and, before long, we were hitting on girls as if we had been each other's wingman for years. At one point, we were split up talking to different girls when his girl came to tell me, "You know what your friend just told me? He said he was two hundred ten pounds of solid steel sex appeal." I have never laughed harder, and, although Derbe has continuously denied the truth of the girl's statement, I have always been sure to bring up the story whenever possible. That night was a fun start to the longest lasting friendship of my life. Overall, my first couple months of college were a bipolar balance between my emerging new interests and my childhood dream of being a college hockey player.

My freshman season was our best year of hockey at Michigan Tech. We won a good share of our games, and I had enough of my passion remaining to enjoy it. One thing that became immediately apparent was how structured our lives were. I would spend my mornings in class, go directly to the rink for a long practice, and then spend the rest of the evening working on coursework, doing research, or reading for pleasure when I was lucky enough to have free time. A desire for freedom and control over my life was definitely starting to emerge, but I was forced to suppress this desire while I took care of my responsibilities. One of the ultimate ironies of our society is that success can often be directly correlated to the number of suppressed desires. Perhaps this is why success doesn't breed happiness. I was focused on being successful but quickly realized my achievements would be greater in the classroom than the rink. School came so easy that I felt almost embarrassed when I was flooded with academic awards. I loved learning in class but hated being too busy with coursework to have time for reading the things I was actually passionate about. It was the same feeling I had towards loving hockey while hating the itinerary it required me to live by.

Despite my brewing discontent with the lifestyle, I had a lot of fun during my first year of college. In addition to the typical parties and girls, the hockey guys in the dorms and our buddy Les would cook weekly Sunday dinners. I loved sitting around on Sundays eating, having a few beers, and telling stories from the night before. Additionally, Derbe and I started going to a local bar, the Uphill, every Tuesday for quarter beer night. The time I spent with Derbe on these nights became the foundation for our lifelong friendship. My favorite story is from the first night we went and got absolutely bombed. Derbe had driven to the bar, and, when we walked outside after last call, he asked if I thought he was fine to drive. Before I could laugh and tell him we were obviously getting a cab, a woman of a hundred percent hillbilly lineage walked out of the bar and face planted in the middle of the sidewalk. Her husband (and probably cousin) followed soon after yelling at her to get up, but she didn't respond. The guy reached down, grabbed a handful of her hair, lifted her head up, and started dragging her across the road. I will never forget how limp this woman's body was as she was being pulled across the pavement, and I don't even want to think about her hangover the next day. When the guy reached the other side of the road (took him forever because he was drunk staggering in a zigzag pattern), he opened the back door and slid the woman onto the back seat of his car. He then got behind the wheel and took off in the worst display of drunk driving I have ever witnessed. After watching this, Derbe looked at me and said "I think we should get a cab" to which I was happy to agree.

My new friendship with Derbe highlighted a first year of college that seemed to fly by. Before I knew it, March had arrived. I will never forget the final day of practice before we left for our opening round playoff games in Colorado. After practice, I went into the training room to ice my shoulder and overheard Mike talking to Bill about their plans for the weekend. The Mike I am referring to was another teammate of mine, Mike Wagner, who had been sitting out after having hip surgery. I liked Mike but didn't really hang out with him my freshman year. It is actually funny since, by the time I graduated college, Mike would become my best friend. Anyway, Bill and Mike told me their plans, and I just listened with a smile. Mike had a way of talking that always inspired me, and, for the first of many times I would spend listening to Mike's future plans, I highly doubted the actual future could match the one he was envisioning in his mind. As usual, I was right.

When we got back from Colorado the following Monday, I learned that Bill was facing expulsion from school. The news came as an absolute shock and added to the sadness I was already feeling for Bill. About a month earlier, Bill had blown out his knee and was informed that his career was over. It was heartbreaking to watch my friend's professional hockey dreams destroyed, and the worst part was the powerless feeling of being a helpless bystander. I had done my best to console him, but hollow sympathy is useless when it isn't accompanied by a solution. Bill had spent his whole life dreaming of playing in the NHL, and, as much as I wanted to help, there was nothing I could do to save his dream. I knew Bill was going through a difficult time, but it wasn't until I returned from Colorado that the full extent of his downward spiral was revealed. Upon my return, I learned that Bill was facing expulsion for stealing prescription drugs. Unfortunately for Bill, Mike was the one who caught him. Bill had done his best to convince Mike to keep the secret, but Mike was never the type of person to sacrifice his integrity. As a result, Bill's actions were reported, and he was now facing expulsion from the university. The coaches were sympathetic towards Bill, but they ultimately concluded that his injury wasn't a sufficient excuse to justify the crime he had committed. Personally, I was disappointed in Bill's actions, but I understood the addiction he had developed and was mostly just worried about his wellbeing.

When I returned home that night, I tried to reach out to my friend, but he just pushed me away. Instead of discussing his problems, Bill sat down at his desk, scribbled something on a piece of paper, and then left the room slamming the door behind him. After he was gone, I walked over to see what he had written. As I read the first sentence, I realized it was a suicide letter. Bill briefly apologized for stealing the drugs, but the majority of the letter stated that he couldn't envision living now that his dreams of playing in the NHL had been destroyed. I immediately panicked and ran out to catch him. When I didn't see Bill in the parking lot, I got in my car and began driving around. I circled through Houghton blindly hoping I would somehow run into him. I unsuccessfully searched all the places I thought Bill could be. I called other guys on the team trying to sound nonchalant because I didn't want everyone to know the situation. When I got ahold of Kevin, one of our goalies, he told me Bill had stopped by about twenty minutes earlier to pick up his shotgun. I was immediately devastated when Kevin said, "Of course I gave it to him. It's his gun, and he needed it for hunting this week." About a minute after I hung up on Kevin, I saw an ambulance racing down College Avenue and turned in a state of silent fear. As I followed the ambulance, Bill's truck passed me in the other direction. I slammed on the brakes, made a U-turn, and started the pursuit. After following Bill for many miles in a high speed chase, he finally pulled over. I went to talk to Bill, and everything worked out in the end as he slowly calmed down during our discussion. As always, it was the look of sadness in his eyes that ultimately broke my heart. Growing up, I was constantly tormented by the pain of people I loved but couldn't cure. Bill and I had a deep conversation, and, after talking through things for a couple hours, I convinced him to come home. As I went to sleep, I was sad for what my friend was going through but thankful he was alive.

The next day, Bill met with the coaches and learned he had been removed from the team. However, they made a deal with the school so he could finish his degree without being expelled. I was happy to see Bill move past this incident, but it would later become clear that he would never recover from the events of that week. My friend's spirit had been destroyed along with his dreams, and it was a tragedy to watch. Even though Bill got kicked off the team, I was just grateful he was alive. Looking back, I realize Bill's survival was an undesirable outcome for his wellbeing. If Bill had died, we would have spent the next few weeks honoring his memory. No one would have uttered a negative word but rather would have spoken softly about the tragedy. Instead of being removed from the team in shame, Bill would have been remembered with fondness. Unfortunately for Bill, he didn't go through with his suicide plan and had to live through the utter hell that followed. As thankful as I was at the time, I regret that I had not yet reached the clarity of mind to understand the effects of my actions, and I am ashamed of the detriment those actions have caused Bill in the years since.

After my freshman season ended, I moved out of the dorms and into a house off campus. Living with Ryan and Drew during my sophomore and junior years was awesome. The three of us had a tremendous time together, and we became lifelong friends. I have so many fond memories in that house. Whether it was the crazy nights we enjoyed or the quiet mornings that followed, my time at home during those two years was a comforting balance to the rink and classroom. We threw quite a few parties at our house, and it was a good thing we had these nights to distract us from hockey because my second and third seasons were pretty rough. We lost the majority of our games, and all the fun was slowly stripped away. For the first time, I dreaded going to the rink. As much as I enjoyed the other aspects of my life, my daily hockey chore was an enormous roadblock preventing my happiness. I got so sick of listening to my coaches and teammates give their massive speeches about conquering obstacles or achieving goals. I would find myself fighting back laughter listening to guys talk about the importance of being a good teammate instead of being a good friend. If any of them are reading this book, I apologize for the fact that I was a nice guy that was inconsequential to your hockey career instead of a cunt that really pushed you to work on those crossovers.

Hockey had been the primary focus of my entire life but was no longer even weakly attached to my desires. The only reason I wanted to win games was to mitigate my stress the following week. I consistently enjoyed my life at home and school, but whether I enjoyed hockey varied from day to day. My fondest memories from this time are stupid little things around the house like arguing with the guys to close the living room windows in the middle of December as they tried to hunt squirrels with BB guns. I still loved the locker room and the friendships, but I no longer gave any value to the illusion that success in hockey had any real importance in the world. I spent this time in a state of intellectual rebellion against the way I was living. As a positive person, I still found joy in every day, but I was unable to become consciously content with the life I was leading. I became a person that loved every day but hated every week. I despised the fact that I was simply following the path laid in front of my feet and lacked the courage to extract myself from my social shackles and pave my own way. To an outside observer, I was on the path to success. However, I realized what people viewed as success was utterly meaningless. I wanted to be free from the constraints on my life and was sick of living on a constant itinerary. I was repulsed by the fact that people were impressed because I was an athlete with a high GPA. I had the choice to become a renowned scholar or a professional hockey player but wanted neither. Two roads diverged in a wood, and I simply stood still. I realized that life is like a treadmill: even when you move forward, you get nowhere. Somewhere along the line, it hit me. I wanted to be a writer. Since the fork in my path was leading to two equally unappealing destinations, I figured I might as well sit down and create the path I desired with my mind since it was the only place where I could control things.

It was at this moment that my mind was opened in a new way. I saw a path to freedom that had been previously hidden. I became content with the fact that I would never be truly free, but at least I could now be liberated in my mind. As a writer, I could create the world I wanted. However, as pleased as I felt about this newly developed desire, I still lacked the courage to take the risk to become a writer. I continued to live my life as if hockey was important and stayed on track to get my Biomedical Engineering degree. I was too weak to completely follow my new desire, but I told myself I would pursue writing as a hobby until I was successful enough to write full-time. In hindsight, this gutless decision set my writing back about five years, but it was an unavoidable part of my development. As a result, I spent my last couple years at Michigan Tech often thinking about books to write without ever putting them to paper.

During my senior year, I moved into my own place. I had broken up with Mary towards the end of my junior year and liked the idea of living alone. This worked perfectly since Ryan and Drew had moved in with their girlfriends, Lindsey and Jordan. By this time, my transformation away from hockey was complete. I still played the games and was a phenomenal salesman for the school when I was interviewed. In my mind, however, I had completely moved on. One of the true pleasures of my senior year that helped me find peace was my friendship with Mike. Mike and I had become closer friends every year as our personalities grew towards one another. Mike was also disillusioned with the hockey lifestyle and ready to move on. Both of us knew our plans for after college and neither involved hockey. I was going to the University of Michigan to get my PhD in Biomedical Engineering while Mike was going to join Derbe in medical school at Michigan State. Since Derbe had graduated the prior year, I spent almost all my time at the rink with Mike, and he soon developed into my best friend.

Before every hockey game during my senior year, when the rest of the team was blasting rock music four hours before the puck dropped, Mike and I would grab a seat in the stands and just talk about life. I think we both valued this time immensely more than the actual hockey games. Our pregame conversations covered a wide range of topics. We would often have talks about religion or politics that would inevitably evolve into elaborate hypothetical discussions until we were interrupted by the drop of the puck. It was a major release to vent my frustrations with society to Mike. Although we rationally agreed on most topics, our demeanors were temporally opposed. I was a long-term pessimist that could see no purpose in any possible life path while simultaneously being a short-term optimist that could turn any situation into an enjoyable experience. On the contrary, Mike was an unparalleled optimist about his future while constantly complaining about each day. When Mike would explain the grandiose plans he had for his life including becoming a doctor and having a family, I would argue that the only purpose in life was to extract as much pleasure as possible out of the present moment. I was quoting Oscar Wilde while he was quoting Walt Disney. I once told Mike that I believed there was no such thing as a happy ending except in fiction. It was Mike's response to this comment that later inspired me to write my first book. Mike, who had heard my parent's love story in the past, made the comment that my mom's death had caused me to focus on the ending instead of the story.

That night, I began to reflect upon what Mike had said and disagreed with his claim. Although I detested the fact that my mom was taken from me at such a young age, this ending was never my focus. I had always thought of my mom as the personification of perfection. I spent my life trying to find the type of love my parents had in their story. In fact, my mom's death was the one chapter of her life that I rarely reflected on which was most likely because it added nothing positive to the story. That night, I opened the *Mom in Heaven* draft I had previously fiddled around with and made the decision to finally write a book about the mother I had lost. A week later, I made another major breakthrough after watching the movie *Atonement*. The movie ends with the main character, an author who had written what was seen in the movie, revealing that, although the movie was the true story of her life, the happy ending was fiction. One of the author's decisions as a child had ruined the other characters' lives, and she wrote the happy ending in her book as a final act of mercy to give them what she had stolen from them in life. I was immediately drawn to this concept. I decided I was going to do the same thing for my mom and give her the happy ending that she never had the chance to live.

As is often the case with an overworked college student, I had little time for anything except hockey, school, and research. As a result, my book got put on the backburner. Although I constantly had thoughts stewing, I struggled to find the time to sit down to write. There was always something more pressing to finish which only added to my resentment of the rat race I was stuck in. I couldn't wait until I was finished with the season and could move on to graduate school. I figured, without the responsibilities of hockey filling my entire schedule, I would have plenty of spare time to write my book. As these thoughts lingered in my mind, I did my best to enjoy my senior year and prevent myself from yearning for the future. I had spent the first twenty years of my life striving to be a college hockey player, and all I now wanted was for it to be over. If it weren't for my daily conversations with Mike, I don't know how I could have kept my sanity through that final year.

Mike and I had more in common than our shared disdain for being personally exalted for something as insignificant as playing hockey. As time passed, I began to learn so much more about Mike. In addition to Mike's views on the world, I heard the most intimate details of his personal life. Mike had grown up in Traverse City, Michigan, with two sisters and a brother. Mike's father was a successful surgeon which provided Mike with a privileged upbringing. Much like my own life, Mike spent his childhood playing sports and dreaming of being a college athlete. Additionally, Mike had always wanted to become a doctor like his father. It was no surprise that Mike grew up with the same optimism about his future that I did. One of the most memorable conversations we had was before a game in Grand Forks when Mike told me about his parents' divorce. Mike and I had grown up with the same delusions about our parents. We both thought of our parents as being completely in love. Fortunately for me, my delusion was frozen in time along with my mom's death. Mike, on the other hand, wasn't as lucky. His parents were both still alive, and it was merely his ideal world that had been killed. The divorce occurred when Mike was in high school after he caught his dad cheating on his mom. When faced with the decision to lie for his dad, Mike proved the extent of his integrity. It is a rare person that is capable of making the right decision in spite of the fact that it is actually worse for everyone. Mike would never be close with his dad after this day. Mike's mom, a truly amazing woman, would instantly see her life crumble. Mike would be left to watch the devastation caused by his terrible correct decision. After leaving home to play hockey in the USHL, Mike turned his frustration with the divorce into a period of youthful debauchery like many of the other young men I had played hockey with during that same period of my life. I heard a lot of stories about how much of an emotional mess Mike was before coming to college and even witnessed some of it firsthand when he had been a freshman. He was truly a different person than the friend I came to know. And then he met Angela.

Mike exactly represented the irrational dream of every woman who is attracted to the bad boy and believes he will change. Fortunately for Angela, Mike was this man. Mike didn't change into this responsible man by a gradual process but was instantly transformed the moment their paths collided. Contrary to the claims of the priest at Mike's wedding during his pitiful speech, Mike won Angela's heart with persistence and honesty. For once, the true story was much better than the fictionalized version although that was partly because the priest was an inept storyteller. In reality, it wasn't the hand of god that caressed their relationship through Mike's incompetence as described at the wedding, but, rather, the calculated courting of a woman by a man determined to prove his worth. Once again, Mike's integrity was evident. Unlike most people who would shrink from their past in fear of prematurely terminating a new romance, Mike began his relationship with Angela by confessing every truth about his being while leaving no skeleton in the closet. Mike took the ultimate risk of revealing the entirety of who he was and shining a light on his every flaw. There is real wisdom behind Mike's approach. Most of the worry in a new relationship rests in the unknown. Instead of Angela having to wonder about Mike's history, she knew every detail. Although it would take time for her to overcome the worst parts of this knowledge, she could be comforted by the fact that she no longer had to fear the unknown. Mike and I often talked about why he was the type of person he was before meeting Angela. Mike basically told me he was just so numb from his parents' divorce that he was void of emotion. Mike's envisioned future had been stolen from him, and he was left hopeless and angry until he met Angela. Angela rekindled Mike's belief in happy endings. She shattered his cynicism and allowed him to finally overcome the lingering sting of his parent's divorce. It is a strange thing for a cynic like me to observe a relationship like Mike and Angela's. They defied the odds and were a perfect couple. Mike had found the love that I had yearned for my entire life.

I loved hearing about Mike's relationship with Angela and their future plans. It became clear that Mike was motivated entirely by Angela's wellbeing. I would listen to him describe his future and envied his devotion to her happy ending. Mike planned to become a doctor, and he and Angela were both accepted into the same medical school. Their life was following an apparently perfect path. I found it upsetting how much time this cute couple spent looking towards the future instead of living in the present, but I guess that is the sign of successful people (at least if you mark success by the number of plaques on the wall of your country club office). The sad irony of Mike's relationship was that he was so in love but forced to wait to completely live that love. Instead of moving in together as they both desired, they remained in separate apartments to avoid an awkward conversation with Angela's parents. I always brought up the stupidity of Angela living with Mike while paying rent at an apartment she never saw. Mike agreed but explained to me, in a fatherly tone, that he just didn't want her family to be in an uncomfortable position. Although this politically correct answer sounded nice enough, it did little to convince me this was a smart move. In reality, Mike and Angela ended up paying a few thousand dollars just to avoid one awkward five minute conversation. Other than a few meaningless criticisms such as this, I was thrilled for them. It was a pleasure seeing the type of person Mike had grown into during his four years of college. The out of control kid had become the responsible man. Mike frequently talked about his desire to have kids, and, most importantly, Mike didn't want to make the same mistakes as his own father. He was a man with only one purpose in life, and that was to become a devoted husband and loving parent.

In my conversations with Mike, I found it difficult to clearly express the way I felt about life in college. Even now, it is hard for me to summarize my experience. I left college as a different person than the one who had arrived. I once wrote in a graduate scholarship application that "of all the lessons I learned in college, time management is at the top of the list." I talked about the challenge of balancing my hectic hockey schedule with my coursework but described how I loved being busy because I felt like I was living my dream. In reality, this was only half truth and half propaganda. Although the claims about my schedule were accurate, I was actually living the dream of a child that no longer existed. There wasn't much time in this busy schedule for fun, and the occasional Saturday night party did little to compensate for what was missing. I had slowly developed an utter disgust towards all the things I had dreamt of growing up. Hockey no longer provided the joy it had when I used to stay up late playing in the driveway. I didn't love hockey anymore, and maybe I never had. I thought I had loved the glow of the red light behind the net, but it was really the glow in my dad's face that made me fall in love with the game. My enjoyment with hockey was now purely tied to my friendships. I enjoyed the locker room and weekend parties more than actually playing the game in front of the big crowds. I don't want to give the wrong view that I didn't love actually playing hockey because it is the one part of my childhood from which I derived my main sense of satisfaction. I always loved the artistry of the game and the understated elegance of a three foot area pass. However, I ultimately found that I enjoyed these things more in a family game of boot hockey at Christmas than I did playing in front of twenty thousand people. The pleasure just seemed to get lost in college as the rink turned into an office where the business of winning was all that mattered and unfortunately didn't happen often. I missed the days when it was all about having fun and making plays. I hated people's obsession with scouts and dreams of The Show. I viewed a hockey career as paling in comparison to my intellectual endeavors which only added to my disillusionment and caused me to further devalue the markers of success in our society. I resented being considered successful because I played college hockey. Nonetheless, I enjoyed the friendships and the Saturday nights that were my one release from the prison I was trapped in. After college, hockey had become like an ex-wife with the extent of my hate being a constant reminder of the strength of my previous love.

Although the rink, lab, and classroom took up the majority of my time, another integral part of my life was solitude. During my senior year, I lived alone for the first time and was surrounded only by my thoughts. Through the quiet, I could feel my desire to become a writer growing ever greater inside me. I truly believed there was nothing of value in life, and I came to understand there was no accomplishment that could satisfy my desires. Instead of letting this truth demoralize me, I allowed it to liberate me from my own selfishness. I decided to contribute my time towards the lives of those I loved. My senior year was the culmination of a struggle to remove my childhood delusions. This year ultimately provided the foundation from which my true character emerged. I would no longer allow myself to be constrained by the norms of society. I had started college with a dream and ended with an alarm clock.

Overall, I had an extraordinary upbringing. No one could have possibly predicted the person that would emerge from this environment. I grew up with an idealistic faith in happy endings that was replaced by the realization that the quickest way to kill a dream is to make it a reality. I saw no value in the achievements of our world and came to the decision that I needed to move beyond the common constraints of society. I wasted a lot of time getting to this point in my life, but it was a valuable process that taught me the truth of the world. I learned that time ultimately devours everything. I came to the realization that, if glory is fleeting and time heals all wounds, everything ends up lukewarm in the end. This lukewarm ending repulsed me more than any bad ending possibly could. A life is better off ended at either extreme than some boring neutrality. I would much rather end up in an adrenaline fueled rage or a passionate bliss than that quiet yawn of regret towards which most lives inevitably crawl. By the time I graduated college, I no longer thought in terms of personal achievements but instead wanted to be a person that prevented others from embarking down the paths of their own demise. I still had an unexplained desire to be a writer, but I wanted to be sure I made an actual difference in the world. I came to believe I could provide the happy endings that reality was unfortunately incapable of delivering. I had spent my entire life dreaming of a world that didn't exist, and my eventual coping mechanism would be to create dream worlds through fiction. The prologue to my story was finished, and it was now time to write the rest of my life.

CHAPTER 2

My Irresistible Desire to be Irresistibly Desired

Love is the delusion that one woman differs from another.

-H. L. Mencken

CHAPTER 2: My Irresistible Desire to be Irresistibly Desired

Before I move on to my life as a writer, I would like to take a detour to talk about my search for love and the women that defined that journey. I am dedicating a separate chapter to these relationships because so much of my personality was shaped through them. As I begin to write this section, I am reminded how valuable these romances were to my emotional development and how my idealistic nature ultimately doomed them from the start. I have often heard girls described as good from far but far from good which is a perfect temporal description of my relationships. Growing up, I truly believed I was destined for the same type of true love my parents had shared. I never once doubted that I was going to meet the love of my life. My dad had found my mom, and it was just a matter of time before I met my own true love. The following is the story of my search for that perfect woman.

The first girl I ever loved was April. I was eight years old, and she was stunning. Every morning, I would scan the entire school bus until I saw her smile. That smile was permanently imprinted in my mind and was the first drug I was ever addicted to. Actually, calling me an addict is an understatement. I was a junkie. I tried to sit by April every day and was tormented by withdrawal each night when I came home. It is funny how a first love never really goes away. I can still picture her beautiful smile as I look back fondly on this crush. When I went through old pictures at my high school graduation party, the first thing I did was look for April. When I saw her, she looked just as wonderful as I remembered. I still feel the same today when I see her picture. I wonder if thinking this image of an eight year old girl is beautiful makes me a pedophile. If a man my age looked at an eight year old girl the way I look at April's picture, he would be arrested, and yet I just cannot help myself with her. Even more disturbing was when she added me on Facebook years later. Although she was still attractive, I immediately pictured that cute little kid and preferred the young girl to the grown woman. I guess this is an issue best left alone until I can get an appointment with Dr. Freud. Overall, my experience with April is just another example of the unmatched passion of a first crush. My love for April shows that a crush can last forever as long as you never actually get to know the person.

My next major romantic milestone was my first girlfriend. I was twelve years old which was an appropriately awkward age for my first relationship. I had just started the seventh grade at a new school, and the first girl I met was Emily. Emily was a year older than me, and I soon learned that her younger sister, Sara, was in my class. Sara and Emily had completely opposite personalities. Emily was an outgoing blonde while Sara was a cute, quiet redhead. In my initial months at school, I was immediately drawn to Emily. I loved everything about her, and she quickly became the only object of my affection. Ninety percent of my free time at school was spent flirting with Emily. If I hadn't been so naïve, I would have asked her out immediately. Unfortunately, I didn't have a clue what I was doing. I was a shy kid that never made a move. This period highlighted the cognitive diffidence that characterized my early days rather than the strength of thought that defined my later life as a writer.

My relationship with Sara was different than my immediate connection with Emily. Sara and I got along in a more proper manner. We would talk to each other like we were addressing someone in a business interview. My formal conversations with Sara were in stark contrast to my passionate flirting with Emily but fit the girls' respective personalities. During this period, my whole excitement for getting up each day was to see Emily. This all changed when the Sadie Hawkins Dance arrived. All I could think about was Emily, but, as soon as the dance was announced, Sara asked me to be her date. I said yes with a regretful smile as I could feel my words destroying any hopes of being with Emily.

After the dance with Sara, I was surprised that things remained essentially the same with Emily. In fact, our flirting actually increased. Emily was the sexiest thing I had ever seen. Even though everyone was asking me about Sara, I could only think about her sister. About a week after the dance, Sara invited me to her house after school. It is weird to think back on seventh grade relationships, but all I know is that, sometime during dinner, one of her parents referred to me as Sara's boyfriend and that was enough to make it official. I now had my first girlfriend. I remember thinking things felt weird, but everything was just a whirlwind and I didn't fight back. I let my life determine itself without any real input from my own desires. I was a character living in a story written in third person. After dinner, I went upstairs with the girls to play a board game. At one point, Sara was called downstairs. As soon as Sara was gone, Emily tackled me onto the floor. Rolling on the carpet with Emily's legs wrapped around me is my earliest memory of being sexually attracted to a girl. That magnificent moment ended with my first kiss. It was the only kiss Emily and I ever shared, and it was better than I could have imagined. That moment got me through the next three years of my life. It was my own cherished secret that my first kiss was with my first girlfriend's sister.

I ended up dating Sara for five months in seventh grade which basically consisted of us hanging out a total of three or four times. The main problem we had was that we were both far too quiet. Another issue was that, the entire time I was dating Sara, my crush on Emily continued to grow. I felt like I was doing the right thing by dating Sara, but those positive feelings were derived from my sense of sacrifice as if I was doing volunteer work rather than a sense of fulfillment. I thought my actions were benefiting Sara, but I didn't know how to balance my charitable relationship with my own desires that selfishly pulled me in the opposite direction. Altruism can't exist when a man keeps himself as top priority. As a result, the good deed I thought I was doing was ultimately unsuccessful. It was painful to observe Sara's sadness when I ended things, but my focus immediately turned to Emily as I was still a young man primarily focused on my own happiness. I couldn't write a happy ending for Sara because she was only a supporting character in the story I was concerned with. Even after Sara and I broke up, I never dated Emily. I can honestly say I have never wanted a girl more than I wanted her. Emily and I remained friends through high school, but I didn't have the courage to make a move. The ever-present sexual tension prevented us from losing our desire to spend time together which, in hindsight, was probably the catalyst to the growth of our friendship and a better result than hooking up and then losing each other. However, this was no consolation at the time. I would have traded anything to be with Emily.

Although Emily was my primary infatuation early in high school, there were plenty others that stole my heart. I would honestly fall for any cute girl that would smile at me. I am not sure if this affliction has ever totally worn off, but I have at least learned to recognize the symptoms. Even though I didn't actually interact with many girls during my first years in high school, my life and mind constantly revolved around them. As I now look back from my experienced perspective, I find it embarrassing how little I knew. I used to go across the street to my neighbor's house and listen to music for hours while we talked about girls. My favorite song was "Rape me" by Nirvana which I would always play an extra couple times before I went home. When I heard that song again ten years later, I realized what the words meant. I had no idea what I was listening to at the time, but I have to wonder what my family was thinking when that sweet young kid was walking around the house singing about rape.

During this awkward period of my life, my body seemed to learn things long before my mind. Like most guys, my dick naturally reacts faster than my brain. One of the best examples of this was the first time I saw a naked girl. It was the summer before my freshman year of high school. I spent the morning working out and then walked down to the local park to shoot some baskets after lunch. When I got to the courts, I noticed a bunch of empty bottles along the far side of the fence. I walked over and saw a magazine tucked into an empty beer box. I pulled out the magazine only to find it filled with naked women. After looking around worried as if I was being watched by the FBI, I quickly grabbed the magazine, tucked it under my shirt, and went home immediately. I walked into my house like I was smuggling drugs across the border and was terrified I was going to be caught. I hustled down to my room, locked the door behind me, and pulled it out. It felt as if I had found a buried treasure. The contents of the chest were foreign to me, but the value was unquestionable. I had never seen anything like this, and things would never be the same. I hid the magazine in the ceiling tiles above my bed and spent the next two years in a constant state of worry that my secret would be discovered.

In addition to what I learned from my nightly reading, I slowly began to experience new frontiers with girls. I had my first slow dance during my freshman year at the homecoming dance. Although we danced like it was a slow dance, the song was almost as unromantic as "Rape me" would have been. The song was "Too close" by Next. Anyone who has heard this song knows that it is an awkward song for a young man's first dance, but it was an accurate one in this case. The dance ended with my first French kiss. About a month after that dance, my learning curve with women increased dramatically when I started dating Jenny, my first high school girlfriend.

Jenny was the star of our high school's volleyball team. We first met when we had to do a photo shoot for the local newspaper after we were both named all-conference. I was drawn to Jenny immediately for many reasons. First of all, she was a junior, and I was only a freshman. No matter how trivial this age discrepancy appears in hindsight, it makes a big difference in high school. Not only was I dating a girl I was lusting over, but she had the added benefit of solidifying my position on campus. Jenny having her own car only added to the feeling of liberation I received from this relationship. For the first time in my life, I could go anywhere.

Although Jenny and I spent a lot of time wasting gas, the only thing on our minds was when we were going to stop. During this relationship, I lived in a constant state of nervous anticipation about what was going to happen between us. Things were probably moving at a snail's pace, but I felt as if I was breaking new ground every time we were together. After a while, our nightly routine became driving around for a short period and then finding a parking lot to stop in. We would fold down the seats in the back of her Ford Explorer and lay in each other's arms. My heart raced the entire time while my mind was in a state of continuous rumination. Although the excitement of these nights was exceptional, I could never fully enjoy them because of the accompanying anxiety. When I think back, I miss that sense of anxiety as much as anything. I always laugh when I remember how experienced I thought Jenny was when, in reality, she was in the same position as me. During the year we dated, I transformed from a completely inexperienced kid that was clueless about girls into a young man that, although still mostly clueless, at least had the delusion of experience.

I dated Jenny for almost a year before we broke up. As with most of my early relationships, I ended things by slowly becoming harder to reach and letting the relationship dissolve naturally as it starved to death. I was too timid to initiate the conversation directly. This has never been a wise approach, but I was restricted by my innate disposition and, at the time, unable to overcome this character flaw. Eventually, Jenny confronted me about things changing between us. When she asked me about our relationship, it gave me the optimal opportunity to break up with her. Once she initiated the conversation, I did the rest. I remember the discussion like it was yesterday. This was the first time I ever added humor into a breakup which is something I continued with my subsequent relationships. We had the discussion in my car with the music turned really low. Right before I broke up with her, I turned the music on my Peter, Paul, and Mary CD to "That's what you get for loving me." Even though Jenny was unaware of the quiet song in the background, it provided a suitable soundtrack for the breakup and allowed me to enjoy an otherwise tense evening. I always relish the chance to create humor out of normally stressful situations even if it is only for my own amusement, and this was merely a preview of that aspect of my character emerging at a young age.

After enjoying my breakup with Jenny, I spent the rest of my sophomore year single. I hung out with a few different girls but was so consumed with hockey that I didn't get serious about any of them until I met Kelly a year later. I was fortunate that most of my dates during this year turned into valued friendships even though none of them led to a love connection until Kelly. Kelly was a transfer student to our school that instantly stole my heart. She was the epitome of the woman I desired when I met her, and the antithesis of the woman I would desire after knowing her. If I had met Kelly later in life, she would have been the type of girl that I would have instantly derided for her naïve nature, her lame views on the world, and just her general outlook on life. I find it a struggle to write this paragraph because I am ashamed of the person I was, but, honestly, I was completely taken by Kelly. I thought she was such a sweet person. I found myself excited that I may have met a girl that matched the perfection of my mom. I was unaware at the time that a lack of character flaws is often the result of a lack of character rather than an indicator of virtue. Regardless of my subsequent feelings, I had a massive crush on Kelly and set out to make her mine. I have never behaved in such a pathetic manner toward a girl in my entire life. I would slip love notes into her locker between class and transformed every inside joke into a thoughtful gift. After a few weeks of pitiful behavior, things paid off, and I took Kelly out. After this first date, she became my girlfriend. I spent many hours with Kelly while we were dating, and it wasn't really much fun. Although we talked often, the conversations were neither of substantial depth nor enjoyment. Unfortunately, these facts weren't acknowledged at the time because I was emotionally blinded. In fact, I am pretty sure my rational mind was not involved in my relationship with Kelly at all. How can you love spending time with a girl when you don't even like spending time with her? It didn't occur to me to check with my brain. During this period, I was controlled entirely through my limbic system and was driven purely by whom I wanted Kelly to be instead of the person she actually was. This was one of my first lessons in a lifelong internal battle between reason and emotion. This relationship was a clear precursor to my later struggle to rise above my basal instincts and gain conscious control over my behavior.

After dating for about six months, Kelly broke my heart. I was devastated. Of all the periods of my childhood, the two months after breaking up with Kelly were the most depressing. I spent every day sulking in a pathetic manner and wondering how this could have happened. I did my best to rationalize why she had broken up with me which only made things worse. I couldn't understand what I could have possibly done to prevent her from falling completely in love with me. I had been the sweetest and most devoted boyfriend possible. I had done so many cute little things for her and was dumbfounded to think why she wanted it to end. Not only was this abrupt end mentally perplexing, but, more importantly, it was emotionally shattering. I am so embarrassed by how I responded to this relationship, but I understand it had a positive effect on me once I was finally awoken from the two months of despair. I think everyone needs to have their heart broken before they can begin to grasp reality. Going through this period turned out to be one of the best things to happen to me and was essential to my emotional development. It is ironic that the girlfriend I was most depressed about losing ended up being the one I liked the least. This was simply my first real taste of heartbreak that occurred during a period when my hormones were in maximal fluctuation. It was the perfect storm.

After finally getting over Kelly, I started to enjoy the rest of my senior year and didn't date another girl until I moved to Lincoln. As I mentioned in the first chapter, things changed drastically in Lincoln. I had previously hooked up with a few girls, but I had always been fairly shy. In high school, it would take me a long time to start talking to a girl and even longer before I made a move. Things changed once I was in Lincoln. We would have team parties where girls would throw pussy at you like candy at a parade. I didn't have to do anything to get a girl because they would just give it away for free. I admired these young altruists. They would hear we played for the Stars, and everything else would be superfluous. I stayed true to my personality and only dabbled with a few girls, but simply being around this environment was a complete culture change.

My first year in Lincoln was a carefree time in which I just enjoyed my newfound freedom. I met a lot of attractive girls but never started an actual relationship. I grew up quickly and benefited from interacting with so many different people. Although I had many new experiences with girls, my focus wasn't on maximizing promiscuity but rather on optimizing my overall experience. I am thankful I didn't get involved in a relationship because the benefits of being single made it much easier for me to mature. This period helped improve my confidence, sharpen my outlook, and throw off my cloche of naivety. Instead of being swept away by life like the majority of my upbringing, I looked upon the world as an outsider. It is hard to see the entire forest when your face is pressed firmly against a single tree. This time of autonomy in Lincoln gave me a broad perspective for the first time and was a precursor to my life after college. Looking back, it is a shame that I didn't transform into this permanent state back then. I patiently pursued my social life, and the results were phenomenal. Overall, life in Lincoln could be summed up as one big party. Although I had hockey, I really didn't have any other responsibilities to cripple my growth. The restraints of my childhood were removed, and I was free to become a man.

When I returned home for the summer, it was clear how much I had changed. Not only was I more confident, but I was now a different person. My views on the world had evolved to the extent that I was ashamed of the person I had previously been. Ironically, a couple years later, I would look back embarrassed of the naivety of this supposedly enlightened self as well. I have come to realize that people are not only self-centric, but temporally partisan as well. When my present-centric self reads this book in five years, I may reflect upon its author and roll my eyes. I spent my summer training hard and enjoying time with family and friends. Although the enjoyment of my family remained unaltered, I no longer had the same feelings around my friends from high school. They weren't my friends; they were friends of my previous self. Every time we would go out, I would get a sick feeling inside me which had more to do with how I felt about my previous self than how I felt about my former friends. Because I liked my current nature more than the high school version they knew, I constantly felt like I was imprisoned by my reputation. As the summer went on, I found myself spending more time with the three friends from my team in Lincoln that were also from MN while spending less time with my high school friends. This phenomenon was isolated to that one summer and most likely just a reflection of my continued desire to separate myself from my youth.

Returning to Lincoln was exciting. I was much more comfortable in my second year and soon had a reemerging desire to fall in love. Although I would daily claim to my best friend on the team, JJ, that I was in love with random girls that would smile at me, I was really looking for the type of true love my parents had. I was still a hopeless romantic with the emphasis on romantic as is common rather than on hopeless as I would later use the phrase. It wasn't only that I thought true love was possible; I thought true love was inevitable. I had a blind confidence that I was going to meet the perfect girl and fall in love instantly. Perhaps this optimistic belief was a self-fulfilling prophecy because I met Kelsey about a month into my second year in Lincoln.

When I met Kelsey, it was love at first sight. Kelsey was a friend of JJ's girlfriend that I hadn't previously been introduced to. On that first occasion, I only saw her briefly, but she left a lasting impression. I made a few jokes with JJ and his girlfriend outside Chipotle, but my attention was glued to the gorgeous girl smiling by their side. It took less than a moment before I was intoxicated with my new diamond. As I joked with my friends, I drew enormous pleasure from the sound of Kelsey's laugh. I have always found it easier to connect with a girl while talking to her friends. It is amazing how the hard to get approach initiates an innate response of envy that makes a woman much more likely to fall in love than when a guy goes directly after her. This first interaction didn't last long, but I had seen more than enough. Before they left, I was formally introduced and immediately told Kelsey I was in love. Her smiling reaction gave me comfort, and I knew it was just a matter of time before we would be together.

Kelsey and I fit effortlessly with one another. There was never an awkward moment as everything about her seemed to align with the girl I had envisioned my entire life. Not only was Kelsey smart and beautiful, but she had a quiet integrity underlying her every move. Kelsey was two years younger than me and still a senior in high school. She reminded me of what I hated about life in high school. Kelsey was the top student in her class and a standout soccer player. Similar to my own life, she seemed to always do the right thing while developing a desire to experience more. What I loved most about Kelsey were the glimpses of that person underneath the surface whose presence was fighting to break through. I became ever more enthralled with her, and, unlike my previous relationships, my mind admired her as much as my emotions. I started to spend as much time as possible with Kelsey while the rest of my time was devoted to thinking about her. After a few weeks, it became clear we were a couple, but we had yet to talk about the obvious roadblock in front of us. I was only staying in Lincoln for another three months, and we would then be going our separate ways for college. Rarely in my life have I looked back on a decision without even the slightest doubt that I did the right thing, but this was one discussion that ended with the correct conclusion. Kelsey and I agreed it would be a bad idea to be in a long distance relationship during our first years in college, but, because there was no way we were going to stop seeing each other, we decided to simply embrace the limited time we had. Kelsey is the only girl I have ever broken up with before we started dating. It was like leasing a girlfriend instead of buying one. After we came to accept the term limits of our relationship, Kelsey and I were free to just be in love without any pressure. Our preemptive breakup allowed our romance to live freely in the moment without being tainted by worries of the future. Robert Frost was correct when he said that "happiness makes up in height what it lacks in length." I don't regret one second of my time with Kelsey and have benefited greatly from having a relationship whose astonishing ascent ended at the summit.

Having Kelsey in my life vastly improved my second year in Lincoln. Dating Kelsey didn't have any of the negative side effects that can often result from relationships. Kelsey fit effortlessly into a life I was already living, and I don't remember having a single argument with her. I still spent the majority of my time with JJ, but my evenings started to increasingly revolve around Kelsey. I was consumed with her in every way and appreciated each precious minute we had together. We both knew it was a temporary romance, and each day was more special because of it. Our time together was short but exceptional and helped shape both my worldview and my writing in the years that followed.

I enjoyed my final months in Lincoln, but, as we moved closer to the end, it became clear that Kelsey was dreading the day I had to leave. During my last week, we spent every night together. When the final evening arrived, we went to a fancy Japanese hibachi restaurant and then rented *Pretty Woman*. Kelsey periodically got tears in her eyes throughout the night. When the song "It must have been love" played during the climax of the movie, she finally broke down sobbing. I just held her tightly with a smile. The irony of listening to this song as I held Kelsey gave me so much peace. I didn't want our relationship to end but was content with every aspect of it. Although we talked often over the next year, I never saw Kelsey again. Since this time, we have periodically sent emails to catch up and wish each other the best. The Kelsey who sends me emails is an impressive person with a nice life, but the Kelsey I loved no longer exists. I knew the person she was but am a stranger to the person she is. I am thankful for my time with Kelsey and was fortunate that it ended before the memory was stained by a typical conclusion. I killed my relationship with Kelsey at the correct moment and learned a valuable lesson as a result.

When I arrived at Michigan Tech, I was on the prowl. Within a week, I met Heidi. It was lust at first sight. Before long, Heidi and I were spending every night together. My relationship with Heidi was filled with passion, but I was oddly not emotionally invested at all. In fact, my outlook with Heidi was unlike any of my other youthful relationships and more similar to the casual relationships that defined my life after college. I had a blissful time spending my nights with Heidi but was wholly disinterested in progressing towards any further commitment. Perhaps my indifference towards the relationship was a result of following my time with Kelsey or maybe was caused by my interests being focused elsewhere during this first year of school. Regardless of the underlying cause, I was unable to give Heidi the commitment she increasingly desired. As time went on, I became ever more annoyed with her attempts to impede my freedom which ultimately led to us parting ways only a few months into our mostly physical romance. After we broke up, I would only hook up with Heidi on nights when we both had enough drinks to forget our previous problems which conveniently occurred once or twice a week.

My time with Heidi ended permanently in January of my freshman year when I met Anna in chemistry class. I would notice her every day and was waiting for my chance to meet her. I finally got my opportunity when Derbe became Anna's chemistry lab partner. I spent most of my time during lab talking to Derbe hoping I could get introduced to Anna. It is scary how quickly a cute smile can induce amnesia. Most days, I would be oblivious to my conversations with Derbe and always tried to initiate things with Anna. After a few weeks of flirting in lab, I invited Anna and her friends out to one of our team parties.

My first night with Anna didn't go as planned as a result of her drinking before the party. Anna had absolutely no experience with alcohol prior to college and was on life support by the time she arrived. Although I could tell she was in rough shape, she still possessed a sweet nature that was immensely attractive. The side effects of Anna being hammered weren't all bad as I was able to witness this normally introverted person coming out of her shell. As time went on, Anna and I started to date. Shyness can be a turnoff, but with Anna it came across as sweetness. Naivety can be a turnoff, but what she had was youthful purity. As we dated, it became evident that everything in Anna's life was changing. I had the pleasure of watching her grow from a young girl that was unsure of herself into a smart, confident, woman. The changes that took place within Anna while we dated reminded me of myself during my first year in Lincoln. She was learning the lessons of life that only experience can teach.

Dating Anna was a new type of relationship. For the first time, I had found a woman I truly admired. Even when I was in love with Kelsey, I had only seen glimpses of her deeper character. In contrast, I could see the entirety of Anna's worth. I didn't love Anna for any outward traits that she possessed, but rather for the nature of her being. My love for Kelsey was passion; my love for Anna was admiration. It is a rare thing to directly observe the goodness in someone's heart. I had always dreamed of meeting a girl who could live up to my mom's memory, and I started to realize Anna might be the one. Anna possessed the best qualities I had heard about my mom. She was calm even when overcome by emotion and hence her beauty shined through even her saddest moments. When I broke her heart, Anna gracefully responded with a painful smile.

Nothing in my memory is more heartbreaking than Anna's reaction when I ended things. Freshman year was over, and I was fighting the dueling desires of staying with Anna or enjoying a summer at home alone. Ultimately, I decided it was best to avoid the inevitable stress of a long distance relationship. I admired Anna but lacked the passion needed to combat the separation. I had not yet realized that my decisions were primarily being made at an adrenal level. I ultimately became jaded with every relationship once the initial period of passion was over. My decision to break up with Anna was a result of my inability to cope with the overall anxiety in my life. Unfortunately for Anna, the only coping mechanism I knew was retreat. The look on Anna's face is still engrained in the back of my mind. Nothing was more tragic than Anna's expression as she made an admirable but futile attempt to hide her absolute devastation. While she tried to smile, I could see the sadness through her eyes and hear the anguish in her cracking voice. My heart broke along with hers. I was completely unaware I would react this way until it was too late. The sad irony is that you often don't know how you really feel about a person until they are gone. The actions of a lifetime can't erase the words of an instant.

After breaking up with Anna, I spent the entire night awake. I was driving home the next morning but was submerged in my rumination. I felt thankful to be single from the standpoint of having my freedom, but I was mostly just tormented by the pain in Anna's final expression. This sour ending had ruined every sweet memory of our time together. I felt awful that I had been the cause of her anguish. When I had first started dating Anna, I gave no thought to the consequences of a failed relationship on my life let alone the effects it would have on her. I immediately regretted our entire relationship and every decision I had made along the way. I told myself I would rather never date again than be the cause of such suffering in another girl's life. I realized I needed to change my decision making process and develop the type of foresight that would allow me to make correct choices. My relationship with Anna taught me a valuable lesson about the consequences of my actions and how I should make decisions that are in the best long-term interests of those I love instead of following my immediate desires. Unfortunately, although this lesson was clear enough, I was unable to change my nature for more than a day before I fell back into my usual routine.

Two days after ending things with Anna, I returned home and went out for drinks with Dillon who was spending the summer with me in Minnesota. I told him all about Anna and my plans to enjoy the summer without a girlfriend. It was dollar beer night at one of my favorite bars, and we were soon feeling the effects of our numerous toasts. Dillon and I started eyeing every girl in the bar, but I was ever mindful of my recent history with Anna and continuously reminded myself to avoid falling for one. We began dancing with a couple scantily clad young women, and, before I knew it, one of the girls was trying to get in my pants. Although she was gorgeous, it was pretty clear she wasn't the classiest broad in the bar. She told me we should go in the bathroom together without making any effort to hide her agenda. It is hard not to appreciate the sincerity of a slut. A woman can only be equal to a man when she has fully disregarded her morality; all other women are doomed to be superior. Before I could respond to this girl's persistent propositions, I saw an absolute diamond walk into the bar. My mind instantly ignored the crazy slut dry humping my leg while simultaneously erasing all recollection of my recent history with Anna. In my future, I would always be aware of the fact that it is irresponsible for an author to begin a story without a clear ending in mind. However, I didn't have this foresight in my early romances. My hockey hopes were crumbling, but finding true love was the real dream around which my life revolved. I would pursue this love with an unwavering faith in my happy ending, and I wondered if this beautiful girl at the other end of the room was the woman I had been waiting for. I left the dance floor and immediately made my way towards the new object of my affection.

Cassidy and I hit it off immediately. I introduced myself with a smile, and she was mine for the rest of the night. We started talking about her job at the Mayo clinic where, as it turned out, she worked with a couple of my friends. The dialog progressed seamlessly as we shared a comforting flirtation that excited every molecule of my body. We only talked for a short while before Cassidy had to leave, but the quality of our connection overshadowed the brevity of our conversation. I was disappointed to see Cassidy walk away but thankful to have gotten her number before she left. I couldn't wait to see her again and called early the next morning to set up a date.

My first date with Cassidy was amazing. I had been out with girls before, but she was a woman. I was not only drawn to Cassidy's maturity, but also her position in life. She had just finished her nursing degree and had begun a new job at the Mayo Clinic. Cassidy impressed me in every possible way on every possible level. I was physically attracted to her while simultaneously admiring the gentle nature and caregiving qualities she possessed. The only negative I could find was the fact that her job was an hour away and she was only visiting the city for a week. As usual, I ignored the obvious initial problem that would lead to our predictable demise and did everything in my power to make her mine. Although she told me from the start that she thought it was a bad idea for us to begin a long distance relationship, Cassidy ultimately was forced to surrender to her emotions in the same way I had done. As we started dating, it didn't even cross my mind that a week earlier I had broken up with a girl I cared deeply about for the simple reason that long distance would be too stressful and unsustainable. I guess a rational romance is an oxymoron. Or perhaps my irrational romances show that I wasn't a victim of an oxymoron as much as simply being a moron. Nevertheless, I began a new and exciting relationship with Cassidy, and, at least for the first few weeks, my entire life was put on hold as I could think of nothing else but this spectacular young woman that had stormed into my life.

It didn't take long before the distance started to take its toll. Having only spent an initial week together, the majority of getting to know each other occurred over the phone. I went to visit Cassidy for a week before returning to Michigan Tech in August. We enjoyed the summer warmth without worrying about the coming winter. It was a wonderful week that seemed to last forever and end too soon. When I got to school, it wasn't long before the same type of anxiety I had feared with Anna began to emerge. Although this underlying stress was steadily growing within me, my relationship with Cassidy outwardly appeared on track. One of the most enjoyable weeks of my life was when she came to visit before Christmas. We spent that week together relaxing and making up for lost time. To end the week, we put on our tackiest Christmas sweaters and went out for a fancy dinner with Drew, Ryan, and their girlfriends. That dinner was the pinnacle of my relationship with Cassidy.

The next day, Cassidy had to go home. She returned to visit three more times that winter and really put a lot of effort into our relationship despite the fact that my hockey schedule prevented me from doing the same. Unfortunately, no matter how much we enjoyed each other's company when we were together, the distance ultimately devoured our intimacy. Phone calls became a monotonous chore as we both discovered there isn't a whole lot for two busy people to talk about. Eventually, the relationship became more of an unwanted hassle than a coveted desire. The storylines of all virtuous characters inevitably approach boredom. Cassidy was a lovely person, but one can't fake passion. She was pretty and nice but had not enough vice. I began to slowly detach myself from the relationship. I called less frequently while unconsciously planning my escape. It was during this period that my eyes were opened to my prior ignorance. I finally realized the irony of repeating the same mistake I had vowed to avoid after hurting Anna. Fortunately (well not in hindsight), I was unable to dwell on my failing relationship for long before I met Mary. When I was first introduced to Mary, I couldn't see anyone else sitting at the table with us. I was in love.

I had never met a person like Mary. Many of the girls I had dated were smart and pretty, but Mary had an added element of energy I had never known. Meeting Mary brought my dissatisfaction with Cassidy into clear view and catalyzed the end of our relationship. The moment Cassidy said she wanted to talk; I had a break up speech ready for delivery. As I broke up with Cassidy, I felt like an idiot for repeating my cruelty towards Anna with another girl I admired. I didn't regret my actions during the relationship since I was confident things failed due to circumstance rather than either of our actions. However, what I did regret was starting the relationship in the first place and my inability to foresee an obviously inevitable ending. Not only had I repeated the same mistake of breaking the heart of a girl who deserved better, but Cassidy had predicted this ending. I had ignored her warning and left her to bear the entire burden of the failed relationship alone. I knew I deserved to suffer more than her, but that was simply not the case as my potential torment was tempered by the fact that I had finally found the perfect person. Never have I seen a relationship end in justice. The punishment undoubtedly falls solely on the shoulders of the victim. As cognizant as I was of Cassidy's agony, I couldn't avoid the feelings of joy accompanying my new crush. Mary had qualities that I had believed were impossible in a woman. She was my fictional heroine colliding with my real world. The eternal ecstasy I had dreamt of my entire life was now just around the corner. Instead of being sad at my failed relationship, I felt overwhelming relief that I was available for Mary. I wasn't the slightest bit worried about the fact that she was dating someone because even my mom had a boyfriend when she met my dad at the beginning of their love story. I still possessed a blind faith in my happy ending. I had removed most of my childhood illusions except for this final fantasy of inevitable true love. I knew that I was meant to be with Mary, and it was only a matter of time before fate would make it happen. Sure enough, she broke up with her boyfriend at the end of my sophomore year, and it was time for the real love story of my life to begin.

I had dated a lot of girls in my life, but they didn't matter anymore. I had tormented myself until I became an intellectual pessimist, but that didn't matter anymore. I was living my childhood dream of playing college hockey, but that definitely didn't matter anymore. All that mattered was Mary. The tragedy of my story is that Mary turned out to be the love of my life. There would be no remedy for this unfortunate fate. After Mary, I could no longer be liberated from life. Death did not arrive in time and was henceforth rendered helpless against this assault of love.

Like most tragedies, what happened with Mary was simple: I fell in love. The early romances of my life were characterized by uncontrolled hormonal desires. My relationship with Kelsey centered on a mutual appreciation for the other person's company without the burdens of the future. Anna and Cassidy reflected my admiration for two genuine young women that shared many of my mother's mannerisms. Those relationships were fueled by the idea that my ideal woman would have the same traits as the perfect woman that never had the chance to raise me. And then there was Mary. To describe my feelings upon falling in love with Mary is like trying to describe the taste of a good smell. My feelings were truly inexpressible. I had never heard a harmony like the sound of her smile. With Mary, it was passion in every sense of the word. After running into her one day during the beginning of the summer, I fell completely out of reality. I loved her on every level. She was the most intellectually stimulating person I had ever met with a sense of humor and extroversion that could match my own. She had a depth of culture that intrigued my intellect. She possessed a million looks designed specifically to trigger each of my million emotions. She was a gorgeous girl with a sexy stare that made me want to rethink every notion of self-control. She was a nymphomaniac with a virgin's face. Her silent pause would scream into my heart. She was a whore with glasses that aroused the mind as much as the body. She was perfect.

The first time I saw Mary after she broke up with her boyfriend was during the last week of June while I was working at the annual seafood festival. Derbe and I were volunteering for a local charity, and, thankfully, Mary happened to pass through my line. After briefly exchanging pleasantries, we made plans for drinks later that evening. My anticipation was indescribable as I spent the entire day checking the time every three seconds. When I returned to my house where we planned to meet, Mary was sitting there with a lovely smile and a peppy attitude that could have overwhelmed the world's ditsiest cheerleader. I was so taken by Mary and ate up every little joke she would make whether it was about her being the cute one while her sister was a flannel wearing lumberjack or when she made her geeky "Geology Rocks" comments that made everyone else roll their eyes while I merely grabbed my chest. After enjoying the delicious food and drinks Mary made, we met some friends down by the waterfront to watch the fireworks. Mary and I were stuck on each other all night without ever actually making physical contact. We spent the entire time in continuous conversation without a second of dead air. In fact, either of us was capable of filling a dialogue single handedly which made the connection even more exciting as we constantly talked and laughed over one another. That night, my love for Mary increased even more than the decibel level of our conversations.

At the end of the evening, I walked Mary to her car and knew it was just a matter of time before we would be together forever. I showered her with sweetness, and we shared a lovely combination of lighthearted flirtation and serious conversation. Looking back, I am repulsed by my behavior during this time, but I guess it is hard not be ashamed of having loved someone once you no longer love them. When we arrived at her car outside my house, Mary and I finished a long conversation we had started about god. Mary came from an ultra-conservative catholic family, and I was an ex-catholic school Atheist which made for an interesting discussion. Mary talked about her family's views but seemed more aligned with my rationale along with her own hint of deistic optimism. It was fun to meet a woman who appeared to handle both extremes of the conversational spectrum with equal ease. After another hour of talking by the car, Mary went home, and I spent the entire night awake.

The next morning, I got a text message from Mary with an inside joke from the night before. I responded, and the conversation began. She was in her garden and I was on my couch as we looked into each other's souls through our phones. After a while, Mary asked why I didn't invite her to stay the night while I responded by saying that I didn't know she was interested. After Mary claimed she was giving me all the signals, the conversation quickly evolved into professing our love for one another. When I told Mary I knew she was the one, she said she had never felt this way before but asked how I could be so sure. I answered by telling her, "god told me" and waited for a reply. Mary responded by saying, "I'll be there in a half hour" which made me leap out of my chair and run around like a chicken with my head cut off. I couldn't contain my excitement as I awaited her arrival. I played out the upcoming encounter in my mind, and, for once, I underestimated the ensuing reality.

When Mary arrived at my house, she looked at me with a smile followed by the first, and only, moment of silence in our relationship. We gazed at each other with intense anticipation. I slowly walked up and kissed her. It was a flawless first kiss. As I held her in my arms, she said she knew we were going to be together forever. We discussed how comforting it was to know the future we had always dreamt of was finally beginning. Mary then told me to make love to her. I was shocked because, before that day, we hadn't even kissed, but she made the convincing argument (not that I needed convincing) that, when you find the one you love, you want to begin your life together immediately. Mary spent the entire day in my bed as we started the rest of our life. I was planning to leave the next morning for my family's annual Fourth of July weekend at the cabin, and I invited Mary to join. She was as surprised by this invitation as I had been when she asked me to make love to her. We both realized the other person meant what they had been saying all day. We were both in love.

Our first weekend together was the peak of my relationship with Mary and possibly the most enjoyable time of my life. I was soaring through the air with neither a parachute nor a magic eight ball and was only aware of the wind on my face. I still remember my feelings when Mary showed up with a cooler of food and drinks. Of all the girls I had been with in my past, none had taken care of me like Mary. This motherly quality was her ultimate attractiveness. I could picture myself loading the car in twenty years while Mary got the kids ready in the house. This was the dream I had imagined my entire life. Mary possessed the selflessness and endless energy of the ideal matriarch. During the six hour drive to my cabin, Mary continually reinforced her perfection. I serenaded her with my favorite songs while she held onto my arm like a young woman in love for the first time. With Mary in my life, the trip was no longer an unwanted obstacle to be endured. The journey was equivalent to the destination (meant literally since metaphorically the destination was grossly disappointing). When we finally reached my cabin, Mary met my family and felt right at home. I had found my other half and was no longer alone in the world.

The Fourth of July weekend with Mary was the realization of a lifelong dream. I had added the perfect girl to what was already my favorite time of year at my favorite place on earth. Life doesn't get any better than a nice barbecue with the people you love. I adored how Mary went out fishing with us and spent time playing with the kids. A good indicator of Mary's worth was how quickly my young cousins were drawn to her. By the end of the weekend, I was completely at peace with my life. It felt strange to have my mind liberated from all concerns. None of my previous worries mattered. Any potential future problems would be utterly trivial as long as I had Mary walking next to me.

The rest of the summer was amazing, and we soon began our first school year together as a couple. Mary had her own apartment but basically lived with me. Having a girlfriend move in can often dampen a man's autonomy. Mary, however, only seemed to improve the efficiency of my life. Instead of adding complication, our relationship simplified things. This comfort blinded me. I became complacent in my life of luxury and hence allowed our romance to slowly approach monotony. Furthermore, I was unable to correct this initial mistake because I was content. This enjoyable repetition was welcome because it was the simple life with my dream girl that I had always wanted. The best part of my romantic fantasy was that I no longer needed a life of excitement. More than anything, I thought love would make me permanently content. My early relationship with Mary epitomized this illusion.

As the passion of our summer romance wore off, we were left with fewer parties and more quiet evenings at home together. I welcomed the opportunity to spend these evenings alone with my love. Spending our nights talking in the darkness allowed me to understand the true character underlying the woman I had fallen for. I had already heard the story of Mary's previous engagement to another geologist and how she had caught him cheating on her. As she described her repulsion towards him and her disgust at ever loving him, I was immediately reminded of my own previous regrets. Our conversations went well beyond talk of our past relationships into every area of science, philosophy, religion, parenting, politics, and any other random topic that crossed into my mind. I found it surprising that this loud girl whose energy overwhelmed crowded rooms would retreat during these intimate conversations. In our deepest moments, I often found myself giving a monologue while Mary casually nodded along. When I would prompt her for more, she usually sat on the fence somewhere between my views and the rest of society's lemmings. I felt a subtle hint of dissatisfaction with her handling of these deeper discussions. As we talked, I would eagerly await the emergence of the dynamic personality that I knew was stewing below the surface just waiting to detonate and encapsulate my mind. However, I soon accepted that this permanent absence of intellectual depth wasn't a result of selective shyness as I had deluded myself into believing.

My momentary criticisms of Mary were quickly removed as my emotional mind refocused on the joy of having found my soul mate. I casually ignored Mary's lack of depth and the other seeds of destruction that had infiltrated her identity. These minuscule doubts were rendered inconsequential as soon as we would go out for our weekly double dates with Mike and Angela. I would watch them laughing at her corny jokes, and it would always remind me of our perfect summer together. Mike and Angela were two years ahead of us in their own love story, and I enjoyed looking at the comfort they shared with one another. I knew that Mary and I would experience that same feeling in the years to come, and I looked forward to following the wonderful example of their perfect love. I was confident that the four of us would be friends forever, and I enjoyed these nights more than anything else during this time. Mike and I were in the process of overcoming our childhood dreams of playing hockey, and these wonderful women were the perfect distraction. After each of these nights, I would drive home drunk with a sense of rekindled passion for the woman I had become intoxicated with.

The first major obstacle with Mary came a couple months into our relationship when her ex-fiancé came to town. It became clear that they had unfinished business when he showed up at her house. I found Mary's emotional response to be strange. If any of my previous girls had visited, I would have laughed at the notion that they could impact my emotions now that I had moved on to the real thing. The night he was leaving town, Mary got a call asking why she hadn't spent time with him. She made plans to meet him, but I put the kibosh on that. I was shocked that my girlfriend was actually considering meeting her old fiancé in the middle of the night. Eventually, our argument ended with us going back to bed and her not seeing him.

The next day, Mary explained that it was hard for her because she still wanted to be friends with him. I gave her the benefit of the doubt because I knew she was a giving person that hated to hurt people. However, I didn't like the idea of her talking to him when he clearly still had feelings for her. Additionally, I forced her to apologize for not being more open about the situation. When she acknowledged her mistake, I was left with no reason to believe she was insincere. I figured this would be a defining moment in our growth as a couple and bring us even closer together. I was wrong.

It took less than two weeks for the ex-fiancé problem to reemerge. I turned on my computer only to find Mary's email open with a flood of messages between the two of them. My heart immediately sunk down in my chest. I looked at the messages and painfully read as she apologized for not seeing him while using me as the excuse. The emails also talked about how she missed him but couldn't forgive him for what he had done. I felt betrayed and confronted her immediately at her apartment. Our ensuing two hour talk was filled with tears and ultimately ended with me leaving both her apartment and the relationship. I walked back to my house in the pouring rain thinking about my fractured world while struggling to appreciate the comical irony of the cliché weather. When I got to my house, I literally wiped rain off my face and metaphorically wiped the rain off my heart so my roommates wouldn't see my pain as I went to my room. Five minutes later, Mary came in with tears in her eyes and crawled into bed. We didn't say a word but simply held each other in mutual sadness. It was a truly surreal night, and I had no idea if it was the final embrace of our relationship or the beginning of our reconciliation.

Over the next week, Mary and I talked many times. She explained how part of her had unwittingly reverted back to an earlier time in her life, but she said I was the only one she loved. Part of my mind told me this was the optimal opportunity to get out of the relationship since I had been feeling increasingly disillusioned with the reality of Mary's character. Mary was a dazzling cover filled with blank pages. I knew she didn't have the traits of my ideal woman that I had optimistically imposed upon her. Despite this knowledge, I was unable to break my love of the book's cover. The after-effects of our first week together were still too powerful. I found myself once again making an ill-advised emotional decision while suppressing my better judgment. Even though her explanation was grossly insufficient to cover her actions, I heard what I wanted to hear and rested in the comfort of my new delusion. She consciously loved me while her limbic system still loved him. My emotions drove me back to her while my cortex had retreated altogether. As my emotional mind forgave Mary and saved our relationship, my subconscious self had already come to accept that our romance was on the path to its demise.

It didn't take long to return to our former routine. Routines are nice that way. I think we both appreciated the stability more than anything. I loved having someone to pick me up for lunch every day, have dinner ready after practice, and, most importantly, be a conversation co-pilot when we were out with friends. Even though we reverted back to our previous habits, my underlying dissatisfaction with Mary continued to grow. By the time spring arrived, I found myself despising the love of my life. I began to hate the woman I loved. I spent my days in a state of constant reflection trying to find a parachute to provide an easy ejection. I started to resent every aspect of Mary's personality. I was repulsed by the utter unoriginality of her jokes. There was nothing that made me want to blow my brains out more than listening to her stupid jokes about her being the cute one while her sister was a flannel wearing lumberjack or any of her embarrassing geology jokes that would make even six year olds roll their eyes. Mary was like a bad comedian with only one act. I thought the act was funny the first time, but I soon started to realize there was nothing else coming. I would often return to the same show and laugh at the old jokes while secretly yearning for new material. After a while, one must recognize that a few jokes are insufficient for longevity in the comedy business. At some point, there has to be more than a single act. A person begins to realize that the only reason the comedian was funny originally was because the audience came looking for laughs. Mary never had the follow-up act I yearned for. There is nothing worse than waking up next to a person after failing in a yearlong attempt to wish them into the person you had hoped for. Mary turned out to be nothing more than a blinding first impression that infected my life for far too long before a proper remedy was discovered. I spent a long time in denial not only to avoid the truth of Mary's vacuous nature but also to cling to the last strands of optimism about my life having a happy ending. In the end, Oscar Wilde perfectly described my relationship with Mary when he said "There is one thing infinitely more pathetic than to have lost the woman one is in love with, and that is to have won her and found out how shallow she is." No other line could better explain the disappointment I felt towards the hollow onion Mary turned out to be.

Despite my jaded feelings, it wasn't easy to find an immediate exit. It is hard to cut down a tree with deep roots. Finally, the day arrived. Three months after I had read the emails between Mary and her ex-fiancé, history repeated itself. When I read the notes this time, I was struck with both anger at her lies and relief that I had found my exit strategy. The thing that actually pissed me off most was not the part saying she still loved him but rather the smaller comments that reminded me how different she was from the person I had hoped for. One of the main comments that really irked me was when she told him she would pray for god's guidance. I couldn't believe that, after all this time agreeing the notion of god was purely a mythical byproduct from humanity's infancy, she was telling him how much she believed. Don't get me wrong, I am not saying I was critical of the belief itself (I actually am critical of the belief, but that is not the point here) but rather was angry that she had lied and hid who she really was for the entire time we had been together. For a person who prided herself on her outgoing nature, Mary turned out to be outgoing only when discussing useless drivel while simultaneously managing to turn cowardly away from all questions of actual value. I read a couple more messages and decided I had seen enough to justify our breakup. I left for practice and decided to break up with her later that night.

When I returned from practice, there was a massive feast waiting for me. One thing Mary was always good at was the domestic side of our relationship. If only I had been a chauvinist from the 1920s, we might have ended up with a model marriage revolving around family dinners and suppressed emotions. As we ate, I realized it would be hard to breakup with Mary and started to have second thoughts. There was no doubt I wanted to end things, but I wondered if I should wait until after the season so I could continue to reap the benefits of having my own personal chef. Ultimately, the cost of listening to Mary for another two months outweighed the value of a few meals, and I decided to go through with the breakup.

As I ended my relationship with Mary, her passionate plea for forgiveness fell on deaf ears. It was empowering to be in complete control. My relationship with Mary concluded a lifelong quest for true love. Mary ended the last shards of faith I had in happy endings. I had been sad in the past when I had broken up with girlfriends, but I was surprisingly not sad this time. In fact, I felt no emotional response at all. She just became some girl I used to know. The end of this relationship broke the monopoly my emotions had on controlling my decisions. After we broke up, I felt a clarity of thought that was previously absent from my life. I began to understand the world not through the delusional view of an optimistic man trying to fulfill his dreams, but through the wisdom of a man that understood those dreams were fictional. Fictitious characters and fictitious storylines can only exist in fiction. They have no place in the real world.

It would have been easy for me to respond to this newfound enlightenment in the wrong way. I could have become completely cynical and fallen into depression. This response would have been amplified during this transitional period of my life by my disillusionment with hockey and the rest of my previous dreams. Fortunately, my enlightenment provided the foundation that created my later identity and brought so much joy to those around me. I would become a person that looked on the world as an outsider capable of making the hard decisions that can only be made with foresight of a greater good.

After Mary, I didn't have another serious relationship until later in life when I met Fantasia. I spent time with many gorgeous girls but carefully guided those relationships into solid friendships or short term physical relationships. In fact, I ended up spending most of my senior year rekindling a romance and renewed friendship with Anna. This time, I was careful to make my intentions clear to avoid aggravating her previous scars. It was comforting to have Anna back.

Although I spent most of my senior year at home in solitude, I enjoyed having her over every once in a while to spend the night. Anna had changed significantly since we had dated. I immensely admired the person Anna had grown into and regretted the fact that I was responsible for the ever-present sadness hiding behind her eyes. No matter how happy Anna appeared to be, this sadness was unmistakably still within her. The effects of a person's first heartbreak can never be erased. I was aware these scars remained with Anna and was therefore sure to avoid escalation into a committed romance. It was clear this type of relationship would now be unattainable based on our history. Fortunately, we started to develop a solid friendship instead. I unquestionably prefer a friendship based on mutual admiration to a relationship based on passion. Whenever it looked like we might move back into something more serious, we were reminded that the past is always present.

By my final year of college, I had developed a view of relationships that would remain with me for the rest of my life. I spent time with Anna without allowing myself to make another fatal commitment. On the night we watched *Atonement*, I observed the main character writing a happy ending that she couldn't give her loved ones in reality and thought about the alternative world I wished I could have written for Anna. I finally understood that all my romances were better in my mind at the outset before they were destroyed in reality. I vowed to never again hurt someone like I had done to both Anna and Cassidy. It was too late to make up for my previous mistakes. Those wounds had scarred and could not be healed. I am proud to say that, since this point, I have never broken another woman's heart. I realized that I had been doomed from the start because of the idealism I had towards my mom. In fact, even when I now rationally defend my uncommitted promiscuity, I am unable to fully appreciate it on an adrenal level because of my emotional connection to my parent's story. My life had taught me that dreams don't occur when one is awake. Instead of hopelessly searching for an impossible life for myself, I would end up spending my time fulfilling the dreams of others. I had no desire to get married to appease my fear of being alone. That fear no longer existed. I could still meet plenty of women to take care of my physical needs without the emotional hassle. Additionally, once I gained complete control over my emotions and became sufficiently trained in the ancient art of masturbation, I really had no need for women at all.

My relationships with Anna and Cassidy taught me a valuable lesson about the consequences of my actions. These relationships helped to create a new person that made decisions in the best long-term interests of those I loved instead of simply following my immediate desires. I wanted to be above emotion and act only for those I loved. My conversations with Mike during my final year of college made me realize that I cared more about his story than my own. It was a wonderful side effect that my egocentrism was destroyed along with my dreams. My admiration for Mike helped me realize that I wanted to make a difference in the stories of the people I loved rather than focusing on myself. I wanted to be capable of making difficult decisions against my own desires to accomplish what would most benefit others. Anybody can take credit for doing a good deed with a good result, but the sign of true integrity is someone who can make sacrifices to achieve a desired objective. My work as a writer would supersede my selfish need for someone to call my own. My time with Mary had taught me the dangers of thinking with emotion and evaluating the present based on a fictional future. Ultimately, another person is only as good as their storyline in your mind, and time turns all stories into tragedies. Glory fades, wounds heal, and everything ends in a whimper. This passionless ending is the true tragedy of life that must be avoided. If Mary had been killed a month into our relationship, I would have spent my life wrongly thinking she was the perfect woman. My illusion would have not only been unbreakable, it would have steadily grown. There is no doubt this fiction would have been better than the ensuing reality.

Ultimately, my relationships turned me into the opposite of what women are commonly attracted to. Women want a bad boy that they can turn into a good guy. Women want the player who becomes monogamous. I was a hopeless romantic that became hopeless about romance. All I wanted growing up was to find a girl to devote my life to. My only fear was that I would end up living a life of lonely torture. I guess it is true that the road to hell is paved with good intentions. I ended up not only living my fear of loneliness but preferring this life to the alternative. I became addicted to a certain type of sadness. Fortunately, there was a silver lining. Loneliness is a virtue both to a writer and a killer. The best work in these fields is accomplished alone. I knew I would never have my parents' relationship that I grew up dreaming of. Instead of chasing that elusive illusion, I decided the best therapy would be to finally write my mom's story. I would give closure to her memory and move on with my life. Instead of the romantic pleasure I previously desired, I found a simple contentment in being detached from the shackles of hope. I had put my dreams back to sleep and would now devote myself to my altruistic occupation. I had lost faith in the real world and would no longer allow myself to be blindfolded by emotion. I had seen the true story of reality and missed my days of fiction. My life would no longer be defined by the love I was searching for. My life would be defined by the love I would create.

CHAPTER 3

Mom in Heaven

Men are what their mothers made them.

-Ralph Waldo Emerson

CHAPTER 3: Mom in Heaven

My youth was in the rear view mirror, and I set out to write the real story of my life. My childhood character had been a kindhearted dreamer with endless potential. This young optimist no longer existed. He was killed by his own success. If hockey had ended after high school, I would have been passionate about it forever. However, something had changed in me over the past few years. I saw no value in the achievements within our society and simply wanted to actually feel life for once. I was fully aware that I couldn't entirely reject society. I wouldn't completely retreat to Walden Pond as that simply wasn't who I was. Instead, I saw myself becoming an outwardly functional member of society while internally overcoming its constraints. I planned to continue with my education at the University of Michigan to get my PhD in Biomedical Engineering, but I knew this career would only be a mask covering the life I lived in my mind's eye. I would exist within the system but live above it. My body was destined to be a prisoner, but my mental freedom was attainable. These liberating feelings grew ever more powerful within me and coincided with an increase in my desire to write. My pessimism about reality collided with my desire to make the world a better place and led me to fiction. Instead of allowing the hopeless emptiness surrounding me to lead me to depression, I used this reality as my motivation to create a better world through text. My relationships had taught me that the fatal flaw in the storylines of reality is that the climax always precedes the conclusion. In fact, stories that peak at the end are referred to as tragedies in our world like a young married couple killed on their honeymoon before they ever have the opportunity to sleep angrily in separate rooms. My insight as a writer was the realization that the real tragedies are non-fiction stories with too many chapters. The first half of a tragic novel is an inspirational story. Even in my own life, the only relationship I looked back on fondly was Kelsey because it ended prematurely. The only way to achieve lasting happiness is for happiness to end. Eternity can only exist for a moment.

My newly-enlightened worldview massively changed the objective of my life. I was focused on becoming a person who wrote happiness into the world and set out to achieve this goal. As a result of my efforts during this period of peaceful crisis, my new personality started to blossom. I found myself on a pendulum between my cheerful nature and depressing thoughts as I continued my struggle to develop a new identity. The majority of this internal battle took place during the summer between graduating from Michigan Tech and moving to Ann Arbor. I spent that summer enjoying as much time as I could with my family at our cabin. My days were spent playing with my little cousins, Ryan and Anna, who never failed to distract me from future worries. We would fish, swim, barbecue, and just enjoy every relaxing minute we had together. There are no greater joys in my memories than these days spent doing nothing with those I love. At the end of each day, I would spend my night reading books or just gazing at the stars pondering the purpose of life. I looked out on my future and could see the life I yearned to live. My blissful days at the cabin provided the foundation for the type of eternal joy I wished to create in fiction. Whenever I had time to myself, I wrote in my first book that was going to be based on my mother's life. I took full advantage of all my older family members that summer as I casually asked questions about my mom's history, habits, and dreams. It was through these conversations that I was able to research my first character, and I finished the first two chapters of *Mom in Heaven* before the summer had ended.

When I arrived in Ann Arbor, my identity crisis was completely unleashed. My days were no longer filled with people I loved which forced me to confront life head on. This growth process had started in the summer but was mitigated by my family's presence. Unfortunately, we are often crippled by those we love. I can only imagine how many people never pursue their goals or move to their dream locations because they want to take care of or be near those they love. It is ironic that the greatest joys in our life can often be its biggest impediment. With my cherished summer days converted to memory, the long-term currency of happiness, I was now free to change into my new self. I had been internally fighting for years to eliminate the roadblocks standing between my reality and the life I coveted. The time constraints of playing hockey were finally removed. My illusion of happily ever after was acknowledged as such. I finally had the time to cultivate my ideas from the last few years in order to create the person I wanted to become. In a way, I was contradicting myself by believing there was no purpose in life while simultaneously trying to determine the goals for my future. However, I like to think this contradiction was superficial as the resulting goals for my life in no way resembled the useless achievements and faulty purposes that are commonly valued in our society. One thing was clear right from the start: I needed to be a writer more than anything. I wanted to be someone who brought joy to the world, and I knew the best way to achieve this end was through the means of fiction. I had discovered the virtue of lying. As a result, I made the decision soon after my arrival in Ann Arbor that my life would revolve around writing.

Life in Ann Arbor was drastically different than the previous worlds I had lived in. I was still busy during the days as I immersed myself in research, but, in the evenings, I would retreat into my solitude to write. My life revolved around research, writing, working out, and going out for drinks with friends a couple times a week. In the lab, I was working on cutting edge cancer research that had the potential to cure thousands of people. At my house, I was writing a book to resurrect my mom. I still remember the first night I spent awake in Ann Arbor writing *Mom in Heaven*. I reread the first two chapters that I had written in the summer which were entirely based upon the true story of my mom. The second chapter had ended on the day she received news that she had gotten cancer. When I finished reading these first two chapters, I just stared at the blank screen in front of me titled Chapter 3. My hands were touching the keyboard, but I was unable to type a single word. I wondered if it was just a case of writers block, but it quickly became clear that I was encountering a much more profound experience. I knew the first two chapters were over. I knew the third chapter didn't exist. The blank page I was staring into was the true story of my mom's life. My fingers so desperately wanted to start the chapter and bring her back, but the tormenting stare of that blank page was impossible to interrupt. I remained helpless against death as I spent the entire night staring into the depths of my mom's nonexistence. It wasn't a sad story. It wasn't a tale of suffering. The real tragedy was the emptiness. I had been four years old when my mom had died, but I was finally facing the loss for the first time in my life as I stared into this endless void. As I scrolled down the page, I could envision words jumping out at me describing laughter that never existed. I pictured my mom on vacations she would never take. I saw the pride in her eyes looking at her kids that she would never watch grow up. I could imagine these words organized on the screen in front of me, but I was physically unable to turn them into reality. When I finally went to bed late that night, my mom was still dead.

It took more than a week before I could open the book again. I found myself constantly daydreaming about the words that had been erased from those empty pages. It was during this time that I was truly able to overcome death for the first time in my life. When I finally opened the book the next week, a miracle occurred in the form of the first word at the start of Chapter 3. My mom was resurrected in a single sentence. Once I brought her back to life, my mom's story told itself. She had waited over twenty years to continue with her life and wasn't going to waste a minute. I smiled as I watched my mom living her happy ending. I never felt as if I was in control of her so much as simply being an admiring bystander observing her story and recording it for the world. It was the story of a perfect mother and the fulfillment of a life spent devoted to one's kids. The book revolved around a mother so miraculous that she could only be described as coming straight from heaven. I have had countless people tell me over the years that the final passage of *Mom in Heaven*, in which the old woman smiles as she gazes out at her family through the kitchen window, brought tears to their eyes and comfort to their hearts. The fact that her story was able to inspire so many people and bring so much joy to the world justified my act of resurrection. I had beaten death. Not only was my mom still alive, it was now certain that she would never die.

Writing *Mom in Heaven* was life altering. I had never written a novel before and found myself excited to open the computer every day. I was surprised how quickly the pages accumulated as the story wrote itself. The best feeling for a writer is to feel as if he is simply reading a book as it comes off his fingertips. I was never able to predict what the next surprise would be. I spent every night writing except for the couple nights a week when I would go out to the bar for drinks. In addition to the great new friendships I was developing in Ann Arbor, my two best friends were only an hour away at medical school at Michigan State. As often as I could, I would head to Lansing to see them. Things never ceased to get out of control on these visits. Since Derbe had already been in Lansing for a year, he had a nice group of friends. Every time I visited, I would leave with another set of priceless memories. I was content with my life in Ann Arbor, but those weekends in Lansing with Derbe and Mike were what I looked forward to most. One of my favorite trips during my first year was Halloween. We kicked off the night with drinks at Derbe's apartment as we all got into our costumes.

Mike and Angela dressed up like Shrek and his princess while Derbe and I dressed up as a cock block with him wearing a chicken outfit and me wearing a block outfit. After taking a dozen shots of tequila at the house, we headed down to the bars. Derbe and I had a phenomenal night staying true to our costume and cock blocking random guys at the bar all night. Every cute girl we saw talking to a different guy became a victim of our costume, and it worked wonderfully as we steadily stole girls away. After about an hour at the first bar, we left with a couple girls and went to Rick's to add a little dirtiness to our Halloween night. Derbe had a full chicken suit on with his head completely covered up, but, when he gave the bouncer his ID, the guy just let him right in. I remember thinking it was the ideal night for underage drinking with the type of bouncers working at Rick's. Any kid could throw on a mask and get right in with no questions asked. Once we were inside, we moved directly to the dance floor. Rick's was packed, and we danced all night. Eventually, the night ended, and we made it back to Derbe's place with a much larger entourage than we had started the night with. During the after-party, I made everyone promise they would make it to breakfast the next morning before I had to return to Ann Arbor.

When I woke everyone the following morning, I saw some of the worst hangovers I have ever witnessed. Miraculously, Derbe and Mike both made it to breakfast. The prior night had been fun, but breakfast turned out to be the real highlight of the weekend. In addition to our usual practice of piecing the stories of the previous night back together, we were able to witness some of the all-time greatest walks of shame. Since the restaurant was directly in the middle of campus, there was an endless stream of people walking home dressed in whatever small fraction of their costumes that had made it through the night. Chirping people as they walked by turned out to be a remarkable remedy for our hangovers. I can't imagine a better day for people watching than the morning after Halloween on a major college campus. The three of us made a pact that we would start a yearly tradition of going out together for Halloween and getting up early for an annual people watching walk of shame breakfast. As I drove home that day, I found myself overwhelmed with excitement to return to Lansing in 364 days for a repeat of that classic night.

In addition to Halloween, I visited my friends quite a few times during my first year of grad school. Although each visit was unpredictable and unique in its own way, there were a few constants. First, no matter where we went, Derbe and I were sure to hunt down plenty of girls. Some of these girls were good for dancing, some were fun to talk to, some were fun to have a drink with, and some just made for a good laugh at their expense. What was most enjoyable was just spending time with my friend. Hitting on girls simply added a nice activity for us to share. I especially enjoyed when Derbe started to like a girl which always made me hope to hear his famous solid steel sex appeal line once again although it unfortunately never reemerged. Another constant in my weekends in Lansing was the continuance of my conversations with Mike. I had missed our daily conversations once the prior year had ended so it was wonderful when we could get together and just talk while we shared a couple drinks. Mike was in the process of planning his proposal to Angela so every weekend I visited I would give him five or six new ideas for the proposal. Some ideas would be funny while others would be heartfelt. Unfortunately, Mike never took my advice which is why his proposal isn't worth including here (I changed it when I wrote my second novel), but, not surprisingly, Angela said yes when Mike finally proposed about half way through the year. Overall, my visits to Lansing consisted of too much alcohol and not enough time. The wine always outlasted the night. Every time I had to leave, I wished the weekend could last forever. The mornings in Lansing were also enjoyable as I would always be the first one awake to assess the damage. One of the best cures for a bad hangover is a friend with a worse hangover, and I loved watching the reactions as my friends struggled to pull themselves out of bed. I was truly at peace with my life during these mornings and would often write in my book while I waited for everyone to wake up for breakfast.

After three months of writing during my evenings and weekends, I finished *Mom in Heaven*. Upon completion, I felt a genuine sense of pride in what I had accomplished. This pride resulted not from the actual book for which I would soon be praised but rather from my ability to give my mom the life that had been stolen from her. I gave the first couple drafts of the book to my closest friends and family whose positive reinforcement pushed me to contact a publisher. I loved my book but was still surprised at the extent of its success. I had not set out to write a bestseller but had written for the love of my mom. The novel was a labor of love that brought the added bonus of financial stability. It was a masterpiece that made it clear writing was my true calling. I am not saying that I became the greatest writer of all time, but what I am not saying is true. What was more important to me than people loving the book was how much people loved my mom. I knew I had been successful when I saw how much more the character was worshiped in comparison to the book itself. The book was selling because people fell in love with the protagonist. I could never have imagined that only a year after beginning grad school, I would be on my way to a research conference in Orlando and see my novel being sold at the airport. It was truly a remarkable experience that would have increased my passion for writing if that was even possible. I decided to finish graduate school and get my PhD, but, in my heart, I was one hundred percent a writer.

After my book was published, my day to day life didn't really change much. I was still a graduate student during the day, wrote books at night, and spent time with my friends as much as possible. People had heard about my book, but it wasn't yet to the point where I would be recognized in public so my privacy was essentially unaffected for the next couple years. In fact, even though my book was selling well, it was mostly through word of mouth, and I was virtually free from marketing events with the exception of the occasional phone interview. The most frequently asked question during these interviews was when I was going to publish my second novel. The truth was I had no idea.

I began to brainstorm different ideas for my next book. I reflected upon the success of *Mom in Heaven* and the inspiration that it seemed to bring. As someone who believed the world was a sad place, I felt amazing about the fact that my book was able to rise above reality and create happiness for my readers. Most importantly, I was thankful that my book was able to bring eternal joy to my mom. As I started to search for ideas for my next book, I decided to keep the format that had made *Mom in Heaven* so successful. I loved the fact that the first two chapters were complete reality while the rest of my book was the fictional happy ending of my character. I felt this structure allowed my character to be anchored in reality but not constrained by it. I wanted my characters to be real people that lived unreal lives. Because of this, I decided I would use the same structure as a model for my subsequent books.

As I began to write my second novel, I found myself growing ever more frustrated with my inability to replicate that first story. During this time, I started and abandoned about ten different books. I ultimately decided to write two chapters about a real person and then make the rest of the story fulfill the character's dreams in fiction. It was an attempt to recreate the same type of inspirational story that had made my mom's novel a success. My hours in the research lab increased dramatically around this time as I was beginning to have a lot of success with my cancer project. However, as every breakthrough led to increasing praise from my colleagues, I started to care less and less. I came to realize that my work was just as likely to cure an idiot as save someone who was truly worthy. It was too late for me to get rid of my mom's tumor, and it really didn't even matter since I had discovered the power to overcome death altogether. My mom's legacy was impeccable. The entire world was beginning to hear her story. In fact, if it weren't for her early death, there is no way she could have possibly achieved this longevity of perfection. I still loved the science behind my research but had to stomach a nice dose of hypocrisy whenever I spoke of the importance of my work at a conference. I knew that curing cancer couldn't save anyone. The only way for them to actually be saved was to idealize their memory. Reality can never compare to a person's image in the memories of those who love them. This is what I created with my mom and what I hoped to continue in the rest of my books.

Finding someone worth writing about was a constant struggle. Whenever I would meet a new person, I would think about basing my second story on them but was forced to give up on most people. At our second annual Halloween breakfast in Lansing, every person that walked by our table looked like they would have been worthy of a story if only I had caught them the previous night before the climax. I ultimately wanted to find a person whose dreams were large enough to inspire the world. I felt as if I had the ability to create a purely fictional person to fill this role, but, each time I would attempt to write a fake story, the character just felt too dishonest. I didn't feel like I was accomplishing anything of value when the characters were purely from my mind. My mom's ending might have been fictional, but she was real. These new characters were fake, and I couldn't understand why it seemed to bother me so much. For some reason, I couldn't muster any passion into writing their stories. I would often sit around talking to Mike about my frustration with writing my second book. He was the one person I really opened up to about my writing. Mike understood how much the first book meant to me because it was based on my mom. No other person has ever known that *Mom in Heaven* was actually based on my own mother. Mike would always love my story ideas and tell me that they didn't have to mean as much as my first book as long as the stories themselves were of value. I understood what he meant and would have given the same advice to another author if I had the opportunity, but I wanted my work to stand for something greater than the writers of the past. I hoped to make an actual impact on the world and not just be a nice distraction from the devastation of reality. As my complaining continued, Mike even suggested that I try writing a non-fiction book. It was a nice sentiment, but writing non-fiction is an unsatisfying undertaking. I thanked Mike for his advice but told him, "I don't believe in non-fiction" and the thought never crossed my mind again. I wanted to write inspirational books, and I could never write about something as unrealistic as a happy reality. If one ever doubts the natural state of the world is anything but suffering, then one is ignoring the obvious truth of evolution. Every single instance of abundance for a species will ultimately lead to increased population until that very abundance has led to destruction. Success only enhances our haste to return to our natural state of competitive starvation. True to nature, a happy humanity won't rest until its misery is restored. The facts of the world made it clear that I would be unable to take Mike's well-intentioned advice. I didn't want to be an author that added to the misery of reality, and non-fiction could only lead me down two roads: a profound pessimist or a hypocritically delusional positivist. In reality, nothing positive is profound; it is merely cliché. There was no doubt that the only path to happiness was through fiction. As much as I loved talking to Mike, I quickly realized discussing my writing with him was pointless. There is no such thing as a literary duet. A writer must compose his work in the company of only his own thoughts.

Despite the fact that we stopped talking about my writing, there was always plenty for us to discuss. Whenever I would visit Lansing, we would play a couple games of tennis before sharing a few drinks and talking about his life with Angela. By the time my second year of grad school started, I had settled into a nice routine of visiting Derbe and Mike every couple weeks. Mike asked me to be his Best Man, and I was honored to have the opportunity to stand next to him when he married Angela. The wedding was set for the following June and during every visit I heard more about their wedding plans. Mike and Angela represented a light in the darkness of my life. Even though I had a best-selling novel and continuous success in grad school, I was delving deeper into a pessimistic depression. I had fun every day but ended each night depressed at the state of the world. I was thankful for my visits to see Derbe and Mike that brought so much joy into my life. I was glad to see how content they were with their lives, but I found myself constantly questioning what I was doing with my own. I was trying to continue my writing career, and my love affair with fiction was growing, but yet I couldn't overcome the sense of pointlessness in my new characters.

During that year, I met a couple impressive people that I thought could be transformed into books, but I was always unable to translate them into success. The problem I encountered was that the people I met contained an unquenchable hope for the future which always made for a promising start but ultimately led to the book's demise in the end. With my purely fictional characters, I could never overcome the lack of emotional attachment. With my real characters, it was the emotional attachment that actually prevented me from finishing their stories. I could see the agony of the real world around me and felt guilty for writing stories that were better than the people's actual lives. The shallowness of my purely fictional attempts wasn't nearly as bad as the tragedy of these quasi-fictional stories that only highlighted the real person's plight. I wished there was a literary Dr. Kevorkian to fix the situation. At least Kevorkian was ending people's misery albeit a little late. I was just ignoring the patients' prognosis and writing false reports about fake cures. Most doctors in the world simply lack the foresight to understand they are unintentionally increasing suffering with every cure. I had thought that writing the happy endings for these people would be doing them some good, but I found that my stories did nothing in reality. I had the emotion and the storyline to mimic their ideal world and create a truly inspirational story, but reality was too agonizing to overlook. I soon found that I had no passion for what I was doing for the simple reason that, although I was creating a separate, better universe for these people, I was not actually changing their prognosis. It was the same problem I had with my work curing cancer while doing nothing to mitigate the real disease of humanity. My cancer research could extend many lives, but I knew that would probably do more harm than good. The only way to really save these people would be to let them die. Unfortunately, many of these patients had progressed too far even for death. The furthest I ever got in creating a second book was a story based on a nurse I met at the hospital during one of our fetal sheep experiments. It was a touching story about a single mom struggling for her kids as she overcame the odds. As I reached the inspirational climax of the story, the real woman that motivated the book lost her job and was evicted from her house. Seeing the pitiful ending of reality made me distraught at the inconsequential effects my book would have. This was the darkest time of my life as a writer, and I ultimately gave up on the whole process after this final failed attempt. I printed one copy of that woman's story and deleted the file. I took this sole copy outside and set it on fire. Burning this story was extremely therapeutic. I watched her happy ending disappear from the earth and wondered if my writing career was fated to end amongst those flames.

Eventually, I realized my mom's book was beautiful because fiction was her only reality. I had actually created a happy ending for her that wasn't trying to cover-up another miserable ending simultaneously taking place. I understood my subsequent failures were a result of my characters' branching identities and my inability to overcome the feelings of regret that those happy endings couldn't stand alone. Once a person's dreams have been destroyed in reality, no false memory can overcome this heartbreak. I didn't understand it then, but I had learned an important lesson in the timing of intervening in a character's life. My mom's death had allowed her to become the perfect story which was what was lacking in my other attempted books. Her death had ironically removed the roadblocks to immortality.

When my second spring in Ann Arbor arrived, I put writing on hold. I accepted defeat and decided to wait for my motivation to be naturally triggered. My focus changed from worrying about my next book to getting excited for the upcoming summer. Mike's wedding was drawing near, and I seemed to have something different planned every weekend. As Mike's Best Man, I wanted to help in every possible way so I spent quite a few weekends in Lansing. Lucky for me, Mike and Angela were obsessive compulsive so there wasn't much for me to do. When I would visit on those weekends, I spent most of the time just sitting around with a beer making fun of their fake fruit (they had bowls of plastic fruit for decoration which always seemed pointless when they could have just gotten a bowl of real fruit for company to actually eat). I loved chirping this perfect pair about how they had become an old country club couple that rarely went out with friends anymore. I knew they were busy with medical school, but it was nonetheless fun to hassle them about their boring lifestyle. In truth, I admired how content these two similar individuals were just being together. Angela had been a college basketball star at Michigan Tech where her team had gone to the national championship. Whenever her friends were around, Mike would constantly hear about their accomplishments while they reminded him that we could barely win a game. After Angela's friends would leave, the three of us would laugh at how much our lives had changed since our years of being consumed by our respective sports. I was extremely pleased that Mike had found someone so similar to him who valued the things that were truly important in life. Angela possessed an unassuming nature that made her look like an outcast amongst many of the medical students that had the humility of Ron Burgundy without actually being a big deal. Every time I visited Mike and Angela, I was amazed at their good fortune to have found each other. They were perfect counterparts and spending time with them was a welcome distraction from the unrelenting rumination that had accompanied my desire to write another novel.

My main job leading up to the wedding was organizing the bachelor party. The original plan was to take a trip to Vegas, but it turned out to be impossible with Mike and Derbe's busy medical school schedules. Even though our Vegas trip fell apart, Derbe and I were able to plan a fun bachelor party in Lansing for the Saturday before the wedding. On the day of the bachelor party, I rolled into town and met Derbe about ten in the morning. We filled a truck with alcohol and went over to Mike's apartment. The plan was to drink by the pool for a few hours, play golf in the afternoon, get a nice dinner, hit up the local strip club, and then let the rest of the night take us where it may. A couple other guys were meeting us for the evening, but it was nice for just the three of us to visit by the pool to start our day. It was the relaxing atmosphere we needed to mix a few jokes with some serious talk about the upcoming wedding. I was proud of the type of person Mike had grown into and didn't think his life could possibly get any better. As the drinks started to empty, the conversation turned to old stories and laughter until it was finally time for golf. We took a cab down to the course and loaded the cart with beer and cigars. Since we were already pretty tanked, golf was a complete debacle. My first tee shot went directly left, Mike's went right, and Derbe's went down the middle. We looked at each other and immediately decided a scramble would be our best bet if we wanted to finish golfing in less than ten hours. For the most part, we just wanted to drink and visit so golf just provided a venue. I have never seen a game of golf in which the players cared less about their shots. There were quite a few holes where Mike just smoked his cigar while Derbe hit on the beer girls and I complained about missing Vegas and told them we better create our own Vegas experience in Michigan. We may not have done much golfing, but it was an amazing afternoon regardless. The only hassle was constantly trying to avoid the country club grandpa who kept trying to give us advice on our swings. This ancient relic just didn't understand that we couldn't care less about golf. The only thing he was good for was the addition of a few Alzheimer's jokes. The guy was dead; he had just forgotten to fall.

After a delightful afternoon of golfing, I told the guys it was time to bring Vegas to the Midwest. However, it was a good thing that dinner was next on the agenda because Derbe was absolutely starving and I could see in his eyes that he was ready to lose it. When we called for a cab and found out it would be a half hour, the Bipolar Bear almost lost his mind. We decided to call Angela for a ride since Mike's sister was visiting that weekend and Angela was spending the day with her. Once they picked us up, we decided to all grab dinner together. There was nothing more appropriate for this perfect couple than for Angela to be there for Mike's bachelor party dinner. I remember looking at them across the table thinking that this perfectly summed up their relationship. Even though I was the one who invited Mike's sister and Angela to join us for dinner, I had a great time chirping them about how they were so close that he couldn't even go to his bachelor party without her. After calming Derbe down with a nice dinner and then riling him back up with a couple tequila shots, we were joined by our buddy Tomo and parted from the girls for the rest of our night.

The strip club had a typical bachelor party atmosphere, and we made sure it was a wild night. Although most of the night revolved around ensuring Mike enjoyed himself, the highlight turned out to be the first girl I laid eyes on when we walked into the strip club. I immediately noticed this rocker type girl on the other side of the stage looking over at us with an intense stare. Once I was able to take my eyes off her neck tattoo, I noticed her tight shirt and screamed with excitement when I saw that it said Las Vegas across her chest. I yelled to Mike, "I told you I would take you to Vegas for your bachelor party," and, from that point on, we referred to the girl as Vegas for the rest of the night. Every time we took a shot together, I would yell for Vegas to join us, and, before long, she was part of our group. I have rarely met a girl so intimidating. She had a scary, sexy stare that made me nervous that she could erupt at any moment. We took a few shots with her before my attention was turned back to Mike, and things soon spun out of control. We even met a bachelorette party at the strip club, and I was able to convince the bride to get up on stage and strip for Mike. As she gave him a lap dance, she stuck a "Team Bride" pin on his shirt. This worked out perfectly at the end of the night when we carried Mike into his apartment, tucked him into bed with Angela, and pointed out that, even at his bachelor party, he was still on Team Bride.

The next morning when Derbe and I awoke, we started piecing the details of the previous night back together. I made a few jokes about how fun it was to run into Vegas except for the fact that she could have taken sin city to a dangerous level. Derbe laughed and said the last he saw of her was when she walked out with Tomo. This image made me smile as there could not possibly have been two more contrasting people than that wild rocker chick and the quiet Japanese medical student in his button down shirt. I couldn't believe that Tomo could have actually gone home with her. We finally got ahold of Tomo and told him to meet us for breakfast. When Tomo walked in, I congratulated him on a job well done which elicited an awkward, sideways smile that revealed everything. I said I was happy that at least one of us got to spend the night in Vegas. Derbe laughed and told Tomo that we wanted to hear all the details. As I mentioned earlier, Vegas was a complete knockout with a solid dose of psychotic. It turned out she was even crazier than we had suspected. Tomo described going back to her apartment in his shy voice. He said that, as soon as they walked in the door, she viciously slammed him against the walls kissing him until they finally rolled onto the kitchen floor. Vegas then progressed to rip his clothes off, scratch her nails across his chest, and wasted no time getting it in. Derbe and I went wild when we heard that Tomo had gotten laid. He tried to avoid telling the rest of the story, but we pressed on and eventually he continued. He said that he tried to put a condom on, but she ripped it off and said it felt so much better without it. When he was almost finished, he tried to pull out, but she grasped the back of his head tightly and yelled at him to keep going. He asked her if she was on birth control, and she said no. When he tried to tell her again that he was about to finish, she grabbed his face firmly and told him to cum inside her. Tomo paused, and we were flabbergasted. After an awkward silence, Derbe asked what he did. Tomo said that he tried to tell her that he couldn't do it, but she said, "it feels so much better when you cum inside me," and, after Tomo hesitated, she slapped him in the face and said, "If you don't cum inside me, I will fuckin kill you." We both froze in shock and just stared blankly at Tomo who didn't say another word. I told him that she sounded absolutely psycho and probably wanted to have his baby. We both said that we hoped he didn't do it and got out of there as quickly as possible. I will always remember the look of terror on Tomo's face when he said, "Well, I was scared so I just did it." I didn't believe what I had just heard. I couldn't think of anything to say in response, but Derbe summed it up nicely when he said, "I guess it is true what they say: What happens in Vegas stays in Vegas!"

After breakfast was over, Tomo began the nine most stressful months of his life while I returned to Mike's apartment for a quiet day as we recovered from the previous night. When I think back on my time with Mike, these moments stand out more than anything. The quiet devotion between Mike and Angela on any average day is what made them such a special couple. Since the wedding was in Houghton, I told them I would see them when they arrived. I was going up the week before to visit friends and basically get the party started. Before I left, I gave a letter to both Mike and Angela to let them know how I felt about them. One thing that has been clear in my life is that a heartfelt message is always easier to convey in writing. I have often been praised for my oratory, but my strength of conversation lies in the art of comedy more so than the expression of admiration. Because of this, I often would write letters to those I loved over the years when I felt the need to let someone know how I felt. For some reason, it never felt right to delete these letters, and, thankfully, I can now look back and be reminded of the people that I have truly cared about over the years. With Mike and Angela, any letters I could write would have been unable to express the admiration I had for them, but I attempted anyway. I'm adding these letters here to give a sense of my feeling for these two leading up to their wedding.

Mike,

Since we'll probably be too busy having a blast during your wedding day, I wanted to write you a letter to get the serious stuff out of the way. First off, I want you to know how truly jealous I am of the life you have, the life you are creating, and, most importantly, I am jealous of the fact that you have found that one person that you can't imagine living without. I like to look at relationships like a business deal where there is always an overachiever and someone who is settling for less. With you two, it is honestly hard not to feel like you're both overachieving. I think Angela is such a perfect person for you, and I could not be more impressed by how genuine she is. It's hard to find someone with such a pure soul in this world especially since souls obviously don't exist but just use it in a literature sense and not the literal ghost inside the body view. You are very lucky to have found her. That said, I think you deserve everything you have. I could not be more impressed with the strength of your character and how devoted you are to creating the life you want with Angela. I hope you can find a way to tell everyone else to fuck off whenever they try to get in the way of the life you want. You've spent the last few years waiting for this moment without a single complaint (yes that was a joke), and, now that the life you've been waiting for has finally arrived, I could not be happier for you. I don't want to hear (although I expect I will and obviously don't mind listening) a fuckin word of your bitching over the next years of school because, no matter how much studying you have to do, at least you are now in control of your life. Remember, there is no happy ending. We will all die and there is no fuckin chocolate heaven sorry to burst your bubble. This isn't a bad thing to know. It is actually a great liberation because now you can focus everything on enjoying the time you have with Angela whether you die next week or live to one hundred. As Robert Frost so eloquently said, "happiness makes up in height what it lacks in length." I hope you are able to enjoy every moment of your life and not waste a single day. You definitely deserve it. Also, I just want to say I hope you don't lose who you are in the next years when you are spending your evenings drinking overpriced wine with the other country clubbers but always stay the genuine person that you are. I'm sure it will be easy to get pulled into that world of who has the nicer car or house, but those things are all fake and are not the real markers of a person's worth. The real things of value are the people that you love, and, in that sense, you are already very wealthy. I can't wait to see how your life turns out. I think you are going to make a great husband and an even better father someday, and I hope I am around to witness it. I think you can be as successful as you decide to be in your career, but I know the things I just mentioned are going to be what actually defines you. As hard as your parents' divorce was on your mom, the truth is that her redemption will be achieved through the way you treat Angela. What a great thing it is for her to know that her son embodies the strength that every family needs but few actually have and has a willingness to sacrifice for those he loves. I have no doubt you are perfectly suited for this role, and I know you will create a solid foundation for your family with Angela. I hope you never forget that this is what is truly important. I hope we remain friends for years to come, but, if that doesn't happen for whatever reason, I want you to know it has been an absolute pleasure knowing you these past few years. I've enjoyed our conversations and getting to know you a million times more than I enjoyed that one time we won that one hockey game. If you and Angela ever need ANYTHING, I want you to know I will be there for you in a second whether you need money, help babysitting the kids, help around your house, help killing the neighbors annoying cat with a sledgehammer, or literally anything else big or small. It is a pleasure to call you my friend, and I am so proud of the person you are (not sure why I should take any pride in it but what else do I have to be proud of these days). I wish you all the best in your future life. Congrats!!!

E

When I read this letter now, it reminds me how truly happy I was for Mike at that time. There is no better feeling than watching your best friend's dreams come true. I may have hidden my pessimism about the probable reality of Mike's life, but one should never allow the present to be injured by the future. The present is a time to enjoy. Whatever discomfort the future would hold for Mike and Angela, they deserved their pleasant present illusion of happily ever after. Mike had truly earned the right to have his ideal world become his reality more than any person I had ever met. Marrying Angela represented that dream. Angela was the culmination of his life's desire, and I only hoped she understood how lucky she was.

Angela,

I wanted to write a letter to you about your wedding because I'll probably be making jokes all weekend and won't get the opportunity to really talk to you seriously. First off, I want you to know how truly jealous I am of the life you have, the life you are creating, and, most importantly, I am jealous of the fact that you found that one person that is perfect for you. If gay marriage was legal, maybe you would be writing this letter to me, but, given the world we live in, I could not be happier for you. I like to look at relationships like a business deal where there is always an overachiever and someone who is settling for less, but it is hard not to feel like you're both overachieving. I know you trust Mike more than anyone, but I want you to know he is in fact everything you think he is and more. Mike and I have talked about our futures for hours over the past few years, and I've never met a person who is more devoted to his girl. Actually, I'm pretty sure the reason his blood pressure is so high is that he spends every minute of his life worrying about you. You could not find a better person to start your family with. He is truly one of the nicest people I've ever met while at the same time being such a strong person. I'm not talking about strength in the weight room but rather the strength of character he possesses. I hope you can fully understand how lucky you are, and, even when he burns the chicken some day or accidentally eats one of your plastic pears, I hope you are able to look past the stupid little things that everyone wastes their lives fighting about and remember how lucky you two actually are. It is easy for us to take the people we love for granted especially after we've been with them for a long time, but I hope you can always remember what you have. Trust me, most people will never find someone that is so right for them. I hope you and Mike enjoy every moment you have together whether you live for days or decades. Please don't waste a single second. I know most often when you see me I'm screwing around and probably seem like a mess, but I want you to know that I would do anything for you two. If you ever need ANYTHING, whether it is as small as a ride to the airport or as big as hiding a dead body, I will be there. I could not think more highly of Mike, and I am happy he is getting what he deserves. I am so impressed by the quiet integrity you possess, and, no matter how many years you spend with the other country clubbers, I hope the two of you never lose the strength of character that sets you well above the rest of us. I wish you all the best in the years to come. Congratulations!!!

E

My letter to Angela was an unsuccessful attempt to express how truly fortunate she was to be marrying Mike. As a writer, the quality of my storylines is consistently undermined by the inferiority of my prose. I wanted to express to Angela that the human being she was going to spend her life with had the qualities of a Shakespearean sonnet, but my words fell sadly short. I hoped the underlying message of my letter could overcome what it lacked in poetry. I thought of Angela as a female version of Mike which was the ultimate compliment that I could give to them both. When her friends on the basketball team referred to them as Mangela, I always smiled at the power of that statement. In reality, their characters had morphed together even more than their names. There isn't a guy in the world that could sit through a movie made about these two. It was a real relationship that was too cliché to be believable. I was happily disgusted by this understatedly excessive display of perfect love.

As I drove to Houghton for the wedding, I found my mind drifting back and forth between my own life and Mike's. I reflected on the paths we had both taken and where our lives were leading. What truly set the two of us apart from one another were goals. My dreams as a kid were the same as Mike's. We both wanted to be successful hockey players, meet our dream girls, fall in love, and have a family. My dreams died at Michigan Tech. I had been awoken to the reality of the world and learned to love this depression. With the exception of hockey, Mike's dreams had been reinforced at Michigan Tech. The second guessing of his worldview after his parent's divorce had been overcome by his introduction to Angela. Mike had endless goals for his future and knew exactly what he wanted in his life, but what about me. In contrast to Mike, I didn't have any goals. I obviously loved to write and wanted to relive the feeling of accomplishment I had gotten from my first literary success, but not even writing appealed to me as a goal in itself. I could care less about the notoriety or monetary gains that fell upon a successful author. What appealed to me about writing was the immortality of the characters themselves. The author of a good book is as inconsequential as the cover. It is the story that deserves the recognition. Great characters and great ideas make a masterpiece. My feeling toward research was no different. I was interested in the science behind what I was doing, but had no emotional drive to win a Nobel Prize. I was actually repulsed by the condescension of successful people who had so much pride in their minuscule accomplishments. I have never met another person who has accomplished anything of actual value. The closest I have ever known to true accomplishment is a standup comedian. Although the success is as transient as the laughter, the motivation behind the career is as noble as any other. No achievement could possibly be more rewarding than the creation of a smile. As far as my previous personal aspirations, those dreams were from a closed chapter in my life. My relationships had taught me that any attempt at achieving personal happiness would only make me a slave to my emotions. I had risen above this emotional hold on my life and was now in the position to make decisions at the level of conscious consideration.

As I continued my drive to the wedding, my emotions fluctuated between jubilation and depression. I was dealing with the fact that I had no goals for my own life while simultaneously finding comfort in my happiness for the people I loved. I increasingly found myself feeling that my role in the world was going to be one of altruism. Unlike most people who attempt to live a life for others, I was in the unique position of not wanting anything for myself. Mike's goal in life was to live his perfect life with Angela. My goal in life was for Mike to live his perfect life with Angela. I wanted the effects of my life to improve things for those I loved. I cursed the world I lived in and vowed to be a light that would shine through the darkness. The world may be a depressing place, but that is no excuse for a person to be depressed. I may be a pessimist, but I have never let it get in the way of enjoying each day. My mood slowly improved as I drove towards Houghton, and my dark thoughts were replaced with light music. There is no shrink on earth that can match the therapy one receives in the solitude of a cross country drive. I had come to terms with my own fate and decided I would strive to bring joy to every pointless day. I would henceforth devote my life to the people I loved.

When I arrived in Houghton, the party started immediately. I was staying with my buddy Hal who I had worked with in the Biomaterials Lab. Hal had a luxurious apartment in the middle of downtown Houghton where he no doubt lured countless young women after he stole their hearts at the bars below. It was great to catch up with Hal and the rest of my friends at Tech. Every minute of my time was quickly filled. I spent my days playing tennis or golf and going out for countless meals with old friends. I spent my nights at the bars reminding myself how much I missed these people. By the time the rest of the wedding party made it to town, I had already spent three days on my vacation and felt as if I was a local again. In addition to my friends still in Houghton, Drew and Ryan made it back for the wedding from Florida and Seattle. It was awesome to hear about their new lives. Ryan had gotten engaged to Lindsey a couple months earlier, and I enjoyed having a drink with them Wednesday night. It turned out their wedding date was coincidentally set for one year from that night so we had a toast to their future and then proceeded to spend the rest of our time at a nice place down memory lane. When Drew showed up the next night and immediately announced he had gotten engaged, I was ecstatic. Both he and Ryan were deserving men, and I knew the girls well enough to support their decisions to enter into this voluntary penitentiary. With Mike busy taking care of last minute wedding stuff and spending time with his family, Derbe and I took it upon ourselves to carry the celebration for the wedding party. Unfortunately, I seemed to be the only one burning both ends of the candle as I would be up early every morning for breakfasts while also pushing my body far past the limit in the evenings. On a normal week, I wouldn't have been able to move by

Friday, but my excitement for Mike and Angela gave me more than enough adrenaline to persevere.

Friday was rehearsal day, and we showed up at the church at two in the afternoon. Since most of Angela's bridesmaids were friends from high school, the groomsmen hadn't met them, and the two sides were quietly sitting separately in opposite pews. When I walked in and saw this pitiful display, it reminded me of a middle school dance. Luckily, this shyness didn't last long as one joke was all it took to break the tension and get everyone together. This jovial atmosphere lasted all the way until the priest walked into the church to do what he did best. He crucified the fun as if he had done it a million times before. As the Best Man, I was asked to go into the back room to get the rings and sign the marriage license. When the priest gave me the rings, I jokingly asked if he felt safe trusting such an important part of the ceremony with an Atheist. He condescendingly looked down on me and said, "It is not my job to judge you young man, but I feel compelled to tell you that nobody in their left mind would be an Atheist." I smiled and made a gentle joke to ease the tension and bring the color back to Mike's face. After the pre-wedding consultations he had endured, Mike didn't want anything to set the priest off again.

The wedding rehearsal was the longest ten minutes I have ever seen. Basically, all we had to do was line up, walk down the aisle slowly with our partner, split to our respective sides at the front of the church, and then listen to Mike and Angela say their vows. The priest quickly made it clear that he was not going to let the simplicity of the task prevent us from working a full eight hour shift. As the priest raced back and forth across the church in a constant state of unwarranted panic, it occurred to me that it was probably about time for him to get laid. I would have suggested beating the bishop once in a while, but I knew he wasn't allowed to assault his superior. It got to the point where it was actually comical listening to the priest's directions. Angela's brother with Down Syndrome even rolled his eyes and asked me, "How dumb does he think we is? Does he think we retarded?" For our walk down the aisle, I was paired with Angela's sister who was the Maid of Honor, and, since she had a two year old daughter, I just droned out the continuous lecture coming from the front of the church and had fun playing with that cute little girl. Three months later, when the priest finished his directions, we all headed to dinner downtown. The food was delicious, and we proceeded to have an amazing evening. This was the first time I got to visit with Mike and Angela since they had arrived, and it was awesome to see their hyperthymia. It wasn't a peak of temporary jubilation that you see at most weddings but rather a look of relief. What made them happy was being together, and I could sense the marriage was just a final barrier between them and the rest of the world. They weren't getting married so the world would know they were together; they were getting married so the world could never tear them apart.

Another pleasurable part of the rehearsal dinner was visiting with Mike and Angela's families. It was such a joy to see the pride in Angela's parents' eyes as they no doubt understood the fortune they had inherited with their new son-in-law. Angela's parents were genuine people that had passed their admirable humility to their daughter. I also had the opportunity to talk to Mike's siblings and numerous members of his extended family at the dinner. It was fun to hear the more conservative relatives making jokes about the priest which comforted me as I realized it wasn't only my religious prejudice that had caused my reaction at the rehearsal. Mike and Angela truly had a fabulous family, and I was positive they would be a strong foundation for that family to lean on for the rest of their lives. Mike and Angela had a type of moral fiber designed for dependability. It was a delight to visit with the extended family, but, most importantly, I enjoyed seeing Mike's mom. This tender matriarch was immeasurably proud of her son and must have known her life would soon be vindicated by his marriage. After all that Mike had told me about his family, I fully understood how much it meant for his mom to see the type of person he had turned into. There was no doubt in my mind that Mike represented the antithesis of what his father had become. As I attempted to express to Mike's mom how much I admired her son, in the back of my mind, his character was always contrasted with the faults of his father. I hoped Mike's mom could understand that her sad story had been superseded by the quality of her son and the life he was proposing to give to Angela.

After I left the rehearsal dinner, I walked to another bar to see the rest of my friends since most of the wedding party was heading back to relax. Derbe was also coming, but, since he had to run back to the hotel with his girlfriend, I was walking alone. On my slow walk downtown, I reflected on my conversations at dinner and thought about Mike and his parents. I wondered what Mike's mom must have been like during her own wedding. She unquestionably thought she was marrying a perfect man in the same way Angela felt on that day. I highly doubted that Mike's mom had simply been misled by a man with bad motives. More than likely, she had just been a victim of time. She had married a good man who promised her the world, but, as usual, life got in the way. My walk was nearly finished, but I was unable to stop thinking about the obvious parallels between Mike and his father when he was Mike's age. Both men were aspiring doctors marrying the loves of their lives and could only be described as having impeccable character. What worried me most as I contemplated Mike's fate was whether or not he was destined to follow the same path. I thought about the fact that Mike was similar to his father in so many ways, and he no doubt had strong genetic connections to that paternal personality. Even though I am primarily a behavioral psychologist, it seemed clear to me that Mike would at least be somewhat predisposed to the same flaws. In addition, I couldn't help but think that the cruel nature of the world would ultimately condemn the idealized future of my presently perfect friend. Two sides of my personality battled each other as my admiration and faith in the quality of Mike's character was lined up against my pessimistic view of the powerful forces of nature that reliably lead all lives to their tragic conclusions. Before I became immersed too deeply in these depressing ponderings, I reached the bar. My last thought about Mike before I walked in the door was simply that the wedding weekend was no time for me to be making an accurate forecast about future realities. The wedding was a time to celebrate the dream.

The night at the bar involved a lot of talking and a lot of tequila. We reminisced about some of the classic lines from our old coaches such as the infamous "Carpe Momentum" speech or any number of famous rants that occurred over the years. It is funny how many of the most joyful moments of my life have resulted in painful memories while the painful times have provided the ideal comedy in the ensuing years. I would much rather talk about running sprints up a mountain at six in the morning than discuss the best day I ever had with Mary even though my experience during the actual events was just the opposite. This fact was never truer than on this night when every story seemed to follow the theme of some dreadful day we had endured together. It was an enjoyable night that never seemed to end. When I finally walked back to Hal's apartment, I wondered if I had made a mistake by drinking too much the night before the wedding. The groomsmen had plans to meet for breakfast while the girls were getting ready, and I feared my reaction to that ever-nearing wakeup call.

Luckily, breakfast turned out to be exactly what I needed. We just hung out for a couple hours while I uploaded as much caffeine into my system as possible. After a relaxing morning, we made our way to the church. We had three hours until the start of the wedding so there wasn't a whole lot for us to do except sit around and relax. Since I knew we would have a lot of free time on the wedding day, I had prepared a letter the prior afternoon to give to Mike. The letter was from a young man named Timmy, and, as soon as I handed Mike the letter, he immediately laughed before even opening it. The story of Timmy went back three years earlier when Mike was working on his application for medical school. Since I had written many personal statements for my fellowships, I told Mike to put a first draft together, and then I would give him some feedback. When he gave me his essay, I thought he had done a good job except for one part in the middle. In an attempt to personalize his charity work, Mike had included the story of a fictional character named Timmy. I forget what disease Timmy had in the first draft, but it reeked of cliché and was absolutely hilarious. I explained to Mike that he was plenty qualified for medical school and didn't need to embellish his story at all. Mike took Timmy out of the essay, but the damage had been done. I harassed Mike about poor little Timmy all the time and figured it wouldn't be right if Timmy didn't get to be a part of Mike's wedding. As we sat in the church basement, I handed Mike the following emotional letter from Timmy.

Dear Mike,

I am writing this for you on your wedding day. First, I want you to know that I wish with all my heart I could be there to see you and Angela on the happiest day of your life, but obviously I'll be dead by then. What I really want to say is how happy you have made my life and how thankful I am for everything you've done for me. When we first met, I had nothing. I was sick with first degree multiple sclerosis and multiple cases of singular sclerosis. I couldn't drink alcohol after my hepatocellular carcinoma and liver were removed. The tumors in my eyes were beginning to blind me. Most people just walked past me but not you. I mean, most fuckin people were so scared of my shingles and the puss seeping from my open wounds that they wouldn't come close to me. What makes you so special is that you are different. I'll never forget the day we met. I had just severed three of my fingers and dropped them down a sewer grate, not to mention the fact that my foreskin was stuck in my bike chain. With your typical doctor calmness, you grabbed my fingers out of that sewer with the chopsticks from your chicken fried rice, sewed them back on using that lock of Angela's hair that you keep with you at all times, and you still found time to remove my foreskin with your mouth. What a guy!!! I hope Angela knows how lucky she is to have found such a giving person. I know we didn't have much time together before I died, but you literally changed my life. Before I met you, it looked like my fate was to die a quadriplegic virgin covered in shingles and filled with tumors, but you changed all that. When Johnny Kivisto cut off my legs with his chainsaw, you were sweet enough to leave the hospital where you had spent the night reassembling aborted fetuses and breathing life back into them to come and give me my legs back. Not only did you remove my tumors, form them into legs, and then train me to walk with them, but you also solved my dying a virgin problem by ass raping me numerous times. Who would have ever guessed that, of all my diseases you cured, it would actually be the ass raping that proved fatal. I was as shocked as you when I learned that you literally fucked my brains out. Who knew that was actually possible? I guess they didn't teach you that in undergrad, but I'm sure you'll learn about it in medical school and know better for the next handicapped ten year old boy you decide to violate. All I can say is I wouldn't want to die any other way. I love you more than you could ever imagine and wish you all the happiness. Have a great wedding, and, on the honeymoon, please remember to stop if you feel your dick hitting Angela's brainstem so the same mistake doesn't happen again. I'll be watching down on you from heaven enjoying my chocolate waterfall and golden pony. I love you Mike.

Love, Timmy

P.S. I gave you Chlamydia

Mike's face was priceless as he read Timmy's emotional note. The best part of writing this letter unexpectedly took place after Mike had finished reading. The rest of the groomsmen wondered what Mike had been laughing at so I told them the background about Timmy. Derbe decided he would read it aloud to everyone, but he quickly regretted this decision. We were in the basement of a church with an uptight pastor just waiting to perform an exorcism on anyone who stepped out of line, and Derbe was fully aware of this as he struggled to read the letter. As the crassness of Timmy's comments grew worse, Derbe repeatedly stopped and looked up at me saying he couldn't read anymore. Every sentence Derbe spoke was an internal battle as he tried to hide his face from the virgin Mary looking over his shoulder. Watching Derbe's moral crisis was especially entertaining since I had never seen him this way before. I guess there is a big difference between bar morality and church morality for some people. Thankfully, I never found this distinction to be necessary in my own life.

After sitting in the basement for about three hours, one of the bridesmaids suddenly burst through the door in a panic yelling at us to get upstairs. She screamed that the whole church was waiting. We raced up the stairs, and I laughed as I pictured the priest's anger at that moment. I guess, instead of practicing walking for ten hours the previous day, he should have taken a minute to hand out an itinerary or at least sent someone to get the guys before the wedding. No harm was done, and we were all smiles as we walked down the aisle. One effect of this last minute clusterfuck was that the beginning of the ceremony felt like a blur. By the time we sat down to listen to the homily, I started to relax and just enjoy the happiness on my two friends' faces as they tied the knot.

The priest started by talking about Mike and Angela's past, and it was immediately evident that he hadn't attended seminary on a speaking scholarship. I have never been a fan of sitting in church, or any type of ceremony for that matter, but this speech was especially excruciating. My main criticism with religion has always been the supernatural claims much more so than the people. I have even found myself able to enjoy listening to a priest talk if he is a good speaker or at least strikes me as a somewhat intelligent, albeit misguided, person. A good example of a smart pastor was the priest at Dillon's prep school who I had met a couple times and was no doubt a person of value that I would have loved to talk theology with. The priest at Mike's wedding lacked the talent of public speaking but made matters worse with his self-confidence in his abilities. The first two hours of his talk droned on about topics that were inconsequential to the event and have thankfully fallen out of my memory. Finally, he addressed the couple getting married and started talking about their story together. There is no easier speech to give than a wedding speech. Everyone is excited for the wedding and willing to laugh or cry at the mention of any random story from the couple's past. It is impossible to ruin a wedding speech. This impossibility, however, was easily achievable for that miracle worker.

The priest began to tell the tale of how Mike met Angela while weaving a common theme into the story as he constantly repeated, "and little did they know god's hand was guiding them." The story of Mike meeting Angela told by the priest described a fictional first encounter. I can't bear to repeat the text of this horrendously drawn out misrepresentation of their relationship, but it basically told the story of two people who not only lacked the social skills to successfully become doctors, but it made one wonder how they were even able to order coffee at Starbucks. The priest described how the hand of god forced Mike to stare at Angela for the entire chemistry class (here he added several terrible "chemistry" puns) and also caused Mike to stalk Angela every day after class until he finally became her lab partner one fateful day in the elevator. The priest's recollection of the elevator conversation ultimately ruined an otherwise awful speech. According to the priest's story, "They were in the elevator during spring break when all the other students were on vacation. After riding up five floors in silence, Mike finally turned to Angela and said, 'Hello Angela, how are you doing today?' Angela responded, 'Good, Michael. How are you doing today?' Mike responded, 'Good, Angela. Are you having a good spring break?' Angela responded, 'Yes Michael. Are you having a good spring break?' Mike responded, 'Yes Angela. Do you have any plans for the rest of spring break?' Angela responded, 'No, Michael. Do you have any plans for the rest of spring break?'

Mike responded, 'No, Angela. Would you like to join me in the library this afternoon so we could study together for eight or nine hours?' Angela responded, 'Yes, Michael. I would like to join you for eight or nine hours of studying.' So, that afternoon, Mike and Angela studied chemistry together for eight or nine hours and little did they know that the hand of god was guiding them (another bad chemistry pun added again) to this day."

I'm just going to move on from the priest's speech because I think the three percent of it I just mentioned paints a good enough picture. The entire time the priest was talking, Mike was visibly laughing while I just smiled. Every word he said made Mike sound less competent and more like a mentally handicapped chimpanzee. I remember wondering to myself how I was going to follow up with my own speech after Mike had already been so embarrassed during the ceremony. I had assumed that embarrassing Mike was my job, but the priest beat me to it. It got to the point where the priest would have to pause for laughter at points during his talk that weren't even jokes. Every time this occurred, he would look up at the audience with a confused expression as if he thought we were laughing at something elsewhere in the church. It reminded me of watching a struggling comedian work out new material at open mic night without realizing he should have stuck to his day job. In any event, nothing this man said could ruin the appearance of Mike and Angela as their perfection could shine through anything. The real shame with the priest's caricature of them was that their real story was already flawless. It is one thing to write a bad story, but it is another thing altogether to plagiarize a great story and then completely butcher your own version as this priest had done. I was most annoyed by his constant refusal to give Mike and Angela any credit in the success of their lives. As far as he was concerned, god's hand had done all the work while these two morons couldn't even tie their own shoes without his help. In reality, it wasn't the work of our unintelligent designer that led my two friends together. Their good fortune had actually resulted from their own actions. They weren't given this gift. They had earned it through their respective virtues. The credit for their joy should have been given to the couple in acknowledgement of their impeccable taste in choosing a significant other and their unyielding persistence in pursuit of that love. The priest was an idiot, but the rest of the ceremony was delightful. The looks shared between the couple during their vows were envied by all in attendance. Seeing the tears in Mike's mom's eyes as he hugged his dying grandmother on the way out of the church was an emotional end to a wonderful wedding. The music was exceptional, and the ceremony ended with a smile.

After the ceremony was finished and the newly married couple shook everyone's hands, the wedding party decided it was time to get greased up. A wedding ceremony is nice if you are over the age of eighty-five, but most people come for the reception. The reception is the real celebration in which the couple is honored. Since we had a two hour break before it started, we loaded the limousine with bottles of champagne, fifths of Johnnie Walker, and plenty of beer as we made our way down to the waterfront to take some pictures and start the celebration. The time on the docks was supposed to be fairly reserved, but it quickly got out of control. I would like to say we were all drunk with love for the married couple, but I am pretty sure a majority of the drinking was done out of thankfulness that the priest was done talking. Whatever it was, we had a marvelous time, and, more importantly, Mike and Angela were overjoyed. I have never seen a couple more in love, and I was thankful they didn't have to wait any longer to be together forever.

As we partied down on the docks, I took pleasure in watching the happiness surrounding me. At one point, I realized that I was the only one without a wife, fiancé, or serious girlfriend. I was forced to look at myself in the mirror and figure out what had led me to this position in the group. I had always been a guy that would meet a girl and fall in love, but that part of my character seemed to be missing in the present. Now, I would meet girls, think they were great, have an amazing night, and then move on. When I was young, I loved with my dick. In college, I loved with my heart. Now, I loved with my mind, and, as a result, I was single. I thought about this for a second and realized that, for the first time in my life, I was content with my relationship status. I had been lonely and alone at certain periods of my life, and I had also been lonely with a girlfriend at other times. For once, I wasn't lonely because what mattered in my life was no longer my own wellbeing. I no longer spent my life trying to satisfy my unfulfilled emotional yearnings. I was starting to get to the point where my happiness was derived from the joy in the eyes of the people I loved. I knew this was the life I wanted, and I figured it was the perfect day to put my new living philosophy into action. I spent the entire time during this celebration downing champagne and taking shots with everyone. My goal was to make sure the entire wedding party got as much pleasure out of that moment as they possibly could.

Once everyone had too much to drink, it was time to head to the reception. When we arrived, I went inside alone to buy some time while the bridesmaids panicked to fix Angela's torn bustle. Although I wasn't sure what a bustle was or how crucial it was to the dress, I had a good time running in and having some fun on the microphone until they were ready to introduce the newlyweds. I walked into the reception with two bottles of champagne in my hands and knew it was going to be a special night when I saw so many friendly faces throughout the room. It didn't take long before the bustle was fixed and the married couple made their entrance. Once we were inside, I immediately started moving around the room to see everyone. You never see more smiles in one room than you do at a wedding (although I have seen a few smiles at divorces too but those are more smiles of relief instead of smiles of excitement). Before long everyone was eating and a steady roar of conversation filled the room as old friends and new friends toasted the deserving couple.

After all the food was served, it was time for the speeches. The first person to talk was Angela's dad. It was a well prepared speech with a nice blend of jokes about Mike's massive stature combined with a heartfelt welcome to the family. Angela's dad was a gentleman that showed a true graciousness as he transferred his most precious asset into Mike's hands for safe keeping. There is no doubt his trust in Mike was justified even more than he knew. While we toasted at the conclusion of his speech, it occurred to me that I better get my head together for what I was going to say. I had thought about my speech on the car ride earlier in the week and had a nice list of jokes that I wanted to weave into a sincere toast to the couple. However, since I was usually comfortable giving speeches, it hadn't occurred to me that I might be this drunk. As Angela's sister started speaking, I thought it probably would have been smart to have written something down like the previous two. At this point, I just relaxed because it was too late to second guess and sat back until it was my turn. The Maid of Honor speech was sweet. Angela's sister referred to their past and nicely combined harmless jabs at Angela's competitiveness within an emotional poem that displayed the love she had for her sister. It was a moving speech that only increased the good vibrations in the room. Finally, it was my turn.

I was glad to be the last one giving a speech because I was the most intoxicated, and, if nothing else, I figured my speech would ignite a spark to kick off the dance party. The following is a reconstruction of this speech.

> Alright let's give a quick round of applause to the Maid of Honor for that moving speech. Well Mike, if only Timmy was alive to see you here today he would have been so proud. Actually before I start my speech, Derbe has asked for a few minutes to read a poem he's written specially for Mike and Angela on their wedding day (I handed the microphone to Derbe while he looked up like a deer in the headlights). Did you not get my email Derbe or is this just stage fright again? Well alright…I guess…hmm…Malcolm, does this mean you and Joe aren't going to sing that duet either? Well, sorry everyone. I guess we'll just have to move on, but at least it will be easier to follow these guys than that Maid of Honor speech so I appreciate the help boys.
>
> Anyway, I just want to start by introducing myself. For those of you who don't know me, people call me E. If you want a quick way to tell me apart from the other guys up here, I am the only one that is allergic to cats, and, as you can see, I'm also the only one who doesn't take anabolic steroids.
>
> Alright, Angela how are you feeling over there? Any second guesses yet? If Angela looks a little nervous right now it has to do with the fact that she has been emailing me for weeks asking to see a copy of my speech so that she could edit it, and, if any of you saw the original drafts covered in her red ink, I hope you'll cut me some slack, but I'm going to do my best to work around it.
>
> First off, I would like to thank the parents of the bride and groom for throwing a great wedding and, more importantly, for raising two great kids. Let's give them a round of applause. Alright, what a great day Mike! We're not in Miami anymore hey fella! I could not be more excited to be here tonight! You know, when I first heard about the wedding and when I look at the two of you right now, I think I can speak for all your friends when I say that we are all really absolutely shocked to see the two of you, of all people, sitting here tonight. I mean never in a million years would I expect to see you two out this late on a Saturday night (big laugh from their friends in the audience that always complained that they never came out anymore). You're not going to regret it. We're going to have a great time tonight.
>
> For those of us who know Mike and Angela well, it became obvious a long time ago that these two are absolutely perfect for each other. I've never met a couple that is more similar to each other than these two. They are both tremendous students. They order the exact same meals at restaurants literally every time. They're both working hard in medical school together. They both played college sports, and, actually, an interesting fact is that, between the two of them, they ended their college athletic careers with exactly .500 record. That's pretty impressive. Not too many couples can say that so you two should be proud.

I've known Mike for the past five years, and he has become one of my absolute best friends. Some of my favorite parts of these last few years have been just sitting around with Mike in the locker room, on the bus, or wherever talking about every aspect of life. Although I was impressed with Mike from the start, I've seen him change a lot in the five years I've known him, and that is definitely a direct result of meeting Angela. In the time I've known him, Mike has changed from a person interested in making a career playing in the NHL to a person whose sole focus is taking care of Angela and doing everything in his power to create the life they want together. I remember when we first met and Mike guaranteed me that in five years I'd be sitting at home listening to them say his name on ESPN, and I'm happy to say that dream recently came true when Angela was shooting free throws in the national championship game, and Mike got his name mentioned. Congrats fella. But you know what Mike, no matter what anyone says, I think you're going to make a great Trophy Wife. No shame in that.

In all honesty, I could not be more impressed by the person Mike has become. I admire how devoted he is to Angela and how every decision he makes revolves around her. In fact, although I was a bit disappointed, I can't say I was by any means surprised when I planned Mike's bachelor party and he showed up with Angela as his date. Even though this kind of ruined the plans I had made for the night, I would expect nothing less from Mike because I know that, no matter what happens, he would never let anything or anybody come between him and Ang. Honestly, all I can really say about you two is how much I admire the people you are and how happy I am for you. You both possess a kind of quiet integrity and genuineness that is unfortunately far too rare. Not only are you great people, and you have been great friends to me, but I'm absolutely sure you're going to make phenomenal parents someday. And, based on the amount of athletic ability between the two of you, I think it is safe to say your kids are going to be tremendous basketball players.

I just want to end by saying that I hope you two enjoy every minute of tonight. My entire life, I've always loved going to weddings and watching the look on the people's faces where you can just tell that it is the happiest day of their lives. What makes you two unique is that I don't see that look on your face tonight. However, I have seen that look on your face in the past when I've seen you walking into the video store on a Thursday night or on your way to one of those early bird dinners that you love. All jokes aside, I absolutely love the fact that you have been looking forward to the marriage way more than the wedding, and no two people are more deserving of a life of happiness than the two of you. I hope you are able to enjoy every minute of your lives and live like you're not afraid to make mistakes. As Albert Einstein once said, "Any man who can drive safely while kissing a beautiful woman is simply not giving the kiss the attention it deserves." I hope you have a long and successful life, but, most importantly, I hope you give that kiss the attention it deserves. I love you both and wish you all the best. Congrats. To Mike and Angela!!!

The speech went even better than expected as the laughter roared and the sentimental part rang true. I meant every word I said and was honored to have the opportunity to speak. I was completely honest when I said they deserved to have their dreams come true and live their ideal life. That perfect life may not have been attainable in the world we lived in, but it was sure a pretty picture. I was overjoyed as I smiled at the thought of their eternal happiness while, on a different level, I could feel my heart breaking with the knowledge that reality could never achieve what they were hoping for. I wanted to embrace their dreams but was somewhat troubled as the vision of Mike's father continued to run through my mind. Nonetheless, this was a day to celebrate the dream, and I've never been one to let my depression get in the way of a good dance party.

Once the dancing started, it didn't stop. The wedding party got a nice introduction out to the dance floor and started the excitement of calling out the bride and groom for their first dance. The lovely couple danced their first song to "I'm yours" by Jason Mraz. From what I heard, it was a cute first dance, but I didn't watch much of it as I used this time to move throughout the room chastising everyone who remained in their seats. I was especially excited to get the older people dancing to make sure the entire family had a fun night and not just the college kids. The dance floor was surrounded by a crowd of people by the time the second dance arrived. The second dance was "I'll stand by you" with Angela dancing with her dad while Mike danced with his mom. This was clearly the most sentimental part of the reception, and I almost worried the emotion of that moment might have a detrimental effect on the excitement level. Fortunately, the DJ followed with an upbeat party song, and we never looked back. I don't remember stopping for one minute all night. This was truly one of the most enjoyable evenings of my life especially when I would catch a glimpse of the smiles on Mike and Angela's faces as they danced the night away.

At the conclusion of the celebration, Derbe and I were the only people left with Mike and Angela. We walked outside to where they were getting a ride and wished them the best. We were all catching our breath and speaking to each other without words. It was impossible to express the depth of our joy at that moment, but we all understood what the look in the eyes of our friends meant. It was a truly surreal moment that will be with me forever. Other than the birth of their son, I don't think Mike and Angela's life was ever better than that calm moment outside the reception when they said goodbye and left in each other's arms. When I wrote the novel based on Mike's life, it was the feeling of togetherness between him and Angela that I was able to successfully build his story around. Whether it was his marriage or his son I was describing, Mike would always be remembered as a man whose life lacked only loneliness.

After Mike and Angela left for the night, Derbe and I slowly walked down College Avenue with a bottle of champagne. The first thing Derbe said was "I think that was the most fun I have ever had" to which I smiled in agreement. It didn't take long for us to start reflecting on the evening and fall into a heart to heart talk about our two friends who had just tied the knot. One thing we agreed upon was that those two were perfect for each other and the potential of their life was limitless. Although Derbe was a friend I could share almost anything with, I hid my true worries about Mike and Angela's future inside my heart and just focused on the current moment. The conversation about Mike and Angela slowly expanded to include our own roles in their future and our desire to remain friends forever. It was clear our futures were destined to be intertwined. Derbe and I looked up at the stars and pondered what our lives would be like in twenty years. We wondered if the three of us would be having barbecues together watching our kids running around the yard. We joked about how many times we would laugh at the same old stories that would never get old. As we passed the champagne bottle back and forth, we enjoyed living this ideal future in our minds. There was no guarantee that life would allow us to achieve this reality, and I obviously doubted it could, but none of that mattered on this night. It didn't have to be reality to be real. We were already living that future as we walked away from the wedding. Our story played out in our mutual imagination, and we were able to appreciate the entirety of our future lives through the eyes of satisfied spectators. It was the same feeling of satisfaction that many of you expressed to me over the years when you told me how you felt after reading my second novel when you unknowingly came to love Mike and the perfect future he was destined to experience.

When we finally got downtown, Derbe went in for the night to see his girlfriend while I continued to the bar on my own. My tuxedo was in shambles, and I looked like a man who had lived a hundred years in a single night. My body was flooded with millions of competing emotions. There was no telling if I would enter the bar feeling elated or dejected. I could have ended up singing at the top of my lungs or been lost in thought sitting at a table by myself. I was completely spent emotionally, and it felt strangely pleasing. When I got to the bar, I saw a crowd of people from the wedding that quickly screamed for me, but I simply waved and went to get a drink. I took my whisky to an open table and started sipping my drink alone with my thoughts. It didn't take long for my table to fill up with friends and a few girls from the wedding who were no doubt unaware that I had outgrown the phase of my life in which I was guided by hormones instead of intellect. The party continued around me while I remained alone in my thoughts. I was fully immersed in the conversation as my personality went into autopilot. I made jokes and said cheers, but my mind was a million miles away. I was still frozen in my contemplation of what lay ahead for Mike and Angela.

The next morning, I felt surprisingly alright as I woke up early to check on the newlyweds. I quickly noticed them struggling to move, and their aching bodies demonstrated their pleasure from the previous night. I made them a couple of sparks to get them going for the day and wished them the best on their honeymoon. I then loaded my car and drove back to Ann Arbor. Once again, I spent the trip thinking about Mike and Angela's future. I am sorry to beat a dead horse here (although, on a separate note, if you have never literally beaten a dead horse I advise you to try it because it turns out to be much more enjoyable than the saying would suggest), but I simply couldn't distract my mind from what I felt would be a truly unattainable future they planned to spend together. My thoughts on the drive home were nothing I hadn't contemplated before. It was just continued rumination as I worried about my friend's future in a way I no longer cared about my own. I had abundant hope for Mike and Angela but couldn't shake my worry that life could never live up to the unblemished picture they envisioned.

When I returned to Ann Arbor after the wedding, I was quickly distracted from my worries as my own life became a hectic rat race between work and moving into my new apartment. My apartment was in the middle of campus, and I started enjoying a lot more nights out at the bar with friends. I had a close group from the lab, and, during this year, I met so many impressive new people as my number of friends in Ann Arbor increased exponentially. I found myself much busier in my free time as there always seemed to be something going on. This welcomed annoyance distracted me from my continued failed efforts at writing a second novel and consumed the majority of my evenings during my second summer in Ann Arbor. I found myself golfing and playing tennis more than I had done the previous year and was thankful to have a nice group of friends to fill the void in my life.

Not only was I enjoying Ann Arbor, but I still visited Derbe and Mike periodically throughout the rest of the summer. They also made some trips to see me, the first of which was immediately after Mike and Angela had returned from their honeymoon in Mexico. It was fun to hear them discuss the trip and just as enjoyable to watch their smiles disappear as they talked about going back to class again. I laughed at the contrast between their two emotional states when talking about their personal and work lives as I could unfortunately relate to how they were feeling. I have always found it ridiculous that, with all the technological advances we have made as a species, everyone still has to work so many hours each week. It would always boggle my mind when I would hear about economic problems being caused by increased efficiency such as improved machinery causing autoworkers to lose their jobs. It always seemed that an increase in mechanical efficiency should make things better for everyone and give us all more time to embrace life. Instead, a couple people made an increased profit, and everyone else scrambled to work more hours with less pay to prevent their children from starving. There is no reason we shouldn't be able to create a world in which the majority of our time is spent living instead of working, but this thought doesn't even seem to enter into anyone's mind. People always talk about creating jobs, but no one really talks about decreasing the need for jobs to begin with. In fact, when I have often made these types of comments to people in the past, they simply laugh it off as unattainable utopianism. I guess I never understood what specific deficiency in humanity prevents us from attempting to reach the ideal. As pessimistic as I am about the nature of humanity, I at least believe a social structure could be developed to utilize our resources to create a more pleasurable world in which we spent more time doing what we want. Unfortunately, I had to settle for my weekend visits with my friends as we were always forced to reenter the rat race Monday morning and put happiness on hold for a little while longer while we chased that illusive imaginary pot of gold at the end of the rainbow.

Like any enjoyable time in one's life, my second summer in Ann Arbor flew by. I had fun going out with friends and no longer seemed to be tortured by my inability to write a successful second book. I came to the conclusion that I simply needed better motivation for writing like when I resurrected my mom. It actually crossed my mind that I could write eulogies for a living, but I quickly realized that a eulogy for most people is just fluffy propaganda that avoids writing the depressing recap of their depressing lives. I didn't want any part in that type of hypocrisy so I nixed that idea without much trouble. I spent a few nights wondering if a second perfect character would finally be revealed. It turned out that my second character was right in front of my face the entire time. I just wasn't meant to know he was my character until the time was right. Although I was completely unaware, this time was quickly approaching.

I was extremely busy when fall arrived, and I didn't get to see Mike or Derbe much during the first few months of the new semester. One thing was sure, I wasn't going to miss our annual Halloween event. The highlight of this trip occurred within ten minutes of my arrival. Mike and Angela were over at Derbe's apartment waiting for me. I surged through the door and immediately poured a round of shots to kick off the night. Angela hesitated to grab the shot, and, before she could even turn down the drink, I looked at her and yelled, "You're pregnant!" Mike and Angela looked at me in shock as they always did when I read their faces like they were some tourists playing in the World Series of Poker. As usual, I could read her like a book and just poured another shot for the three of us guys to toast the baby. Mike and Angela laughed at their failed plan to not reveal their news until after dinner, and we all just had a wonderful time talking. Mike and Angela were still a little nervous about being parents, but I was just excited to watch their child grow up. It is an incredibly wonderful and irrational feeling to be in love with a child that hasn't yet been born. In reality, I loved that kid years before he was even conceived when he was simply the foundation of Mike and Angela's perfect vision for their future. It wasn't my child, but I knew I would love it as if it was my own. My admiration and love for the parents would develop into an even greater love for their offspring. We had a fun night out for Halloween, but the real highlight was that announcement of my new favorite person coming into the world.

Over the next year, I became even more active in Mike's life. I found out he was going to have a boy and spent my nights picturing this little man's future. I didn't know who he would be or what kind of life he would want to live, but I knew I would be there to help him accomplish it. The conversations I had with Mike during this time were amongst the most precious moments of my life. I would love to be able to fully express the depth of Mike's concern for his unborn son and his desire to be a better father than his own dad had been. Mike feared nothing more than following in his father's footsteps. Mike always told me that he could endure anything that might happen to him other than failing as a parent. I would always look him in the eye and honestly tell him that I would never let that happen. Mike knew I was serious when I said I would always be there for his family and often expressed to me how much my friendship meant to him. He even told me that they had wanted to ask me to be their child's godfather but knew better than that. I laughed as Mike recounted his conversation with Angela in which they both wanted to give me the honor of being the godfather but feared the response of their aggressively Atheistic friend and hence figured it best to avoid pissing me off. We had a good laugh about it, and I assured them I didn't need a title to be there for their son.

My conversations with Mike became increasingly about his desire to be a perfect father and the hopes he had for his unborn child. Mike would repeatedly explain how much he wanted his son to have a life that would be envied by all. Mike often struggled to turn his feelings into words as he would be overcome by emotion during these conversations. I was always there to assure Mike that he was a remarkable person and his son was going to be lucky to have had such an amazing father. Mike never failed to thank me for all I had done for him and often asked me to promise I would be there for his family in the years to come. I made a vow to Mike that I would do everything in my power to ensure his son had an unequaled life and that Mike became the best possible father he could be. I promised Mike that he could always count on me to put the best interests of his family even ahead of my own wellbeing which is a promise I am proud to say I have kept ever since.

When Mike's son was born the following spring, I was right by his side. It is hard to explain how inspiring it was to see this young man come into the world and watch the look on Mike's face as he held his new son, Jamie Russell Wagner. It was such a unique experience that stands out in my memory as one of the most indescribable moments of my life. As I watched Mike's face looking down at his newborn child, I instantly knew I had found the main character for my second novel. I felt stupid for not seeing the perfection in his story before, but this was truly the climactic moment in an amazing character's story that I was witnessing unfold before my eyes. I was the first person to hold Jamie and made an unspoken promise that I would do everything in my power to give him the life he deserved. When I handed him over to Derbe, I could see a similar look in his eyes. As I drove away that night, I once again found myself conflicted as I thought about the life Mike was living. I was overcome by his present pleasure while, at the same time, I feared for his future. There was really no way the coming years could ever compare to the present. I admired every aspect of Mike and the future he envisioned. I knew the world would prevent him from achieving this ideal life, but that didn't make his vision any less perfect. The future ceases to be perfect once it becomes the present, but, at that point in time, Mike's life was flawless. I wished he could be frozen in the moment forever. Not only did I care deeply about my best friend's wellbeing, but I now had the added burden of worrying about the main character of my second book. I wanted to write another inspirational story and immensely feared the inevitable tragedy that Mike would never again be as perfect as he was on that day.

When I returned to Ann Arbor late that night, I immediately sat down at the computer and begin writing the story of Mike's life. I felt passionately that Mike was the ideal person to base my second novel on since he was truly the only human being that I could possibly envision living up to the standard set by my mom. Much like the first few chapters of *Mom in Heaven*, I found myself flying through the story as I reconstructed Mike's life into the beginning of my book. The parallels of the first two chapters to my previous novel were everywhere. Not only were these initial chapters non-fiction, but Mike had the same strengths that had made my mom's character so admirable. I spent that summer writing the first half of my novel, and, by the end of August, I had reached the climax of the story as Mike held Jamie in his arms. It was this moment around which the emotional substance of the entire story ultimately revolved. The day Mike became a father was the defining moment of his story, and, as a result, the book would be titled *Father's Day*.

I had reached the point in Mike's story where the novel crisscrossed the real world. I found myself not only at the turning point of the book but also at the turning point of my life. I once again found myself stalled at the intersection between fiction and reality. When I had experienced this transition point while writing *Mom in Heaven*, I had found myself staring into the empty future of my Mom's life that was just begging to be filled. Her tragedy had been the emptiness of her story, and my therapy was to give her the life she never lived. The tragedy staring back at me in the blank pages of Mike's future represented something infinitely more heartbreaking than the nonexistence of my mom. Mike's tragedy wasn't that he would die before seeing his dreams come true. Mike's tragedy was that he would live to see his dreams didn't come true.

My next few weeks were spent contemplating a way around this immoveable roadblock standing in the way of an otherwise amazing story. I fully understood Mike's predicament couldn't be overcome in reality. I knew the story of Mike's dad all too well to blindly assume Mike could be an exception to the harsh rules of our world. My literary struggle was not unfamiliar as I had reached similar live ends in my prior attempts to write a second novel. The difference with *Father's Day* was that I cared too much about the character to allow him to undergo the same fate as these previous protagonists. The real world of these former characters had ruined the potential of their fictional stories, and it broke my heart to think this would be Mike's fate as well. I spent every second of this two week period fighting for an answer to the problem. I wanted to believe there was a way to save my friend through my book. I knew that fiction was the only path to a happy ending, but I didn't want this to be a fake conclusion that simultaneously took place as my friend was tortured in the parallel universe of reality. This internal struggle consumed my mind and drove me into a depression that challenged the very foundation of my identity. This would turn out to be the true test of my life. I wanted to be a person who could overcome emotion and bring light into the dark abyss of reality. Saving my best friend from his future would be my chance to prove I was up to the challenge.

I spent a lot of time during these weeks thinking about my best friend. I admired Mike as a future parent as much as I had admired the idealized memory of the mother I had never met. Unfortunately, I knew the progression of Mike's life would make my book more tragic than all of my prior attempts at a second novel combined since Mike was the greatest character of all the potential stories I had ever concocted. In truth, the only way Mike's story could live up to its potential and be told correctly was if Mike would somehow die like my mom. It was a strange feeling when this chilling thought ran into my mind late one night as I reached out for ways to achieve a happy ending. It was the fictional projection of Mike's life that seemed to be the only story worthy of this character. This fictional future was the story I wanted for my friend's fate.

After two weeks of tormenting myself with the future of *Father's Day*, I found myself up late at night on September 11th watching an anniversary documentary telling different untold stories of heroism during the terrorist attacks on the Twin

Towers. One of the stories that immediately caught my attention was an interview with a man that had killed a close coworker as they were trapped underground in the rubble. It was a Kevorkianic story that described the utter torture the man was undergoing as he begged for his friend to kill him. The two had been trapped under the rubble for three days when another beam snapped and crushed half of this man's body beneath its weight. The man being interviewed described his internal struggle as he watched his friend dying before his eyes. He was utterly helpless in his ability to change his coworker's fate. Each time his friend asked him to end his misery, this man refused. Finally, he said his coworker intensely looked him in the eyes with a painful expression of hopelessness and begged him to stop the pain. Before he dug his pocket knife into his companion's chest, he promised that, if he ever made it out of the rubble alive, he would take care of the man's young daughter and tell his family he loved them. He then proceeded to stab the man in the chest with his knife and allow his friend's suffering end along with his life. After six more days buried under the massive debris, this individual was one of the few lucky survivors that was dug out of the depths of Ground Zero. I was captivated by the psychological conflict the man endured before he conducted this mercy killing. I wondered if I would have the courage to commit such an admirable action. I had never been an exceptionally tough person and predictably avoided altercations whenever possible. I always considered this non-confrontational aspect of my personality to be a character strength but wondered if I would have the audacity to face the type of situation in the documentary. Could I kill a person if they begged me to do it? Would I kill a person if I knew it was for their own benefit? It was at this moment, as I fell asleep on my couch, that the thought of killing my best friend for his own good first crept into the back of my mind.

When I woke up the next morning, I remembered my last thought from the night before. I went to the kitchen to make some cereal as the idea lingered in my mind. For most of the morning, I held the thought in my consciousness without directly addressing it. I allowed myself to dwell on things for a long time before I attempted to judge the meaning of this clearly wrong idea that had been sparked in the back of my brain. The idea stuck in my mind was that killing my best friend would ultimately save his life. When I finally confronted the meaning of this idea, the outcome became undeniable. Ever since college, I had claimed to no longer care about the outcome of my own life. I simply wanted to be a force for good in the lives of those I loved. I no longer wanted to be a slave to decisions made by my emotions, but, instead, I vowed to become a man that transcended human nature. I would make tough decisions with a consequentialist morality capable of withstanding the onslaught of my personal desires. I was an author who cared deeply about my main character and made a decision to think rationally about the effects of my potential actions. I was determined to show the courage to follow through with my decision no matter how tough it might be on me personally.

I began to weigh the options about the best possible outcomes for Mike. There was no doubt in my mind that he was currently living at the high point of his life.

I was unsure if this pinnacle period would last for weeks or months, but I knew the eventual downward trend was inevitable. The beginning of his story had been written both in my novel and in reality. I figured I had three options. The first option was to finish the inspirational novel of Mike's life describing the perfect life ahead of him while deciding to simply live with the tragedy of watching Mike's real life unfold. I found this first option to not only be immoral, but, ultimately, unbearable. I had decided to leave my own feelings out of the equation, but the thought of watching Mike's life deteriorate while at the same time enshrining his perfect future in text seemed an immeasurable cruelty. The main character of the novel would be doomed to look out at the real world like Dorian Grey staring into that grotesque picture every night. It was the same conclusion I had made with my previously failed second novels taken to infinity and multiplied to the depths of forever. This option led to a repulsive conclusion that was unquestionably off the table. The second option would be to stop writing the book altogether and simply allow Mike's life to take its tragic course. When I thought of the effects of this choice, I was surprised to find the results seemed even worse than the first option. I had vowed to make the world a better place, but, if I made this choice and became an innocent bystander in Mike's life, it would be the worst possible outcome for everyone. Not only would this decision lead me to stand by passively as Mike's real world unraveled, but his beautiful dreams would be lost along with him. This second choice would cause Mike to be destroyed twice: once in reality and once in fiction. Mike would be robbed of his impeccable illusions, and the world would be deprived of a truly incomparable character. I found option two to be an absolutely absurd conclusion. There was no rational or moral route that would allow me to make one of these first two choices at the expense of my best friend's eternal happiness. I was left only with the third option. It was the option that had not yet been spoken aloud and was muted even in my thoughts. The option was handcuffed in the back of my mind waiting to emerge victorious but held hostage by my limbic system's love of its best friend. I continued to look at all possible outcomes for Mike's life. In both options one and two, I saw Mike's life leading down the tragic path towards a painfully disillusioned conclusion. He would die at the end of this long, miserable journey slightly remembered by the world as another flawed man who lived an all too familiar story. In these first two options, he wouldn't be worshiped for the glorious spectacle of his current character. Even more tragically, the greatest part of his life, his fictional envisioned future, would never even exist. It was clear that there were only two possible outcomes for my best friend. Mike could either become his dad or he could become my mom. I loved this man far too much to allow him to become his dad. I loved his son far too much to prevent him from having the perfect father as I had with my idealized mother. Option three was clearly the only choice I could make: I had to kill my best friend.

CHAPTER 4

Father's Day

Murder is born of love, and love attains the greatest intensity in murder.

-Octave Mirbeau

CHAPTER 4: *Father's Day*

I had no choice. I had to kill my best friend. I wasn't driven to murder by vice but rather by virtue. That virtue was compassion. Killing Mike would be a truly altruistic act. I was tormented by my decision but knew it was the right one. Nothing would be more catastrophic than living the rest of my life without my best friend, but I had to do the right thing. Killing Mike would be an undeniably admirable action. I was completely confident in my decision, but yet I found myself instantly out of my comfort zone. I had never done anything wrong in my life. I often talked about deviance and rejecting societal constraints, but I rarely acted contrary to accepted behavior and certainly hadn't committed an act on the scale of murder. Even though I knew it was the right thing to do, I was fully aware this action would be antagonistic to the primitive morality of our world. There was no doubt our myopic society would struggle to appreciate the long-term benefits of my decision. These two influences, my own emotions and societal acceptance, constantly weighed on my conscience as I thought about killing my friend. However, as powerful as these forces were, they ultimately provided no rational argument against murder. Murdering Mike would give him the immortality he deserved, and I could care less about the effects on my life or the rest of the world. I knew it would be hard to overcome the resilient emotions fighting against my decision, but this was my chance to prove I could do the right thing even when it wasn't aligned with my own happiness. Anybody can make the right decision when it is easy, but it takes a stronger moral character to follow through with a correct action when it goes against both the norms of society as well as one's innermost desires. This was the case with killing Mike. I didn't want to do it, but there was no other option to save his life.

Once my decision to kill Mike was complete, I started to realize that there were plenty of other issues to address in addition to the personal emotional challenges I would have to overcome. Most importantly, I would have to face fear. The most obvious fear I would face would be the fear of being caught. I knew what the potential consequences of my actions would be and by no means did I want to go to jail. Nonetheless, this type of fear was the easiest to conquer. I wasn't doing this for my own wellbeing, and I wouldn't let fear for my own future get in the way of this good dead. The other element associated with the fear of being caught that was harder to deal with was the effect it would have on the story. If I was sloppy in my murder and convicted of killing my best friend, people would tell Mike's story as a tragedy before I ever had the chance to write his real story into fiction. My main worry was that Mike would be transformed into a tragic figure if the story was ruined before it was written. Because of this, I knew it was imperative that I did not get caught. It would be a disaster if my carelessness as a killer stole Mike's eternal bliss. The final aspect of fear I was dealing with revolved around my lack of self-confidence. I was afraid I might lack the courage to commit this noble action. In my mind, I knew the person I wished to become but worried I might lack the internal strength to do what was necessary. I had never before faced confrontation head on but instead had been the type of person who would talk his way out of conflicts. Talking wasn't an option that could save my friend, and I could only hope that I had enough strength within me to accomplish this kill.

Although I never fully conquered my fear until the actual moment of the murder, I eventually came to terms with the fact that this constant rumination was accomplishing nothing. Thoughts can only take a person so far before they must be proved by action. I had a firm confidence in my ability to go through with the kill, but I knew it meant nothing until demonstrated in reality. Instead of wasting more time contemplating my internal struggles, I began to focus on the logistics of the kill. I had never been a violent person and didn't have a clue how to start planning a murder. I thought about looking for ideas online, but my constant fear of FBI surveillance and police tracking my internet history prevented me from doing any outward planning. I had seen enough CSI type shows to understand the challenges of pulling off a murder without being caught (although later in life I began to realize it is much easier than I had initially thought), and I began to worry about the details. During this time, I must have thought up hundreds of potential murders that all fell short as a result of too much risk or the feeling that something was missing. Ultimately, I decided that the only poetic justice in killing a best friend would be to stab him in the back. It was a simple method of killing a person, but the symbolism made this the clear method of choice. I also decided to do it in a place with a lot of people so that there would be plenty of suspects. I wanted there to be numerous suspects since the police would know I had no motive. I admired Mike far too much to do him any harm and knew I wouldn't be at risk of being caught as long as I was careful not to leave any other traces at the scene.

Once I developed a broad outline for my kill, I started thinking about the timing. During this planning period, I went to Lansing and spent a weekend in early October with Mike, Angela, and Jamie. I had wonderful discussions with Mike during this visit and was inspired by the current status of his life. With every word Mike spoke, I admired him more. With every increase in my admiration, my resolve to kill him was strengthened. I saw the love in his eyes when he looked at his son and was comforted by the knowledge that I would be giving that child the perfect future. One interesting observation during this trip was an unspoken stress that I had never before seen between Mike and Angela. They were clearly still in love, and it wasn't anything obvious, but I could see the beginnings of their degeneration in the little subtleties and slight annoyances that were previously absent. They both loved their son deeply, and it was obvious this love superseded their prior romantic life. I began to fully understand the limitations they faced in fulfilling the entirety of their dreams. The feasibility of maximizing both romantic and parental love would be too daunting a task even for this ideal couple. There simply wouldn't be enough time in the day to fulfill all their desires. Fortunately, this was no longer a reason for despair since I knew they wouldn't be forced down this path. I would give them everything they wanted in their lives, and they wouldn't have to settle for reality. This knowledge provided peace of mind that allowed me to enjoy every minute of this visit with my friends. When the weekend was over, I made plans to return in two weeks for our annual Halloween bash and knew it would be the right moment to end Mike's physical reality. The time had come to kill my friend at the pinnacle of his life. I had to act before it was too late.

I finished planning the murder and knew exactly when I would strike. When the week arrived, I spent most of my time in quiet reflection and found myself surprisingly calm. I envisioned the reaction that would ensue after Mike was found dead. I knew there would be a grieving period in which I would have to be there for Angela and Jamie. I remembered listening to my dad describe the period after my mom had passed away years earlier. My dad had nightmares for over a year in which he would be searching for my mom unsuccessfully. Everyone he would hunt down would tell him they just saw her but she didn't want to see him anymore. My dad was struggling to raise his three kids during the day while being tormented every night as he searched for his eternally elusive soul mate that had been stolen from him. I knew Angela would have to go through a similar excruciating period. As much as it hurt to think about her initial grieving, I knew it was in the best interest of her chronic health, and I would be there to help her through this trying period. Eventually, the nightmares simply stopped for my dad. This would be the same for Angela, and, at that point, she would move forward with an unblemished vision of Mike engrained in her memory forever. This memory would be the only husband that Angela would ever have and the only father that Jamie would ever need.

Angela's reaction wasn't the only one I contemplated. I wondered how I would personally feel after killing Mike. I knew my motive was justified, and I was doing a good dead, but it occurred to me that my emotional response might be enough to change my mind. I wondered if I would regret my decision. I figured I would most likely be as devastated as Angela afterwards, and I was completely prepared to drop into depression as soon as Mike was gone. Mike meant so much to my life that living without him was obviously going to be tough. I feared my upcoming reaction but was also curious to what the extent of my suffering would be. Would my rationalization provide some comfort against this regret? Since I was the person killing Mike, one would think I would be better equipped to deal with the consequences, but I highly doubted that would be the case. As I said earlier, I never wanted to kill Mike. I simply saw no other choice.

As the execution date drew closer, I organized everything I needed for a successful kill. I was going to Lansing Friday morning and planned to kill Mike that night. I spent all day Thursday alone in my apartment. I opened my computer and reviewed my most recent draft of *Father's Day*. I wanted to begin filling in the blank pages of Mike's story, but that time would come soon enough. Those pages still represented Mike's condemned future which would no longer be the case after the weekend. I knew I would soon be able to finish writing my second book as I had desired to do for so long. As a result, I closed the file, opened an empty document on my computer screen, and spent the rest of the day writing Mike's eulogy. I knew I would be giving this speech within a week, and I wanted to be sure I did the best job I could. A proper eulogy would be the first step in resurrecting Mike in the eyes of those he loved. I poured my heart into the eulogy and did my best to express what Mike meant to me. It was an odd feeling to spend the day writing the eulogy of someone who was still alive. Even though I knew he only had one more day to live, it still felt strange. However, writing Mike's eulogy turned out to be surprisingly satisfying. With every sad line I wrote, my happiness increased. Writing the eulogy prior to the kill helped put the entirety of my plan into perspective and gave me the reassurance to push forward. When the eulogy was finished, I closed the file and dated it November 1st.

When I arrived in Lansing, the stage was set for Mike's big night as his earthly life was nearing its gorious conclusion. Mike and Angela were hosting a pre-party, and then we were going to Rick's to end the night as was tradition. Our crew was getting older and weren't regulars at Rick's, but, every Halloween, we willingly regressed into lower class citizens for one night of dirty dancing. As Angela prepared for the pre-party at their apartment, Mike and I played tennis and then spent an hour having a bite downtown. During this meal, I had a conversation with Mike that surpassed all of our previous talks. It was almost as if Mike knew he was dying that night instead of that knowledge only residing with me. For some reason, Mike poured his heart out in that conversation as he described his pride as a father and his love for Angela. I was so moved by Mike's words, and I was thankful he had a friend like me to make those dreams come true. The feelings Mike expressed during this talk were later funneled into *Father's Day* to create the emotional backbone of the story and ultimately made it into the masterpiece it became. As I looked across the table at my friend, I experienced many emotions including respect, admiration, and envy, but, above all, I simply felt love. I loved the character that was looking back at me and would do anything I could to give him what he deserved.

After our heartfelt conversation was finished, it was time to give Mike one last celebration. I was killing Mike at the end of the night so I wanted to be sure he went out on a high note. It didn't take long before Mike and Angela's party was packed with crazy people in a wide range of costumes. Mike, Angela, and Jamie were dressed in cute matching kangaroo costumes that made for a fabulous photograph of their final day together as a family. The picture of Mike with his arm around Angela while Jamie was in her pouch is still the background on my computer screen as I am writing today. When the baby sitter came to get Jamie, Mike leaned down to give him a final embrace. As I watched Mike kiss Jamie and say his last goodbye, my heart was overcome with satisfaction. Moments like that rise above description. Mike's love for his son was immeasurable. Jamie was truly lucky to have Mike as his dad. He was a father who would never disappoint. No matter what the future would bring, Jamie would be able to find comfort in the love of his perfect father.

Once Jamie left, Mike and Angela began partying like a couple making up for lost time after their love had been put on hold for the past couple months while responsibility had controlled their lives. The rekindled romance was beautiful.

The entire room was envious of their love as we watched them dance together without ever taking their eyes off one another. In that moment, they were consumed with love just as they had been on their wedding day. In the years that followed, this final dance would provide the comfort in Angela's mind as she recalled her immaculate marriage. I was thankful to have spent the day with my best friend but was careful not to interrupt his time with Angela. Although they interacted with the group periodically, the majority of Mike's time was spent with Angela in his arms. I was happy that he had this final evening with her, and I am confident he wouldn't have spent the night any differently had he been aware that it was his last. I didn't want that party to ever end, but all good things must die at some point, and, before long, the entire party began the long walk towards downtown Lansing, Rick's, and the final resting place of Mike Wagner.

When we got to Rick's, I found myself nervous as I stood in line. I had a huge knife hidden inside my costume and was worried it would be discovered as I tried to get inside the club. I eventually had to laugh when I realized how small this infraction would be compared to the murder I planned to commit. If I was caught, I would probably get fined, but, eventually, my unblemished record, good nature, and history of joking would provide an easy defense to avoid major punishment. It was ironic to worry about getting caught with a weapon before the murder was committed when I wasn't even worried about potential repercussions for the actual murder. As irrational as it was, I couldn't avoid my anxiety as the bouncer grabbed my ID and the sense of relief when he quickly let me in. When we got inside Rick's, it was even more crowded than I had predicted. Each of the hundreds of people inside the club dancing in serial killer costumes provided potential suspects in the future search for Mike's killer. The only people in the room that wouldn't be suspects would be Angela, Derbe, and me. I no longer had any worries about being able to successfully pull off this murder without being caught. My only remaining concern was becoming a coward in the moment as I wondered if I would have the fortitude to fulfill my task. We danced for a while, and, eventually, I saw Angela leave with Derbe's girlfriend while Mike talked to a friend from med school in the VIP room they had reserved. Once this friend left Mike alone at his table, I made my way into that dark room alongside my friend. Mike saw me coming and looked up in a sentimental mood that he had developed over the course of the evening. Before I could say anything, Mike put his arm around me and thanked me for being such a good friend. I smiled and told him I loved him and would always be there for him. Mike's final words to me before he died were, "E, I owe you my life." As he said those words in the dark corner of the club, I pulled out my knife and delivered a fatal blow into my friend's back. Unlike many knife wounds, this was a clean kill, and Mike was gone in an instant.

I had just murdered my best friend, and I felt nothing. My emotional response wouldn't be felt until the next day. Tonight, I simply sat next to my best friend's corpse in numb silence. I should have left the crime scene immediately to safely return to the crowd, but I didn't want to leave. Mike's lifeless body was resting peacefully in his chair next to me, and he said nothing. We had shared many memorable discussions together in the past as well as many quiet moments such as that one. Nothing needed to be said. The dead had been done, and Mike had been saved. We simply sat next to each other in the back of the club in unspoken communication. As I looked at Mike's motionless body, I was struck by the peace in his eyes. It wasn't the look of a person whose life had gotten the best of him. This was the look of a man in all his glory. Mike was at peace with his life, and the world could never destroy the specialness of his character. I knew I should leave but simply didn't want the moment to end. I was with my friend for the last time and didn't want our friendship to be over. Eventually, I knew it was time for me to go. I took one last look at my best friend, but all I saw now was a series of blank pages. The person I was looking at didn't exist. It was no longer the body of a hopelessly doomed character; it was now the body of a perfect character whose story was waiting to be completed. I stood up from the table and walked away. The time had come to finally fill in the blank pages of Mike's life. Mike's happy ending would soon be more than a dream. Fictional happiness would be his new reality.

After leaving the table, I quickly immersed myself into the crowd and made my way to the bar to grab a drink. While I sipped my Johnnie Walker with Derbe's roommate, Jafar, Angela came up to ask if I knew where Mike had gone. I told her he was probably sleeping with another girl which made her roll her eyes and laugh. After she smiled at my joke, I asked Angela if she wanted to dance. We went to the dance floor together and had an amazing time dancing to the only slow song played at Rick's that night. I had danced with Angela numerous times over the years, but this was different. As we danced, we talked about Jamie's future, and I assured her I would always be there for that young child. It was a privilege to have the honor of being the first person to dance with this newly widowed woman. Angela smiled like a woman completely content with her life. I was saddened by the knowledge that this beautiful smile would have to be locked away for the near future but comforted by the long-term prospects for Angela's life. She would have to endure pain, but that pain would blossom into the strong memory of her deceased husband. This acute agony was infinitely better than the chronic degeneration she would have otherwise endured. Still, it was a sad sight to watch this doomed smile shining so bright on her face. It was yet another moment in which I failed in my desire to stop time. The world kept spinning and that smile was lost forever from reality. That is exactly why reality can never compete with fiction. When the dance was over, I couldn't reread the chapter. The dance was simply over.

Angela and I made our way back to the bar where Derbe was sitting with his girlfriend. Derbe complained that he wanted to make a toast but was waiting for Mike. Immediately after he finished his sentence, the music stopped, and the club was filled with bright lights. I heard screams coming from the back room and asked everyone what they thought was going on. We made a couple jokes about people getting caught having sex and were in an altogether jovial mood as we waited for the music to resume. I knew the truth and just waited for it to be revealed. After about ten minutes, the room was flooded with police, and it wasn't long before we were told what had happened. Angela cried in my arms and I stood in disbelief as the police blocked off the VIP area and began taking pictures and gathering information from everyone in the bar. I held Angela and did my best to whisper comforting words in her ear. I could feel her emotions flowing into my body and felt the tears began to trickle down my face as well. I looked up at Derbe and saw a ghost. I have never seen such a pale face in my entire life, and that's saying something considering I have seen more than my share of corpses over the years. After the police finished collecting everyone's information, they slowly allowed people to leave without making any arrests. We were the only ones remaining with the officers as they tried to console us and said they would do everything possible to investigate the murder. This did nothing to comfort us as we all knew there was no way they were going to find the killer. Actually, the knowledge did comfort me but not the rest of the group. Eventually, we left the club and took Angela to get Jamie from the babysitter. When we picked up Jamie, he looked so cute and oblivious to what had just happened. It reminded me of my own memory of watching cartoons the morning my mom had died. Angela was going through torture, but Mike had died soon enough that Jamie could avoid this pain. Angela held her baby in her arms with a strength through tribulation that showed I had judged her character correctly. I knew it was just a matter of time before she would grow into an even stronger person and give Jamie the life, and the father, he deserved.

Derbe and I spent the entire night on the couch with Angela and stayed until her family arrived the following evening. She was completely devastated. I had to return to Ann Arbor but was sure to tell Angela that I would help with anything she needed. I felt alright leaving her because she had plenty of family present, and I knew Derbe would take care of her as well. After I left Lansing, I finally had the chance to deal with my own emotional response to Mike's death. I was initially numb when I had killed Mike and then had spent the next two days entirely focused on Angela's emotions so I had not yet dealt with my own reaction. As I began to think about my feelings, I felt surprisingly pleased. I had expected to sink into a regretful depression, but that simply wasn't the case. Instead of feeling sad after the kill, I felt an overwhelming sense of accomplishment. The same rationale that had led me to kill Mike was unaffected after it was finished. I remained confident that I had done the correct thing and was excited to write the rest of Mike's story. I was proud of the fact I had been successful in such a noble endeavor and hadn't cowered from the moment. I found myself overcome by a sense of liberation. I had gone against the conventions of society for the first time in my life. I had never done anything wrong before. This murder would clearly be viewed as wrong by the rest of the world. I had no doubt they would incorrectly view my actions out of context and be unable to appreciate the complete consequences. By writing Mike's happy ending, I would turn his death into his salvation. I would turn his humanity into his immortality. What I had done was wrong, but what I was about to do was write.

When I returned to Ann Arbor, I immediately submerged myself into writing the conclusion of *Father's Day*. Unlike my previous book, I didn't have to dwell on the blank pages of Mike's future before I filled them in. This story's demons had already been conquered, and the rest of the process was easy. I finished an entire chapter during the single day I was home in Ann Arbor before attending the funeral in Traverse City. I didn't regret my actions and was able to write the happy ending to Mike's life with a smile on my face. It got to the point that I was so excited to finish the book that it was actually hard to stop writing to go to the funeral. As I drove to Traverse City, I had to remind myself to hide my jubilation during the next few days as I needed to demonstrate my remorse to those around me who were not yet ready to experience the true glory of Mike's death. The effects of Mike's resurrection would be experienced by all these people in due time, but I had to allow them to undergo the grieving process and arrive at that endpoint naturally. I was taking pleasure in Mike's fate because I knew the end of the story while simultaneously being cognizant of the fact that everyone else was stuck in the middle of the book under the illusion that the story was over. Time would heal the wounds within those who loved Mike. With each wound that was healed, Mike's legacy would continuously grow until his destiny was finally fulfilled. In addition to the natural longevity Mike would experience in the memories of his loved ones, my book would recreate Mike's dreams and lift him to an entirely higher level of existence by giving him immortality in fiction. The world may not have realized the story they fell in love with was based on my friend, but this perfect character was remembered forever in their hearts nonetheless. I was content with what I had done and happy that Mike was finally on the path to get what he deserved.

When I arrived in Traverse City, I was immediately struck by the sadness surrounding me. Angela's fragile body tenderly greeted me as I stepped out of my car. I gave her a long embrace and told her everything was going to be alright. After ten somber minutes of comforting Angela, I went inside to see the rest of the family. There wasn't a dry eye in the place. Everyone mourned the needless death of this innocent young man and cursed the evil person that could have committed such a crime. I walked through the grieving crowd and consoled everyone I encountered. Every person expressed the same sentiment about the tragic nature of Mike being taken from the world far too soon by that senseless act of violence. No one realized that they were actually crying in the murderer's arms. I insincerely expressed my regret at what had happened but was honest when I said that everything would work out for the best. I told people things had gone according to a plan that was beyond their comprehension, and they simply needed to have faith. Little did these people know that I was talking about my plan rather than that of some fictional deity. The last person I talked to before the funeral was Mike's mother. I had seen the joy in her eyes at Mike's wedding and hated to see her discomfort as she dealt with her son's death. I wished she could appreciate the whole picture of Mike's life rather than focusing on her current loss. I hugged her tightly and wished with all my heart that I could sit her down and explain to her that Mike's death was a blessing. She had already lived through the real tragedy with her husband years ago. Instead of focusing on what she had lost in her own life, I wanted her to realize the gift that I had given to Angela, Jamie, and the future readers of Mike's story. I knew she would be incapable of understanding this reality, and I was obviously unable to tell her, but yet I wished she could find the peace she deserved. Her son would be remembered as the greatest father the world had ever seen, and yet she was standing there mourning his life. All I could do was embrace her in this emotional moment as we walked into the funeral together.

The church was filled to capacity. Everyone sat in silence looking up at the front of the chapel where a giant picture of Mike hovered over his coffin. I quietly walked Mike's mom to her spot in the front pew and then sulked back to into the shadows. I wanted to observe Mike's funeral from a distance to gain a real appreciation for the value of his life. I could see so much love for Mike in the hearts of everyone in attendance and felt proud of the fact that I was responsible for this outpouring of love. I listened from a distance as the speakers praised Mike's character and described what an outstanding husband and father he was. It was refreshing to hear people speak truthfully at a funeral about a person for which lying was completely unnecessary. The truth of Mike's life had been so beautiful that there was no need to embellish. I was set to give the main eulogy for the ceremony after the priest spoke, but, in the meantime, I was comfortable standing along the back wall observing the moment. Mike deserved the response he was getting, and I hoped this love would someday be funneled into Jamie's memory of his amazing father.

The ceremony was beautiful right until the priest began to talk. This was the same idiot who had previously tried to ruin Mike's wedding. This time, the priest got up on the stage, pulled down his pants, and attempted to piss all over Mike's memory. Once again, the priest decided to give Mike absolutely no credit for the glory of his character and instead kept describing Mike as a vessel for god's will on earth. To make matters worse, the priest said god had decided it was time for Mike to die which infuriated me even more because he was now giving god credit for my achievements as well. I found myself getting continuously angrier as I listened to this idiot trash the legacy of my perfect friend. The story of Mike's life was beautiful, and it was mine to write. I wasn't about to sit back and let this priest give a badly plagiarized version of Mike's time on earth that ended long before the actual conclusion in my book. This speech was attacking the core of what Mike's life stood for. The priest was trying to murder my friend in front of everyone, and I found his actions completely reprehensible. Before long, I decided enough was enough and started walking up the aisle as if I had just heard my cue. Although the priest was surprised when I interrupted before he was finished, he cared more about his appearance than anything else so he tried to play it off as if my walking up was part of his plan and handed me the microphone. Those who realized he had not finished undoubtedly assumed I had been drinking my way through my grief, and, instead of being offended by my poor etiquette, they were moved by the emotional torment they assumed I was going through. I took the microphone and delivered the eulogy I had written the day before Mike's death with an added response to the priest's nonsense mixed in with the original draft.

> Alright. Where do I begin? Mike was an incredible man, and I would be doing him a disservice if I didn't first address the grossly inaccurate description of him that was just expressed by father Knob Job over here. I was honestly offended when I heard Mike's legacy described as a journey that took him on the path to heaven. There is no way Mike would end up with such a minuscule eternity as a typical heavenly existence. I have no doubt Mike is not in heaven. Heaven doesn't deserve to hold the strength of Mike's character. To end a story like Mike's in heaven would be to sell the man short. Mike transcends death. Mike may have died, but he still lives today because Mike stood for something greater than himself. Mike was an ideal, and it is hard for people like us to appreciate the extent of his excellence. As Virginia Woolf once said, "It is far more difficult to murder a phantom than a reality" and that is exactly why Mike's murderer was unsuccessful in ending his story. We were but the extras in the movie of Mike's life. He was the star. Mike was a perfect husband and a devoted father. I have never seen a man who loved his wife as honestly as Mike. There was nothing fake about his love for Angela. Mike was pure love manifested into human form. His love for Angela was only outmatched by his love for his young son, Jamie. If any of you want to regard today's events as a tragedy, then this is the aspect of Mike's death that you should focus on. Jamie was extremely blessed to have Mike as a father, and there is no question Mike would have been the greatest dad the world had ever seen. I hope you will all be there as Jamie grows up to tell him how magnificent his father was and constantly remind him of this paternal perfection. Jamie deserves to know that his father loved him more in his short life than most people are loved in a millennium. A moment of love is taller than the length of eternity. Jamie deserves to know about his father, and, through Jamie, Mike will live on forever. I am not going to stand in front of you a sad man because my friend lived a great life and I don't believe he is dead. Mike lives on through us all. Mike's past rests in our memories. Mike's future remains in our hearts. He may no longer sleep next to Angela every night, but his strange loop resides in her brain. Mike's identity lives in the minds of everyone he touched. At Mike's wedding, I told him I hoped he lived his life according to some of my favorite words by Albert Einstein: "Any man who can drive safely while kissing a beautiful woman is simply not giving the kiss the attention it deserves." I hoped that Mike would give that kiss the attention it deserved, and that is exactly what he did. Mike loved Angela to capacity every day of their lives. Mike didn't wait until he was financially secure to start living his life, and, because of this courageous lifestyle of living in the present moment, Mike and Angela brought Jamie into the world. Mike didn't shy away from life until it was too late which is why Mike's life didn't end as a tragedy as our incompetent priest so rudely suggested earlier. The value of a person's life is measured by the quality of the storyline and not the length of the book. Mike's story is not one of despair but rather one of hope. Mike proved that a person can live an entire life with his integrity securely intact. My friend will be remembered long after we are all forgotten because he represents a life of which we could only dream. We may be sitting at Mike's funeral today, but I have no doubt we will all die long before he does. I was selfishly sad to lose Mike, but I know better than to stand here depressed for myself. I came not to mourn, but rather to celebrate the life of my best friend. The story of Mike Wagner is one of joy. Mike was a great man. Mike is a great man. I hope you all honor this man by celebrating his life in a manner deserving of his character. Thank you.

When I finished my eulogy, the church was filled with applause for Mike. The reception afterward included the ideal blend of tears and laughter that I had hoped for. As I spoke at the front of the church, I could see Angela smile through her sadness as she was reminded of the truly marvelous man she lost. Angela's smile was exactly what I needed to reinforce my decision to have killed Mike and write his story. I spent the rest of the day drinking with people who loved Mike and telling stories about the man we missed. I always made sure to refocus the discussion on the future Mike would have lived. We told a lot of stories about his past, but I wanted to make sure everyone realized the best part of Mike's life was the part he would never experience in reality. None of these people ever realized that my second novel was explicitly the story of Mike's life, but I have no doubt those who knew him best suspected the motivation for this inspirational story was drawn from my long lost friend. Although, I suppose it is entirely possible that this connection was never made because none of these people ever asked me if *Father's Day* was based on Mike once it was published. Even Derbe didn't make the clear connection between my second novel and the death of our best friend. I guess the emphasis of the story on the rest of Mike's life helped to hide the character that had started the story.

As I reminisced with friends at Mike's funeral, I kept a constant eye on Angela. I watched her facial expressions intently to ensure things were going as planned. Although her pain was outwardly obvious, I could see her character strengthening with each person she talked to. There was no doubt everyone was trying to comfort her by saying how great Mike was, and I could see Mike's character growing ever stronger in her long-term memory. Mike was being transformed from a mortal man into an immortal myth right in front of my eyes. Mike had been a doomed person with a flawed future but was now becoming a perfect character preparing for an immaculate eternity. Everyone took their turn hugging Angela and trying to help her move past this seemingly tragic event. My friend Hal, who had worked with Mike in the Biomaterials Lab at Michigan Tech, even offered to let Angela stay with him for a couple months while she got over Mike. Hal tried to explain to Angela that it was time for her to move on and that his apartment would be an excellent environment for her to forget Mike. What started out as a seemingly sweet sentiment quickly turned ugly as Derbe and I had to convince Hal that hitting on Angela at Mike's funeral wasn't appropriate. I guess a ladies' man like Hal just has a one track mind and couldn't help himself around a single woman even at her husband's funeral. Nonetheless, the ordeal gave Angela a good laugh and helped distract her for a bit. The night of Mike's funeral ended with Angela, Derbe, and I taking a long walk and having an emotional conversation about my friend that was no longer with us.

As we walked, Derbe and I vowed to be there for Angela and Jamie for the rest of their lives. This conversation between the three of us reminded me so much of the conversations that Mike and I had shared in the past. Angela talked about her determination to overcome Mike's death and give Jamie the life he deserved. The best part of this night was listening to Angela say that she was going to make sure Jamie always knew what an amazing man his father was. Angela expressed her desire to always keep Mike a major part of Jamie's life, and, at that moment, I knew my first murder had been a monumental success. I hadn't even finished writing the actual book that would give Mike his immortality, but I could already see everything lining up exactly as I had planned. We walked together in conversation about the future, and, eventually, Derbe brought up the investigation of Mike's murder. Derbe was completely appalled that the police had no leads and refused to accept Angela's accurate assessment that it was hopeless. Derbe talked nobly of justice and was tormented by the fact that Mike was dead and the man responsible was out walking the streets. I smiled inside when I laughed at my friend's obliviousness that the killer was not only walking the streets but actually walking right next to him on that exact street.

We took Angela home and then continued just the two of us. Mike and Derbe had been my best friends. It was now just the two of us, and we walked in quiet conversation as we recounted our history together as friends. It was Derbe that brought up our previous walk after Mike's wedding in which we had looked out at our future together as friends forever. Neither of us had expected forever to end so soon. Derbe and I were now left only with each other and the shared memory of our deceased friend. I promised Derbe I would make sure Mike's life wasn't in vain as I vowed to watch over Jamie in the upcoming years, and Derbe vowed to change his life to make sure he honored Mike's memory. I remember being a bit unsure of exactly what he meant, and I think he was unsure at the time as well, but it was a noble statement that made me admire this man even more than I previously had.

The morning after the funeral, I said goodbye to Angela, kissed Jamie on the forehead, and drove back to Ann Arbor. Although I still spent my days in the lab, my life became consumed with writing. I was so intensely devoted to writing Mike's story that I would often go days without sleeping. For the next month, I avoided all social activity as I immersed myself in the book. The only breaks I took were to visit Angela and Jamie in Lansing once or twice a week to ensure they were doing alright. Every time I would visit, I noticed how much Derbe had been taking care of them in Mike's absence, and I was so thankful he was there. Derbe was in his final year of medical school, and it would have been easy for him to focus on his own life, but he never missed a moment to be there for Mike's family. I did my best to be there as well, and I could see the positive effect our presence was having. Mike had been dead less than a month, but Angela's lovely demeanor seemed to return much quicker than expected. There was no doubt her sadness remained in the quiet hours of the night, but I was no longer worried about the timescale of her healing. Every time I would visit, I was further energized to finish *Father's Day* as quickly as possible.

Before long, the book was finished, and I took it to my publisher. I had spent the last two years being pestered to write a follow-up novel, and it was well worth the wait. After this book, I was never again forced to write on anyone's timescale except my own. It is a good feeling to have achieved the literary status at which one can write without anxiety. My first book had been a success, but this would be the novel that ultimately propelled me to fame. The book sales soared. Two months after giving the book to my editor, I found myself with the top two bestsellers in the country. Not only was *Father's Day* setting book sales records in an era when books no longer seemed to sell, but *Mom in Heaven* sales rebounded as my newly extended readership bought my original novel as well. I was almost finished with my PhD but was forced to slow the process as I went on a nationwide book tour and made the talk show rounds for the first time in my life. I was careful not to misattribute the success to my own achievements. I knew this success was a reflection on the main characters, and I was always sure to focus my interviews on the quality of the book's message rather than my individual accomplishments. Despite my best efforts, I became known as a talented new author and was constantly worshiped for my work. I found this praise as unwanted as when I was a hockey player being praised for a good saucer pass. At least this time, I was grown up enough to overcome the pitfalls that often accompany a good compliment. I conquered my emotions and stayed intellectually centered in my life. I was proud of what I had accomplished, but I didn't just want to sit back and be praised for my work. I wanted these first two novels to be the start of a long writing career. I hoped this was just the beginning.

Three months after I returned from my book tour, I finished my dissertation and received my PhD. Upon graduating, I immediately retired from the medical field and became a fulltime writer. I had waited a long time for this moment and was thankful to have the financial stability to live the life I wanted. I had no need to work as an engineer now that I had two top selling books and a true passion for writing. Although my financial success was a welcomed surprise, I had no desire for the amount of money I had accrued. All I really wanted was enough money to live a simple life with those I loved, write my books, and have a little extra money set aside for a sunny day. I was proud of the social effects my books had on readers much more than the monetary gains they provided. All money meant to me was the freedom to continue writing which excited me tremendously. I once again began to think about my next novel. *Father's Day* was a best seller, and my popularity was skyrocketing. I was at the point in my career that I could probably write any book and sell it purely on reputation, but I cared more about the quality of my books than commercial success. I always felt a rush inside me when I went on the talk shows and they asked about the motivation behind my stories. I would constantly deflect the questions with references to my love of the characters and my desire to create happy endings for them. I had written about two of the greatest characters the world had ever seen. They were two dead people that were now living happily ever after.

My mind soon turned to finding my next character. I obviously had a great method for success, but it had not yet been optimized. I was unsure if my next character would die of natural causes and simply fall into my lap or if I would have to kill another person to achieve the desired result. One thing that was clear was that timing was important. The person had to die before their dreams were killed by the world. My last book was the result of killing my best friend and was a monumental success. Not only was Mike honored by millions of people around the world, but his wife and son were benefiting from his death in so many unseen ways. As a result, I thought seriously about killing Derbe for my next book. I figured that if killing one best friend worked well, it was bound to work again. Ultimately, I decided not to kill Derbe after thinking seriously about it for a few days. I'm not entirely sure why I didn't want to kill Derbe. It may have been selfishness inside me wanting to preserve at least one best friend, or, perhaps, it was simply the result of his outlook on life. Mike had impeccable dreams that could never be reached in reality. Killing Mike preserved this happy ending. Derbe, on the other hand, was a realist, and I ultimately saw no upside in murdering him and fulfilling his pessimistic story. A realist deserves to live in reality; a dreamer deserves to live in his dreams.

I decided I wouldn't kill Derbe, and I was left without my next character. I was once again at a crossroads in my life as I tried to determine the person I wanted to become. I was pleased with the progress I was making but was ready to fully immerse myself into my new career. I no longer had the constraints of graduate school and was free to pursue my passion with all my energy. After significant soul searching, I came to the conclusion that I would be a force for good in the world. I saw so much pain around me every day. The most tragic type of torment was watching people as their dreams were destroyed. I would be a dream defender. I decided I would continue the trend I had started with Mike and kill people I admired before it was too late. I made the decision that it was probably smarter to kill people who I didn't know instead of continuing along the path of killing those closest to me. This choice was made for two reasons. First, there was much lower risk of being caught killing people to whom I had no connection. Second, I felt my gift for restoring people's dreams should be shared with the world and not reserved for those closest to me. There was suffering throughout the entire world, and I wanted to make as big a difference as I could. My plan for the future was to live my life until I met someone I truly admired at the pinnacle of their story. I would then kill them and create a proper ending to their life. I would write a wide range of inspiring stories while drastically improving the future lives of the loved ones who were left behind. I was going to kill, but I would do it for the right reasons. I would be an author with an assembly line of inspirational characters. My writing would be the penance for the lives I ended. I would be an altruistic killer, a murderer with a heart of gold. I had risen to a higher level of morality. I was willing to do what was wrong in order to accomplish something truly brilliant, and there was no telling how many dreams I would save in my new career. It was now time to choose my next character.

CHAPTER 5

Alone Together

If you are afraid of loneliness, do not marry.

-Anton Chekhov

CHAPTER 5: *Alone Together*

Mike was dead, but his life went on. Angela began to piece herself together, and I could see the foundation of Jamie's perfect story taking form. It was hard to watch Angela struggle with school while simultaneously attempting to take care of Jamie and overcome the heartbreak of losing Mike. I did my best to follow through on my promise to be there for her and spent a lot of time in Lansing during this period. Between Derbe and me, someone was always available to babysit. I cherished every second I had with Jamie. He was still just a baby, but I could see the life that stretched out in front of him and felt enormous pride in my contribution to the quality of his life. My time with Angela and Jamie provided the positive feedback needed to motivate me to start my next book. I hadn't yet found the protagonist for my next novel, but I was constantly on the lookout. However, it was important for me to finish Mike's story before I moved on. The book had been written, but I wanted to also ensure I created the perfect life for Mike's son. The world admired Mike without knowing his original identity, but Jamie's life would be an equally important part of Mike's legacy. With that in mind, I set out to create a controlled environment around this young man to ensure every aspect of his perfect future was fulfilled.

The first thing I did was purchase a house in Lansing. My new lifestyle as an author allowed me to travel the globe with ease, but I made sure to keep a continuous presence near Angela and Jamie. I knew I needed to keep a close eye on Mike's most valuable investment. After moving into my new house in Lansing, I gave Angela a million dollars. She was struggling to work through medical school, and I wanted her to be free to simply raise Mike's child. I had more than enough money flowing into my accounts and preferred that the money was used to create the environment Jamie needed to grow into the person he was destined to become. I always loved the quote by B.F. Skinner that said, "Give me a child, and I'll shape him into anything" which was exactly what I was doing for Jamie. I was trying to design his environment in such a way that he could live a perfect life. The final aspect of this ideal life was just being there to constantly remind him of Mike's character. This ongoing process played an integral role in preserving Mike's legacy.

During the time I was helping Angela shape her new life, I was also in the process of building a new life for myself. I had the financial security to live out the rest of my life writing books and making the world a better place. I used this newfound freedom in every way possible. I traveled around the globe to places I had always longed to see and visited friends I had missed for too long. Everywhere I went, I found myself praised for my work as a writer and had to do my best to keep on level ground. I found it ironic that people would call me a genius for my writing without even knowing the true value of the books. In reality, the most profound part of my literature was the necessary deaths needed to write them. I was thankful my books resonated with the public, but only I knew the secret recipe. I had grasped what millions before me had failed to see and turned it into something beautiful. I had discovered the certainty of life's tragic character and transformed it into a happy ending. One might contend that my means were wrong, but no one could argue with the results. The response I got from *Father's Day* was all the evidence I needed to justify my next kill. The only thing I had to do was sit back while waiting to be inspired. I no longer searched for inspiration as I had done in the first year following *Mom in Heaven*. It was just a matter of time before I would find my next subject naturally. I didn't need to create a timetable for my next book as I had plenty of money. Even so, I was overwhelmed with delight at the thought of beginning a new project. The excitement for my next book quickly became the main addiction in my life and has been a constant ever since.

About a month before I began my third novel, Derbe finished medical school. I was extremely proud of his accomplishment as I attended the hooding ceremony. As a graduation gift, I planned a five day vacation to New Orleans for just the two of us. We left the week after he finished his final requirements to enjoy a relaxing trip together. As the plane took off, I congratulated Derbe on finishing medical school and made a toast to our vacation. The first thing Derbe said was that he wished Mike could have been with us. Until this moment, I hadn't realized how hard Derbe had taken Mike's death. I had known he would be there for Angela, but I never imagined he would be impacted in such a profound way. For the rest of the flight, Derbe described the full spectrum of emotions he had experienced in the time since the murder. Derbe felt a mixture of guilt and inspiration. The guilt came as a result of his own success in medical school while Mike was no longer there to experience the same achievements. The inspiration came as he expressed how he was going to change his life to make sure he didn't waste the time he had left on earth. Derbe vowed to make his own life a tribute to Mike. I was amazed at how hard Derbe had taken Mike's death but impressed that my murder seemed to have yet another positive side effect. I knew murder was the only way to give Mike his happy ending and Jamie his ideal future, but I never imagined it would alter the course of Derbe's life as well. I was shocked to hear he had decided not to become a general practitioner as originally planned. Instead, Derbe decided to go into forensics and use his medical expertise as a detective solving cases such as Mike's. Derbe talked passionately about his anger that Mike's murderer was never found and claimed the real tragedy of Mike's death was that his killer was still out there living his life. I nodded as I listened to my misguided friend express his plans to get another degree and become a forensic detective. I didn't blame him for this response as he was unaware of the big picture of Mike's life. Years later, Derbe would often reopen Mike's case file in the hopes of uncovering some missing information and would constantly put his arm around me and tell me he could feel he was getting close to Mike's killer. This always made me laugh as I knew how true that statement really was. Derbe could never get over losing such a close friend, and I felt the same emotional turmoil inside myself. I wished I had lived in a different world in which there would have been an easier alternative. Unfortunately, great achievements in the real world rarely come without sacrifice. Derbe was focused on his new future, and I loved watching him become a diligent detective in the years that followed.

Derbe remained my best friend for the rest of my life as he fought for justice in Mike's honor.

I have had the privilege to travel all around the globe in my life, but this trip to New Orleans with my best friend was truly special. We spent our time experiencing the entire range of emotions that New Orleans has to offer. There is nowhere else on earth quite like the Big Easy. We enjoyed quiet days listening to depressingly beautiful music and talking about life. We had wild nights in the French Quarter. Ultimately, the trip allowed us to fulfill all of our most honorable and most sinister desires. We spent our days meeting with kids at a charity I hosted in the area while spending our nights in complete debauchery. It was an amazing vacation.

Our last night in New Orleans was a night to remember. Unfortunately, I have forgotten most of it. The one part of the evening that made a lasting impact on my life was the first two hours that were spent visiting at a quiet bar. There is nowhere on earth I would rather be than sitting in New Orleans listening to the best undiscovered acoustic music in the world. A single guitar player singing a slow song triggers the resonant frequency of my soul. The overall musical environment of New Orleans perfectly aligns with my ideal night out with friends. The music is quiet enough to enjoy a friend's company while, at the same time, allowing one to simply sit back and soak in the emotion behind the music. During this evening, Derbe and I sat quietly and allowed ourselves to be inspired by the sounds in the air. We had been together four straight days and had left no subject untouched in our discussions. As a result, we were free to just enjoy this relaxing final day without a word.

As Derbe and I sat at the bar, we eventually struck up a conversation with a cute couple at the table next to us who were also on vacation. The couple lived just outside Atlantic City, and we got along with them right from the start. Before long, Derbe and I had heard their entire life's story and listened to them describe their plans for the future. The couple had just gotten engaged and was planning to be married in an extravagant wedding in six months. It was easy to see that these two were excited for the wedding as everything we talked about was rerouted into a conversation about some aspect of their ceremony. Fortunately, I was able to hear about more than just wedding plans in our two hour conversation. I always relish the opportunity to hear people's histories and understand the real driving forces in their lives. It quickly became apparent that this couple was driven to one another by their desire for togetherness. They were high school sweethearts but hadn't followed the usual route to marriage. This couple had actually broken up after high school as they desired to forge their own lives. Ultimately, these years apart brought them back together as they both found loneliness without the other. I had a knack for understanding people's true feelings beneath the surface, and this couple was no exception. As they described their breakup and subsequent reunion, it was clear they were impacted by their time alone to a much greater extent than their time together. When I looked a layer below the surface, I could clearly see their motivation to be together was simply the lessor of two evils. They told us how they had broken up the first time because, as much as they liked each other, they just didn't feel the connection they had always envisioned with their soul mate and wanted to explore the world separately in search of that complete connection. It was during these years apart that the sting of loneliness had changed their perspective and helped them understand what they had not previously appreciated. I immediately felt pity for the plight of these two who were no doubt struggling with a problem common to us all. We can either be alone by ourselves or alone with someone. I knew that their lifelong struggle against loneliness would be an insurmountable obstacle standing in the way of their happiness and wished they could experience the connection they truly desired.

Derbe and I spent the rest of the night drinking and dancing all over New Orleans with this couple, and, although most of the details are lost to me now, I remember getting invited to their wedding before the night was over and woke up the next day with the wedding date and address written on a napkin in my pocket along with their contact information. I threw the napkin in my suitcase with my dirty clothes and didn't give this couple another thought for the next few weeks. Upon our return to Lansing, Derbe immediately immersed himself into pursuing his future as a detective, and I spent the week helping Angela and Jamie move into a nice new home just outside the city. Once they were settled, I left for New York to do a taping of the *Daily Show* to discuss my books and help create some hype for the *Mom in Heaven* movie planned for the following year. One of the questions in the interview was if I had an idea for my next book and if it was going to be the same type of story as the first two. At that moment, my mind turned to the couple I had met in New Orleans, and I knew my next story. I answered honestly that my next book was going to be a romance.

It was a comforting feeling to have decided upon my next story, and my adrenaline was immediately spiked. The first thing I did when I returned home was search through my suitcase for the couple's address to make sure I had directions to the scene of my next crime. I found the napkin and placed the address inside my desk drawer for safe keeping. I then began brainstorming the details of the book. My first two novels were similar stories, and, this time, I wanted to write a different type of book. There was no doubt the theme had to be love. I had written my first two books focusing on the strengths of my mom and Mike both in their marriages and as parents, but the primary focus of both stories had leaned towards the parenting aspects of their lives. I wanted this book to be about the absolute connection between two lovers. The book would focus on the love shared by two young people and tell the story of how they came together to conquer loneliness. These two separate individuals had planned to transform themselves into a single entity on their wedding day so I decided this would be the appropriate day for them to die. Even the wedding day wouldn't actually have given them the connection they wanted, but, since it was the closest they would ever be in reality, I figured I would kill them at the peak of their lives. I remembered Mike's wedding and how it had been special because it wasn't the best day of their lives as he and Angela truly loved being with one another. This couple's happiness, on the other hand, would never be greater than on the day of their nuptials. I figured I might as well end the romance before the downfall. I marked the murder date on my calendar and booked a weeklong trip to Atlantic City. One of the charities I had started was expanding rapidly, and we had just opened a youth center in New Jersey, so I figured I would kill two birds with one stone. Just to be clear, the last sentence was just a metaphor. Animal lovers can be comforted by the fact that no birds were killed on this trip, only people.

Once the logistics of my trip were planned, I sat down to begin the book. It was a nice feeling to get a start on the writing process, and I wrote a large majority of the book before the characters were killed. Most of you have no doubt already guessed that I am referring to *Alone Together*. It was the first true love story I had ever written, and it was a joy to create. True love is actually an oxymoron. True love is the most beautifully tragic paradox the world has ever created. As I wrote the story, I loved the irony that true love could only exist in fiction. Although the book was remembered primarily for the cliché love lines constantly quoted from it, my ultimate goal in writing the story was to highlight a complete connection between two people. The book's title suggested that this couple was alone together for the simple reason that their love was sufficient. It was the story of two people who only needed each other for their happiness while, in reality, the title represented the tragic irony that, in their real life, they would have remained lonely no matter how much time they spent together. Unfortunately, science has never come up with a way for us to connect two brains. It would be amazing if we were somehow able to not only share a conversation with another person, but actually share their thoughts. If this could somehow be achieved in reality, complete chronic romantic happiness could feasibly become theoretically possible again. The sad fact for this couple, and the rest of us for that matter, is that we are constantly imprisoned within our minds while being simultaneously tormented by the concept of togetherness. The gift I gave this couple in the book was to provide a remedy for a life spent permanently isolated from one another while being in such close proximity.

As I wrote the story, I constantly returned to my own desire to share another person's thoughts. If we could only connect brains, there would be so many amazing possibilities. In addition to creating a real connection in a relationship, we might develop a true empathy that could have so many positive repercussions. As long as people are trapped within their own skulls, world peace is utterly hopeless. There appears to be no route to a collective morality in an egocentric world. Even more interesting than these societal consequences of connecting brains would be the personal benefits we could enjoy if this technology was developed. I imagine brain sharing would allow us to communicate on completely different levels such as an emotional communication in which we could feel another person's feelings. Honestly, experiencing simultaneous shared orgasms should provide enough motivation for us to pursue this possibility by itself. Unfortunately, any type of brain connection seems to be a long way off, and, in the meantime, this couple's only hope was fiction. If we had Avatar connectors built into our hair to directly connect us with our lovers, murder may not have been necessary, and I wish that was the case. In fact, I actually got a lot of grief from friends when Avatar came out and I continually expressed my crush on the cute blue alien with whom I could share my thoughts. This desire for complete connection with another human being is forever present in our lives and impossible to completely eradicate. I have spent my entire life attempting to gain rational control over this desire and am consistently finding myself falling short in this endeavor.

Before long, the story was almost finished, and it was time to fly to Atlantic City. When I arrived, the first thing I did was scope out the wedding location and then spend the rest of the day visiting the youth center we had set up about twenty minutes away. My mind was preoccupied with murder plans, but I found the children at the youth center to be an inspirational distraction. There is nothing more admirable than the dreams of a young child. I spent the entire day playing games with the kids, helping with homework, and listening to them talk about their dreams. It was so uplifting to listen to these kids talk. However, it also gave me an uneasy feeling in the pit of my stomach as I contemplated the magnitude of unfulfilled dreams that awaited these incredible children in their futures. The most inspirational moment of the day was when I met three young kids with disabilities. Two of the kids were paraplegics struggling to regain use of their lower extremities. Fortunately, both prognoses were good, and the doctors expected these kids to partially recover in time. The final girl I met was a blind girl with a truly bright spirit. This young child had recently lost her dream of being an artist along with her eyesight. Unlike the two young boys, her blindness was ensured to last forever. As sad as her story seemed on the surface, talking to this young girl for fifteen seconds reminded me what dreams are all about. Against all odds, she held to the hope that she might somehow see again. It was a rejuvenating feeling to listen to this young girl, and I could feel my entire mood lifted. That night, I went to dinner with a couple friends in the area and was totally at peace. I was excited to kill the couple on their wedding day and finish *Alone Together*, but I wasn't anxious at all. Instead of worrying about the next day, I sat comfortably and embraced the moment at hand. I had everything planned, and it was now just a matter of waiting patiently for the time of death to arrive.

On the morning of the wedding, I was up early and ready for action. As I ate breakfast, I went over the murder plan in my head. Killing Mike with a knife was a messy murder necessary only for the simple fact that killing a friend is the most obvious example of stabbing him in the back. Even though that kill hadn't taken long to plan, I was proud of its poetic nature. In a similar way, killing these two people on their wedding day was symbolic of the peak of their togetherness which was exactly what I wanted to achieve. I had the freedom to go through with the kill in any way I desired and decided to make sure it was a wedding gift specially designed for them. I liked the idea of providing an additional element of symbolism to their deaths in addition to the immortality I would give them. It had taken a little work, but I felt extremely pleased with the murder I had planned.

After breakfast, I looked through my supplies and found everything in order. I didn't attend the wedding ceremony but observed from a distance as the couple walked out of the church and got into the limo. During the reception, I made my way out of town to an abandoned crematorium that would host their after-party later that night. Two months prior, when I had developed the idea for the kill, I had chosen this location for an additional youth center to be built and hence forced the crematorium out of business. After buying the property, I changed the construction timeline under the guise of scheduling conflicts so that I would have this crematorium available on the date of the wedding. I arrived at the crematorium around seven and turned everything on in preparation for the night. Once the stage was set, I returned to my hotel and awaited the arrival of the newlyweds.

When they returned from the wedding, I was ready. I waited about five minutes to make sure they were inside their room and then went to knock on the door with a bottle of champagne. When the door opened, the celebrating couple looked out in absolute shock. I walked right past them, said congratulations, and asked if they were ready for champagne. The blank looks staring back at me were priceless as the couple tried to gather their composure. They were obviously excited to see me but confused about what I was doing there. As I filled their champagne glasses, I explained that I was in town working with my youth center, had remembered their wedding date, and wanted to surprise them with a toast. We had only met once six months earlier in New Orleans, but we had an obvious connection, and they were thrilled that I remembered. We briefly caught up as I asked how they were feeling, and I smiled when they responded that they had never felt closer. I then raised my glass and toasted to the transformation of two people into one. They smiled with pride, raised their glasses, and drank up. Two minutes later, I found myself looking down at two poisoned corpses resting motionless on the floor. They had been wrong about their wedding. They hadn't become one which was clear from the symbolic three feet of separation between their lifeless bodies. Those three feet paled in comparison to the miles of separation between their identities in real life. I was happy to have the opportunity to toast their fictional dream and observe their special final moment together. That moment was over, and they were now dead. They had been killed simultaneously but even that was inadequate to unite them as they collapsed separately on the floor. It was now time to bring the couple together. I put the bodies into a large hockey bag to load them into my car downstairs so they could be transported to their next destination.

As I left the hotel, I felt a rush of adrenaline as I smiled at people in the parking lot. I got a strange excitement thinking about the oblivious people smiling back at me and wondering how they would react if they later found out the nice gentleman they met was carrying the corpses of his two victims right past them. It was a fun thought that added some enjoyment to my night as I loaded the car and drove to the crematorium. The murder was unfolding exactly as planned, and my anxiety started to fade away. In the days leading up to the kill, I had been most concerned about the portion of the evening in the hotel room. Now that I was on my way to the next stop, I felt completely confident. I had mapped out every step of my trip in detail to ensure I was fully prepared for the night. As a result, I felt like I was on autopilot once the evening finally arrived. The car ride to the crematorium was one of the most cheerful of my life. I had burned a CD earlier that week specifically for that trip. This murder soundtrack was made in honor of my victims and represented the gift I planned to give them in their novel with all the songs being about two people becoming one. I actually had to circle the block a couple times when I got to the crematorium because I wanted to finish "Come Together" by the Beatles. Once the song was over, I parked the car, grabbed the bodies out of the trunk, and took the newlyweds inside for the final step of their union.

As you have probably already guessed, the point of the crematorium was to bypass the physical separations between these two lovers and finally allow them to become one. I turned the fires on and unzipped the bag. I pulled out the bodies, propped them upright next to the furnace, sat down in my chair facing them, and took a few minutes to think about the beautiful future they had to look forward to. I ended up sitting alone in silence with the bodies for a good hour without moving a muscle because of the internal peace this setting brought me. It is an amazing feeling to see the look of relief in the eyes of a corpse. The couple's struggle was over, and they would soon be together forever just as they had always dreamt. In addition to the comforting feeling of staring at the peaceful bodies, I wanted to make sure I gave the ovens enough time to preheat. I had never cremated a person before so I wanted to be sure I didn't rush anything. Most people probably just assume that burning a person into ashes is simple, but this was a controlled process and I was no expert. I had read a little about it, but how was I supposed to know all the details of cremation? Too bad they didn't teach us that back in Home Economics. If bodies came with cooking instructions tattooed on the back like a frozen pizza, it would have made my life a lot easier. Anyway, I erred on the side of caution and waited an extra few minutes before throwing the bodies into the fire. As I slammed the oven door shut, I saw the flames engulf the two lovers stacked on top of one another. They had lived their lives as prisoners inside their respective bodies while futilely trying to escape this loneliness and become one. That was what their marriage was all about. They wanted their wedding to transform them into a single body. As I watched their bodies burn into ash and blend together, I realized that, thanks to me, their dream was coming true.

An unexpected thing happened as the bodies burned. I found myself starving. It had never crossed my mind that the savory smell of burning human flesh would make me hungry. I wondered if Hannibal Lector had simply planned to cremate his first victims and then undergone the same experience. If that was the case, I could definitely empathize with him even though I personally still had no desire to eat the people. Instead, I left the crematorium and went down the road for a pulled pork sandwich at a barbecue joint nearby. Just as with the preheating, I was unsure how long it would take to fully cremate the bodies so I just left them in the oven and went out for dinner. I have often had the same problem when cooking a nice roast at home. You never want to undercook, but there is only a limited window before a meal is burned and the roast is ruined. Fortunately, this time I didn't have to worry about burning anything since that was the whole point. As a result, I was in no rush to get back to the bodies and took my time enjoying a nice meal. After I finished eating, I returned to the crematorium and shut off the ovens. I spent the rest of the night collecting the newlywed's mixed ashes, putting them into a nice urn, and cleaning the place up. The first sight of the ashes was unbelievable. These two separate people were now a single mound of ash with two wedding rings resting on the top. I was so moved by the visual that I ran out to my car to get my camera and eventually made this photograph the cover of *Alone Together*. Although people argued about the symbolism of that picture, no one came close to realizing the truth of its origin. After the picture, I packed up the ashes and was on my way.

The next morning, I woke up and saw the urn sitting on my desk in the hotel room. I smiled at the couple and asked if they were ready for their honeymoon. They didn't reply, but I knew the answer. The hard part was over and now the fun was beginning. I packed for the flight home and brought my laptop down to breakfast since I couldn't wait to continue the novel. I had a nice meal but was unfortunately unable to write since the lobby was buzzing as people from the wedding party began to panic at the news that the newlyweds were missing. At first, most people insisted that they had probably gone out for some time alone together, but, once news arrived that a poison had been found in a champagne bottle and blood was on the countertop (the bride's head hit it on her way to the floor), people began to break down. I asked the waitress what was going on, and she explained the entire story in much less detail than I already knew. I told her it was crazy and then asked for a side of bacon which I had been craving ever since I smelled that long pig burning the previous evening. I spent a few more minutes listening to people screaming in the lobby and thinking about the pointlessness of their sadness. They had no way of knowing that the couple was actually better off, but I just wished they could somehow realize that, although it might be sad for them, it wasn't a sad morning for the couple. The couple's lives ended on a high note, and they would never have to feel loneliness again. I felt terrible for the loved ones who were sad, but this collateral damage was minuscule compared to the positive effects of my good dead. Before long, I had heard enough and decided it was time to leave.

When I returned from Atlantic City with the two lovers, I spent about a month writing the ending to their romance. The book vividly described the couple's yearning desire to become one entity and their subsequent success achieved through their marriage. The entire time I wrote the book, I had the couple sitting together in their urn on my desk as a reminder of the story's message. The book turned out to be a two part story with part one describing the struggle of two individuals while part two portrayed the comfortable life of a connected couple. They had been together at the beginning but were unfulfilled. They then broke up and were apart but unfulfilled. Now they were together and forever fulfilled in fiction.

When the story was completed, I felt the usual sense of pride one gets after doing a good dead. I looked up from my computer screen and saw the urn staring back at me. At this point, I wondered what I should do with the ashes now that I had finished the book. The whole point of the novel was for the couple to be together forever in their fictional happy ending. The cremation of the bodies had been symbolic of the merging of the two characters from part one into a single protagonist in part two. I felt as if the murder and book were perfectly aligned, but yet the ashes were still sitting on my table. Finally, after an incandescent intervention, I knew exactly what to do. Two months later, after the editing of *Alone Together* was complete, I mixed the couple's ashes into the ink of the first edition of the book. As the book was printed, the couple became their story. They lived forever in their happy ending.

Writing a story centering on the idea of loneliness gave me the chance to reanalyze my own life. A lot had changed since I had graduated from Michigan Tech, but my fundamental views on relationships had remained primarily unaltered. I no longer spent time searching for a nonexistent ideal woman to fulfill my desires. I knew this was a complete impossibility and moved on with my life. When I first came to this pessimistic realization about my future after breaking up with Mary, I was a bit despaired at the turn life had taken. I was pleased with the rational conclusion I had made but still remained emotionally disappointed in the result. As time went on, I had begun to address the deeper issues affecting the situation. It wasn't the ideal woman that I had actually been searching for. In reality, I had been pursuing a feeling of comfort and completeness that I thought this ideal woman would provide. Once I was able to acknowledge that the root of my problem was an emotional quest for connection with another human being, I was able to realize the fundamental flaw in my outlook that had driven me to unhappiness in the past. This empty feeling of loneliness is ever present in our lives and writing *Alone Together* allowed me to address the issue head on. In the book, I gave the couple what they had always wanted. In the process, I came to realize that I no longer needed this fictional ending in my own life. Even if I would have achieved that type of connection with a woman, I am fairly certain we would have spent our lives yearning to connect with another couple to put an end to our lonely life alone together. In the end, I came to terms with the fact that there is no cure for loneliness. From that point on, my life was spent as a completely satisfied individual and not a missing piece waiting to fit into a bigger puzzle. I was sufficient living by myself within my own mind. My relationships with women during this period were frequent but brief. I would blow through the lives of these different women, ironically often after they blew me. I tried to nurture long-term friendships but not romantic relationships. I was content being alone. I became like a starfish; I was asexual. I had no need for another person to fill a void in my heart. I still experienced women for passion but never for emotional comfort.

As my life went on, my desire for a complete connection with another person would constantly reemerge. Instead of allowing it to control my actions or destroy my happiness, I was simply cognizant of the impossibility of this desire and worked to rise above it. In fact, my intellectual view on this issue actually trained my emotions to the point where I became quickly repulsed by the notion of exclusivity. I often found that I could go no more than a couple nights with a girl before I began to reject any further intensification of the romance. My emotions became so tightly tied into my pessimistic view of relationships that I no longer saw potential in any girl. I could admire the person looking back at me but knew she couldn't give me what I desired. My focus on what was important in life was sharpened as I wrote *Alone Together* and found stability in the new identity I had created for myself. I would not end up like the couple in my novel, and so I moved forward alone.

As my newest novel began racing off the shelves, I realized the value of my life was beyond my original comprehension. I had started as a selfish author fighting to bring my mom back from the dead. I then grew into a selfishly altruistic friend that was addicted to giving happiness to those I loved ultimately manifesting this love in Mike's story. I had now risen to an entirely new level. I was a completely altruistic murderer. *Alone Together* was written about strangers and still brought so much joy into the world. By following the same process that had led to success in my first two books, I had stumbled upon a greater calling. My everyday life was still consumed with my addiction to making life better for those I loved such as helping Angela and Jamie through their lives, but my work had risen to an infinitely larger scale. A person who wants to make a positive difference can either try to make individual lives better or fight to make a major global impact. Either of these goals could be argued as the noblest cause for one to live their life. My writing was accomplishing both. Each book I wrote transformed the tragic story of an individual into an inspiration for the world. My books provided a global comfort to readers while saving an individual in the process. I was moving forward on a path that would make the world a better place. One thing was clear: life was short, but there was still plenty of time to kill.

CHAPTER 6

Blind Faith

It is a terrible thing to see and have no vision.

-Helen Keller

CHAPTER 6: Blind Faith

I killed a blind girl, and she didn't even see it coming. Barely a month had passed since I had murdered the lonely couple on their wedding day, and my productivity was increasing. I didn't need to spend months waiting for inspiration before I found my next protagonist because I decided to make a simple change in the way I would choose my next story. Rather than waiting passively to be inspired, I decided to pick a theme for my next novel and then find the right character to fit that theme. It was only a minor change in my approach but greatly improved my efficiency. For this book, I decided I wanted to write about a child. I had written about parents and lovers, but a book about a young person could portray the unlimited extent of a child's dreams. Once the decision was made to center my next book on a young character, it didn't take long for me to choose this child. I quickly remembered my visit to the youth center in Atlantic City and the inspirational blind girl I had met. I looked back through the records and found out her name was Faith.

As I read through Faith's file, I was once again inspired. I remembered the tragedy of her story involving her recent vision loss. As it turns out, this was just the tip of the iceberg. This young child was an inspiration to her entire community. There was no question sadness would have been justified based on Faith's history, but, instead, she lived a life of optimism. Faith's file described a person who had entered our youth program to cope with her disability but had instead become a natural therapist for those around her. Faith never doubted the certainty of her redemption. I was moved by the unshakable optimism of this tragic figure. There was no rationality guiding Faith. Her history was characterized by devastation, but yet she somehow retained her positive worldview. Faith believed that miracles were not only possible but inevitable. She represented the optimism I had grown up with in my own life without the flawless childhood that had led me down that path. Unlike me, Faith had every reason to be depressed but simply waited patiently with an unwavering hope for her future.

Faith was the correct character for my next novel because she represented the optimistic dreams of a child better than any person I have ever met. The only problem facing her life, the same problem that tormented all of my characters, was time. Miracles don't exist in the real world, and there was no doubt her blindness was permanent. I could picture the sadness on her face when she would one day reach the end of her life and realize that her optimistic nature remained unrewarded. This thought tortured me as I contemplated Faith's fate. It is impossible to describe how much I admired her vision of the future. Her idealistic outlook was contagious to everyone around her, and she deserved to see again and have her dreams fulfilled. I knew neither of these was likely to occur without my help. Whenever people would ask why she couldn't accept her terminal prognosis, Faith told them that she was just waiting patiently until her miracle arrived. I was inspired by this young woman's story and decided I would be that miracle.

As I reflected on Faith's story, I was reminded of the hopelessness of the world we live in. If the world of Faith could actually exist, it would be an amazing place. She had lost her sight but not her vision. She could no longer see, but she still believed. In my own life, it had ironically been an increase in my vision that had caused me to lose my faith. What a pair we made, the optimistic child and the cynical adult. No one could have guessed that it would be this cynical author that would make this child's unrealistic dreams come true. I believed in Faith. I admired her outlook and wished she hadn't been forced into hopeless optimism by her lack of options. Everything Faith had seen suggested the world was a terrible place, but she simply refused to accept that conclusion. None of her experiences could support her worldview, but Faith remained steadfast anyway. Faith is what is left when evidence is unavailable. Faith had developed out of helplessness, and I couldn't help but envy the persistence of her belief.

I had quickly decided to kill Faith, and the task was completed within a month of murdering the couple at the crematorium. Faith was incapable of seeing the unavoidable future that extended inevitably in front of her, but this no longer mattered once I killed her to prevent that future from taking place. She was trying to hope her dreams into reality, and, thankfully, I came to her rescue. Planning the murder and book turned out to be surprisingly fun. There were numerous elements of Faith's character that could potentially be exploited so I had no shortage of ideas running through my mind. In the end, I decided to have a little fun by planning a humorous kill with plenty of ironic elements that would be symbolic of the life she was leaving behind and the story she would soon become.

On the morning of the murder, I got up early and rechecked everything. Faith was spending the day at the youth center, and I used this knowledge to my advantage. No one from the center was informed that I was in town, and I was careful not to run into any of them during my trip. I stalked out the youth center for an hour until I finally saw Faith listening to music alone in the back room. I snuck into the room, slipped a pill into her drink, and she quickly passed out on the floor. I then hurried out the back door with her body, threw her in my car, and we were off.

When Faith awoke from her slumber, she began to call out for the counselors. I responded in a comforting voice, told her everything was okay, and asked if she needed anything. To my surprise, this little girl recognized my voice from the one time we had met a month before. She told me that she hadn't heard I was returning so soon and asked about the purpose of my visit. I explained that I was in town helping out for the day. I informed her that we were planning to do some trust exercises with everybody, and she had been picked as my partner before I found her sleeping in the music room. I told her that she had looked too peaceful to disturb, but, now that she was awake, we could proceed whenever she felt ready. The life immediately returned to her face as she looked up (well she didn't actually look up but you get the point) with an expression of excitement only seen in a person who doesn't want to waste a single moment.

She asked me to explain the rules of the game. I had planned for us to do both a trust walk and a trust fall. The trust walk was a game in which one person was blindfolded and had to trust the other person to guide them through a maze. Before I could make the joke, she stole it away from me as she laughed and said it would probably be fine if we skipped the blindfolding part with her. I agreed, and we began our first game.

As we moved through the maze I had prepared, I had a wonderful discussion with Faith about the future she believed she would have. Anyone who has read *Blind Faith* should know how impressive her dreams were. The highlight of the walk was Faith's response to my question of how she could have such a strong belief in her happy ending. Faith ironically responded by saying that the signs were all around her. Little did she know, at the exact time she made that statement, she was walking through an obstacle course with hundreds of large signs lining her path. Some of the signs were subtle hints of what was to come such as the "stop," "wrong way," and "one way" road signs that I had put up. Other signs were more direct saying things like "beware of death next 500 feet" or, my personal favorite, "dead end." I even included some funny signs just for my own amusement such as "Do you see what I see?" and "If you are reading this, your blindness was greatly exaggerated." I thought I might feel bad about taunting Faith on her final walk, but it was funny and one should never apologize for harmless comedy. It wasn't as if the jokes hurt my oblivious victim, and the signs brightened my day so I definitely don't regret it. The entire time she walked through the maze, Faith told me about her plans for after her miracle arrived. It was a pleasure listening to her future while simultaneously watching her move peacefully past signs foretelling her impending death. She was a walking metaphor for so many oblivious people moving eagerly towards death without ever noticing the signs along the way.

Before long, we reached the end of our walk and stopped for one final conversation. The more I tried to talk with Faith, the more annoyed she got as she wanted to get right into the next trust game. I laughed at her eagerness since I knew what was coming. I didn't have the somber sentiment of my previous kills, but, instead, I had a feeling of relaxed excitement. I told Faith we could go ahead and start the trust fall. Anyone who has ever been to a retreat or a team building seminar knows how the game works. One person stands behind another and catches them while they fall backwards into their partner's arms. Faith also knew the rules and told me she trusted me with a smile. I thanked her and joked that maybe she only trusted me because she hadn't seen all the signs. I moved Faith into position and told her she could fall back whenever she was ready. Before she fell, she reiterated her trust that I would never do anything to hurt her. She then leaned backward and proceeded to fall off a cliff as I watched her plummet to her death from a few steps away. I could have easily killed her myself, but I heeded Woodrow Wilson's words: "Never attempt to murder a person who is committing suicide." As Faith soared through the air, I felt a sense of relief that she didn't have to live in the dark anymore. She had spent her life ignoring the signs that clearly showed the mortality of reality. She refused to accept the fact that her blindness would be with her until her death. Her life was now finished, but her story was far from over.

After watching that final leap of Faith, I packed up my stuff and headed to the casino. I hadn't played poker in a long time and figured I might as well take advantage of my trip to Atlantic City. In honor of Faith, I played one in every ten hands blind (without looking at my cards). To make things simple, this blind hand turned out to be my big blind hand which made me smile even more. I obviously don't believe in supernatural events, but it would have been easy to attribute my huge wins on these blind hands to Faith. It felt as if she was helping me as a thank you for the Lasik surgery I had just provided her. That afternoon, I won a few thousand dollars before leaving on my flight left for Mexico where I planned to sit on the beach and finish writing *Blind Faith*.

Faith's story was easy to write. The book followed the life of a young blind girl with a clear vision for the future. I was able to create an optimistic story that gave the world an example of the power of Faith. Faith strongly believed that her happy ending was destined to occur as long as she held on to hope. The way her miracle would occur was simply an inconsequential detail that she was confident time would expose. The most inspirational part of *Blind Faith* was that her faith wasn't blind. Faith believed in the people around her and was confident medical advances would eventually allow her to see again. In the book, this is exactly what happened. I cured her blindness, and she now has perfect vision in fiction.

By the time my vacation was over, I had completed a draft of *Blind Faith*. This was the first book that was really effortless to write. My writing style and personality had evolved to a point where I knew exactly what I was doing and why I was doing it. The internal struggles that had accompanied my early novels were now absent from my writing and really didn't return until my final novel years later. On the plane ride home, I reread the draft of *Blind Faith* and remembered how much I loved the fact that this blind girl claimed to see the future. I was pleased that this facet of her character fit so nicely into the message of the book. She had an unjustified positive outlook on life that was impossible not to envy. I can only imagine how much happier my life would have been if I had retained that same type of ignorance myself. Thankfully, Faith will never be awoken from her beautiful illusions.

When I returned from Mexico, I finished editing the story, and, before long, it was published. The book was optimistic to the point of annoyance, but the world loved it. I was proud to have saved another person, and, for the most part, I was content with the results of the murder. The only thing that bothered me about the story resulted from a random thought that entered my mind during the writing process. I loved the appropriate title of *Blind Faith*, but, somewhere along the line, I had the idea that it would have also been fun to kill a blind boy named Steve and call the book *Stevie Wonders*. It should have simply been a funny thought that entered my mind, but, for some reason, I was tormented every time I saw *Blind Faith* on the shelves. I knew *Blind Faith* was actually a better title than *Stevie Wonders*, but I just loved that other name for some weird reason that was impossible to explain. Eventually, I was able to force my mind to hush this ridiculous criticism and appreciate the inspirational story I had written.

Other than my disappointment in not being able to use *Stevie Wonders*, killing this little girl was a satisfying experience. This was the first time I had killed a child, and it was incredibly agreeable. This murder and my subsequent child kills represent some of my best work. I loved killing kids because they had the most ambitious dreams and were really the most loveable of all potential characters. Faith was only one example, but anyone who has ever listened to a young person talk about their dreams understands exactly what I mean. Every time I listen to children talk about their goals and watch their faces light up, I can't help but think that this is what life is all about. I always wish I could stop time and let them spend their entire lives locked in that moment forever.

These thoughts were racing through my head one day as I ate lunch at No Thai in Ann Arbor about a month after I killed Faith. I was sitting at my table editing *Blind Faith,* and, as I thought about the virtuous dead I had done, I couldn't help but smile. Before long, I found myself lost in thought as my mind drifted away from the restaurant and into Faith's world. She was a child with an unblemished future that I had protected from being tarnished. All of a sudden, I was pulled away from my daydream when one of the cutest little girls I have ever seen came up to my table and said, "Excuse me sir, do you know what time it is?" Her question snapped me back to reality and brought a smile to my face as I told her the time. As she walked away, I thought to myself that this little girl could never be cuter than she was then. She was perfect. Her smile conveyed a happiness the world has not matched since. How could I sit there writing a book about having Faith in the future while letting this pretty little girl pass through my life without intervening on her behalf? I figured I should probably kill this little girl simply because she was so cute. She was too beautiful a character to pass up.

When this cute little girl left the restaurant with her mom, I followed slowly behind and watched as they pulled into their driveway about a mile away from the restaurant. I then returned to my friend's house, and we made our way to the bar for a night out with a group of friends. The bar was packed, and, after about an hour, I slipped away and made my way back to Kerrytown to murder the little girl. I could see her sitting with her mom in the living room watching television, and I awaited my opportunity to kill her. The family soon went to sleep, and I watched the girl shut off the lights in her first floor bedroom. I waited a little longer before cutting through the screen covering her open window. Once I was inside, I quickly anesthetized the young girl and injected her with a high dose of a euthanasia drug that I had stolen years earlier from the hospital when I had been observing another lab's animal experiments. I loved the fact that this girl experienced a painless death in her sleep that reminded me of *Sleeping Beauty*. She truly was a sleeping beauty, and the peaceful corpse was symbolic of the eternity of that beauty. I admired her for a moment, and then left the house, disposed of my sterile lab clothes in the dumpster behind the hospital, and quickly returned to the bar with my friends who merely thought I had been drinking with others in the group during the time I was gone. I spent the rest of my night enjoying the company of my old friends while internally smiling at the secret detour I had taken to Kerrytown.

The next morning, I woke up early and thought about the best way to write this cute little girl's story. It was a weird feeling to have killed a person on an impulse compared to my other well-planned murders. I knew nothing about this young child other than the beauty of her nature and the fact that she deserved a protected future every bit as much as Faith. As I contemplated this cute little girl's fate, I realized I would never have killed her if it hadn't been for Faith. It was the timing that had highlighted her beauty. I have taken credit for saving many lives through my kills, but it was Faith who was really responsible for saving this little girl. As a result, I decided not to write a separate book about the cute little girl from No Thai but instead made her into a character that most of you know well, Faith's best friend Katie in *Blind Faith*. At the climax of the novel, Faith saved Katie from dying. The world saw Faith save Katie's future in the book; I saw Faith save Katie's future from reality.

CHAPTER 7

The Diction of Fiction

Silence is safer than speech.

-Epictetus

CHAPTER 7: The Diction of Fiction

What a person says is often not as important as how they say it. The right words can change the world, but only if they are heard by the right people. If Martin Luther King had a dream in a forest and no one heard about it, would it really make a difference? Fortunately, I never had to worry about my books falling on deaf ears. The entire world was hearing the tales of my flawless characters and embracing their happy endings. I was empowered by the effects of my work, and it didn't take long before I found my next project. I had looked for stories in the past, but this time I found my victim by listening. I first heard Tham's voice as I drove from Ann Arbor to Lansing for Christmas. Tham was a sad story of a young man struggling to be heard, and, the entire weekend in Lansing, I couldn't get his voice out of my head. I spent my time in Lansing celebrating Christmas with Derbe, his wife Abbey, Jamie, and Angela. Jamie was four years old, and it was the first Christmas in which he started to be aware of the festivities. This weekend will always be marked in my memory as the turning point in Mike's life. The last remnants of Angela's sadness were absent from her eyes and replaced by the pure joy of watching her son. As the weekend went on, memories of Mike were undoubtedly brought up. In contrast to my previous visits since Mike's death, I watched as Angela fully delighted in the stories of her soul mate. The room was filled with laughter as we told old stories, ate and drank too much, and opened presents on Christmas Eve. In addition to the usual group in Lansing, there were nearly a hundred other family members crowded into the house. It was awesome to have my entire family fly into town for the holidays and even more special that our three families could come together for Christmas. The night was filled with love and slowly dwindled down to a few of us remaining by the fire. These tired moments at the end of the evening are always my favorite part of a long night. There is something peaceful about these quiet endings. The last two people awake with me were Mike's sister Jennie and her husband, who was Jamie's godfather.

Once these two went to sleep around one, I spent the next hour cleaning up the house and reflecting on the evening. I felt so special to have such an incredible family and be an adopted part of this other amazing group. I knew I was more fortunate than most people in the world who didn't have the same joy in their lives. As I thought about those less fortunate, Tham immediately came to mind, and I wondered how this young man was spending Christmas. I knew from hearing about his struggle on the radio that he wasn't content with his life, and, wherever he was, I imagined he was dreaming of a better world. Over the course of my life, I have always wanted to help sad stories like Tham transform their tragedies into triumph. As I continued to clean, my mind bounced back and forth between Mike and Tham. It was therapeutic to reflect upon both a character I had already saved and a character I wanted to save. I decided I would hunt Tham down after the holidays and find a way to save his life. In the meantime, I was going to enjoy my time with the family and make sure everyone had a Christmas they would never forget. When I finally finished cleaning, I went out to the car and brought in all the Santa presents for the next morning. I always enjoy giving gifts to those I love, and the success of my books allowed me to take full advantage of the large crowd in Lansing. It took me over an hour to get all the gifts into the living room, and it was a spectacular sight when I was finished. The entire wall behind the tree was covered with gifts four rows deep rising up like a pyramid towards the ceiling. When my head finally hit my pillow, I was completely exhausted and slept deeper than I had in years.

Because of my late night, I was one of the last people to get up the next morning. The rest of the family that wasn't staying at the house had already arrived, and I could smell breakfast coming from the kitchen. I rolled over and looked at the clock. It was only nine, but the excitement of Christmas had awoken everyone bright and early. I closed my eyes until I heard the door open and saw little Jamie walking in to wake me up. I pulled him up into the bed and asked him if he was ready to open his presents which brought a huge smile to his face. I then jumped up and began one of the best mornings of my life. Santa gave out so many gifts that morning and every reaction is eternally engrained in my memory. I have always had the good fortune of receiving more in return for the gifts I have given, and this morning was the perfect example as I felt like the luckiest person in the room. The best gift reaction was Jamie's face when he opened his first pair of hockey skates. It was a joy watching him walk around the living room wearing his skates the entire morning. Once the gifts were opened, Derbe and I took all the kids down to the outdoor rink and let the rest of the house deal with the cleanup. I held Jamie up on the ice as he skated for the first time, and I continually told him how proud his dad would have been. Like all kids' first time on the ice, it was an uphill battle for Jamie, but you wouldn't have guessed it from his face. This young man was such a cheerful kid, and I continued skinnering his life as I positively reinforced his joyful nature and told him how special he was. Before we left, I took Jamie on one final lap around the rink concluding with a trip into the snow bank reminiscent of my own first time on the ice.

After skating, we returned to the house for Christmas dinner, and I repeatedly told Angela what a flawless job she was doing raising Jamie. He was such a cute kid, and I was thankful to see him so often. Derbe expressed a similar sentiment and was even more present in Jamie's life. As usual, Derbe was unconsciously doing more work to complete Mike's story than I could possibly have accomplished alone. Throughout the day, I would continuously notice the subtle way Jamie would lean on Derbe and me. I knew Mike would have been thankful that we were there to look after his son. Before I knew it, the weekend was in my rear view mirror as I drove to the airport with the rest of my family. I flew with them to Minnesota for a nice New Year's celebration before going to New York for two weeks to meet with publishers and discuss my next project. As I flew away from my family, I had a familiar feeling of appreciation for the newly formed memories combined with an excitement for our next visit. I had taken a nice break to enjoy the holidays, and I was now ready to get back to work writing books and helping people. And so my mind returned to Tham.

Tham was a young man who was fighting a severe speech impediment. I felt bad as I listened to Tham on the radio fighting to express the life he wanted. Tham had always wanted to be a politician and make a difference in the world. He had been taking speech classes his entire life in hopes of improving his speaking skills so that he could achieve this goal. Tham's story reminded me of *The King's Speech* movie I had once watched. I wanted to give Tham a happy ending and made sure to look up his information when I returned from New York. As it turned out, Tham lived in Detroit which made finding him extremely convenient. Additionally, I felt relieved that the murder plot could be simplified since another dead body dropped in the middle of Detroit would barely turn any heads. Of course, I was mostly joking to myself with that last comment, but I still felt relaxed as I contemplated a way to kill Tham and write his story. I was probably just confident since my first few kills were so seamlessly successful that I no longer felt anxious when thinking about murder.

On the first week of February, I drove to Detroit to kill Tham. I caught him as he walked home after speech class and pulled him into a dark alley. I planned a simple and quick kill that would look like a common mugging in the middle of Detroit. To pull this off, I didn't need an elaborate plan like when I killed the couple in Atlantic City, but, instead, I simply cornered Tham in the back of the alley and put a knife to his throat. Instead of killing him immediately, I told him I was going to give him a chance to save his life. Tham looked up at me in fearful optimism and struggled to express his desire to live. I looked Tham in the face and told him I planned to kill him in five seconds unless he told me to stop. Although he quickly responded with numerous words in the tone of a beggar, I couldn't understand anything he was saying so I slit his throat. As I walked safely out of the alley and drove away, I acknowledged that Tham's final words definitely rhymed with stop, but it was just too bad he couldn't articulate the word before he died. It didn't matter anymore since I had acted as the ultimate speech therapist when I cut the lisp out of his throat like a surgeon extracting the pathologic vocal cords from my patient.

When I returned to Ann Arbor, I started writing Sam's story. Just as in real life, Sam struggled to speak as a child, but, in the novel, he grew into one of the world's most renowned orators. Tham was a young man who had an abundance of ideas but was simply unable to express them because of his lisp. In the novel, Sam grew into a person that could not only speak his thoughts eloquently but could even transform a lie into truth through his oratory. The book was titled *The Diction of Fiction* and told the story of Sam's dreams coming true. If the story had been written about the real character, it would have been titled *The Fiction of Diction* because his speech had simply been non-existent, and he was probably the worst speaker I had ever heard. Tham was truly miserable in his life, and I was proud to put him out of his misery and teach him to speak to the world. Because of this book, Sam's speeches have now been heard clearly by millions of people.

The response to *The Diction of Fiction* was mostly positive, but I found myself unprepared for some of the criticism that accompanied the novel. I had included many of Sam's political views that I remembered hearing on the radio and found numerous pundits upset that I was trying to use my success as an author to push my politics. The ultimate irony of their comments was that I actually disagreed with most of Sam's opinions but had written them into the novel because the story belonged to him. It wasn't in my control to change his beliefs. I was simply the vessel through which his story would be told, and I found it comical that I was catching so much flack for Sam's views. This turned out to be only one of many times throughout my life in which I was criticized by people completely unaware of the true meaning behind my work. Ultimately, this type of criticism just made me laugh. Another side effect of Sam's story was the perspective it provided on the value of communication in our lives. It is unfortunate that we live in a world that rewards the way something is said more than the quality of the idea. The great thinkers of our time are the ones with the ability to create witty bumper sticker sound bites to be continuously repeated on cable news. The politician with complicated solutions to complicated problems will ultimately be unsuccessful unless he hires a marketing team to shorten that solution into four words that a crowd can chant in unison. The appearance of a person seems to be valued more than the substance of a person, and I found this to be a true shame. For this reason, it felt gratifying to write Sam's story.

Those of you who have followed my career closely are probably wondering why I passed over the two books I wrote between *Blind Faith* and *The Diction of Fiction*. Some of my novels were simply less important to me and will be skipped as I move forward with this autobiography, but I will quickly address those two stories before I move on. From the time I started writing *The Diction of Fiction* to the time I finished was actually two years. Unfortunately, the book was delayed by two unexpected car accidents during the first year of writing. The first accident happened three weeks after the murder in Detroit when I was visiting friends in the UP and hit a deer with my car. My car was severely damaged, and the deer was killed. As I looked at the deer lying on the side of the road, I figured it was only right that I wrote a book about that deer which led to *Bambi 2*. This book was filled with fluff and only took so long to write because of an ensuing copyright hassle. Once *Bambi 2* was published, I returned to writing Sam's story but was again interrupted with another car accident. This time, I killed a person instead of a deer. There was no doubt I was not at fault in the accident as the man had fallen in front of my car as I passed. I felt terrible that I had killed this man and went to offer my condolences to the family. His family turned out to be extremely gracious and understood I could not have avoided the collision. I heard all about this man from his family. He was a truly ordinary individual who had an average job and lived an average life. There was nothing exciting about his life, and it wasn't a moving story by any means. Even those who loved him struggled to muster excitement as they described his life. Nonetheless, I knew I had to write his novel if only because of the precedent I had set after killing the deer. I wrote the story of his life and prepared for the reaction. The book I had written was a truly boring book and got a horrible response just as I expected. The book was titled *Day after Day* and was the monotonous story of a man who continued along his boring routine every day. The book is well known as the worst book I have ever written. One critic ironically said it was as if I didn't even want to write the book which was actually quite correct. I never wanted to write this boring story but sometimes tragedy strikes and all we can do is deal with it. Most people I talked to really hated *Day after Day*, but it is probably the most accurate portrayal of life I have written. As Mencken once correctly stated, "The basic fact about human existence is not that it is a tragedy, but that it is a bore. It is not so much a war as an endless standing in line." The problem with the story was that it lacked the beautiful fictional ending of my other novels because this man's dreams were dead before I killed him with my car. The novel was too real to be a good story. People close to me who heard the story of me killing this man were concerned when they read *Day after Day*. These people were worried that I had fallen into depression and couldn't emotionally handle the feeling of being responsible for ending another person's life. I assured them this was not the case, but they continued to worry. Derbe even asked me, "Is this book because of the guy who died?" and then he proceeded to tell me I needed to move on and not let this unfortunate event affect my work. Derbe told me I couldn't change what happened and did his best to help me through it. I smiled at my friend's ironic concern which made me thankful I had decided to write this terrible novel simply for the humor it provided me.

Once *Bambi 2* and *Day after Day* were published, I was finally able to return to Sam's book. Two years after his death, Sam's story was finally being sold in stores. When people read the novel, they described it as my return to inspirational writing and considered it the resurrection of my career. In reality, the two books in the middle hadn't been passionate novels but were simply necessary hassles that had entered into my life and needed to be written. I was thankful to finally finish *The Diction of Fiction* which had consumed so much of my time, and I was ready for my next character. Sam's voice was finally being heard, and I wondered who would inspire me next.

CHAPTER 8

Stevie Wonders

I started being really proud of the fact that I was gay even though I wasn't.

-Kurt Cobain

CHAPTER 8: Stevie Wonders

My next character was an excellent example of why you shouldn't judge a cover by its book. I had loved the triumph of Sam's story and decided to write a follow up novel with a similar structure following a person's life as he overcame a struggle he couldn't conquer in reality. Sam was now busy giving his speeches to the public, and I was looking for the next person who needed help. When I met Steve, I knew he was the right character to fill this role. Steve was a seventeen year old gay kid that was volunteering at a police fundraiser that Derbe was hosting. Derbe was now the lead detective in the Traverse City Police Department. He was also connected with the FBI murder investigation unit facilitating their work in Michigan. Derbe had passed on the opportunity to take a full-time job with the FBI to stay in Traverse City where Angela and Jamie had moved to be closer to Mike's family. With a little help from me, Angela was able to buy a gorgeous house right on the water. It was the perfect place for Jamie to grow up, and I visited whenever I had the chance. That weekend, I spent time playing catch with Jamie who was now seven years old, and I also volunteered to flip burgers at Derbe's police fundraiser on Saturday night. It was nothing new for me to be in Traverse City. I visited my friends multiple times each month as I continued skinnering Jamie's perfect world, and I now observed the happiest seven year old I had ever met. Jamie had the athleticism of his parents and was an astonishingly sharp young man. Every time I visited, I was shocked at the depth of his thoughts and loved talking to him about his future and his father.

At the fundraiser Saturday night, I was running the grill with the help of a young man named Steve. As we cooked, I asked Steve about his life and heard about his success in school and future plans. Steve was a sweet kid, but I could sense an unexplained sadness within him that didn't fit his character. When I asked him if he had a girlfriend, the source of his sorrow became clear. His reaction betrayed his homosexuality, and I wasn't shy about my newfound insight. I immediately asked Steve if he was gay which turned his face pale as he scanned the area to see if anyone else had heard. I had been careful to make sure no one else was around when I asked, and, after ignoring his halfhearted denial, I told him his secret was safe with me. Our conversation progressed awkwardly for a half hour or so until I eventually gained Steve's trust and the comfort level between us was established. When we took a break to eat, Steve became an open book as he described the internal turmoil he had been going through while hiding his sexuality. He was such a nice kid but was unable to come out because his parents and friends would never have accepted him. An interesting comment he made during our conversation was the astute observation that even if they could accept his homosexuality, his life would still change forever as his sexual orientation would become his identity. People would always think of him as being gay first and Steve second. It was a catch-22. He had the choice to live as Steve with a secret or as an openly homosexual man unrecognizable as Steve. I felt bad but agreed with his assessment. Prejudice in the world can be a terrible thing, but the prejudice of loved ones is an infinitely bigger obstacle to overcome. Steve dreamed of a world where he could be comfortable and open about himself without losing the intimacy with those he loved. It was an impossible thought, and I felt bad for this sweet young man with no possible route to happiness.

I offered some comforting words to Steve and told him things would work out for the best. I had already decided to help him but wasn't sure when. I had plans to spend Sunday with Jamie and was going to Minnesota on Monday morning so I figured the murder would have to wait until I returned in three weeks. This would give me plenty of time to plan out the kill and prepare the necessary details. I was aware of my growing overconfidence in my last few kills and knew I needed to be extra careful not to leave a trace when I killed Steve since Derbe would be on the case. My biomedical background was very helpful to me in these endeavors as I was an expert in the types of clothing needed to prevent leaving any evidence at the scene. My other piece of confidence came from the police officers themselves. Even if there was a sign at the crime scene saying I had committed the murder, I knew Derbe would never believe it. He thought too highly of me and lacked the ability to comprehend my doing anything wrong. Although the rest of his police unit wasn't as attached to me as Derbe, I got along with them all and knew I wouldn't be a suspect unless I made an obvious mistake. With that in mind, I began planning the murder during my trip home to Minnesota.

I came up with a simple plan and liked the irony that would be involved in the murder. The one thing that continued to trouble me was his name. I couldn't help but renew my frustration that he wasn't a little blind kid so I could use the ironic title of *Stevie Wonders*. That irrational regret still lingered in me, and, finally, I just decided to use that title for this novel even though it wasn't the ideal situation. He wasn't blind, but I had a weird attachment to the title and just went with it. I began writing the novel before I returned to Traverse City and found the storyline inspirational right from the start. Steve had the foundation for a story about overcoming prejudice. The climax of the novel would be the point when he finally gained the courage to come out of the closet. I stopped writing at this point in the story to wait until Steve was dead, but I already knew the ending. In the novel, Steve would be fully accepted for whom he was, and his identity would be unchanged by his sexual revelation. This was the comfortable life that had been unattainable for Steve and the life he deserved to live. The story of this gay man would be a true fairy tale.

When I returned to Traverse City, I spent the first two days with Jamie and Angela before the right moment for the murder presented itself. I purposely accidentally ran into Steve on his way home from school and asked if he wanted to grab a quick bite to eat. He told me he would love to and just needed to drop his stuff off at home. I walked the rest of the way with him and told him I had to use the bathroom before we left. I quickly changed into my murder gear while I was in the bathroom. I then proceeded to Steve's room and saw him looking for a shirt inside his walk-in closet which precisely fit into my plans. Steve turned around with a look of shock on his face as he saw the knife I was holding. I told him to relax and it would all be over soon. Steve was right when he had told me at the police barbecue that he didn't think he would ever come out of the closet. I was going to kill him in that closet where his spirit had been trapped for years. His entire life had been a battle to come out of the closet and be accepted by the world. Today, he was finally going to lose that battle. I wasn't homophobic but loved the irony of a fag being murdered in a closet. I was moments away from killing Steve and leaving him in that closet while I wrote *Stevie Wonders,* but, once again, I found myself wishing Steve had been a blind kid instead of just being gay. Before I killed him, I decided to cut his eyes out to blind him so that the title would have the irony it was meant to have. This blinding part didn't really have anything to do with Steve's story, but it gave me a good laugh so I figured it was worth it. Although I was never fully satisfied, blinding Steve before killing him helped ease my internal criticism of using the title. After his eyes were gone, I quickly finished the murder and returned to Angela's house.

When I got back to the house, I played with Jamie for about an hour before Derbe and Abbey came over for dinner. We had a nice meal and then sat around watching a game on television and visiting a bit. At about seven in the evening, Derbe got a call from work, and I watched his face drop as he heard about Steve. When he hung up, Abbey asked him what was wrong, but Derbe glanced at Angela and then told us it was nothing. He said he had to go to work to help a couple officers find a file that had been misplaced. I smiled and chirped him for being such a workaholic while secretly admiring the fact that he was hiding the real story to save Angela from hearing about another murder and being reminded of Mike. It was an otherwise unnoticed but noble action by my friend. I felt bad that he was going to spend so much energy over the next few weeks investigating Steve's murder in vain. I would have liked to tell him that it was hopeless to save him the time. Unfortunately, that wasn't an option, and I just had to let things take their course. I stayed in Traverse City for the rest of the week and then flew to LA to discuss another movie that was being planned based on one of my books.

On the flight to LA, I thought quite a bit about the murders I had committed. As I had grown into a successful killer, the obvious thought of getting caught was bound to creep into my mind, and, on this flight, I lingered on that possibility. As I thought about it more, I realized that there wasn't a jury in the world that would convict me even if I got caught. I had no motive for any of my murders and lacked the characteristics needed to hurt another human being. I was a loving person down to my core. The very fiber of my being was built upon my desire to create happiness. I got to the point where I almost believed I would be able to achieve my innocence in court through a confession of guilt. Even though I was confident I was never going to get caught, I felt comfort in the fact that my actions were morally superior to the world I was living in. Lesser minds might find my actions reprehensible, but that would represent the limitations of their own mental capabilities rather than a flaw in my superior morality. My work was reinforced by the fact that I was an author of unequaled achievements. Had I been arrested for murder, I have no doubt the case would never have made it to trial as jury selection would have stretched on indefinitely as the prosecution labored in vain to find a jury of my peers. The world would have cowered at the task of supplying even one individual, let alone ten, that could live up to the moral code required to serve on the jury for my trial, and none of them could come to any conclusion except the fact that my work was a divine gift that turned suffering into joy. Putting me on trial would be more likely to end with the creation of a new religion than the conviction of a criminal.

I was soon able to finish *Stevie Wonders* and move on. It had taken a long time to write *The Diction of Fiction* so I was thankful to have returned a sense of urgency to my work. Other than an upcoming movie release, my schedule was wide open so I hoped to quickly find my next protagonist and take advantage of the free time in my schedule. I placed Steve's book on my mantle next to my other characters and set off in search of the next admirable person to add to that immortal group resting in eternal perfection on my bookshelf.

CHAPTER 9

Pretty Ugly

A man's face is his autobiography. A woman's face is her work of fiction.

-Oscar Wilde

CHAPTER 9: Pretty Ugly

My next novel got off to an ugly start, but it didn't take long for it to develop into something beautiful. From the time I found Jane to the time I finished writing *Pretty Ugly* was only about two months. I met Jane in a coffee shop on one of my visits to Los Angeles. She was sitting across from me and drew my attention immediately. Jane was a hideously unattractive creature, but I couldn't take my eyes off her. She was wearing designer clothes and reading magazines filled with gorgeous women. I was instantly struck by what a tragic a figure she was. She was just a plain Jane dreaming of being a supermodel. I never knew her real name but simply referred to her as Jane in my mind as I watched her reading those magazines while constantly checking her make-up with her pocket mirror. Jane reminded me of a quote I had once heard saying that a woman's greatest asset was her beauty. It was horrifying to watch Jane take care of her worthless asset. I was sad to observe a woman putting on make-up when she really needed a mask. I examined Jane intently from a distance for a couple hours in the coffee shop and started writing her story on my laptop.

As I sat writing Jane's story, I knew I had to quickly come up with a plan to make sure I didn't miss my chance to kill this ugly girl. I had nothing prepared and tried to think of a way to be alone with her. I have always been a killer that prefers to experiment with different types of unique or ironic murders, but, when in doubt, you can't go wrong with stabbing someone. Stabbing someone is always an intimate way to commit murder and convenient for those spur of the moment type kills. As I contemplated a way to get Jane alone, I suddenly realized I was overcomplicating things. She was an ugly girl doing her make-up in a coffee shop. How hard could it be to get her alone? She had been glancing at me for the last few hours, and I knew she would jump at the opportunity to leave with me. However, before I asked, I had to somehow find a knife. I looked around the coffee shop, but all I could see was the cheap plastic silverware that came with my blueberry muffin. I then had a great idea. I picked up the plastic knife from my table and walked over to say hi.

I told Jane she looked cute sitting there and asked if she wanted to take a walk. She said yes with an ugly blush. I packed my computer and told her I was going to use the bathroom before we left. In the bathroom, I quickly sharpened the plastic knife to a point so that I could soon use it to stab Jane to death. When I finished sharpening my weapon, I returned to Jane's table, and we went for a walk to a park nearby. We found a bench deep in the woods where we could be alone. Jane had a look of anticipation on her face, and she was completely unable to hide her eagerness. I lied to myself believing that her excitement was for the beauty I would be giving her in my book. She was one of the ugliest girls I had ever met, but she would soon be remembered as a model. I looked at her one last time and then slipped on my gloves, pulled the plastic knife out of my pocket, put my hand over her mouth, and stabbed her about fifty times until she stopped moving. This was the first and only time that I ever performed plastic surgery.

The results of this plastic surgery were astounding. I left Jane's bloody body in the woods and returned to record her new beauty in text. In the book, I transformed Jane into her alter ego, Janet. Janet was a stunning model with an unparalleled attractiveness. All other women wished they had Janet's natural beauty. There is a quote by Emerson that says, "Love of beauty is taste. The creation of beauty is art." That is exactly what my novel accomplished. I had turned this ugly girl into a gorgeous woman. My novel was a work of art and another triumph of fiction over reality. A woman in a magazine is never as beautiful as the description of a woman in words. The beauty we imagine can never be replicated by nature.

As I continued writing the book, it turned into a critique of the fashion world alongside the story of this beautiful model rising above the common pettiness of the industry. The industry was pretty ugly, but this lovely woman was unaffected by it. Janet possessed a natural beauty both outwardly and inwardly. She had the look of a supermodel with the humility of the ugly girl she had evolved from. I enjoyed exposing the superficiality of our society as I wrote the novel. It was therapeutic to have the opportunity to express some of my actual views in a novel as I vented about the stupidity of valuing a person for their appearance. It is such a shame that being good looking is a better predictor of success in our society than being smart. We definitely don't live in the meritocracy that many people claim exists in America. Beauty may only be skin deep, but that is more than enough depth to satisfy the shallowness of humanity.

Around the time *Pretty Ugly* was published, my schedule started to spin out of control. I have continuously made an effort to include leisure in my life, but, even for someone with money, this can be an uphill struggle. During this period, I was losing this battle. I had made the mistake of starting too many charity groups around the country in which I was directly involved. I found my free time continually destroyed by different mandatory events. I was passionate about the charity work, but it was beginning to consume my schedule to an annoying extent. Finally, I told the directors of my charity that I couldn't play such an active role. I explained that I simply didn't have the time to attend so many events and needed to focus on writing. Although I was constantly praised as one of society's foremost philanthropists, I knew my greatest contribution to the world came through my work as an author, and I didn't want to sacrifice that part of my life. I still planned to attend random charity events, but I was focused on removing my mandatory obligations. I decided to celebrate my newfound freedom by taking Angela and Jamie on a vacation to Greece. Before I left, I had to attend one last charity event I had already agreed to attend at an Indian Reservation by my cabin in Northern Minnesota. I had built a new school for the tribe and was going up for the opening. I kept this last event on my schedule since it would only take two hours on Friday, and then I would have the rest of my weekend up north with my family. I organized all the details of my vacation with the Wagners and smiled when I saw Jamie's enthusiasm. It was still a week away, but Jamie had everything packed and sent me text messages every hour asking what we were going to do. I was excited for our trip to Greece as well as the weekend I had planned at the cabin. There was nowhere on earth I would rather be than up at the lake with my family. I couldn't wait to put my life on hold for a couple weeks while I just enjoyed my trips with the people I loved. Even murderers deserve a vacation once in a while.

CHAPTER 10

The Little Injun that Could

Society attacks early, when the individual is helpless.

-*B.F. Skinner*

CHAPTER 10: *The Little Injun that Could*

Our lives are shaped by the world around us. I had a delightful time visiting my family at our cabin and soaking in the beautiful world around me. Not only was it a wonderful weekend, but I also found my next character on Friday during my visit to the Reservation. The storyline of the novel became clear as I presented a college scholarship to a young Native American girl named Onida. I immediately knew Onida was the one I was searching for. Onida was the highest achieving student in this poor community and would now have the opportunity to attend college at the University of Minnesota. What Onida had accomplished with such a weak support system was amazing, but she was still clearly below average compared to the rest of the population. This was not a negative reflection upon Onida but rather a limitation of her community. The greatest quality Onida possessed was her perseverance. The extent to which Onida had been able to overcome her environment was inspirational while it was simultaneously a tragedy that her environment had still left a terminal wound. The ceremony was wonderful as the entire tribe gathered to celebrate the opening of the new school and wish Onida success in college. I smiled as I handed Onida the award while being fully aware of the obstacles she would soon encounter. I felt confident the school was a long-term investment that would allow many young Native Americans in that poor community to reach their potential and live a successful life in our society, but I was fully aware that it was too late for Onida. The scholarship was a well-intentioned gift, but she was simply going to be pulled out of the frying pan and thrown into the fire. Her previous education had not prepared her for what was to come, and I knew even her unwavering perseverance would be unable to overcome the handicap of her history.

I continued to think about Onida throughout the ceremony as I pictured how I would write a better future for her. She would come to represent the triumph of nature over nurture. Onida would become the prototypical example of a person overcoming the limitations of her surroundings and reaching her impossible dreams. After the ceremony, the real celebration began as I experienced the full spectrum of Native American culture. I had to fight my despair as I thought about the tragic fact that the ancient lifestyles of these people no longer existed. I was always attracted to the mystic nature of a group of people living in harmony with the earth, but it was sad to watch these people clinging to a way of life that could no longer provide for their needs. Luckily, these thoughts were unable to linger long in my mind as I was continuously pulled into the celebration and had a wonderful time dancing at the festival. After a couple hours of celebrating, I said my goodbyes and wished them the best. I then made my way back to my cabin to spend the rest of the weekend with my family. Before I left the Reservation, I stole a huge box of traditional Native American souvenirs. With the amount of money my charity had pumped into the community, I felt justified in taking these things and didn't give it much thought. I threw the box in my car and drove back to the cabin where my family was waiting.

It was another wonderful weekend at the lake. We must have caught over fifty walleye, and my cousin Anna even caught a massive Musky Friday night. She was fishing with a bobber off the end of the dock while I was grilling steaks at the top of the stairs watching as her brother helped her reel in the fish. I have never had a bad weekend at my cabin with the family but certain memories stand out above the rest. Sitting by the fire recapping Anna's catch was a memory that will always hold a special place in my heart. The combination of roasted marshmallows and laughter was a splendid end to a summer evening. We stayed up late by the fire, and, as usual, when the rest of the family fell asleep inside the cabin, I retreated to my solitude under the stars. The only therapy that has ever worked for me has been laying back on a clear night gazing at the sky. We can only understand our place in the universe if we at least attempt to contemplate the extent of our insignificance. I looked up at the stars, thought about the vastness of the universe extending beyond my comprehension, and appreciated how laughable our earthly problems actually are. People spend their lives so passionately fighting for what they believe in and rarely stop to realize how little any of it matters. We are microscopic life forms that live for less than an instant. I spent the night removing the cares from my mind and finding peace in the pointlessness of life. I was proud of my accomplishments in the context of the world I lived in, but I knew the odds were small that my stories would ever extend beyond our little globe.

I spent the rest of the night moving in and out of thought as I allowed my mind to drift freely through the universe. I contemplated things as big as the beginning of time and as small as my own purpose on earth. I spent time thinking about everyone I loved. I smiled as I thought about the characters in my books and the special place they held in my heart. I reflected upon Onida and the other unknown characters that I would be able to help before I died. I also thought about the millions of people who probably deserved my help but would never meet me. I have always loved people to a fault and was unable to shake this sad image of so many promising characters surviving into old age and waking up every morning cursing the stars for the fate they inherited. In the end, a single person can only do so much in the limited time, and I was optimizing my experience on earth as best I could. My mind continued to circle in thought until eventually I drifted into a comfortable slumber in my chair.

I was awoken on the dock at a quarter after four the next morning as my phone alarm jostled me back into consciousness. I snuck inside the cabin and quietly grabbed a Mountain Dew for the car ride. I drove to a well-covered location about a mile from the entrance to the Reservation and got out. I grabbed what I needed out of the box in my trunk and cut through the woods towards the water. I reached the lake and followed the shoreline to the Reservation. When I neared the edge of Indian land, I saw Onida reading down by the water all alone just as I had hoped. The previous day, one of the elders had praised her for being the first one up every morning to study down by the lake. He described her commitment to success and said he couldn't remember a single day in which she had ever overslept. Lucky for me, the rest of the tribe was fast asleep at five in the morning recovering from the previous day's celebration. I looked down at this young woman reading and was saddened by her predicament. She was starting to study for the future she would soon be thrown into. She had such an admirable desire to be successful in the large world around her but was too wounded by her culture to reach those goals. I admired her passion too much to allow her to suffer the inevitable disappointment that college would bring. I hadn't planned an elaborate kill for Onida since the culture she was raised in had already killed her future long ago. I simply wanted the murder to reflect this fact so I scouted the area to ensure there were no witnesses, snuck up behind Onida, and shot her in the back with the bow and arrow I had stolen the previous day. I wasn't a well-trained warrior with a bow, but, from that range, my accuracy was spot-on and the arrow pierced right through her heart. I retreated to my car only turning back once for a final glimpse of this young Indian lying dead on the shore of the lake. Onida's body lay bloody on the ground with the arrow in her back while her face rested on a college brochure. Nothing could have captured the symbolism of her life better than her lifeless body killed by the weapon of her community. She was a victim of the failed system she lived in and no longer had to fight in vain to overcome this reality.

When I returned to the cabin, I found my entire family still asleep. I decided to go for a ride in the boat to take in the peaceful morning. I cruised across the water and admired the beautiful shoreline and newly-arrived sun above my head. The gorgeous new day brought warmness to my heart that is difficult to express. The sense of insignificance that had overcome my body the previous night as I gazed at the stars was replaced by simple amazement at the bright blue morning sky. There is a subtle difference between the melancholy insignificance felt in a dark night and the positive insignificance one feels on a new morning. Instead of feeling overcome by the vastness of the universe, I felt amazed that I was even a small part of this greater whole. There was no change in my outlook but simply a change in my emotional response to it. It was the difference between night and day. Both were wonderful, but one created a sense of tired meditation while the other provided an inspirational excitement for the new day ahead. The night sky made me want to dream; the morning sky made me want to live. The rooster is ever the enemy of the dreamer. The morning light reminded me I was fortunate to see the arrival of another new day, and it was time to live.

After an hour of natural therapy on the lake, I returned to the cabin to spend the day with my family. Everyone was asleep so I moved quietly into the kitchen and started cooking breakfast for the entire crew. The smell of eggs and bacon was an effective wake-up call, and I soon saw some glossy eyed individuals make their way to the table with smiles on their faces. I whispered good morning to each of them and asked how many pancakes they would like. There were three separate breakfast groups that seemed to congregate as the cabin slowly awoke from its slumber. It turned out to be a wonderful weekend with my family that reminded me how phenomenal life can be when one has the luxury to spend a day busy doing nothing with the people he loves. It didn't matter what we did to pass the time because we were together and enjoyed every minute.

When the weekend was over, I drove to the Twin Cities to catch a Monday morning flight to Detroit where I was meeting Angela and Jamie. On the drive, I got a call from a member of my charity telling me about Onida's tragic murder. I was shocked when I got the call and told him so repeatedly. I said I was leaving for Greece the next day but to send my condolences and let me know if the charity needed any further resources. When I hung up the phone, I thought about Onida's novel and put the storyline together in my head. I wrote the story on the airplane during the next two days and filled in the details during breaks on the vacation. Onida's story was about overcoming one's environment which was fitting for a kid from a poor Reservation that hadn't provided her the tools needed to succeed. She had lofty aspirations and unwavering perseverance but simply lacked the resources to achieve her goals. We are all ultimately slaves to our environment, and Onida was thankfully freed from hers. I was the world's premier abolitionist. Onida's dream was now free to be fulfilled in the novel, and she was no longer a victim of her environment. She would be forever remembered as *The Little Injun that Could*.

The focus of Onida's story on how the environment affects one's life led to a great deal of reflection about Jamie as I watched him during our vacation in Greece. As much as I was saddened by the circumstances surrounding Onida's existence, I was equally pleased with the state of Jamie's world. I had truly created a perfect life for this young man, and it was a pleasure watching him reap the rewards of my hard work. Jamie was a nine year old clone of his father. The trip to Greece was a nice blend of touring the ancient world and breathing in the scenic landscapes the country had to offer. We took Jamie to some of the most beautiful beaches in the world, and every place seemed to outdo the last. On the final night of the trip, we put Jamie to bed early as he was worn out from two weeks of activities and could no longer keep his eyes open. That night, Angela and I sat outside our hotel room and were accompanied by the most beautiful sunset over the water. For the first time in years, Angela and I talked about Mike. As Angela spoke, it felt as if she was expressing a part of her that had been dormant for a long time. Her love for Mike had never wavered, but she no longer expressed it even to herself. It was buried deep within her soul and could only be extracted by a truly special moment like that night in Greece. I remember every word of my conversation with Angela that evening, but it was one discussion that is simply too special to share with the world. I will take this conversation to the grave. I was moved by her love in a way that I didn't know was possible. After our talk, I gave Angela a hug, wiped the tears from her eyes, kissed her on the forehead, and left her on the deck with Mike. I then went for a walk through the enchanting streets of that small town and was thankful for everything that had happened in Mike's life. Anyone who thinks Mike's life was cut short or that he could have done more in the world is completely mistaken. The value of a person's life is not a result of the number of chapters but rather the quality of the storyline. Mike's love continued within Angela long after he was gone. Mike didn't need to be alive to be the perfect father for his young son.

Mike was accomplishing more from the grave than he could have possibly accomplished with a pulse.

When we returned from Greece, I could see yet another change in Angela's demeanor. She had moved past her despair years earlier, but I could now see her making a further transformation into real happiness. That last night in Greece had obviously given her the final closure she needed to move on with the rest of her life. Her love for Mike would always be present but would never again be a source of pain. Angela was a devoted mother and deserved her wonderful life. I was thankful to have had the opportunity to take the two of them on vacation and was excited to see what the next few years held for Jamie's life. He was getting more involved in both academics and athletics and was successful at both just as his parents had been. I drove Angela and Jamie back to Traverse City, and, the next morning, departed for Minnesota to spend a month with my family while I finished writing *The Little Injun that Could*.

The book came together nicely, and, before long, I had a final draft completed. As I finished editing *The Little Injun that Could*, I found myself thinking about another famous Native American named Ira Hayes. I had read the story about the flag bearers and knew the Johnny Cash song by heart. I was always moved by the tragedy of Ira's story as he was forced to act as the hero he never believed he was. Ira was one of the flag raisers in the famous picture from Iwo Jima who were portrayed as national heroes. Ira was tormented by the fact that so many of his friends had died in the war and didn't receive the hero's welcome that was given to him. One of the famous quotes of Ira Hayes was, "I am not a hero, but the brave men who died deserved this honor." Anyone who has heard the story understands the tragic ending to Ira's life. I have always thought this story had the ability to teach us a lot about our perceived identities and how difficult it is to change them. Instead of simply being known for the good person he was, Ira was turned into a heroic caricature to promote a political agenda. It was the same thing the government would try to do years later when they pissed on the memory of a great American named Pat Tillman. The real shame in the Pat Tillman story is that he was, by all accounts, a truly amazing man that dwarfed the one dimensional image that characterized him after his death. The Pat Tillman story is a perfect example of the power of death and the danger it can pose when a person's life is placed in the hands of the wrong author. One thing I have always done is taken care not to push my own beliefs into my characters' stories. I have been torn apart by critics disagreeing with messages in my books, but these criticisms were misplaced as I myself disagree with certain things I have written. The eulogist should be a vessel through which the true story of a life is told. A eulogy is not the time to change the character into something they weren't. I merely projected the rest of my characters' dreams into reality but never changed the beauty of their lives. I highlighted great lives and didn't capitalize on someone else's death for my own selfish benefit. Ira Hayes was destroyed by his portrayal in public, and he was the most famous modern Native American story I knew. I was thankful that Onida would now become the much needed motivational story to inspire youth within that community. Onida was a victim of her environment, but her story created a better environment for those who were left behind while she lived her happy ending in fiction. Her inspirational story provided the seeds that helped a poor community slowly grow into a success. The Reservation needed a savior, and Onida was the one they were searching for. Onida's story shaped the future of the community that had shaped her story.

CHAPTER 11

Life by Choice

If men could get pregnant, abortion would be a sacrament.

-Florynce R. Kennedy

CHAPTER 11: Life by Choice

Potential is inversely proportional to time. I had saved Onida at just the right time to prevent her potential destruction. Onida's story renewed my interest in the arguments between nature and nurture. I think we are all wired uniquely and the genetic impact on our lives is huge. However, although an enormous amount of us is reliant upon our internal make-up, it is dwarfed in comparison to the effects of our environment. Our genetics may predispose us to certain character traits, but the real cause of who we become is the way in which our world molds us. I am definitely a behaviorist, and there is no doubting the fact that we are constantly being trained by the world around us. This training is not always evident, but it is always present. The training is most often not consciously conducted by another person but rather a result of millions of ping pong balls bouncing against each other and changing the directions of the other balls in the terrarium. Most people grow up as slaves to the environment they were fortunate, or often unfortunate, enough to be born into. I will stop here as I have elaborated on these types of psychological issues throughout my life, and those curious about my views on psychology and child development will find no shortage of resources. However, I wanted to mention this behavioral psychology briefly because I devoted a great deal of thought to the issue and my next book actually originated in an argument that started with a simple discussion of developmental psychology.

The topics of psychology and childhood development came up while I was at a bar with a large group of professors from the University of Michigan. I expressed my opinions at length and debated a naïve notion of divine destiny proposed by a woman I had not previously met. It turned out that she was a major abortion activist, and she made sure to turn our psychology discussion into an argument about abortion. She did this by making the claim that every aspect of our personality is determined at conception, and she believed my view completely discounted the presence of the human soul. I responded that she was correct in saying I was accurately ignoring an imaginary ghost residing within the body. I further expressed my belief that our personality is only established at conception from a deterministic view of the universe in which I believe we don't really have free will to change our personality. However, I added that, although I believed we are all on an unchangeable path set by the current conditions and the laws of the universe (although the factors are much too large to allow us to predict what this path will be), the fact that we will become a certain person doesn't make it true the future person has already been developed at a prior point. A personality is clearly formed over time through experience.

The conversation quickly made a complete turn to abortion as the woman asked me when I believed life began. I said a new life starts at the emergence of consciousness. She then asked if that meant I was pro-choice, and, when I responded in the affirmative, she said, "So you are a murderer?" What an ironic statement this woman had just made. I paused for a second and was unable to respond. The room fell silent as the others in attendance expected me to be offended at this woman's comment. In my mind, I was thinking, "Yes, I actually am a murderer but not for the reasons you are suggesting." After a nice chuckle to myself, I simply responded with a rational argument that abortion should only be legal up to a certain stage in the developmental process at which point I believed it should then be banned. The woman jumped on this viability argument by chastising me and condescendingly asking how I was going to decide that cutoff. In a calm voice, I told her that I only supported abortion up until the point of kindergarten. This comment got a roaring reaction with thirty people laughing and one woman fuming. Before she could respond, I followed up by asking her, "How else are you going to know if the kid is a little shit?" My nemesis, unfortunately, couldn't realize this wasn't a discussion she could win and continued to try to convince me of the immorality of my opinions. I simply sat back sipping my whisky and spent the next two hours making jokes at her expense to the delight of those around. Even people in the group that were pro-life were laughing at my increasingly satirical comments and the fact that this woman couldn't grasp the sarcasm.

I had fun arguing the morality of abortion, and the subject lingered in my mind the next day. My favorite part of the pro-life argument was this notion that life has potential. Human potential was a core theme in my literary career as I exploited characters filled with potential and transformed that potential into their eternity. The idea of potential had grown even greater in my novels based on kids. I wondered if it would be a good idea to focus my next novel around the murder of unborn children. I loved killing kids and figured killing potential lives before they were tarnished at all would probably be even more rewarding. I loved the idea of writing a potential life book, but I needed to figure out what perspective I would write it from. I knew I would somehow kill an unborn child and then write a pro-life story, but I didn't really know where to start. A major pillar in the pro-life argument was that life starts at conception, and I thought seriously about attempting to kill a baby on the day it was conceived. This plan posed two serious problems. First, there was the obvious challenge of guaranteeing conception had occurred right after sex and then finding a way to quickly kill that single cell. An even bigger problem was the flaw I saw in the conception argument in general. I saw conception as such a false time point for an abortion argument because it was simply an intermediate between a hard line stance and a viability stance. A viability argument makes sense because it represents a distinct change in survival ability as the fetus would then be capable of surviving outside the mother. The same could be said for the emergence of a new individual at the onset of consciousness if that point could be determined as a distinct moment rather than a gradual emergence. Conception, on the other hand, didn't represent much of a moral change to me. I don't believe in the ridiculous notion of a soul, and the argument that after conception a cell has potential for life didn't seem distinct from the potential moments before the sperm penetrated the egg.

Instead of using this intermediate stage of conception as the motivation behind my novel, I decided to take a harder lined pro-life stance and respect all potential unborn human lives that didn't have a voice. The next day, I went to the sperm clinic, masturbated into a cup, and was told I had a sperm count of five hundred million lives. I then proceeded to commit mass murder on an unprecedented scale. As I discarded these five hundred million potential lives in the trash can, I found it surprising that this mass murder hadn't elicited a response of outrage from the seemingly moral doctor in front of me. How could a man who had vowed to spend his career defending life just stand there as he watched me murder a half billion defenseless unborn children right in front of his eyes? I left the clinic, and two thoughts came to mind as I walked to my car. First, I wondered if my murders had finally gone too far. Second, I wondered how in the world I was going to pull off a novel with five hundred million protagonists. It was this second question that stuck in my mind as I drove away trying to formulate a storyline for my next novel.

After much thought, I decided on the plot that would become *Life by Choice*. This book was the story of five hundred million extraordinary individuals. For the first time, I slightly dabbled into the fantasy realm as I created a world in which each conscious fetus in the womb was given the choice to live or die. It was a pro-choice story that pro-life supporters could fully embrace because, for the first time, it was the fetus that made the choice whether it wanted to live or die. In the novel, I made every single one of the five hundred million babies choose life and justified their decisions based on a simple evolutionary argument that all of us are wired to pursue survival. If the book had allowed the children the added benefit of viewing the entirety of their future lives before making a decision, I expect there would have been many babies choosing to skip life altogether. However true this may be, it was not the point of the novel, and I moved forward with five hundred million new children choosing life. The thought of deciding whether or not to live one's life was appealing to me. I had always been critical of the notion that there is any purpose to life. I have heard many people argue that the purpose of life is simply to live it or to enjoy it or to help one another, but all of these answers ultimately lack any real insight. Even the idea of purpose itself seemed to be a byproduct of human evolution. It is one thing to say the purpose of college is to prepare us for future careers, but I have yet to hear a fulfilling answer to the purpose of life itself. The closest thing I can see is that the purpose of life is to ensure the beauty of death. We are all born terminally ill, and the only thing we are adequately prepared for is death. Not only have I struggled to find meaning in our ill-fated existence, but I see no real purpose in the universe itself. Even if the universe was some type of perpetual motion machine, to what end would it have any purpose? There are many variations to these questions of purpose, but all I've ever learned from them is that purpose is a human question that does not need to be answered by the cosmos. I learned to simply accept the extraordinary extent of my incredible ignorance. Ultimately, life is but a means to an end.

Writing *Life by Choice* brought many questions about the purpose of life into my mind, but, ultimately, the message of the book was straightforward: everybody chooses life. Every single person on earth, with the exception of suicidal individuals, is pro-life when it comes to their own existence. The five hundred million fetuses in my novel were no different. After I finished the portion of the novel describing the unanimous decisions of the babies to live, the rest of the book became a sociological overview of the glorious results of this influx of life into the world. The majority of the novel provided a fictional statistical analysis of the future lives and careers of these young children. Additionally, I added my usual optimistic twist to get rid of all the horrible people that were no doubt amongst the five hundred million survivors while I highlighted numerous individual lives within this population. I completely ignored any potentially negative sociological effects such as increasing overpopulation. I also ensured all of these five hundred million people lived perfect lives. There wasn't a single bad person in the millions that chose life which helped make the book successful but definitely wasn't an accurate portrayal of our real world. I always laughed when people repeated the message of the book that every child was a blessing. In reality, I highly doubt every child is a blessing. Every seems to be a hideous overestimate. Even a person like me who loves kids more than anyone has still met quite a few little shits in my day, not to mention all the assholes in the world that were once kids. It's hard to imagine that kids who grow up to be assholes can really be considered blessings. Thankfully, I wrote fiction and didn't have to worry about this reality corrupting my story. The book was written quickly, but editing took a long time. This was the first time I had undertaken a novel that hadn't followed a biographical structure. The logistics and flow of the novel were eventually ironed out, and *Life by Choice* was ready to be published.

The first thing I did after the book was printed was send a copy to the pro-life woman whose passionate arguments at the bar had catalyzed the creation of *Life by Choice*. I attached a letter to my gift telling her I hoped this book would allow us to move past our argument and signed the letter as being from her "Life starts at Kindergarten" friend. From what I have heard, she read the letter and immediately threw my book into the trash expecting it to be a pro-choice book to further anger her. I expect the story is most likely true because it wasn't until the book had become such a famous pro-life manual that this woman responded with a note thanking me for the wonderful work I had written.

The success of this novel is well-known, and my net worth was nearly tripled as a result of it. I didn't need any more money, but, on the same token, I didn't complain either. The book has since been a staple of the pro-life movement and has caused me constant grief as I am continually asked to speak at pro-life rallies throughout the country. The book also caused me to be viciously attacked by those on the other side of the issue who suggested it was morally wrong to write the novel. These pro-choice people would constantly try to corner me into a conversation about abortion and were always flabbergasted when I not only agreed with their views but was actually much more pro-choice than they were. My close friends that were pro-choice were puzzled by my book that seemed to fly in the face of my claimed beliefs, but I tried to express to them that I loved exploring different sides of issues and wanted to write a book from the point of view of the fetus. A fetus doesn't have the ability to speak for itself so I allowed it that platform in my fiction. If a fetus was a conscious being, I imagine it would want a say in the future of its life. The subtle difference between the novel and my actual beliefs can be found in this last point. I believe a distinct human life really begins at the emergence of consciousness. Whether we should protect the potential for life may be a question worth asking, but I do not think it is morally equivalent to the protection of a developed human life and definitely shouldn't be decided simply because we have evolved a strong emotional response to the look of a baby. Real moral decisions shouldn't be made with emotions but, instead, should be made with intellect. I was the master of these types of decisions, and I found it comical as I was criticized so strongly from both sides of this ridiculous debate.

Depending on who you talked to, I was either against a woman's freedom or supportive of murdering a fetus. When pro-life people would hear that I was pro-choice and come to confront their fallen hero, I would constantly hear about research showing a fetus can feel pain in the womb. These people failed to realize that we were talking about two different things. A dead fetus doesn't feel pain. I don't support hurting a fetus any more than I support hurting a grown human, but the truth of the matter is that the only way to completely mitigate the suffering of life is through death. Unfortunately for those pro-life supporters arguing with fetal pain, their comments eventually turned me from pro-choice to pro-abortion as I grew to realize how much pain could be avoided simply by ending lives before they started. I never expressed this view and simply moved on with my career leaving the supporters on both sides to continue their hateful arguments against one another while using me to support their cause. It was an emotionally charged shouting match rather than a rationally driven debate, and I simply wanted no part in it anymore. I had done enough and was ready to move on to my next project. The last thing I will say about *Life by Choice* is that it was a fun book to write but caused a whirlwind that ripped through my life and put me on a two year rollercoaster ride that changed me forever. I was ready to get back to my previously relaxing work as a writer. One thing is for sure, after writing *Life by Choice,* I never looked at masturbation in the same way again.

CHAPTER 12

Walk like a Man

The Olympics are not about medals, but the pursuit of medals.

-Herb Brooks

CHAPTER 12: *Walk like a Man*

Success is the enemy of solitude. The response to *Life by Choice* only increased my desire to detach myself from the world. I have constantly struggled to maintain a relaxing pace to my life, and, after *Life by Choice*, I made a conscious effort to get out of the limelight and retreat into solitude once again. The people I love and the success of my books constantly impeded my efforts to find social autonomy. Every time I published a book or opened a successful new charity, the free time would slowly be sucked out of my life. I never minded the hectic schedule when it came to being there for people I loved, but, when it came to work obligations, I loathed the strain it put on me. The huge success and controversy surrounding *Life by Choice* was the worst example of this I have ever experienced, and it felt marvelous to put that hectic time in the rearview mirror. I continued my visits to Traverse City and kept a close eye on Jamie, but, otherwise, I spent a solid year at my cabin in the woods of northern Minnesota. During this time, I reflected on my life and found peace by my own Walden Pond. My weeks were spent alone with only nature and my computer to keep me company while the weekends were filled with welcome visitors and the people I loved most. This was probably the most pleasurable year of my life. I planned to take an entire year off to simply live life to the fullest or, more accurately, to live life to the emptiest. I knew my altruistic nature was bound to reemerge and drive me back to writing, but I was so worn down from the past couple years that I didn't care how selfish it was. I was going to take a year off for myself.

As it turns out, I couldn't stay self-interested for long as I starting writing *Walk like a Man* about two months into my year of selfish solitude. The idea for the book originated when Derbe visited my cabin after spending a week in the Minneapolis working on some federal investigation. Derbe talked for hours about his life in Traverse City and updated me on his current cases. I think he really enjoyed the chance to talk with me and have his friend around to listen again. At one point, Derbe told me about a young handicapped boy he was mentoring. Derbe always had a gentle heart, and I could tell he was moved by this young man. He described the kid's struggle to find an identity amongst his peers. This young man's story wasn't abnormal for a kid in a wheelchair, but the personal characteristics Derbe described immediately gave him a special place in my heart. I felt terrible as I heard about this young man's struggle to be thought of as one of the guys. Derbe said this kid was a huge sports fan and always envied those around him who could be part of a team. He was a high school student but couldn't get a girlfriend or even an invitation to parties because of his handicap. When Derbe finished venting his frustration, I patted him on the back and told him he was doing all he could. My encouragement was honest as I knew there was nothing else Derbe could do to help him find a path to his dreams. On the other hand, I also knew I could easily change this kid's fate. At that moment, I decided I would take a break from my break to kill this paralyzed young man.

Two weeks after Derbe's visit, I traveled to Traverse City to kill the paralyzed boy. I billed the trip as one of my usual surprise visits to see Angela and Jamie, but the real motive behind the trip was murder. Nonetheless, the added bonus of seeing Jamie was obviously welcome. I always enjoyed watching Jamie dominate on the hockey rink, but this paled in comparison to the pride I felt when I heard about his perfect grades in school or listened to the depth of thought that exuded from that twelve year old kid that I watched grow from a baby into a magnificent young man. On the second night of my visit, I took Angela and Jamie out for dinner and then tried to gather my thoughts on how to kill the paraplegic. I had run into a couple problems with my plan since I had failed to check Derbe's schedule and he was of town. This would have worked splendidly if Derbe had mentioned the young man's name, but, unfortunately, I only knew the storyline and was now left with no path to my victim. I decided to simply go to Derbe' precinct and ask his fellow officers if they knew the name and whereabouts of the paraplegic boy Derbe was mentoring. The first person I ran into when I got to the police office was Carl. Carl was an officer who I had gotten to know well over the past few years when he had been working with my friend. I told Carl I wanted to pay this young man a visit, and he gave me all the information I needed. I nearly soiled myself when I found out the kid's name was Christopher. I had planned on using my next novel to fulfill this young man's dreams of being an athlete, having a girlfriend, and being accepted for whom he was. After hearing his name, I wondered if a Superman sequel would have been more appropriate. It was such a tragedy when the world had seen Superman become paralyzed, and I felt enticed to use my literary method to reverse the process and resurrect Superman from Christopher's paraplegic body. I ultimately decided against the Superman novel because it was Christopher's story, not my own, and I wanted to do his dreams justice. However, as I later wrote *Walk like a Man*, I always had this inner desire to write the superhero story which is ultimately what led to the Olympic sprinter protagonist of the novel being commonly referred to as Superman by his peers. Giving this nickname to the hero of the novel allowed me to fulfill my obligations to Christopher while still enjoying the irony of turning a paraplegic into Superman. It was an inside joke shared only with myself, but it gave me immense pleasure.

After getting the information on Christopher, I immediately went to his house. I knew the police would now be aware of my visit so I decided to postpone the murder for another couple days. On that day, I merely went inside to see Christopher and give him a gift I had brought. Christopher loved sports and had always wanted to be an athlete so I had already decided that he would be a champion Olympic runner in the book. The gift I presented him was an Olympic gold medal that was given to me by a swimmer who had previously attended one of my charities. This was one of four swimming gold medals this woman had won. She had given me the medal as a thank you for everything my charity and the college scholarship I had awarded her had done for her life. I figured Christopher would appreciate the medal so I put it around his neck and had his mother take a nice picture of the two of us. She then took a second picture that caught the smile on his face as I handed him two tickets to the upcoming summer Olympics. I told him I planned to fly him to the games with me. Christopher could not have been happier. His mother thanked me for the generous gift and asked how I had come to drop in on their family like an angel out of the sky. The first emotion that arose inside me was pride in the fact that I was, in fact, an angel. I was what the Angel of Death should be. I brought death to those who deserved it most. As these thoughts went through my mind, I simply smiled at the woman and said a friend had told me Christopher's story, and I felt compelled to help.

Two nights later, I returned to Christopher's house as he slept. I broke in through the garage and made my way to Christopher's room. I saw him lying in his bed with his gold medal still around his neck. I slipped him a drug to keep him asleep and then moved his body into a bag. When Christopher awoke an hour later, he found himself sitting in the middle of the running track outside his high school. He looked up and saw me standing in front of him with a gun pointed at his head. I could see the adrenaline began to race inside this young paraplegic, and I asked him, "Well, aren't you going to run?" I already knew the answer, but the question made me smile anyway. The answer to the question was yes. He was going to run. However, he wasn't going to run until the next day when he started his new life in fiction. I looked at this handicap kid sitting on the starting line of the track, and I said, "On your mark, get set, go." Christopher never heard the word "go" as the noise from the starting gun drowned out my words. I left Christopher's body lying on the track with the gold medal still hanging around his neck. For once, a character in my novel ended his real life at the same point his life was ended in the book. Those of you who have read *Walk like a Man* know the ending well. The crowd was chanting "Superman, Superman, Superman" as the hero of our story lined up to race in the moment he had dreamt of his entire life. It was a fulfilling feeling when I later wrote the final lines of *Walk like a Man*, "On your mark, get set, go."

After killing Christopher, I returned to his house and put the gun back on his father's shelf where I had noticed it two days earlier. I then disposed of my murder attire and returned to my bedroom at Angela's house. The next morning, I said my goodbyes and gave my usual motivational speech to Jamie. As always, I was sure to tell him how proud we all were of what an amazing kid he was and how proud his dad would have been. I then drove to the airport, flew back to Minnesota, drove up north to the cabin, and continued with my year of relaxation.

Writing *Walk like a Man* was easy and didn't intervene with my comfortable lifestyle at the cabin in the slightest. I breezed through three chapters in the first week and was poised to finish the novel in no time. However, nine days after I killed Christopher, I awoke to quite a surprise outside the door of my little cabin in the woods. The place was surrounded by about ten police officers and a half dozen FBI agents. As soon as I noticed the men outside, I heard a knock on the door and opened it to see my best friend with Carl by his side. Derbe's eyes were bloodshot, his cheeks were tearstained, and he had less life in him than any corpse I have ever seen. I immediately gave him a hug and asked if he was okay. I followed up my concern by asking what was going on and if everyone wanted to come inside. Derbe couldn't muster a response, but the officers made their way inside and, in the process, informed me that I was suspected of murder.

I laughed so hard at the thought I could have committed a murder, and it made for a really awkward moment for the officers. I could see in their eyes that they didn't know if they were in the process of a mistaken murder accusation or in the presence of a genius killer responding to the allegations. I told Derbe that his acting was better than expected but the prank wasn't going to work. One of the FBI agents then told me to sit down and showed me a picture of Christopher's dead body lying on the track. I was immediately sobered and didn't say a word. The officers proceeded to recap the circumstances of finding Christopher's body, and, midway through, I interjected to ask how they could possibly imagine I would have been the one to do something like this. I looked across the table at Derbe and asked him to tell them who I was. Derbe looked up at me in excruciating pain but, once again, was unable to speak. I could tell he had been pleading my innocence relentlessly in the previous days, and I didn't push him any further. The FBI investigator continued his recap and answered my question at the same time. He told me my finger prints had been found at the crime scene, Carl had told them I had been looking for Christopher earlier in the weekend, and I was currently the only suspect in the case. He showed me the picture of Christopher again and said my fingerprints were all over the medal found around the victim's neck. I told them in a panicked voice that of course my fingerprints were all over the medal because it was my medal. I raced through my explanation about hearing Christopher's story from Derbe and being so inspired that I had brought him the gift and was planning to take him to the Olympics the following year.

As I fumbled through my words in a fake panic, I could see the life return to Derbe's face. My friend had been through hell standing by me for the past two days, and his faith had just been vindicated. I showed the officers the pictures that had been taken two days before the murder and asked if they had talked to the mother about my visit. The officers said the investigation had been completely internal, and they had no knowledge of a previous visit between me and Christopher's family. I could see I was already in no danger of being arrested but let my fearful act continue for a while. Derbe stood up and began to speak in my defense saying that he had already told them there was no possible way I would ever do something to harm another person. I asked the officers if I was going to be arrested or what they needed me to do and offered to cooperate in any way. As I expected, they told me my story seemed to cover all the bases, and, if it was corroborated by Christopher's mother, they had no cause to arrest me at this point. After that, the mood slowly turned from an intense confrontation to a somber, relaxing, and almost jovial atmosphere as I fired up the grill and cooked lunch for my visitors. Derbe became increasingly talkative as he continuously chuckled at the morning's events. He had been in so much anguish at the thought that there was any possibility I could be involved in the murder, and he was now laughing that he ever let that notion enter his mind. I smiled at my friend and thanked him for all he had done. We had a nice meal, and I wished the officers well assuring them I would be available if they needed to follow up with me in any way. I never heard about the case again except for a funny letter of apology from Carl and the rest of Derbe's unit in Traverse City.

I was thankful to have once again gotten away with murder, and my confidence grew even bigger than it had previously been. However, I realized it was probably safer to stop killing people around Michigan to avoid any further conflict with the same cops. Other than that, I didn't worry about the episode at all. As I thought about what had happened, I smiled at the power of a person's identity. The world knew me as a brilliant writer, a giving philanthropist, and a genuinely caring person. This was why it had been so easy for my story to be accepted that morning. The evidence itself supported my explanation, and I have no doubt I would have prevailed anyway, but it was my reputation which made everyone accept the story so quickly. On the same token, it amazed me how quickly those men who knew me had changed their opinion when they first arrived at the cabin. Many of them had known me for years, but yet they came to my cabin prepared to arrest me. If I had been a little less careful with my murder and left an actual trail of guilt, these men would have had no problem characterizing me as one of the worst human beings they had ever met. This single new piece of evidence would have been enough to override years of building my immaculate identity. I have always been amazed at how fragile a good reputation is. The only reliable reputation is a bad reputation. A good reputation can be taken from a person in an instant, but a bad reputation is nearly impossible to remove. A good reputation is a fragile egg that can be broken in a moment. As for a bad reputation, well you can't unscramble scrambled eggs. A single act of weakness by a spouse can ruin them forever in the eyes of someone who has loved them exclusively for decades, but no single good action would allow a person to overcome a bad reputation. Once that stigma is applied, it takes years to remove, and the residue of that reputation will never be fully erased. There would be nothing harder for me than to have attempted to kill a person with a bad reputation and turn them into a beautiful story. A good reputation takes only a moment to shatter, but even death struggles to combat a bad one. I smiled that morning as I fed my story to the cops and was thankful for the way in which I was perceived.

The concept of identity controlling one's view in the eyes of the world was nothing new to me. For most of my life, I struggled to simply be known as me instead of being known as a hockey player, a biomedical engineer, a philanthropist, or a writer. The stereotypes that come with these titles create a view of a person before they have even spoken. I always try to wait to understand the depth of a person before I create an image of them in my mind, but, more often than not, I am just as guilty as the rest of the world. The problem with stereotypes is that they are often accurate. I don't know how many times I would see a girl with a designer bag, immediately create an image of her in my mind, and feel justified as she vindicated my guess moments later. Even though I was often correct in my assumption, I hated the role superficial identities played in the world. I first came to despise this identity effect during my college hockey career. This notion that people would hear I was a Division 1 hockey player and instantly give value to me greatly benefited me and greatly repulsed me at the same time. I loved playing hockey and enjoyed telling stories about my time at the rink, but I wanted people to appreciate the person I was instead of my quasi-accomplishments. The more I tried to separate myself from this identity, the more I realized how impossible it was. All my clothes were covered with hockey emblems. So many of my memories and stories were inseparable from this identity. Even after I was finished playing hockey, I constantly would notice myself making references to my team or other subtle lines within my stories that would prompt my listener to ask and then be impressed that I had been an athlete. These hockey references would always jump out in my mind as they came out of my mouth, and I became aware of the fact that these comments were a subconscious way for me to translate my previous identity to my new situation. I think this ability to portray one's previous identity rather than starting from scratch creates a sense of comfort in a new situation. Throughout my life, I have worn my hockey shirts and clothes that portray my previous life like a billboard for all to see. I started to realize how difficult it was to start fresh with a new person in conversation without giving a description of things I had done as opposed to just being myself in the moment. Even after I began to loathe the identity pushed upon me by society, it was still impossible to break my social place in the world.

As I reflected on the impact of my own identity, I realized I was much better off than my current character. Christopher's story had been filled with identity issues from the moment he was paralyzed as a child. I have already described how a person can be crippled by his or her identity, but the reverse can be true as well. Being crippled became Christopher's identity. All of his classmates, teachers, and the girls he desired looked at him firstly as a paraplegic instead of just another kid in the class. Christopher was crippled by his crippled identity. More than anything else, he wanted to be treated as a normal kid without the handicap stigma. Christopher loved sports and always dreamed he could be out competing with everyone else. I felt sorry for Christopher and looked forward to the day when he would no longer be looked at with pity but instead would be the star athlete on the track with a pretty girlfriend sitting in the stands and a social life envied by all. Christopher's dream was nearly destroyed that morning when Derbe and the FBI had confronted me at my cabin, but, thankfully, everything worked out for the best, and I was now free to return to writing my book and enjoying my relaxing days up north.

After my run-in with the law, I returned to Christopher's story. The novel followed a young man in pursuit of Olympic aspirations. I used Christopher's desire to be an athlete as the underlying emotion behind the story. I have always loved the quote at the beginning of this chapter because I think it exemplifies what sports should be and often are not. The desire for greatness is a form of greatness in itself. I admire a dreamer as much as a dream. Christopher's novel demonstrated the difference between merely hoping for success and striving for it. It was the comeback story of a young man overcoming the odds to fulfill his dreams of competing in the Olympics. What made *Walk like a Man* such an admirable novel was the dedication that the main character took to reach his goals rather than the moment of achievement itself. It was for that very reason that the book was ended with Christopher at the starting line of his Olympic race. At that point, his story was already complete. The glory was in the journey, not the result. The ending was inconsequential. So often we value a person's success by the results instead of the process. This book demonstrated the value of the pursuit.

I slowly finished *Walk like a Man* and sent it to my publisher. I refused to cut my year of relaxation short to go on a book tour which was a decision I have never regretted. I spent the rest of the year centering my life and reenergizing my passion for writing. During this time, I reflected on how far I had come in the past few years. It was impressive what I had accomplished in such a short time and how much joy I had brought into the world. My passion was returning during my time alone at the cabin. Every day, I grew more excited to get back to work. As I thought about my next books, I made a few key decisions about how best to proceed. First, I was no longer going to kill anybody around my usual locations to avoid another risky run-in with the law. I also realized I had probably been a little selfish in the past by not extending my work to a wider region to help a broader audience. Finally, I decided I was just going to enjoy myself. Sometimes, people who spend their lives helping others get so emotionally invested in what we are doing that we forget to have fun along the way. I had enjoyed parts of my previous work such as the ironic twists I added to the murders or the feeling of fulfillment when I finished a novel and watched the person live happily ever after. I had also spent a lot of time in sadness leading up to these murders as I felt terrible for the doomed reality of the characters. It was often not until I killed them that I would get the full pleasure out of their lives. I ultimately came to the conclusion that there was no reason I couldn't commit my good deeds and enjoy my work at the same time. After all, I was spending my life helping people and helping people should be fun. It was time to let the fun begin.

CHAPTER 13

The Pursuit of Purity

What men desire is a virgin who is a whore.

-Edward Dahlberg

CHAPTER 13: The Pursuit of Purity

I returned from my yearlong sabbatical but kept my sense of solitude within me as I resumed my work. I had spent the last year reenergizing in the woods and returned to society feeling good about the future. This time, I wouldn't get caught up in the same hectic lifestyle, but I would instead focus on having fun with my writing. I made up my mind that I was going to enjoy my next book from start to finish, and that is exactly what I did. The lead role in my next novel would be given to a young woman I met in Las Vegas. I had taken the trip to Vegas to meet a couple old friends from grad school who were now spread out around the country. The four day vacation with my old lab crew was wonderful as we took in the full Vegas experience of shows, food, and gambling. It had been too long since I had last seen these friends, and I had a blast hearing how well their lives had turned out. Life is unpredictable, and it was fun to learn about the strange twists in each of their stories. The only member of our initial group still working in the medical field was Simone who was doing safety tests for the FDA. Years of killing pigs in her lab experiments pushed her down the path of suspicion towards people's published results, and she seemed to like her current work. The rest of us had somehow ended up in completely different fields as I had become an author, Adam had retired early and opened a 90's karaoke bar outside of Seattle known for its infamous boyband nights, and Tim had recently taken a job brewing beer at Samuel Adam's which fulfilled a lifelong passion although you may now have to wait two years to get your Winter Lager if I remember his process correctly. The other two former lab members on the trip were Yohan and Ryan whose lives had taken completely unexpected paths. Ryan had always been an amazingly loving father and family man, and no one could have predicted the path his career would take. He had started fighting in local UFC events as a hobby during his final year in grad school under the alias of Radar's Rampage and found considerable success locally that propelled him to a career on the national stage before he retired to his current job working in the UFC front office. Yohan had moved to the heartland of Nebraska and started a sheep farm. He lived a quiet life raising his sheep, and I could tell he was excited for our trip to Las Vegas. I never would have imagined my friends' lives would have turned out the way they did, but we sure had fun telling old stories and experiencing everything Vegas had to offer.

After four days in Vegas, I said goodbye to my friends. I didn't want the vacation to end so I decided to stay another few days to play poker and relax. The first day after my friends left, I spent the entire day playing cards and soaking in the sun by the pool. In the late afternoon, I took a long nap and then went downstairs to have a few drinks. I found a nice bar on the casino floor at Bally's to drink and play video poker. The bartender was a hybrid between a butler and a British Royal Guard that never smiled. I liked this guy from the start as I observed his serious demeanor and fancy attire including a freshly pressed shirt and bow tie. I had a feeling that behind his expressionless face was a guy who loved his job and enjoyed watching the different people that passed through each night. I put forty dollars into video poker and started betting a quarter each hand to pass the time as I sat and drank. I had a good time striking up discussions with people as they stopped by and even the bartender got involved in a couple conversations as the night progressed. It was hard work to break his stoic nature, but I was doing my best and could see the beginnings of a few grins on his face as the night wore on. I was a multi-millionaire that didn't care about gambling and was just having a fun night. I was on quite a streak and had more than doubled my forty dollars. It was at this point in the evening that the heroine of my next novel, *The Pursuit of Purity*, made her way into my life.

I had been causing a great deal of commotion that hadn't gone unnoticed as I celebrated my video poker victories. Two gorgeous women soon sat down at the far end of the bar and ordered drinks. At that moment, I hit another big hand and won thirty dollars to bring my total winnings over two hundred for the night. I screamed out in excitement and even forced the bartender to give me a high five although he appeared extremely uncomfortable doing this. As I celebrated my winning hand, the more attractive of the two women made her way around the bar and sat next to me. She didn't say anything but just sipped her drink waiting for me to initiate the conversation. I turned and told her she better not be coming to steal my machine because I was on a roll and wasn't leaving. She smiled while saying that she didn't even know how to play and asked if I could show her. After playing a couple hands together, we started a nice conversation. She asked where I was from, and I told her I was visiting from the Midwest and was born and raised in Minnesota. When I asked where she was from, she told me she lived in Las Vegas and had been there the past six years. We chatted a little more, and, after hearing a reference to work, I asked her what she did for a living. She replied by saying that she gave naked massages. My mind perked up as I was suddenly aware of the fact that I was talking to a hooker and she had actually been at work the entire time. When she made the massage comment, she gave me a serious stare with her seductive eyes. I quickly responded by asking her if there was good money in naked massages these days, and she told me that she did alright. I laughed and continued with the conversation feeling bad that she was wasting her time on a hopeless client like me. Unless there was a hooker that could fuck me in my mind, I wasn't going to pay. Finding someone for sex was the least of my problems. Finding someone to stimulate me mentally and give me an intellectual climax would have been a different story altogether, but I figured that wasn't really an option.

As my conversation with this lovely prostitute continued, she introduced herself as Chastity. I nearly soiled myself at the irony in her name and instantly knew she was a magnificent character for a book. From then on, I continued our conversation with increased interest in Chastity's life. I was making jokes the entire time and watched as the bartender did his best to fight off laughter. Finally, Chastity had enough of the pleasantries and was ready to get down to business. She asked me if I wanted her to join me in my room, and I responded by asking her how good her massages were. In one of the sexiest voices I have ever heard, she told me that she never had any complaints. I knew I wasn't going to become one of her clients, but I really admired how well she had mastered her craft. Instead of stopping her right there, I asked how much she would charge for a massage. She said that, because she liked me, she could go for as little as six hundred dollars. I literally laughed out loud and told her to look down at the video poker screen. I then proceeded to loudly advise her that, if she was going to charge six hundred dollars, she shouldn't be wasting her time talking to someone betting quarters. I then pointed to the business man sitting at the end of the bar and told her that she should be talking to the guy wearing the Rolex instead. I felt bad I had laughed out loud at her price so I was sure to follow up my comments with a series of compliments on how sweet I thought she was as well as how smooth she was at her job. We parted ways with a smile as she returned to work and followed my directions down to the guy at the end of the bar. The best part of this encounter was when I made the comment about the guy with the Rolex and the bartender unknowingly laughed out loud before catching himself and trying to play it off by straightening his bow tie and looking the other way. I caught his eye a second afterword, and he gave me a little smirk which made my day.

I spent the next hour playing video poker and visiting with a host of new people as the bar started to fill up. Every once in a while, I would glance over at Chastity and could see it was just a matter of time before she was up in Rolex's room making money. When they finally left together, I was talking to someone next to me and almost missed the moment completely. I looked over just in time to see them on the other side of the casino floor waiting for an elevator. I immediately sprinted over to them and yelled for Chastity to wait. She turned around with a look of concern on her face. I asked her if I was entitled to some sort of finder's fee for my referral. She laughed and gave me a hug before getting in the elevator with her client. Before I broke our hug, I whispered for her to meet me the next morning for breakfast at the hotel restaurant. She didn't say anything, but, as she walked towards the elevator, she glanced back and gave me a subtle nod that told me I would see her in the morning.

Breakfast with Chastity was a pleasure. Other than the fact that she was a whore, I have rarely met a more innocent person in my life. She was a gentle and sweet soul with a wonderful warmness. As we ate, she told me the story of her life and the path that took her to her current career. It was a story that was as old as the profession itself. As I have said thousands of times, it is always a pleasure to hear someone's story and gain a glimpse into their identity. Chastity was a perfect example of the William Blake quote: "Every harlot was a virgin once." I don't know if it was circumstance or convenience that led Chastity into prostitution, but, either way, it was nice to see it wasn't having a negative impact on her personality. I still saw her purity shining through and felt bad when she told me that she felt dirty every time she had sex for money. If only she could have embraced her lifestyle completely, I think she could have been content with her life. I have no problem with her behavior in a moral sense. Prostitution is capitalism at its finest. The government can make all the laws it wants against prostitution, but Adam Smith's invisible hand is going to keep reaching out until he finds a girl and gets laid. Chastity was simply making a profit from fulfilling people's desires. I wish she could have guiltlessly accepted her identity so I wouldn't have needed to kill her. Unfortunately, Chastity missed her previous life as that sweet virgin she had been in high school. Our society puts such an emphasis on women being pure that many of them, like Chastity, end up feeling bad about themselves when they are simply following their nature. I wonder if Chastity subconsciously chose her hooker name as a result of her internal desires. I empathized with her feelings, and, as breakfast progressed, I began to concoct a plan to kill Chastity before my trip was over.

After finishing breakfast and our heart to heart conversation, Chastity and I parted ways but made plans for later in the day. I made sure she was aware this wasn't a business meeting and told her I would understand if she had to work, but she just smiled, and I could tell she was excited to see me again. That evening, I met Chastity for dinner and a nice walk along the Strip. As we walked, I heard even more about Chastity's life and couldn't wait to shape it into the world she wanted. I spent an amazing evening with Chastity and accompanied her home at the end of the night. In a way, I felt guilty that Chastity was going to have sex on her day off, but I figured she might as well get one last lay before she died.

Years of training had paid off. Chastity was phenomenal and did things in bed I had never even heard of. She had undersold herself the previous evening as this was definitely the best naked massage of my life. I was the last person ever to make love to Chastity. Unlike most men, I wasn't going to pay her. Instead, I was going to give her something infinitely more valuable. As she reached her climax, I grabbed my belt and put it around her neck. She screamed with pleasure as I fastened the belt around her throat. I tightened the belt and choked Chastity to death as she orgasmed for the final time. Once my chastity belt had saved her life, she was never a whore again.

Chastity's life soon became the story of the virgin heroine in *The Pursuit of Purity*. As the title suggests, the novel was designed to follow a young woman on a lifelong pursuit of purity. Chastity set an example that proved a woman could still live a life worth admiring. She was a fictional representation of what so many women try to achieve. My description of Chastity in the book was an accurate portrayal of that hooker. I didn't have to embellish her sweet nature as she already possessed the qualities that made her so special. I only changed the results of her life, not the goals of her life. I enjoyed exploring the topics of sex and temptation in a novel. Chastity represented the triumph of discipline over temptation. I have always had an interest in our struggle between what we desire and what we feel we should be doing. This constant struggle is one of the fundamental aspects of the human experience, and it was satisfying to write a story that followed a person who was able to overcome her instincts and follow her rational desires instead.

As I finished *The Pursuit of Purity*, I thought about the differences between real life and Chastity's story. The book put an emphasis on controlling desire in order to achieve a preferred reward at the end. Chastity blamed her lack of purity for the fact that she hadn't had a happy ending (although her clients did). Chastity was a victim of our society's control over desires. We are constantly being told what kinds of actions are considered appropriate, and it was disconcerting that not even this hooker in Las Vegas was immune to the guilt. We live our lives constantly suppressing our innate desires whether it is the desire for women, food, or any number of deviant behaviors. I understand why society suppresses certain types of deviant behavior that could negatively affect other people. The majority of our suppressed behaviors, however, consist of victimless crimes that would have no effect on anyone but the individual. There is no reason a prostitute like Chastity should have felt bad about her job. Chastity should be able to use her job to bring joy to men with an excess of both money and loneliness. Instead of being free to pursue this almost altruistic life, Chastity's profession was illegal and would have landed her in jail had she been caught. It amazes me how many people are in jail for actions that only impact their own lives. The best example of this is drugs. I fully support laws preventing people from drinking and driving, but what is wrong with a person smoking pot in their own apartment? I have never been into drugs, but that is not because I think drug use is morally wrong. If I was assured of my safety, in both the short-term and long-term, I would try every drug at least once. I still remember the first night I had alcohol and how different being drunk actually was from what I had imagined. I expect the same would be true if I were to try other drugs for the first time. I would try them all simply out of curiosity.

When I think about deviance and the question of controlling desires, I do my best to follow Oscar Wilde's timeless advice, "The only way to conquer a desire is to give into it." I have spent my life trying to maximize my happiness while doing the same for those around me. Instead of fighting my emotions, I have focused on understanding them and cultivating the desires that are truly of value. The primary theme of Chastity's life, sex, is an excellent example of a desire that I have gained control over in my own life. In Chastity's novel, I allowed her to move through life without being victimized by the effects of sex. Instead of being a hooker whose identity was tarnished by sexual misconduct, the woman in the story was characterized by purity. She was an example of discipline in the face of unwanted desire. She said no when she wanted to say yes and would live to reap the rewards in the form of a perfect relationship that was worth the wait. In my own life, I had also overcome the common pitfalls of sex. Because I lived in the real world, however, I was forced to take a much different approach than Chastity took in *The Pursuit of Purity*. Instead of spending life fighting my desires, I was able to understand them and beat them through thought. I was consumed with the pursuit of the perfect woman but was finally able to look inside myself and realize the hopelessness of this chase. Even after my college years were over, I would often find myself enamored with a new girl. I was no longer naïve enough to believe she was the perfect woman, but I would still pursue her to the point of a sexual relationship until I reached the point of repulsion usually within a week or two. I often regretted sleeping with girls I admired when they quickly lost all appeal to me. I started to regard women in the same way as W.C. Fields when he said, "Women are like elephants to me. I like to look at them, but I wouldn't want to own one." I still believed in love at first sight, but I no longer ruined the view by staring for too long. I had dated many women that brought a spark to my life but never ignited the fire I had hoped for. Women were like luggage: I liked to put things inside of them, but, once I did, I could never get rid of them.

These thoughts about women ran through my head as I finished writing *The Pursuit of Purity*. I realized that Chastity had been one of the best relationships of my life. Not only was she fabulous in bed, but I didn't have to feel guilty when we were finished. There was never any question of where the relationship was going, and my opinion of her only grew stronger in the time after we had sex. I had slept with plenty of women but rarely had enjoyed it as much in hindsight. Most often, I would look back on sex and wonder why I didn't just stay home and masturbate to save myself five hours (by the way that five hours includes more than sex and I am not trying to say that's how long it usually lasted). The truth is I have never met a girl that was as good at having sex with me as I was at having sex with me. I could easily rub one out in a tenth of the time, and, once I was done, whether it was sex or masturbation, the last thing I wanted to do was have sex. If I could have removed my sexual desires from my life completely, there is no telling how much more I could have accomplished. It is sad to think about the time I wasted and how many people are still alive today because I was too busy jerking off to focus on my work and kill those additional people. I guess even a person like me is incapable of fully overcoming all desires although I know I came closer than the vast majority of the world. Most people simply don't understand the purpose of sex. Sex causes three things: orgasms, babies, and the desire to sleep alone. I guess I could easily add abortions, STDs, and a few others, but the ones I listed seem to be the most common. Relationships aren't that much different than sex and masturbation. All three start with anticipation (fortunately much less time is wasted on foreplay in masturbation). All three then develop into passion (sex for sex, masturbating for masturbation, holding hands for relationships). In each case, a climax is eventually reached at some moment of unadulterated bliss whether in the form of an orgasm or a wedding. Finally, all three eventually end with regret of what you have just done whether it is the desire to sleep alone after sex, the desire to sleep alone during relationship, or just going to sleep peacefully after masturbating. Once a sufficient amount of time passes, we reenter the anticipation phase, and the wheels on the bus go round and round. Fortunately, I have been able to get out of this vicious cycle in my own life and just have an orgasm every once in a while for old time's sake.

I would be remiss if I didn't admit my views on women have never been jaded completely. I have lived my life based on many beliefs described above, but I never fully killed my previous self. Against all odds, I am still a romantic. I don't believe there is a woman on this earth that could fulfill my desires, but I still dream of her. In *The Pursuit of Purity*, Chastity found the eternal love I used to dream of. I was now repulsed by the pursuit, but yet the desire remained. Thanks to fiction, I could still dream about my ideal woman. Even after everything I have learned about women and relationships, to my amazement, my dreams haven't changed at all. The only thing that has actually changed is the fact that I used to think I was awake. Now, I know I am dreaming.

At no time in my life was this dream rekindled more than when I was writing *The Pursuit of Purity*. In fact, during this period, I took a break to write the only completely fictional book of my life. It was a book about the woman of my dreams. I started with a blank slate and created the woman I wanted from scratch. I hesitate to begin my description of her here because the novel about this woman turned out to be over seven hundred pages and the story still fell short of doing her justice. I molded everything I desired into a perfect woman and fell in love. I named my dream woman Fantasia as she was truly a manifestation of my greatest fantasy.

Fantasia possessed every facet of female perfection that I could imagine. As with most women one falls in love with, the description of this woman began with beauty. Fantasia was physically, mentally, and emotionally beautiful. Physically, I had never seen a woman as breathtaking as Fantasia. The first thing I noticed about her was a smile that could light up my heart. Fantasia was so generous with her smiles and could accomplish more with a simple glance than most people accomplished in a lifetime. A single smile from Fantasia meant more than the entirety of my previous relationships combined. In addition to her enchanting smile and flawless face, Fantasia had the perfect athletic body without an ounce of fat. Her body was the physical manifestation of her personality and was a direct result of her energetic lifestyle. She had a petite and toned body with a trim but muscular build. Spending my life with Fantasia, I would never have to deal with an out of shape tired woman but, instead, would spend my life trying to keep up with her. I have always been attracted to girls with pretty faces and athletic bodies, but Fantasia made the rest look like hideous slobs. She was a stunning specimen that could turn heads from miles away. She had an innocent face with a guilty expression. She was the extremes of Chastity's story and allowed me to be the only exception to her purity.

More impressive than Fantasia's physical attributes was her mental beauty. I was enamored with the full spectrum of this woman's mind. Everything Fantasia said would effortlessly hit the mark. When others struggled for hours to describe a thought, my girl would show up and express the depth of an issue in a single statement. Even Fantasia's shallowness was deep. She could comfortably control every type of conversation whether we were contemplating the meaning of the universe or were at a bar chirping people as they walked by. Fantasia's depth directly mirrored the broad range of human experience as she could be the life of a wild party just as easily as she could be the perfect partner for a quiet conversation in my arms at the end of the night. Fantasia's intelligence was only overshadowed by her creativity. I was never bored with Fantasia as she taught me to experience life in a way I hadn't dreamt of before.

The final aspect of Fantasia's appeal was her emotional perfection. I have met many beautiful women and a couple semi-intelligent women in my life (granted none came anywhere near Fantasia in either of these qualities let alone both), but I have never met a person with Fantasia's emotional makeup. Fantasia had a wild passion for life while containing an unfalteringly calm temperament. Nothing is more important to the success of a relationship than the respective temperaments of two lovers which is why Fantasia and I made a perfect match. We both loved life without taking it seriously. There was never a single instant in which Fantasia was in a grouchy mood. We could go to the depths of intellectual depression together through our shared pessimism with the purpose of life but never experienced a dip in our emotions as long as we were together. In Fantasia's story, we were completely consumed in each other's lives and didn't waste a single moment on sadness. Every minute was filled with stimulating conversation, passionate lovemaking, or overpowering laughter. Fantasia completed my personality and provided the perfect partner for me in the world. I was completely comfortable with her and was free to express the entirety of my character without worrying about her response. I knew there wasn't a single joke she couldn't handle. More importantly, she wasn't simply a cute girl standing next to me laughing at my jokes as previous women had been, but rather she possessed the unequalled ability to make me laugh. I have never met someone who was as hilariously clever or seriously sarcastic. We both made each other laugh and didn't need anyone else to complete our journey. Her energy level and passion made me seem like a bore. Instead of spending every night singing to her and making jokes, I would often find myself lying down with a smile as she provided her equal share of entertainment. Every moment with Fantasia was blissful, and this was made possible by the trust we shared together. This wasn't the type of trust present in most relationships but, rather, a deep trust in every aspect of the other's identity. I knew everything about Fantasia was real, and I never had to worry that I had been misled by who she was. We knew we would still be in love that next morning when the night hit the morning sun which gave us the comfort we needed to love without fear.

The last thing I will say about Fantasia is that our dreams were completely aligned. Everything Fantasia offered me in the present was amplified in our future. Fantasia was more than a perfect woman and passionate lover that I wanted to spend every day with. Her dreams directly matched everything I wanted in my happy ending, and she epitomized my eternal desires. Fantasia was undoubtedly designed to be to be the perfect mother. In the dream world I had envisioned, she was the woman I knew I would spend my life with. We would live a blissful life raising our children and never have a need for anything more than what we had under our roof. In reality, I had been forced to fulfill many of these desires as a father figure in Jamie's life, but Fantasia allowed me to relive my original fantasy. We were truly in love, and our joyful life together was the outward reflection of our immeasurable affection. We became completely immersed in each other's souls. We became one entity without losing any of our respective autonomy. She took care of me as much as I took care of her. For the first time in my life, I felt as if I was getting as much in return as I gave to a relationship. She took care of my needs on every level. Our relationship was built on want rather than need. The feeling I had for Fantasia was an eternal crush. After the day we met, the rest of my life would be consumed with this one person. I asked her to marry me on that first day, but we would never have time for a wedding. We were too busy living to take a day off for a ceremony to say what we already knew. Once I met Fantasia, there would never again be a need for my mind to stray to any other topic. I had found my perfect woman and simply wanted to dance my way through life with her. The sadness I had previously experienced as a result of never finding Fantasia in my reality was replaced by happiness as I wrote her into existence.

When I finished writing Fantasia's story, I read it from start to finish. As I read through her story, I realized she was even more beautiful than I had assumed while I was in the process of writing. Each individual quality that Fantasia possessed was worthy of praise, but the full extent of her character was overwhelming. It was such a relief to finally meet the woman I had been waiting for my entire life. I was extremely proud to have created what the world was lacking. When I reached the end of the story, I fell into a strange emotional state of empty happiness. I realized that, no matter how lovely her story was, my woman didn't exist in the real world. I spent a solid month of my life staring at the book resting on my kitchen table and didn't know what to do. I could publish her story, but I selfishly wanted her all to myself. Fate had intended for Fantasia to be with me forever, and I refused to give her to the rest of the world while I struggled forward on my lonely path without her. My decision not to publish this book was further justified by the philosophy behind my work as an author. I wrote books to give real characters the stories they deserved. Fantasia was perfect, but she wasn't real, and it didn't feel right to publish such a dishonest novel and pawn it off as truth. The story warmed my heart, but I knew it wasn't reality. There was no place in my fiction for falsehoods. I decided the only justifiable option was to burn the book. I was simply fooling myself by taking pleasure from a fictional heroin. When I set out to burn Fantasia's story, I immediately realized how difficult it would be to commit this crime. The previous murders I had committed paled in comparison to killing my dream woman. I knew it had to be done, but I couldn't bear the thought of parting with my love. In the short time since meeting Fantasia, I had lost all focus on the rest of my life. Instead of pushing to get *The Pursuit of Purity* published, I left it sitting on my shelf as I thought only about my new romance. It was time for me to move on, and I knew it would be therapeutic to rid myself of this fantasy once and for all. I will never forget the feeling of burning that book. I held the flame about an inch away from the surface for a few minutes before I finally gained the courage to proceed. I then set it on the ground in front of me and drank a glass of whisky as I watched my perfect future go up in flames. This experience was the opposite of everything I had done in my prior literary career. Instead of creating an immortalized perfect version of a person that previously existed, I was killing a perfect person that never existed. The contrasting nature of this experience convinced me that burning the story was the right thing to do, but I couldn't help missing my love. Rather than being a therapeutic way to forget my irrational hopes, I found my anger focused on resentment that my dreams had never come true. I was finally forced to deal with the sadness inside me. This despair only lingered a short while but was enough to have a lasting impact.

Although it was painful, burning my dream girl helped me to gather my thoughts and learn to fully accept my life. I had long believed that I had already overcome my emotions, but it wasn't until I wrote my dream girl into fiction that I fully understood them. I had yearned for this woman my entire life but hadn't met her until that point. I was thankful to have known her even if it was only in fiction. I was truly in love. It was like parents who claim to love their children before they are conceived. My girl was perfect, and the tragedy of her nonexistence was overshadowed by the quality of her character. I would have given up everything to live a moment in her book. I knew I would never hold her in my arms, but I struggled to keep her out of my mind. Burning the novel of my perfect woman turned out to be the only failed homicide of my career as she was impossible to keep in the grave. It is hard to recreate a story from scratch after it is lost. Something will inevitably be different when one attempts to rewrite a book, but this was not the case with Fantasia. Her entire story was written on my heart. I knew every inch of the object of my affection. She was part of my identity and never ventured far from my thoughts. About a month after burning her story, I got drunk one night and rewrote the entire book. I was amazed at the clarity of my memory and the efficiency with which the new edition was written. The second time through I didn't burn the book but simply printed a tiny single copy to be kept in my pocket at all times. I may not have found the girl of my dreams, but I found solace in the fact that I could still have dreams of my girl. I remained the same cynical man when it came to women in my reality, but I lived forever as a romantic in fiction. Rarely did I dwell long on my woman, but her presence was never far away. I loved Fantasia in the same tragic way that I loved my mom. It was a hopeful love for a person whom I will always yearn for but never know.

I guess for me this chapter wasn't as much about purity as it was about the pursuit. I killed Chastity because I admired her pursuit that had fallen short. My pursuit had also fallen short. As I revived Chastity's pursuit and the dreams she had lost in reality, she returned the favor by providing the catalyst to save my lost dreams as well. We were both vindicated in fiction. I had taken a year off from my life before I returned to kill Chastity, and I was once again reminded of the power of my words. I had forgotten how fulfilling writing could be and how much joy I could bring to the world. This time, I was fortunate enough to reap some of the rewards myself. I was freed from my chronic emptiness as a byproduct of saving Chastity from her own torment. Killing this virgin hooker was a success in every possible way. I was back from my year off and once again excited for life. This kill had reenergized my career, and I felt better than I had in years. Unfortunately, the world has a way of correcting for happiness, and I would soon be pulled back to reality when I met the characters for my next book.

CHAPTER 14

Child Rearing

When a man has been found guilty of rape, he should be castrated.
That would stop him pretty quick.

-Billy Graham

CHAPTER 14: Child Rearing

My next novel was one of the books I have ever written. My experience with Chastity had reenergized my work, and I was back on track as a writer. I had already accomplished more than I had expected, but I was also far from finished. My next project was *Child Rearing*. Although this was a novel, it basically functioned as a manual for raising children. As someone who loved kids, this book was a joy to publish and set an excellent example for society. I had helped raise Jamie for years and always wanted to write a book about the topic of molding a young child's life. My years of shaping Jamie's world became the foundation of *Child Rearing*. The only part of this project that wasn't enjoyable was meeting the main characters that would inspire the book. Of all the people I have written about, I had to do the most manipulation to make these characters inspirational. These men didn't deserve to die, but I had to make a judgment call. It is hard to decide the fate of people who don't deserve to exist but also don't deserve to die. I decided their spoken goals in life would be adequate for the basis of my story even if their reality was lacking. Although unnoticed by the critics, making these despicable creatures into loveable characters was the pinnacle of my literary ability. This novel was the most fictional of all my published work. It was a joy to kill these people, a joy to transform them into positive characters, and a joy to spread such a positive message to the world. The only negative was having to meet the characters.

The first main character from *Child Rearing* was father Matt Rasmussen. Father Rasmussen was a roman catholic priest at a parish in West Virginia. My first contact with Matt was through an email from a friend. The email contained a link to a CNN video of father Matt talking about his work with children. In his interview, father Matt was arguing that religion was the greatest force for good in the world. He then made the baseless claim that no secular charity could possibly compare to the work he was doing. When the host mentioned my well-known national charity and sighted the impressive number of students we had sent to college, father Matt refused to back down from his ridiculous original claim. I had gained a lot of respect from my appearances on the program, and, as a result, the host refused to ease up. He noted that the founder of my charity was an admitted Atheist. Father Matt defended his initial claim by throwing a few personal attacks at me. Matt claimed I was a bad example by making people believe they could be fulfilled without god. He then assured the host that the people working for my charity, and actually making the difference, were religious. Before I finished watching the interview, I got interrupted by a phone call. The call turned out to be from CNN asking if I would come on the show to respond. Since I was a bit annoyed, I made plans to appear on the program the next evening.

During my interview, it became clear the host wanted the show to be an argument of whether religious or secular people were a greater force for good in the world. I tried to avoid the issue and, instead, simply highlighted the accomplishments of our charity. When the host continued pestering me, I finally decided to take the bait and made the claim that no religious charity could ever accomplish more than mine. I guaranteed my charity would send more kids to college and put more money into youth education in the next year than all religious charities combined. This was a safe bet since my charity had grown to be much larger than its founder. As the years had passed, our success gave us extensive publicity, and this notoriety had caused many other successful individuals to come on board. We were now the largest children's charity in the world, and I knew it would be a daunting task for anyone to match our success. I told the host I would give one million dollars to a school of his choosing if I was proven wrong. I figured my money was safe but actually wanted to lose the bet. I wasn't likely to lose, but I hoped my comments would anger people into action. One of the most notable characteristics of the religious is their self-pride. My comments were harsh, and I knew criticizing religious people for their lack of virtue would anger them more than commenting on their vices. I was interested in seeing what type of response my comments would get and wondered what father Matt would say. I claimed religion was doing little to help society, but, in reality, I was just trying to trick them into doing more. I knew their pride would motivate them to prove their superiority which, in the end, would improve the world and hence justify my means. My comments were just a better way of motivating them than relying on their own good nature.

The religious community didn't disappoint. An entire movement started to emerge across multiple religions as people put aside their differences to show their collective superiority. I went back to my life but was pleased at the passion I had created with my brief comments. The religious world is inherently divided, but, during this year, they transcended their petty arguments and came together to help the children. All of these good deeds that I induced were done with the common goal of making me eat my words. The results proved my longtime suspicion that the best way to bring people together is to give them a common enemy. It is a shame people act the way they do, but I was proud that I understood human behavior enough to trick them into accidental altruism. Not only were religious people coming together for a good cause, but the workers in my own charity took my comments as a challenge as well. The charity I had begun ten years earlier expanded more in that one year than all previous years combined.

The only disappointment after my comments was that I never got to hear father Matt's response as he was hit with a major controversy two days later. A young boy in his parish had accused father Matt of rape. This story was nothing new for the church, and, as a result, it only briefly made headlines. It is perplexing how quickly the news stations will stop reporting tragedies when the storyline gets stale. As bad as father Matt's actions had been, people had heard the story before, and it wasn't particularly newsworthy in an industry increasingly driven by ratings. When I had first seen father Matt's interview, I was annoyed with his dismissal of our charity's work, but I mostly just smiled at his comments. I had no problem with someone striving to help more people than me. Once I heard about the reality of father Matt, I became extremely angry. Nothing repulses me more than the idea of a child suffering, and, as far as I was concerned, this man was the scum of society. He was a person people trusted to guide their children, and, instead, he committed those horrific acts. As with many religious messages, there was a massive disconnect between his inspirational words and repulsive actions. It reminded me of when I once heard that if Jesus was alive today there is one thing he wouldn't be and that is a christian. This statement perfectly represents what was wrong with this pastor. He wasn't living his message, and I decided it was time to fix that problem.

Once I decided to kill father Matt, I thought of all the other similar stories about pedophile priests. I started reading about some of them online and was absolutely appalled. This was a systemic problem that had plagued society for years. I remembered hearing about a similar child abuse case in our local parish when I was a kid. I'll never forget, about a week after the incident, I was waiting in a long line with "The Walker" at the church pancake breakfast when he leaned over to me and said, "The more these priests fondle little boys, the more people seem to show up." I had always laughed when I thought about that comment, but I wasn't laughing anymore. I read the endless stories and tried to comprehend the real scope of the problem. I had already decided to kill Matt, but that no longer seemed adequate in comparison to the huge numbers of documented cases. Sure, I could use Matt as a symbol, but I really felt a single priest wouldn't convey the systemic message I needed. I therefore decided to look through the records of convicted priests (convicted in the sense that there was sufficient evidence even though the church had protected them) and planned to choose a couple more characters to complete my story. I found no shortage of inexcusable cases similar to Matt's in which the priests somehow managed to get away without punishment for their atrocious actions.

After doing my research, I narrowed my list down to ten final priests. They all deserved to be punished for their actions, but that wasn't why I wanted to kill them. My decision to commit these murders would be purely driven by my desire to transform these men into the people they claimed to have been for society. Instead of being pedophile priests preying upon young children, they would become celibate protectors of our youth. As I looked through my list, three names jumped out along with father Matt. These four priests were from four different countries spanning three continents. Father Matt was American while father John was now located at a church in South America. Father Luke and Mark were from Germany and Ireland, respectively. When I saw the names amongst the list of ten, I knew these four murders would lead to an appropriate inspirational novel about four priests coming together to help the children of the world. What could be more fitting than Fathers Mathew, Mark, Luke, and John as my main characters? At that point, my entire mood changed from anger at these vile creatures to enjoyment in writing their story.

At first, I was undecided about the best way to go about my kills. The priests in my novel would be connected to one another so I wanted it to be clear these murders were not coincidental. I figured it would be best to kill them all at the same time to help ensure the connection was made. One problem I faced was geography. It wasn't going to be easy to travel such long distances in such a short period of time. As a result, I decided the timing would be less important than the manner in which these men were killed. What I lacked temporally, I would compensate for in symbolism. I had plenty of ideas for the kill so it was now just a matter of organizing the details to optimize my success. Since I was planning on killing the priests in order of their gospels, father Mathew was first on the list. I have commonly looked at my victims with sadness as I think about their lives, but, with father Matt, I only looked at him with disgust. It was such a pleasure looking forward to a murder without the burden of caring for the initial character. Unlike my previous work, I envied only what these priests would become and not what they were.

I am sure, by now, you have become fully aware of the four murders that provided the inspiration for *Child Rearing* as they garnered quite a bit of press. I can still remember the hype during the week before I killed father John when the whole world was put on watch for the final kill. As you know, I decided to kill each of the four priests on a date chosen based on the chapter and verse of the most famous line in their respective gospels. After the first three had been completed, all the news channels began to buzz with the FBI's theory that the murderer would strike again by killing a priest named John on March 16th. I remember watching the pride in the investigators faces as they were interviewed on television discussing how they had figured out the motivation behind the murder dates. However, what you don't know is that I actually left a copy of the bible on top of each corpse with the passage highlighted to make sure they would catch the symbolism. Either way, the entire world waited in anticipation for this final kill and was shocked when father John turned up dead a day early. I have always liked the fifteenth verse of the third chapter of John's gospel better than the sixteenth so I chose that for my final kill. The symbolism of this verse on top of a dead corpse filled my heart with laughter. I took pleasure in every aspect of these kills and have never enjoyed looking down on victims more than these four pedophiles. I was offended with what these trusted individuals had horrifically done to such helpless children. They weren't worthy of existence. The world deserved to have a better example from our clergy. My murder and book accomplished both of these things.

The book was considered an inspiration amongst a religious community in utter confusion about the motives of an Atheistic author. The murders were widely debated, and I was described by many people as a hero. Although the church expressed their extreme condemnation of the kills, the majority of the world was absent of sympathy for these hideous creatures. These were the only murders I ever committed that were described somewhat positively. In reality, every kill was for the benefit of the characters and the future readers. Nonetheless, it was fun listening to comparisons made between these four murders and the *Boondock Saints* movies. The only thing holding people back from fully embracing my actions was the graphic nature of the murders. Even people who seemed to care less about the priests expressed their disgust at the torture they had to face before their deaths. It was this torture that had provided the poetic justice they deserved. I enjoyed castrating each of the priests, but, most of all, I enjoyed cutting the dick off my first victim. I chose an especially dull knife for father Matt and cut slowly to make sure I had plenty of time to get his confession. After all, I did kill him in a confessional booth so I figured it wouldn't be appropriate not to ask him to confess. I made father Matt tell me about each of the victims he raped in detail, and, with each confession, I cut another piece off the end of his penis until it was all gone. When it was finally over, I gave him his final penance and smiled over his lifeless body. The murders of the other three priests followed the exact same process. I enjoyed every minute of these kills and wished I had time to murder every pedophile priest in the world. Unfortunately, it wasn't practical to waste my life cleaning up after the clergy so I had to be content with this small symbolic sample.

When I began to transform the priests into fiction, I started to realize how much I had previously relied upon the virtues of my characters. From a purely creative and artistic standpoint, this was the biggest writing challenge of my life. I worked hard to turn these priests into role models for children while retaining at least some of their previous characteristics. I became ever more discouraged as I started to realize the futility of this task. There was a point at which I actually thought I was going to fail to finish the novel, but a quote by Edgar Degas gave me the inspiration to finish. He once said, "Art is vice. You don't marry it legitimately, you rape it." Not only was this an insightful comment about the artistic process, but the thought of raping these rapist characters out of their characteristics struck me as being perfectly appropriate. I immediately returned to the book, and, this time, I completely stripped the priests of their previous identities. The only connection between the priests in fiction and reality was in name. The book justified another quote I read around that period by Giuseppe Garibaldi: "The priest is the personification of falsehood." When I finally finished the novel, the newly improved priests had been transformed into the force for good that they had claimed to be in reality. As the final line of *Child Rearing* correctly stated, "no one had touched more children than these four priests."

The response to *Child Rearing* was mixed. As far as the book was concerned, people loved the message. I explored themes of parenting and mentorship. The book convincingly conveyed the responsibility adults have to care for kids in our world while acknowledging the obvious challenges in being successful in this endeavor. We have come a long way in our knowledge of developmental psychology, but we are still faced with the difficult challenge of teaching our children to follow directions while also creating independent thinkers. I have always envied those who have mastered this difficult art or at least dedicated their lives in a noble attempt to do their best. At one point while I was writing the novel and struggling to turn the priests into admirable characters, I actually gave up and started writing an alternative book in which I simply gave the priests what they wanted. This was a dirty pornographic pedophile novel that fulfilled the priests' dreams of violating every child they could lure into the sacristy. I eventually found my inspiration to push forward with the original novel, and, once I heard the response to the book, I was thankful for my decision. The readers loved the devotion these priests showed to children in their communities and admired their discipline that manifested itself in their celibacy. I knew these priests had been tempted continuously since taking their vows, and I was glad to help. I figured it would be easier for the priests to remain celibate after I castrated them, and, sure enough, they never again broke their vows. Overall, the priests were immortalized as everything they were not in life, and the world was better for it.

The other half of the response to *Child Rearing* was the reaction to the murders. As I mentioned earlier, the response ranged from full support to outright rage. However, everyone seemed to agree on one thing: these murders were the work of a serial killer. Some people sympathized with the manner in which this killer identified his victims, but they still agreed he should be given this label. I was in shock when I heard the news describing me as a serial killer. I had only killed four people as far as they knew, and the only reason for the multiple victims was symbolic necessity. It wasn't as if I was out of control or continuing indefinitely although I was curious as to what the response would be if I moved forward. When most of society hears about a pedophile being killed, they think it is a good example of karma. I would be willing to bet their views would change if all of a sudden I did the same thing to a hundred or a thousand. I have always exploited the gaps in the moral vision of our society. There is no ethical change that occurs when one simply multiplies the same action. You could argue that the results are scaled accordingly, but there is no reason a noble action should be considered an immoral action simply because it is repeated extensively. I have also noticed the reverse to be true as well. Many people are repulsed when they see the face of a starving child and yet aren't nearly as distraught when reports of thousands of starving children are heard on the news. We seem to have evolved to care more about personal stories compared to a more society-driven moral code which could explain many of the problems we continually face in our world. I have always exploited these irrational gaps in morality as I attempt to improve my outlook. I understand my views are far from perfect, but I am proud of the fact that I have developed a rational moral code that has allowed me to function at a far superior level than the rest of society and hence bring so much joy to those around me.

I felt proud of the impact my writing was having on the world, but yet I couldn't seem to get away from this constant talk of serial killers. I had really enjoyed the last couple murders but wasn't a fan of the incorrect label I was given. People referred to me with numerous nicknames after the murders of the four priests, and I even turned into a bit of a cult hero for a while. The reason I was opposed to being called a serial killer was because it seemed so inaccurate. My disappointment ultimately caused me to become interested in what it meant to be a serial killer. I started noticing all kinds of serial killer movies, books, news stories, and documentaries. I starting watching these programs and was appalled by what I saw. The stories about real life serial killers were depressing. Every single story I heard described a dark killer with a scowl on his face. I also started to hate watching the news. The news was so depressing and gave murderers such a bad reputation. Hell, people made murderers out to be entirely bad people. It was like they thought we were politicians or something. The more stories I heard about different serial killers, the more I started to understand why there was such a negative stereotype associated with them. I couldn't find a single example of a serial killer that was a nice guy. I would only rarely see a killer with a smile, and, even then, it was always a sadistic smile. I thought about all the positive effects of my own murders and couldn't believe there weren't at least a couple other killers doing it for the right reason. It bothered me that there wasn't a single serial killer with a justifiable motive. The only serial killers that seemed to enjoy themselves were those who took pleasure in other people's pain. This could not be further from me. I was tormented by the pain of others and had dedicated my life to relieving as much suffering as possible. I continued to search for an example of a good serial killer but was unsuccessful. This was an awful group, and I was disappointed in what I saw. I had always been told how immoral the act of killing was and obviously was aware of the demonization of killers, but, as I had progressed in my own murders, I had always assumed that there had to be some well-intentioned serial killers somewhere in the world. Unfortunately, I was unable to find a single example so I did what I have always done when I find myself in a hopeless situation: I turned to fiction.

I began to comb through literary and cinematic history in search of another altruistic killer. I knew I could easily become a serial killer if I cared less about my victims. I could have written short essays to fulfill their dreams and then moved on to other victims, but that wasn't what I had done. Each of my victims had taken a considerable amount of time. They were killed in a specific way, and their stories were written into novels with attention to every detail of their dreams. I was not a serial killer, but I still wondered why there wasn't a mass murderer somewhere that was driven by his care for others. Since the serial killers I read about fell horrifically short, I hoped this good-hearted killer would emerge somewhere in my literature search. I soon found fiction to be nearly as depressing as reality. The fictional killers I continuously read about were merely caricatures of those on the news. For the most part, the motives of these murderers were no different. I had hoped to find a different breed of killer mixed in with the bad guys, but, instead, they were simply amplified versions of the terrible murderers from reality. There was nothing redeemable about these individuals, and I didn't find a single one to envy. The only serial killers with marginally positive motives were those that killed bad guys such as Dexter or the Boondock Saint type killers. Although these characters were billed as heroes, they did little to fulfill what I was looking for. They were driven by creating justice and punishing bad guys instead of being motivated by love. Although they may have provided a good service to the law, they didn't possess the virtue driven approach I was looking for nor did they have the same passion for their kills as I possessed. Revenge can never be as powerful a motive as love.

The other type of killer that appealed to me was the killer with a smile. I always felt happy after I murdered someone so I could relate to these types on some level. I disliked the grumpy killers most of all. I never understood the appeal of living a depressing life killing people with no sense of humor. Even worse, many of these killers would murder people and then commit suicide after. This was beyond my comprehension as I would never kill myself. No matter how hopelessly empty the future is, I always enjoy my present way too much to end my own life. Even if one was killing people to make a statement, it made no sense to commit suicide. I always wondered why they wouldn't want to stick around to defend their actions afterwards or at least try to get away. These sad looking serial killers that would cause so much destruction and then kill themselves were the worst example of murderers and, unfortunately, the most common. I guess that is why the happy killers always made me smile even when they were smiling for the wrong reasons. Two well-known examples of this type of killer are Hannibal Lector and the Joker. I had always enjoyed watching those movies with a killer that seemed to break the mold. I loved the intelligence behind Hannibal Lector and the enjoyment behind the Joker. The Joker may have lacked my compassion, but he shared my disgust at the structure of society and the extent to which we are controlled. I have similarly always wondered why everyone has to be so serious and loved watching the Joker wreak havoc on the world with a smile on his face. Of all the murderers in fiction, the Joker probably stood out as my favorite which only added to my depression since he wasn't even close to the type of killer I had set out looking for. It was hard for me to believe there wasn't a single example of a kindhearted killer.

After spending time learning about the disappointing killers in the world, I began to wish I could have been a serial killer to set an example for the rest. Not only were real life serial killers depressing, but people didn't even have a good example to look to in fiction. I had killed a few people in my life, but I wondered if I could really do it on a larger scale. The limited number of kills I had already committed had brought immeasurable joy into the world so I figured I would amplify those feelings if I tried out serial murder for a while. I made up my mind to at least try being a serial killer to see how it felt. Once this decision was made, my attention turned to what type of serial killer I would become. Up until this point, my murders were individualized for each victim. I was much more of a writer than a killer, and I wasn't really sure how I would translate my approach to this larger scale. I decided I needed to include both writing and murder into my work as a serial killer to stay true to who I was. Additionally, I knew I wanted the murders to be ironic and fun. Most serial killers followed some type of pattern, but they weren't really much fun. I was going to change all that.

My first attempt at becoming a serial killer was a lot of fun but ultimately failed in the long run. It wasn't that I didn't like the approach, but it wasn't perfect and eventually I figured out a better way to transform my previous style into a large scale operation. Sometimes it takes a couple attempts before we figure things out, and my first try at serial killing is a good example. Even though I ultimately abandoned this first method of serial murder, I still killed fifty-five people. I like to think I stopped at fifty-five because it is a common speed limit and hence a good place to slow down and think. In truth, I had actually only made fifty-five cookies in my initial batch so it was just a natural break in the process. This first attempt at being a serial killer ultimately failed because it was skewed too much towards humor without enough emphasis on writing. Although the kills were fun, they didn't have quite enough meaning for my victims, and I regretted the lack of writing involved in the process. I wanted to have fun but still fulfill dreams. My previous victims had won the lottery with their death and subsequent resurrections so I wanted to include both aspects in these murders. As a result, I had begun my first attempt at serial murder and became known as the Fortune Killer.

My method as a killer was simple but enjoyable. I murdered people at Chinese restaurants by poisoning their fortune cookies. I figured I would be called the Fortune Cookie Killer and was always surprised that the "Cookie" was left out. I guess some cop must have liked the poetic nature of me killing a victim's fortune as I stole their future away. Perhaps this misinterpretation of my work was one of the reasons I quickly moved on after killing fewer people than planned, but I definitely understood the mistake from a poetic standpoint. In reality, I wasn't really stealing people's fortunes, but, instead, I was giving them one final view of their dreams before they were killed. For my first batch, I made sixty poison fortune cookies (broke five in the process in case you are wondering where the discrepancy comes from). A specialized message was added to each cookie for the specific victim. The first few cookies included inspirational true messages about the victim's future that stayed true to my previous work such as "You will live forever in the hearts of those you love." However, I soon began to have a little more fun with the messages as I wrote things that made me laugh such as "You will soon overcome one of your biggest fears." I always found it humorous to think about the irony of someone reading their fortune and dreaming of their future when, in reality, they had but a moment to live. Eventually, I started having fun with the fortunes and wrote messages such as "Things aren't looking good" or "I wouldn't make any plans for the weekend." My favorite fortune was one I gave to an obese man that said, "Do you really think eating another cookie is a good idea? These things are going to kill you." I watched from two tables away as a scowl came over his face while he read the message before he scarfed down the cookie without heeding the warning. As his massive body hit the floor, I laughed to myself and was pleased that I had at least given him a chance to save himself.

Overall, the fortune cookie murders were extremely enjoyable but lacked the passion of my other work, and I felt the response I was getting wasn't enough. I think people appreciated the humor of the kills, but I didn't feel the single line fortunes were enough to justify continuing the method. I actually found myself writing a short story for each of my victims and published them in a weekly series on my website. Everyone seemed to love these short essays that basically contained the same inspirational stories of my novels shortened to a single page. This work seemed to ease my internal criticism with my fortune cookie kills, but

I hated how the writings were so separate from the murders. I wanted to find a better way to incorporate the stories with my fortune cookie approach but was ultimately unsuccessful because I only had one or two lines of text to work with. As a result, I scrapped the project after the first batch.

I learned an important lesson from my initial attempt at being a serial killer. I loved the humor that accompanied the fortune cookie murders but wanted the victim's stories to play a larger role. I didn't want to just be another serial killer with a gimmick but instead be truly unique. It hadn't been easy to come up with my first method, and I was worried I would be unable to incorporate inspirational writing and a humorous murder method into a single approach. Finally, the idea came to me, and it was as if my spirit was awoken from a long hibernation. I have always been amazed when a genius idea seems to drop into my head out of nowhere. I decided I would become a Cereal Killer. Once the idea entered my mind, the rest of the details seemed to flow steadily, and the entirety of my plan was quickly developed. I wanted to be a serial killer that people knew was having a good time and nothing could be better than a serial killer that only killed people while they were eating their cereal. My Cereal Killer plan had the humorous irony I was looking for in my murders but would also give me the opportunity to incorporate my short stories. The previous stories I had written after my cookie kills had gotten great reviews, and I had received numerous offers to write more. One of the most unique job offers was from Kellogg's asking me if I would be interested in writing inspirational stories to be featured on the backs of their cereal boxes. It was actually reading this letter that first put the idea of being a Cereal Killer into my mind. I immediately responded to the job offer, and, two weeks later, I signed a contract to write a series of inspirational stories for Kellogg's over the next year. My plan was to choose each victim ahead of time and write their happy ending on the back of their favorite cereal. I would be a Cereal Killer that only murdered his victims while they were eating their morning cereal and reading their perfect future on the back of the box. I now had everything I was looking for including a positive motive, a funny murder, and a happy ending in fiction. The table was set for the Cereal Killer to begin serving breakfast.

CHAPTER 15

The Cereal Killer

I believe the only way to reform people is to kill them.

-Carl Panzram

CHAPTER 15: The Cereal Killer

Some people cheer for the bad guy in a movie; I cheer for the bad guy on the news. I simply couldn't figure out how the news media could possibly butcher the story every single time I killed someone. At no time in my life was this injustice more prevalent than the period after my first few cereal kills. I knew I could be portrayed negatively for my murders, but I had no idea how bad the coverage would get. I was fine with people disagreeing with the murders, but it was as if they didn't get the joke at all.

It is hard to describe the complete incompetence of the reporting that surrounded the Cereal Killer. I was amazed when I first heard of the Breakfast Killer on the news. I couldn't believe my ears. I set the bar for society pretty low, but people always seem to go below and beyond my expectations. In my opinion, you would have to be an absolute idiot to hear about six people murdered while eating their morning cereal and not get the joke. I thought about writing a note to the news networks telling them to immediately fire whoever came up with the Breakfast Killer nickname. However, I soon learned my anger was misplaced when the author of this nickname arrived at my door.

I was on one of my usual trips to visit Jamie when my best friend walked in. Derbe had his usual look of distress across his face, but it soon went away as I threw him a beer and our favorite young man ran up to give him a hug. We heard all about Jamie's most recent success in school, football, and hockey. Derbe and I unloaded endless praise on Jamie, and we could see the blush on his face as his humility revealed itself. We didn't let him off the hook and made him tell us every single one of his accomplishments. I was so proud of that young man sitting in front of us and could see the same pride in Derbe. Jamie was truly a remarkable person. After a nice visit, Angela took Jamie to his hockey game while Derbe and I following close behind. Once we were alone, Derbe and I had a nice discussion about Jamie's future and remembered how exciting it was when we were his age. The stress was absent from Derbe's face as he talked about Jamie. It wasn't until we were in the stands at the hockey game and finished our conversation about Jamie that I had the chance to ask my friend about his own life. The look of concern returned as he told me about his stress at work. He said the majority of his time was now spent on federal cases, and the most recent case was driving him crazy. I wondered if he was perhaps talking about my recent cereal kills but didn't press him for information and just let him continue to vent. I quickly found out my suspicions were correct. He described a new serial killer that murdered people in the mornings and said he had started calling him the Breakfast Killer. I had suspected that Derbe may have been on the case, but it didn't occur to me that he could have been the one to ruin the joke by naming me the Breakfast Killer. I couldn't believe my ears. I tried to make him clarify by asking why the murderer referred to himself as the Breakfast Killer, but Derbe corrected me and said it was just a name he had come up with that seemed to stick. I knew Derbe was a smart person, but this was fuckin stupid. I have never been more upset with him in my life, but yet I was forced to be silent as he continued to describe the investigation.

I was amazed how misunderstood the Cereal Killer was. The murders were conducted by poisoning the cereal inside specific boxes that I would give the victims, but yet they still couldn't seem to connect the murders with cereal. As frustrating as it was to be mislabeled in my work, it was also comforting to hear how far off the agents were. Derbe described their psychological profile of a demented killer and their plans to catch him. I loved my friend, but I knew he was totally outmatched in his chase. They were looking left while I was going write. The happy endings of the victims weren't even noticed on the back of the cereal boxes. I had expected the cops would assume the killer read the stories and chose victims to fit them rather than writing the stories to fit specific victims as was really the case. As it turns out, they missed the connection altogether which made getting away with these murders much easier than expected. I have always been meticulous in covering my tracks, but, looking back, I wonder if my hours of stalking each victim and covering every angle of the murders were really just a waste of time. Either way, I figured it was better to be safe than in jail so I went a bit overboard on the planning. After spending an hour talking to Derbe about the Breakfast Killer, we returned to watching the hockey game and enjoying the rest of the night with Jamie.

When I returned from visiting my friends in Traverse City, my immediate goal was to find a way to get my name changed from the Breakfast Killer to the Cereal Killer. I figured the best way to go about this would be to kill a couple people while they were eating cereal in the evening. Three of my next six cereal kills were thus performed at night, and I hoped Derbe would pick up the trail and correct his mistake. At first, nothing changed as the news reported the Breakfast Killer was changing the time of his murders out of fear of being caught. I listened to the report and just rolled my eyes. From that point on, I made sure to choose victims eating cereal at a table with others eating different breakfast foods. The change made it more difficult to isolate my victims, but it was ultimately worth it to shed light on the fact that only people eating cereal were killed while those eating eggs were left untouched. The fact that the cereal itself was poisoned seemed extremely obvious to me, and I just hoped someone would soon pick up on the symbolism. My attempts to correct my mislabeling once again went unheard. I was extremely frustrated and finally said the hell with it. I decided to just call Derbe and tell him directly. After exchanging pleasantries with my friend for a few minutes, I transitioned the conversation to his work and waited until he brought up the Breakfast Killer. I listened patiently as he vented about his frustration chasing down this murderer and did my best to console him. I assured him that he was doing all he could and told him not to be so hard on himself. Finally, I told him that it sounded like a Cereal Killer to me. Derbe responded that it was obviously a serial killer based on the patterns of the Breakfast Murders. I then told him I meant the term as in the breakfast food and told him straight up that he didn't sound like a fuckin Breakfast Killer as much as a true Cereal Killer. There was a silence on the end of the phone as I could tell

Derbe was thinking it over, and, finally, I heard him laugh. He said it hadn't even crossed his mind. When Derbe laughed, it made my day. Finally, someone else got the joke. Even though he quickly returned to his disgusted attitude towards the killer, his initial reaction cheered me up and betrayed a part of him that he wouldn't show again. After my conversation with Derbe, I continued with my murders and started having a lot more fun. Two weeks later, the Cereal Killer was correctly identified to the public, and people were finally able to appreciate the joke. The dialogue changed from a debate on the motive behind the Breakfast Killer to talk about catching a man who seemed to be killing purely for fun. I was pleased with this discussion because it showed the world finally understood at least part of the motive and started to realize how difficult it would be to catch this murderer. It is hard to predict where a murderer will strike next when he appears to be choosing victims at random. The only noticeable similarity to the public was that the victims all ate cereal. In reality, my murders were further specialized to the same type of admirable characters I had previously targeted with the added constraint of picking futures that could be completed in a single page on the back of a cereal box.

After approximately five months of cereal murder, I had killed over eighty people. I mildly resented the fact that no one noticed the stories about the victims' happy endings on the back of the cereal boxes. This was the one time the public could have been given a glimpse into the true value of my literature. I did my best to make my next few stories as obviously about the victims as possible. I even attempted to localize the stories to the region where the victim was killed, but it was no use. The stories continued to go unnoticed so I simply gave up on my attempt at transparency. I knew I could probably call Derbe and simply tell him directly again, but, this time, the risk seemed too large. I rarely showed interest in his work unless he initiated the conversation, and I didn't want to seem too involved. Once I accepted the fact that the stories weren't going to be noticed, I began to care a little less about the detailed connections to my characters which allowed me to have much more freedom with my writing. As usual, my favorite stories were the ones about kids. One story about a young singer with a beautiful voice got a five star review. I wish the world could have known that deaf girl from New Hampshire whose murder provided the inspiration. I continued these ironic kills for the remainder of my time as a Cereal Killer. I got so smooth with my process that I progressed almost effortlessly through the murders and even started killing multiple people for a single story in instances where I could include more than one character on the back of a single cereal box.

In addition to the fun I was having with my murders, I was also enjoying the response to my stories. I was being paid a large sum of money for a minimal amount of writing. People would constantly express their eagerness to read my next story on their cereal box each week, and I really started settling into my life as a Cereal Killer. Even though I missed the intimacy of writing novels, I loved how many different lives I could now touch. My life constantly fluctuated between hearing people praise my writing and listening to the news chastising the

Cereal Killer. There was a long period in which I dominated the headlines, and the entire society seemed focused on my murders. Every day, there seemed to be a new expert on some talk show discussing their opinion. The vast majority of these supposed experts were completely off base in their assessment. I loved hearing them quote other serial killers as a means to understand me which made no sense since I was the complete opposite of these boring, heartless murderers. However, I did like a select few of the quotes such as the David Berkowitz statement, "I didn't want to hurt them, I only wanted to kill them," or the Albert DeSalvo quote, "It wasn't as dark and scary as it sounds. I had a lot of fun. Killing somebody's a funny experience." These and a few other quotes seemed to capture the spirit of what I was doing, but only after I would twist the meaning to fit my own approach. In my case, I was actually doing something even better than not hurting people, I was healing them. I was curing the disease of degenerating life they were suffering from and giving them a positive diagnosis for the future. In response to Albert, I can only say that I had a lot of fun as well, but, in my case, I deserved to have fun. Doing a good dead should always be enjoyable, and it definitely was. Of all the serial killer experts interviewed on television, the most memorable was Pat Brown. I was actually visiting Derbe when I watched the interview which is probably the reason I remember the episode so vividly. Derbe was obviously interested in Pat's assessment and kept commenting on similarities and differences between her statements and the actual investigation. There are a couple lines that stick out in my memory such as "All serial killers want to win. They choose victims they can kill successfully" and "There are two kinds of serial killers as far as the victim is concerned: the kind that you don't see before they pounce on you and the kind you see and don't expect to pounce on you." I liked both of these lines because I was the kind of serial killer who you wouldn't expect to pounce but also would never be seen coming. Pat's statement simply showed how superior I was to the average killer and demonstrated why I could pick any victim I wanted. I also chose victims that I could kill successfully. The difference was that I was good enough to kill anyone. These comments brought a smile to my face, but the highlight of the interview was when she said, "We assume people we know can't be serial killers." When we heard that line, Derbe and I turned to look at each other awkwardly and then burst out laughing. I asked him if he was a serial killer and told him I just thought it was safe to check. After we joked back and forth a bit, he got serious and told me he agreed with Pat's comment which was why he never assumed anyone was innocent and followed every lead. We then moved on with our evening and didn't waste another moment talking about murder.

After spending a year as a Cereal Killer, I felt unstoppable. I had written fifty stories and killed a total of ninety-seven people while they ate breakfast and read their dreams on the back of the box. I missed writing longer stories and being more invested in my characters but couldn't imagine ever stopping. I was so efficient that it seemed selfish to quit. My yearlong writing contract had just finished, and I had a meeting scheduled to discuss a renewal. I decided I would sign on for at least one more year. I knew they would be thrilled to have me back since there had been such an outpouring of positivity in response to my stories. To my surprise, the meeting turned out to be the exact opposite of what I had expected. My plan was to act a bit unsure until they offered a little extra money at which point I would sign the contract. It turned out they had asked to meet with me not to offer another contract but rather to explain that they were basically firing me. I was immediately taken aback by their comments, but I could see from their apologetic nature that they felt bad about losing me. They went on to tell me that my writing was the only upside to the past year, but their sales had plummeted so much as a result of the Cereal Killer that they simply couldn't afford to pay that kind of money anymore. I had heard that cereal companies had lost business from people fearing to eat cereal, but it hadn't occurred to me that my job might be on the chopping block. I had plenty of money so it obviously wasn't a financial problem, but I knew I would no longer be able to continue as a Cereal Killer without my writing. It was frustrating to be forced to stop. I hated being controlled by society. This was just another example of a time in my life when I was unable to make my own decision. I have always hated the control economics has over our decisions. I had planned to continue for at least another year, but, in the end, the Cereal Killer was stopped by the invisible hand of the free market.

CHAPTER 16

Born Again

Question Y.

-The Walker

CHAPTER 16: Born Again

Once the economy accomplished what Derbe had failed to achieve, I came to accept the fact that the Cereal Killer's time was over. In a way, I was happy to be moving on from that phase of my life. I liked the frequency with which I could kill people as a Cereal Killer, but my real legacy was as a novelist. I loved the connection I had with my earliest characters and decided I would only write again when I was truly inspired. There was no longer a reason for me to write unless my passion was completely aroused. If I never wrote another sentence, I would have been content with my career. Nonetheless, I was hoping to be truly inspired once again. There was something special about meeting a person worthy of writing about. Many of my victims in the past year had to be forced into their roles simply because I liked one aspect of their dreams or thought they would make a funny or ironic story. That part of me was in the past. My focus was now completely on finding the next novel that would once again touch the hearts of my readers. I wanted to return to more admirable murders and more inspirational stories.

As I began to decompress from my hectic period of mass murder, I fell into a peculiar emotional state. I spent most of my time reflecting on life and took as many trips as I could to visit my family in Minnesota and my friends in Traverse City. On all these trips, I found myself awake late into the nights staring up at the stars contemplating questions that no mortal man should torment himself with. I tried to round up the energy to write but continuously found myself drifting into a reflective leisure. It became clear that I was simply not in the right emotional state to begin my next project. It was the middle of winter in Michigan, and I finally decided I might as well be sitting around thinking about life in a more pleasant location so I bought a one way ticket to visit one of my favorite places in Greece.

My room in Greece overlooked a scenic landscape with the vast ocean extending out from my window. I spent four or five hours a day just sitting in my chair looking out over the gorgeous view in silence. The rest of my time was spent walking slowly along the city streets and having quiet dinners alone with my thoughts. I would occasionally pick up a cute woman that passed into my life, but these evenings were less frequent than usual and primarily involved deep conversation rather than deep penetration. I always kept in touch with my loved ones, but, as usual, they didn't know where I was. I think they liked the mystery of my whereabouts, and it always made them smile to know I could be anywhere in the world. I had traveled extensively but always seemed to return to a few favorite places. I loved to vacation, but this trip felt different. I found a sense of peace that I had never experienced before. It occurred to me that I could retire at that moment and never return. There was really nothing stopping me from casually drifting off into the twilight of my life. I was still young to be thinking about retirement, but I didn't feel there was anything left for me in society. I got very close to following through on this retirement idea, but something told me it wasn't quite time. I convinced myself my story wasn't finished but made an internal promise that I would soon return to my quiet happy ending. As a reward for the good I had done for others, I would give myself many years of quiet bliss to end my life. I never wanted to go out in a blaze of glory but instead saw myself simply disappearing into a happy haze. The world would never know what happened to me. I knew I deserved this ending, but I also knew my work was not yet complete. I don't know why I felt as if I had unfinished business, but maybe it was just the author inside me that wouldn't allow me to leave until my story was properly concluded.

I didn't know what I was returning for, but I followed my heart away from my solitude after a couple months in paradise. Instead of returning home immediately, I took a detour to Italy that turned out to last for almost four months. Initially, I was only planning to visit Rome for a couple days, but I was still stuck in a reflective mood and decided to wander around a bit longer. After two weeks of travelling aimlessly, I found myself in a unique town in northern Italy. It was a beautiful place with interesting people of all ages. I got along with two people in particular right from the start. One was a retired college philosophy professor and the other was a semi-retired priest. The retired philosopher was a woman named Anne who had taught in Ireland for many years before retiring to this town with her best friend, Peter, the aforementioned priest. There was a strange connection between these old friends that I instantly appreciated. They often felt like an old married couple in spite of the fact that they were never romantically together to my knowledge. It was obvious they enjoyed finally having the companionship that they had probably craved their entire lives. I immediately connected with these two and loved joining their conversations. They spent every day sitting around talking philosophy which fit my current mood perfectly. My return home was put on hold as I started spending every day with my new friends.

I have often been critical of the feeble philosophical views of many priests, but father Peter was different. Peter had an overwhelming theological curiosity which was complemented nicely by Anne's deistic nature. Both of them loved when I quoted Denis Diderot as saying "The philosopher has never killed any priests, whereas the priest has killed a great many philosophers." Anne constantly would repeat that line to heckle Peter which would just make him smile. He was a different type of preacher that spoke of scripture with hope. Peter never portrayed the arrogance of claiming to know answers to the imponderable questions of the universe that is often seen on the pulpit. Instead, Peter was what I had always wanted from a priest. He was a man of hope who spent his life searching for a connection between the wonders of the world and his optimistic theology. Father Peter was in a constant struggle between his desire to fully embrace scripture and his acknowledgement of the limitations to our minds. This man would have been a brilliant example of what religion should be if his natural scientific inquiries didn't contradict many of the things he was fighting so strongly to believe. Fortunately, Peter had Anne in his life to prevent him from losing his natural curiosity. Anne was a prototypical example of an Atheistic person that had converted to Deism purely as a result of her hopeful nature.

Anne often expressed the reasons why she thought it was irrational to believe in god, but yet her wonderment in the intricacies of the universe kept her religious journey alive. Anne worshiped the beauty she saw all around her. She was a true follower of the type of faith Einstein professed when he said he believed in Spinoza's god and described himself as "a deeply religious nonbeliever which is a somewhat new kind of religion." Anne might have clashed with other members of the clergy, but not with Peter who seemed fascinated with everything about her. Most religious people are a combination of narcissism and optimism. I am a combination of altruism and pessimism. Peter and Anne fell somewhere between the extremes. There are many positions on the religious spectrum from deeply religious radicals to staunchly pessimistic Atheists like me, but, in my opinion, the high point falls somewhere around these two old friends. There is little doubt the evidence supports the worldview on my end of the spectrum, but this position is much harder to admire. There is very little beauty in being right. The Atheist is forced to sacrifice fiction for truth and, for that reason, falls short of the Deist. A Deist walks the fine line between rationality and hope. I would often win the discussions with Anne and Peter, but my victories would be vacuous. I loved contemplating the vastness of the universe that extended around us which was exactly what Anne's religious view was. Deism is Atheism plus poetry. The difference between Anne and me was simply that, although we shared an appreciation for the elegance of the world, I couldn't bring this passion into my rational religious views. Peter had the same problem from the other side. In the same way I wouldn't allow my love of the unknowns in the universe to affect my judgment, Peter wouldn't allow the knowledge of the universe to affect his religion. When Peter's faith was shaken, his religion remained intact.

As my time in Italy progressed, I started to enjoy the new lifestyle I was living. Anne and Peter had such a close friendship, and I was thankful to be adopted into their inner circle. The three of us spent leisurely days in conversation, and I was even more relaxed than I had been during the earlier part of my long vacation. The days of living with a mountain of stress on my shoulders seemed like a lifetime ago. There were entire weeks during my time in Italy that I did nothing except wander aimlessly through town admiring the world as it moved around me. Peter and Anne provided an excellent escape from this solitude whenever I needed it. The three of us had a unique dynamic and were much more ideologically aligned than our religious labels might suggest. Although we spent time arguing about minor disagreements and large conclusions, these things paled in comparison to our shared love of the beauty surrounding us. I admired the depth of thought and gentle nature of my two friends. We spent more time laughing than arguing and even the arguments were conducted on a backdrop of smiles. There was no animosity in our disagreements and our love for one another was never threatened. The three of us would often find ourselves dwelling for entire days on questions we knew were impossible to answer. We were usually very close in our opinions as well as our passion for asking the questions. However, whenever the topic was finished, we would each retreat to our respective beliefs as our agreements would do little to change our overall worldview. I loved contemplating things such as space, eternity, or the notion of infinity itself. All of these topics are hard for a human mind to comprehend and hence led to many interesting conversations. I could never accept a belief that the universe could be either infinite or discrete. The thought of coming to the edge of the universe seemed idiotic to me. There must be something on the other end of that boundary. On the same token, the notion that the universe could be infinite in nature seemed equally ridiculous. Perhaps there is an answer to these questions, but I am limited by my four dimensional mind and severely myopic view of the universe. I have always been tormented by these types of questions, but it is an enjoyable torment. I get a kind of intellectually sadistic pleasure from being stuck on the edge of my mental limits, and it was fun to share this with Anne and Peter. I wish more religious discussions addressed these interesting questions instead of repeating ancient mythologies too ridiculous to even be considered good fiction any longer. We should spend our Sunday mornings asking questions that invoke thought instead of preaching answers. Someone should write a scripture that consists purely of interesting questions with no answers because the subject matter is beyond our comprehension. This is the type of religion I experienced during my time in Italy, and it was an absolute pleasure. Much of the philosophy that arose out of these conversations was used to provide the foundation of *Born Again* especially when Father Peter embarked on his search for truth in the first two thirds of the novel.

My time in Italy had lasted longer than expected, and I once again felt as if I might not return. I was comfortable living my quiet life away from the world. The desire to return to writing and give my story an adequate conclusion was still present, but I was emotionally inclined to exchange it for the comfortable retirement I was now experiencing. No one could have ever found me hidden away from the world, and I knew I could find the same sense of anonymous comfort in numerous other places. I was completely on the fence about my future and lived each day for that day and left the future to the future. The nice thing about the future is that one doesn't have to make it happen. The future will come no matter what we do so I simply sat back and waited.

As always seems to be the case, the future arrived faster than expected. There had been many times when I had searched for victims to kill, but this time the roles were reversed as my victim searched for me. It all started one evening when I arrived for dinner at Peter's house. I immediately knew something was wrong when I saw the lights off. I walked over to the neighbor's and soon learned Peter had suffered a seizure. When I arrived at the hospital, I got a big hug from Anne. The doctors soon informed us they were moving Peter to a hospital in Rome more equipped to take care of him. I accompanied Anne to Rome where we found out that Peter had a rare type of brain tumor and the outlook was grim. When I went with Anne to see Peter, we found him in good spirits as he spent more time consoling us than vice versa.

Over the next month, I spent as much time as possible with my two friends while I tried to find a doctor capable of saving Peter. That first seizure was only a small precursor to what he was now going through. Peter was having multiple agonizing seizures every day, and they were increasing in both pain and duration. It was hard to watch. When Peter was able to talk, I could see the strength of his character emerge as he tried to hide his pain. Even though he made a valiant effort, Anne and I were tormented by Peter's fate and wished he could find comfort in his final days. Peter talked increasingly of death and an afterlife during this time, and I found myself wishing there was a heaven for this deserving man. More importantly, and more realistically, I simply hoped he would find peace in his own belief. To my disappointment, Peter's last days did not give him the comfort he was searching for but, instead, led him to confess his disbelief. Peter was a man of hope, but, in the end, he simply couldn't believe the story he preached. I had spent the last few months arguing for my Atheistic worldview, and I have never been sadder to have won an argument. I wished Peter could have been rewarded for his long struggle to convince himself that his faith was justified. More than anything, Peter had wanted to be a good christian, but he was tormented by his inability to consolidate this desire with the facts of the world. I looked down at my friend in pity as he suffered in his hospital bed. Anne's agony was just as heartbreaking as Peter's pain. After another month, Peter's condition was so bad that we rarely got a glimpse of the man we loved. A week before he died, Peter struggled to speak and told Anne he wanted to go home. We honored Peter's last request and brought his hospital bed back to his house to spend his final days in the place he loved.

When we moved Peter home, I hired a couple nurses and a doctor, but, for the most part, Anne and I took care of our friend. Peter's condition was terminal. The doctor told me the pain and seizures were only going to get worse, but it was likely he could still survive a considerable amount of time. It is a strange feeling to hear that someone you love isn't going to die and have that sadden you. All I wanted was for Peter's pain to cease. Peter had lived a loving life, and I decided to tell his story. There was no doubt how Peter's happy ending would manifest itself in fiction. I would give Peter a comfortable ending in which he would find the true belief he had coveted his entire life. Instead of a surprise trip to a hospital in Rome, Peter would make a trip to Vatican City where his faith would be reborn at the climax of the story. Peter's story did become my next novel, *Born Again*, but it wasn't until I spoke to Anne that I decided to kill Peter. It was the third day after moving Peter home when Anne came to me in tears. I comforted her as best I could but realized this wasn't the usual grief she had been experiencing. Anne was hysterical and kept saying that she couldn't do it. It took me a long time to get the entire story, but I eventually found out that Peter had asked her to kill him. Anne loved Peter with all her heart, and I could see how much his request had broken her. She couldn't bear to see Peter die while, at the same time, she couldn't bear watching him live. Anne told me she had agreed to end Peter's life, but then she simply couldn't bring herself to go through with it when the moment arrived. I told her I understood what she was going through and felt as bad as she did about Peter's predicament. Finally, Anne asked me the question I knew was coming. She asked me to kill her best friend. I answered Anne by saying I didn't know if I could do it either, but she continued to beg me and convinced me to talk to Peter.

I will never forget the horrific sight of walking into Peter's room. He was in severe pain, and I was surprised he recognized me. His seizures had grown much worse, and I knew killing him was the right thing to do. Not only would I soon be giving him the ending he wanted, but I would be getting rid of the continuous pain he was currently facing. Peter was the perfect example of the altruistic nature of my murders. I constantly removed people from their excruciating lives but never before had one of my victims been in such obvious physical pain. I held Peter's hand, and he looked up at me with a hopeless expression on his face. He forced out a few words asking me to let him die. I told him we would take care of him and asked Anne to give him his last rights. It was a unique sight to see an Atheist and a Deist giving a final blessing to a christian priest. Once Anne finished, I gave Peter a sedative to put him to sleep and then suffocated him until he was no longer breathing. This Kevorkianic murder brought me much needed comfort, and there was relief in Anne's face as well. She promised she wouldn't tell anybody I had killed Peter, but I told her that I knew it was the right thing to do and would have done it even if I knew I would be caught. I laughed inside as I thought about Anne's concern. Of all my murders, I am pretty sure this would have been the easiest one to get caught committing. The world wouldn't blink an eye at two passionate friends' final act of mercy towards this dying priest.

During the two weeks following Peter's death, I started to compile his story. Once Anne was doing well, I decided it was best for me to finally head home. It had been a long time since I had written a story about a person I loved, and it felt phenomenal. I always enjoy writing, but there is a different level of satisfaction writing about certain characters that hold a special place in the author's heart. I gave Peter a perfect ending to fit his character. He spent his whole life hunting for god which is exactly what he was rewarded with. Peter wanted to believe his faith but constantly struggled with it in life. Peter's hope led him to become a religious man, but he never became a truly faithful man. As Oscar Wilde said, "Religion is the fashionable substitute for belief." Peter exactly fit this description as he simply couldn't believe his own religion when confronted with the facts. In the novel, he finally found God at the end of his long journey. Instead of ending with the terrible trip to Rome of his reality, Peter's story ended with a trip to the Vatican where his religious and scientific worldviews finally aligned. I decided to name the book *Born Again*. The title was not only perfect for the new strength of faith I gave to Peter in fiction, but it was also a perfect title for my books in general. The title *Born Again* was exactly what I had given to each of my characters after I had killed them. Every time I look at this book on the shelf next to my other characters, it brightens my day as I think of the appropriateness of that title.

When *Born Again* was published, I once again found myself in a crossfire of praise and criticism. It is always fun listening to people I disagree with use my novels to justify their false beliefs. I have even had people quote my own novel to me to support their arguments without knowing that I was actually the one who wrote *Born Again*. Many Atheists chastised me for writing a book of faith, but they simply didn't realize that the book wasn't about my beliefs. The book was about comforting a suffering friend. I didn't mind writing a book about Peter going to heaven because that's what I wanted for him. I think it is silly to believe heaven exists, but that is no reason to prevent me from creating it in fiction. I may have been extremely criticized for writing the modern christian novel, but that was what my character had desired so I made this baseless fantasy into a reality. What my critics didn't understand is that religion isn't wrong, it's simply fiction.

When I returned to America, I found myself happier than I had been in a long time. I moved into the basement at Angela's house and totally immersed myself in Jamie's life. I was in touch with him weekly while I was gone, but it still felt incredible to be with him every day. Jamie was living the life I designed for him, and I took such pride in the person he had become. It was also comforting to spend so much time with my family now that I was back. There was nothing that meant more to my life than the family I loved, and I am so appreciative of this time. The people I loved were the only thing important to me now. I knew I would soon be ready to retire to some far end of the earth, and I wanted to soak in every last moment with those I loved. Jamie was now a teenager and seemed like such a grown up as I talked to him. At the same time, I could still picture him in Mike's arms as a baby. Every time he smiled, it reminded me of my best friend that I had lost years ago. I missed Mike immensely. I wished he could have seen what an amazing young man Jamie had become, but I knew that was impossible. Jamie was so much like his parents, and his potential was limitless. He had become one of the best athletes in the region, but yet I had no idea which path he would choose for his future. He was a gentle young man whose greatest quality was in his nature itself.

The next year of my life revolved primarily around Jamie, Angela, and the rest of my family. I didn't have much desire to travel during this period since I soon planned to retire and would have the rest of my life to wander around the globe. Jamie was still young, but he was getting increasingly interested in his future so I planned a few college trips to give him a taste of what his life might hold. I had connections at all of the top universities in the country so I had Jamie make a list of ten schools he was interested in and planned to take him the following summer. Derbe said he would join us on the trips as long as it fit his schedule. Jamie was excited to see the schools but was probably even more excited for the vacations themselves. It made me smile to see his excitement as he truly deserved to be rewarded for his hard work. Jamie was so dedicated to achieving his goals, and it was rewarding to be such a large part of his life. It was also nice to be close to Derbe again. We stayed best friends over the years, but it is always better when you live in the same area. Derbe had become extremely successful in his work. I loved hearing about the different cases he was working on and was impressed with all the arrests he had made. We are all fortunate to have people like Derbe protecting us. Detective Felidae stood for justice above all, and his life's work made the world a better place. Every once in a while, I would hear him complain about a couple killers he wished he could have caught, and it would make me smile when he mentioned the Cereal Killer. Derbe told me it was just a matter of time before the Cereal Killer struck again, and he planned to catch him when he did. I knew the Cereal Killer would never murder another person, but I didn't bother to tell my friend. Another surprise during one of my conversations with Derbe was when he told me he was investigating Mike's murder. I looked at him in shock as he described all the time he had put into finding Mike's killer over the past years. I asked him why he never told me before, but he said it was something he hadn't told anyone. It was surprising to hear how many hours Derbe had spent investigating Mike's death. He had used his federal access to organize all the evidence from the initial police report. Derbe had started investigating Mike's murder illegally, but, eventually, he had officially reopened the case as his stature as an investigator had grown. Derbe told me he had a profile on every individual from the bar that night (other than Angela and me) with every aspect of their lives prior to and after Mike's murder included in his report. For over ten years, Derbe had been tracking these people hoping some clue would surface and reveal the guilty person.

I was shocked to hear about Derbe's investigation into Mike's murder. I knew Mike's death was the primary force that drove Derbe away from medicine and caused him to become a detective, but I had no idea how much it had consumed him since. Derbe was a great man with a nice life, but I now saw how disappointed he was with the way things had ended up. Derbe's life was the opposite of Mike's as he never had the opportunity for his dreams to become his story. Derbe was haunted by the fact that he had been unable to catch Mike's killer and spent his whole life fighting this feeling. If there was ever a risk of my regretting killing Mike, Derbe's life pushed that thought out of my head. I could see the stress he was under and how too many years on this earth had tarnished the young man I had once known. As our conversation about Mike's murderer turned to reflection about our old friend, Derbe told me something I will never forget. He told me his job was hard on him because he had to see all the suffering in the world. He then said, "Looking back, I really think Mike was lucky. He lived a perfect life." Although it was a small comment in the middle of a long conversation, Derbe's words lifted my spirit. It was a moment in life where a simple comment can give the positive reinforcement that reminds you why you spend so much time working towards your goals. I hated to see Derbe going through the agony he was facing, but I knew there was no remedy. He had simply lived too long and was feeling the natural effects of time. When we reach a certain age and finally gain a clear view of the world, we are all forced to realize that everyone is either depressed or delusional. Unfortunately for Derbe, he had lived too long to be delusional anymore. Mike was killed, but Derbe was alive. Mike had survived, but Derbe had departed.

CHAPTER 17

Publish or Perish

May you live all the days of your life.

-Jonathan Swift

CHAPTER 17: *Publish or Perish*

Mike was ever-present in my mind as Jamie's summer college trips approached. Jamie's excitement was contagious and reminded me how it felt to be a young man waiting to see the world for the first time. I had taken Jamie on vacation before, but things were different now. He was fifteen years old and had a growing curiosity that I admired. I remembered having that same feeling when I was Jamie's age. Jamie was optimistic about his future and the world he lived in. Nothing seemed impossible to that young man, and I could feel the energy radiating from him as he talked about the schools we were going to see. Although Jamie was still too young for official athletic visits, he had plans to meet with a few coaches during our trips, and it reminded me of my own college recruiting visits. Jamie had the option of playing Division 1 hockey, football, or baseball and seemed to revel in the thought of being a multiple sport college athlete. Jamie was a young man that never lacked ambition. I couldn't wait for the summer to arrive and was thrilled that Derbe was able to free up enough time to join us on our first trip. I planned a ten day vacation to the University of Washington, Stanford University, and the University of Texas that included three days of camping at the Grand Canyon.

Our trip was even better than expected. Derbe and I have been on many vacations together, but none were as special as that trip with Jamie. We had fun watching him think about his future and were constantly telling him how proud we were. There was no doubt Mike's presence was everywhere during that trip. Derbe and I reflected on our own college days and told countless stories about Jamie's fabulous father. Jamie always wanted to hear about his dad, and the sentimental nature of this vacation kept Mike present at all times. It was pleasing to see how much Jamie had gotten to know his father over the years. I loved watching his face as he talked with pride about Mike. On our visit to Stanford, we took a short detour to visit the grave of Mike's dad, Jamie's grandfather, who had moved to California after his divorce. As I looked at this grave, I couldn't help but pity the man buried beneath. Jamie had never known his grandfather, but I knew we were standing over a man who had lived far too long. There were weeds covering his tombstone and not a single flower in sight. What a contrast it was to Mike's gravestone that was well taken care of and visited often by those who missed him. As we left the cemetery, Jamie asked me about his grandfather. He had heard a small part of the story from his mother but wanted a more honest answer. I told him the truth. His grandpa was simply human and made some mistakes that he paid dearly for. I told him what made his own father special was that Mike lived a better life than Jamie's grandfather which is all we can hope for in each generation. I told Jamie, in that sense, he faced one of the greatest challenges I had ever witnessed. In my eyes his father was perfect, and it was his task to be even better. Derbe echoed my sentiment and added his usual sad speech about what a tragedy it was that Mike was not there. With every word Derbe spoke, he breathed new life into Mike. With the exception of me and Angela, Derbe was more responsible than anyone for Mike's immortality.

After Stanford, we drove to the Grand Canyon for a couple days. I had reservations at Phantom Ranch in the bottom of the canyon so we had a nice relaxing hike down when we arrived. I have always been a sentimental person, but seeing something as vast as the Grand Canyon brings this reflection to an entirely greater scale. As we made our way down the trail, we sang camping songs the entire way. There wasn't a happier group anywhere in the world. Every turn on that hike brought a new valley into view. We would stop at each point and be in awe of what we saw. It was fun to look down at landmarks below and then find ourselves standing in those places moments later looking back at how far we had come. When we finally made it to the bottom, Jamie went racing ahead and jumped into the river screaming. Derbe and I burst out laughing and followed closely behind. We were sweating from the hike and were also ready to cool off. As we swam in the river, we were joined by a couple from Czechoslovakia that stripped down completely naked before they jumped in. It wasn't anything I hadn't seen before, but Jamie's eyes were glued to the woman as she walked into the water. I knew the trip would be a growing experience for Jamie, but I hadn't expected him to see his first naked woman. Fortunately, she had a gorgeous body so I was glad his first look was a good one. Derbe and I laughed as we needled Jamie later in the night and listened to him talk about girls. He had only recently started to get interested in women and took full advantage of the trip with us. Without Mike, it was our responsibility to teach Jamie about women, and we gave him the full sex talk by the fire that night. I can't imagine a better environment for a kid to learn about sex. Derbe explained women to Jamie with his serious demeanor while I constantly chirped him. Every time Derbe would say something, I would tell Jamie not to listen since Derbe didn't know what to do anyway. Jamie was laughing hysterically at my comments while being entranced by what he was learning. Derbe ignored most of my jokes but finally responded by saying, "Hey E, if this was a gay sex talk, we would care about your opinion, but Jamie wants to hear about women from an expert like me." I will never forget how hard Jamie laughed at Derbe's joke, and he repeated it to me all night. After we answered all Jamie's questions, we spent the rest of the night quietly gazing at the spectacular view above us. It was a clear night with millions of stars filling the sky. Jamie fell asleep by the fire, and I enjoyed a relaxing night talking with Derbe and thinking about Mike.

The next morning, we woke up early and had breakfast overlooking the river. All three of us were fully aware that it was Father's Day as we sat in sentimental reflection. I had spent every single Father's Day with Jamie since he was a baby, but this one was the most special. It meant so much to see the love Jamie had for the dad he had never known. Hearing Jamie express his thankfulness that Derbe and I had been his new fathers gave me more pride than anything else in my life. After a sweet breakfast, we surprised Jamie with a white water rafting trip down the Colorado River. I'm not as much of an adrenaline junkie as the other two, but I still had a good time. At the end of our trip, we had a nice meal on the shore and set up camp for the night. Jamie was constantly thanking me for taking him on the trip and being the father he never had. He was such a humble and appreciative young man, and I could not have been any prouder of him. It was the perfect end to another Father's Day with the boy I loved, and I knew Mike would have appreciated everything I had done for his son. I loved Jamie so much and was happy to see him enjoying every second of his vacation.

The following day, we hiked out of the canyon, stayed one last night at the top, and then left for Austin. We took a nice tour of the university, but I could tell that Jamie didn't like it as much as the previous two schools. Even though he wouldn't be picking Texas, the visit was still fun. We took Jamie out on 6th Street late at night and watched his excitement as he got to see college nightlife for the first time. Every gorgeous girl that walked by would turn Jamie's head and ours as well for that matter. It reminded me of my first time at a bar when I was only a few years older than Jamie. I told Jamie that we would take him for a drink at Pete's Dueling Piano Bar, a favorite place that I always visited in Austin. The owner saw me before we even walked in and raced out to give me a hug. I had gotten to know this man years ago when I held a charity event at his bar. Together, we raised a lot of money for music education in Austin, and, since that time, we had opened three local music centers for children in the area. I always loved these types of after school programs geared at providing education for children in the areas they dream about. My admiration for the dreams of children had combined with my depression with the facts of the world to create programs that would make these hopes more feasible. The owner of the bar gave me updates on the programs as we made our way to the table and ordered a round. My friend asked for ID's and looked at Jamie as his face turned pale. The owner then smiled at Jamie's response, walked away, and soon returned with our drinks. I figured this was as good a time as any for Jamie to have his first beer. He was surrounded by people that loved him in a bar with an ideal atmosphere for a night he would never forget.

There are two things I will always remember about my trip to Austin. The first memory is watching Jamie drinking at the bar and asking me to bring girls over. Every time I would get a couple girls to have drinks with us, he would act so shy at first, but, eventually, he wouldn't be able to stop talking. I am pretty sure Jamie thought he fell in love at least a hundred times that night. The other memory was watching Jamie's hangover the next morning as we boarded the plane. Derbe and I smiled at each other as we watched him sleeping peacefully on the flight. When we arrived home, Jamie gave his mom a hug and went right to sleep while Angela thanked us for all we had done. Angela would constantly tell me what a difference I made in her life and how she could never have made it as a single mother without me. The thanks was unnecessary as I considered it an honor to watch over Mike's family.

It didn't take long after our return before Jamie was already talking about our next trip in three weeks. This time, we were doing a road trip through the Midwest to Jamie's favorite Big Ten schools as well as Michigan Tech. Derbe had to work so I had the entire car ride alone with Jamie. On the first part of our trip, we talked extensively about the things Jamie wanted to accomplish in his life. I loved Jamie's dreams and couldn't help but appreciate how close his goals aligned with his father's. Jamie talked more about meeting his dream girl and the type of family life he wanted than he did about sports and school. We had enjoyed visiting the first few schools, but I was most excited for Jamie to see Michigan Tech. I didn't think he would necessarily choose my alma mater, but I knew it would be an important experience for him to see where we went to school and learn more of his father's history. When we arrived in Houghton, I gave Jamie a tour of campus and showed him his father's statue on the wall at the rink. After Mike's death, the team had named a perseverance award after him. Additionally, Jamie got to see the Mike Wagner Medical School that I had raised money to help build at the university. Jamie had heard a lot about his father over the years, but Mike's image grew even larger in Jamie's mind during our time at Michigan Tech. The impact of Mike's life was greatest through my fiction and Jamie's life, but this medical school was one of many other positive effects of Mike's memory. As we walked through campus, I told Jamie stories about his father and reiterated the type of character Mike possessed. It was a trip filled with reflection. Jamie's life validated everything I had hoped for when I killed Mike. Jamie had grown to love Mike just as I loved my mom, and he benefited from the same perfect childhood I had known. Even better for Jamie, I had consciously created an entire world around him specifically to give him a perfect life.

A month after we visited Michigan Tech, I took Jamie on our final trip of the summer to the East Coast. I planned to give Jamie a full Ivy League experience and then end our trip at the University of Connecticut where my old friend Dillon was coaching hockey and teaching economics. During our visit, I got the feeling Jamie would end up somewhere in Boston. He seemed to love the area which made me envious. I always wished I had spent a couple years around that area as I enjoyed my visits over the years. Of all the schools we saw that summer, Jamie seemed to like Harvard the most, and I secretly hoped he decided to go there. Nonetheless, I kept my thoughts to myself and let Jamie soak up the experience and make his own decision.

The last stop on our East Coast trip was the University of Connecticut. Dillon had been the head hockey coach at UConn for the past six years and had already won four league titles and a national championship. Even more impressive, in my opinion, was that he was the only Division 1 college hockey coach also working as a full time professor including both teaching and research. Dillon always had a contagious energy, and he definitely needed it to be successful with his overbooked schedule. I was always proud to call Dillon my friend, and I loved bragging to everyone about his success. There were no other college coaches that even came close to setting an example for their players in the way Dillon did. Many preached the value of being both an athlete and a student, but the players at UConn were led by the perfect example. I was so excited to see Dillon when we arrived. On the first day, Jamie and I scrimmaged with Dillon and his team. It was fun for me to relive some old glory days, and Jamie made an impressive impression by holding his own on the rink. Afterwards, I went out for dinner and drinks with Dillon while Jamie spent the night with some of the players. At the bar, Dillon and I reminisced about old times and caught up on our respective lives. The conversation was great, and it was fun to hear a few entertaining locker room stories for the first time in a while.

Although we had an enjoyable evening, one part of the conversation left a bad taste in my mouth. Dillon had gone off on a tangent about one of his colleagues that had moved there from Harvard about a year earlier. The man Dillon was talking about was Edward Burton, a famous economist who had served two years as an advisor to the President while working at Harvard. I had previously met Mr. Burton a few years back when I visited the White House and distinctly remembered our conversation. He was the kind of person who constantly recited his resume but didn't seem to understand the irony of his fame. He was a person who had been given everything in life and had achieved unequaled mediocrity. I have often run away from success in search of a simple life so, in a way, I envied Mr. Burton. I had to work to be insignificant, but yet it came so naturally to him. As soon as Dillon brought up his name, I remembered how much I had enjoyed talking to this unjustifiably conceited man and laughing at his expense. The irony of his arrogance was priceless. There was no reason he should have been proud of his accomplishments as he simply plagiarized his way through his profession without a single novel contribution. The reason Dillon brought up Mr. Burton was because he was set to receive a large award the following day. Dillon began to express his dislike for the man, and I initially figured it was for the same reasons as me. However, Dillon's disgust with Mr. Burton turned out to be based upon something much worse than him merely being a pompous professor. Dillon told me the reason Mr. Burton left Harvard for Connecticut was not for a large sum of money as reported in the paper, but rather as part of a cover up after he had been caught having sex with a twelve year old girl. I asked Dillon if he was sure, and he proceeded to lay out the facts in gruesome detail. It turns out this wasn't a single case of committing a appalling crime but just another day in the life of a terrible, disgusting scumbag. Dillon's wife had become friends with Mrs. Burton and soon learned of the abuse she faced daily. I was mortified as Dillon described the life of this woman. She was viewed by the public as a happy house wife but lived every day in terror. There is nothing that angers me more than people who commit horrific acts on those who are helpless. Mr. Burton represented everything that was wrong with the world. He had a wonderful family, but, instead of loving them, he abused them. I don't support any type of spanking or child abuse and would soon be repulsed by the beatings I saw Mr. Burton commit with my own eyes as I staked out his house. Dillon described his efforts to hold Mr. Burton accountable, but his attempts had been futile as the authorities refused to listen. Dillon had come to realize that part of the deal when Burton was hired had included the assurance he would be taken care of. I understood how much Dillon had risked in his own career by continuing to pursue the issue, and I could empathize with his frustration. We eventually returned to more pleasurable topics, but the story of Mr. Burton never really left my mind.

The following day, I attended the ceremony Dillon had mentioned. Mr. Burton was receiving an award from the university for his contribution to his field and for being a man of virtue in the community. I could feel my blood boiling as the speaker listed his virtues. The chief virtue described was Mr. Burton's devotion to his work. People applauded the speech but didn't realize the price that was paid for this devotion. Mr. Burton put his own success above his family and lived a self-centered life while those around him were destroyed. It was true that Mr. Burton contained many of the virtues described in the talk such as ambition, but they were all propagandized virtues that hid the devastation he brought to the world. He was a man whose vices weren't nearly as bad as his virtues. Those supposed virtues were the reason he was able to destroy everyone around him with impunity. Every positive comment that was said about Mr. Burton concealed the true evil of his character. As they listed the notable publications on Mr. Burton's resume, it reminded me of the famous research maxim, publish or perish. Mr. Burton had plenty of publications, but there was no doubt the world would have been a better place if he would have perished instead. I could feel the sentimental emotional state of my past two years replaced with a pure rage that I rarely encountered. Mr. Burton was a complete asshole, and I wished he didn't exist. My blood pressure rose as I thought about killing him. This was the first person I really wanted to murder out of pure hatred. I became an emotional wreck as I couldn't get the thought of killing him out of my mind. I pictured the pain in his eyes with anticipation as I thought about him suffering at my hands.

I nearly fell victim to my emotions and killed Mr. Burton in rage, but I stopped myself just in time. I had spent my life acting at a level above emotion so I forced myself to take a step back to think before I killed him. I returned from my trip with Jamie and began contemplating the best option with regards to Mr. Burton. It was clear this man didn't deserve life. I thought about simply making him disappear from the earth. I considered burying him alive to avoid killing him. Instead of immortalizing him in fiction, I would write his story and burn the only copy so that he would be erased from the world twice. There were a few problems with my plan. If I killed Mr. Burton, he would be left in a painless state that he didn't deserve. He would become a martyr while further devastation fell on the shoulders of his family who had already been victimized enough. I decided I couldn't bear the thought of bringing any more pain to these people. Mr. Burton had done enough of that already. He was a worthless person proficient only in the art of underachieving. This was a man who could ruin the reputation of assholes. I wanted to kill him, but he hadn't earned the honor. The one thing my murders had in common was their beautiful stories. These were people who deserved to live in fiction. Mr. Burton deserved to live in a torturous reality, and that is exactly what I prescribed. I gave up on the idea of murdering him and came up with a more appropriate plan.

As I finalized my plans for Mr. Burton, I struggled to suppress my anger. I was usually an easy going person that was friendly to everyone, but I became extremely ornery during this time. Every little thing would get under my skin. The most memorable of these experiences was when I was sitting in a coffee shop thinking about Mr. Burton and writing the outline to my next novel. Some guy was making all kinds of noise yelling at his wife, and it reminded me so much of the other asshole in Connecticut. Finally, I couldn't take it anymore and politely asked him to shut the fuck up. Apparently, assholes don't follow directions well. I calmly listened to threats from this idiot for ten minutes until I eventually just rolled my eyes and tried to move on with my day. Just like Mr. Burton, there wasn't anything wrong with this guy that a miracle couldn't fix. He called me a pussy and I said, "Well, you know what they say, you are what you eat." I tried to walk away, but he followed in anger and said he was going to kill me. When he said those words, I looked up with a smile. This guy really had no idea who he was talking to. If you're going to run your mouth about killing people, you better be prepared to follow through especially when you're threatening someone like me. Death couldn't scare me. I controlled death. Killing me was the nicest thing this man could possibly do for my future. I was already loved by the world and many had said I was the best author of my generation, but I might have become the greatest of all time if I was murdered. I laughed in the guy's face and left before I accidentally killed him and gave him a gift he didn't deserve.

This coffee shop confrontation was a catalyst to refocus my mind. I realized I needed to be in control of myself to be effective for my next novel. I made all the arrangements and went over the plans relentlessly until I felt confident in every detail. I felt guilty that it took so many weeks to get my plan together, but it had to be perfect. When I finally put the plan into action, everything went flawlessly as usual. I set out to commit murder and ruin Mr. Burton's life. I had two goals in mind. My first goal was to watch him suffer for a long time, and my second goal was to end the suffering of his family. Contrary to my usual methods, I proceeded anonymously in pursuit of these goals and wore a mask the entire time to hide my identity. I decided to strike while Mr. Burton was on his family vacation at their cabin in Maine. I had followed his whereabouts for a few weeks, learned of his vacation plans, and thus arrived ready for action.

When I got to the cabin, I hid in the woods and awaited their arrival. It was a sad sight to see the dynamics of this family when they arrived. I could see the anguish in the eyes of Mrs. Burton and the children as they unloaded the car. It was almost as if the family was only comfortable in public when the patriarch was forced to adhere to his image. In their private lives, things were obviously much different. There was a constant look of fear on the wife's face. Once the car was unpacked, Mr. Burton drove away and left his family at the house alone. At first, I didn't know if I should stay to take care of the family or follow Mr. Burton, but I decided it was best to see where he was going. I ran back to my car and tracked him to a motel nearby where he was joined by an obviously way overpriced piece of pussy. I can empathize with certain people cheating (such as if his wife decided to cheat), but it never makes sense when a person cheats with someone worse than their spouse. This went far beyond the need for a little variety and seemed absolutely irrational. I had seen enough and returned to the woods.

When I got back to the cabin, I saw Mrs. Burton playing a board game with the kids. They were a cute family but didn't have a single smile between the three. I looked at them in pity and drew comfort from the fact that they would soon be dead. Their agony would be over as soon as I murdered them. I sat back and waited until Mr. Burton returned three hours later. He was drunk and made a big scene when he entered the house and started hitting his kids. I could feel the anger rising within me, but I took a deep breath to regain my composure and realized things were going according to plan. After watching Mr. Burton toss his wife around for a few minutes, I had seen enough. I broke into the house and put a gun to his head. I then proceeded to tie him to a chair and made him watch as I shot his wife and children in front of his eyes. Instead of pleading for their lives, this scumbag only seemed to care about himself. He tried to offer me anything I wanted to let him go. I killed his family but told him he would be spared. He was the reason they were dead. He was the disease they had suffered from for too long, and the only cure was fiction. I would give them a happy ending to pay the penance for the horrific world from which they had just departed. As for Mr. Burton, I simply threw my gun on his lap, untied him, and told him he had the choice whether he deserved to live or die. I already knew the decision he would make. As I walked away, I heard the trigger click. Instead of appropriately ending his own life, he had tried to shoot me in the back, but all three bullets had already been used to kill his family. I left the crime scene and didn't look back. I always wished I could have seen the look on his face when he realized he was holding the murder weapon, and it was actually his gun I had used.

When the news broke about Mr. Burton beating and murdering his family, I got a call from Dillon immediately. The evidence was irrefutable, and the world soon learned the terrible history of Mr. Burton. Dillon had worked unsuccessfully to expose Mr. Burton in the past, but stories were now emerging from everywhere. It was a horrifying history that extended far beyond my original knowledge. When I think about this man, my initial response is always anger, but the feeling that remains after adequate reflection is pride. I had wanted to kill this man out of rage but was able to transcend my emotions and create the justice his family deserved. While Mr. Burton was tortured in jail, his family lived happily ever after. Instead of the man now rotting in prison, I gave them a husband and father who loved his family above all. In honor of the noble professor that should have existed in reality, the book was titled *Publish or Perish*. The world has always loved the happy endings of my stories, but reading the Burton family's fiction brings me more comfort than almost any other book and always brings an extra smile as I think about the suffering I left Mr. Burton as a parting gift.

After writing *Publish or Perish,* I spent a lot of time thinking about my life and career. I had grown into the person I had always strived to become and finally proved I was above emotion. I could have easily acted rashly, but, instead, I took my time and did the right thing. Not only had I withheld my desire to kill Burton, but I also found a way to both make him suffer and stop the suffering of his family at the same time. An additional aspect of the murder that I was proud of was the fact that I had the foresight to frame him for murder in Maine to prevent him from getting the death penalty. Maine didn't have a death sentence like Connecticut so I knew he wouldn't be given the easy way out. I loved the thought of Mr. Burton suffering in jail for the rest of his dreadful life.

Setting aside the direct effects of this murder, the biggest thing I took away from *Publish or Perish* was the power I finally had gained over my emotions. My entire life was moving constantly towards this point, and I was proud of the self-restraint I had shown in not killing this asshole. I believe it is impossible for a person to become completely analgesic, but I had come as close as possible. I considered my life a constant battle against my evolutionary deficiencies. The true power of the human intellect can only be realized when one is able to overcome the evolutionary byproducts inherited from the lower animals. I had made extensive progress in this struggle over the years, but the futility of the task was obvious. I could rationalize my way around many emotions, but so much of my life was still controlled by my physiology. I always wished I could have conscious control over every aspect of my feelings. Even things as common as sleeping pissed me off when I thought about them. Anyone who supports the idea of intelligent design needs explain the purpose of sleep. There is no reason we should be forced to waste eight hours each day asleep when that time could instead be spent living. An omnipotent creator could have done a much better job than the impotent being that designed the human body. It is bad enough that we have to live such short and pointless lives, but the added inefficiency of sleep only adds to the stupidity. From an evolutionary perspective, it makes sense that we sleep. Our ancestors grew up in a world without artificial lights, and it made sense to spend the nights dormant, but, like many of the traits we have inherited from our past, it no longer makes sense for our lives. It boggles my mind that more people haven't joined my war against sleep and found a way for us to overcome it. I have always kept an eye out for new scientific research to address this issue and even funded a couple preliminary studies over the years, but the results have always been disappointing. There seems to be a complete lack of will to look at medical research from a eugenic perspective. The focus is always on curing disease, but research on improving the average person's function is consistently lacking. Sleep is a small symptom of this bigger problem. We have made few attempts to gain control over our hormonal cycles in general. Not only should we try to destroy the circadian rhythm, but we should try to overcome the limitations of the entire endocrine system as well. Our goal should be to control every aspect of our hormonal functioning. I am disappointed the research community has failed in this area, and, as a result, I am stuck in a constant battle with my hormones as I try to gain control over emotion, sleep, sex, hunger, or many other things I often desire against my own will. I doubt I will progress much further in this struggle before I reach that final flaw in human design. Like all the others, I will fight off death as long as possible, but, eventually, I will have no choice but to accept my inevitable fate. As Groucho Marx once said, "I intend to live forever or die trying."

I may not be strong enough to overcome my evolutionary past, but at least I am able to understand my reality. As weak as I have felt in my battle against biology, the small victories such as *Publish or Perish* have been a source of enormous pride. I overcame my desire to kill a man who didn't deserve to live and instead killed his family that deserved to die. This murder brings up a good point about all of my characters. The obvious criticism will be that justice would have been to kill Mr. Burton, but my kills have never been about justice, punishment, or revenge. My kills have been about mercy and love. The murders behind each of my novels are a reward given only to a select few that deserve it. Any attempt to interpret my kills as heinous in nature would be completely inaccurate. My victims were chosen out of pure admiration and given the gift of eternal happiness. In fact, it is probably inappropriate to even refer to them as victims since their lives were forever better as a result of their deaths. If I was functioning out of hate, I would have killed the asshole. I never acted out of hate; I only acted out of love.

CHAPTER 18

United We Stand

Literature is my utopia.

-Helen Keller

CHAPTER 18: *United We Stand*

The only way to unify humanity is through the creation of a common enemy. The world was unifying against Mr. Burton as they watched him suffer in jail, and I began to take a serious look at my life in order to decide if it was time for retirement. My two most recent novels, *Born Again* and *Publish or Perish* were getting great reviews and selling like pancakes. It was always rewarding to hear positive feedback from my readers, but most of my pleasure was derived from the process of actually writing the stories. Over time, I had come to assume the books would sell, but the most gratifying part was always the process of creating happiness. I loved the career path I had taken and was proud of my many accomplishments. My life had been spent bringing eternal fiction to the terminally real. My work provided lasting comfort for suffering characters and made the world a better place. I was content with my career and ready to begin my transition to retirement. My entire life had been devoted to others, and I desired to spend the rest of my time living for myself. I wanted to transform the delightful relaxation of my vacations into the permanent state of my life.

Once the decision to pursue retirement was made, I began to think about the things I needed to take care of before I left. My plan was to get completely off the grid and simply fade into the memories of those I loved. I wanted my final deterioration to occur in the solitude of an anonymous life traveling the world. Before I was ready to leave, there were a couple things I would need to settle. My two main concerns were the long-term well-being of the people I loved and the conclusion of my career as an author. I had always watched over my loved ones, and there was no way I would leave without ensuring their futures were taken care of. Most of my family was content with their lives so it wouldn't take long before I was comfortable moving forward with retirement. My major concern was making sure Jamie was taken care of. I had invested the majority of my life into creating the perfect world for Jamie, and there was no way I was going to abandon Mike's son before I was sure I had done everything I could to give him a perfect life. I decided to focus first on finishing my work with an adequate final novel and then spend however much time I needed to take care of Jamie before I left forever.

As far as my work as an author, I hoped to end with a bang. I have always had a flare for the dramatic and wanted my final novel to be a climactic conclusion to my literary legacy. I knew it was going to be tough to raise the bar from my previous books. The quality of my prior novels had created the almost impossible task of finding someone worthy of being my final character. I couldn't comprehend the possibility of a person more impressive than the characters I had already written about. It seemed inconceivable to envision the type of person that could provide an adequate counterweight to my first two novels about my mom and Mike. I wanted my career to end on a level comparable to its beginning, but I soon came to the conclusion that I would never find a single character to fulfill this role. My process of killing characters and writing their happy endings was well established, but I wanted my final story to function on a much larger scale. Although it wasn't easy, I was finally able to decide the subject of my last book. Instead of another inspirational story about the life of a perfect person, I would write a novel about the perfect society. I have always been critical about the world, and the thought of creating utopia struck me as the correct conclusion to my career as a writer. I had given the gift of eternal happiness to a select few, but my final novel would extend to all of society. Instead of a single beacon of hope shining through the darkness, I would illuminate the entire globe. It was this initial idea that eventually led to the creation of *United We Stand*.

One of the hardest parts of *United We Stand* was determining who I would kill. I wanted to write about a better world, and, at first, I figured that meant I must blow up the entire earth. If my novel could create an entire world of peace and prosperity, it would be the crown jewel of my life. Although the thought of killing literally everyone entered my mind, it was soon pushed away by the simple logistics of such a massive murder as well as the fact that I didn't want to immortalize the entire human race. I had chosen to give eternal life to a select few that had been deserving of the honor, but the whole of humanity was clearly not worthy of such a privilege. As a result, I decided my final novel would be about a smaller society coming together and setting an example for the rest of the world. Although I hadn't figured out if this would be a small town, a big city, or even an entire country, I liked the notion of my final book giving hope to readers living in a hopeless world. I loved sociology, and the notion of creating a utopian society was extremely attractive. I read a lot of social philosophy and social evolution books over the years and have always been sad that our human deficiencies have prevented us from developing an ideal world. I remember being attracted to the ideas in books like *Walden* by Thoreau or *Walden Two* by Skinner and wondering why those ideas had failed to impact the world to the necessary extent. In reality, the world only seemed to change drastically when there was a major tragedy. There are countless examples of communities coming together after natural disasters, and no one forgets the unbelievable unity in America following the attacks on September 11th. It is a shame that war is able to unite the world so much more than love. The only way to bring the world together is to tear the world apart.

I soon began to develop a general plan for my final act. It was clear I would need to kill a large number of people in order to write adequately about a utopian world. The brilliance of my final novel was that the fictional world I planned to create would not only provide a great guide for the world but would have the added benefit of once again uniting the world as society rallied around those lost in the attack. My major focus was now centered upon choosing the correct victims. I wanted to include a variety of people so that I could create an all-inclusive utopia. Among the options that crossed my mind were a major political debate, a sporting event, a high school graduation, or a Red Cross building. The political debate appealed to me because it included people of opposing viewpoints arguing like they were on reality television. Nothing could provide better contrast to utopia than the current political environment. Additionally, there was no question a mass murder of our political leaders would highlight what was wrong with our violent world and potentially bring our divided planet together. The appeal of blowing up a sports stadium was primarily the same as the political debate. Sports should be a symbol of people coming together in teamwork, but, instead, it seems to breed so much hate between fans of different teams. I always felt world peace would be unattainable as long as Michigan fans were unable to hug their counterparts at Ohio. An even more appealing option was the idea of using a high school graduation as the backdrop for my next novel. There is no other event that is as synonymous with hope and the potential to change the world, and I loved the thought of committing my final murders on a group of young adults about to enter the real world. My final idea was the Red Cross simply because these hard working people represented the best of our world. The deaths of these volunteers would shine light on the guiding principles behind their work and provide a unique hope that could be exploited in my novel. Overall, I was attracted to certain aspects of each of these possibilities, but none seemed to contain everything I wanted so I decided to combine my favorite parts of all of them into a phenomenal final chapter in my life as an author.

The first thing I did when planning my mass murder was create an overview of what the event would look like. I knew the best way to include the positive aspects of the Red Cross was to use my own charity as the backdrop for the event to ensure sufficient volunteers would be present. I met with members of my charity and told them I wanted to plan the largest gathering of honor students in the history of the charity for a huge event honoring their hard work. I was planning to gather a considerable amount of money for paid trips for all the honorees to the event at the Verizon Center in our nation's capital. Over the next couple months, we began to plan our event. I was soon able to get numerous celebrities to volunteer including professional athletes, politicians, and many prominent scientists including six Nobel Prize winners. I was extremely pleased with the way the event was coming together, and I knew it would be an extraordinary location for utopia to begin.

Once we set a date for the event, I left the rest of the planning to the committee and focused primarily on organizing the details of my mass murder. For those of you who might think killing people is easy, I can assure you that it is not always the case. It is not an easy task to plant a bomb in a large building anywhere in our country let alone in our nation's capital. All my murders up until this point had been on a small scale, and I knew the type of kill I was now planning was nearly impossible. My usual attention to detail would need to be significantly magnified if I planned to succeed in this endeavor. My main worry wasn't that I would get caught afterwards, but rather that my plot would be prevented during the process. The simplest way to kill such a large number of people would be for me to bomb the building with everyone inside, but I had enough knowledge to doubt that this method would be successful. Earlier in my life, I was fortunate to have spent a week touring the FBI and Secret Service facilities with Derbe, and I remembered the vast capabilities of these two groups. I have constantly benefited from the good nature of others, and the top secret access from that visit was essential to my current planning. There is nothing more valuable than having the trust of others, and I was greatly indebted to these people for the trust they had given to me. The primary question remaining in my mind as I planned my attack was the CIA. I have always considered myself a conspiracy theorist without a conspiracy theory. I believe those in power control our lives in so many ways that we are completely unaware of, and I wondered how much reach the intelligence community really had. I feared the possibility of them discovering my plan. For the first time in years, I found myself nervous for my next murders. I wondered what would happen if the CIA discovered my plans. I was pretty sure the mass murder I was considering would be viewed as business as usual in the intelligence world as they wrote the book on spinning tragedy into the desired societal response. I was almost curious to see if I would be arrested or if the CIA would simply ask for a piece of the action. These thoughts ran through my mind as I cautiously proceeded.

While I organized the details of the attack on my charity event, I spent three months writing *United We Stand*. Unlike many of my novels that couldn't be written until the characters had perished, this novel was completely finished a month before the event. The book was the story of a community coming together to create the perfect world we should all be living in. I erased the real world and built utopia from scratch. This world was the meritocracy that America had often falsely claimed to be. My new world was one of comfort and love without the terrible virtues of ambition, competition, and patriotism that prevent the world from matching fiction. There is nothing poetic about the nature of the world we live in. All attempts at glorifying the world are doomed to either fall short of their goal or wander into the realm of fiction. I was heartbroken by the world around me so I created the world I had always hoped for. Unfortunately, I couldn't write the story of reality. The real world was either written by a sadist or a comedian although I can never make up my mind. Either way, I think the world is proof that god is a satirist. I have never met another author who can match the tragic comedy of the world that surrounds us. Reality is the purest form of satire. I am not claiming that satire illuminates reality as many would suggest, but that reality itself is a true satire. In my own work, I have found that the secret to writing satire is to exclusively tell the truth. It has only been through fiction that I have been able to create a world of inspiration.

When I finished *United We Stand*, I was proud of what I had accomplished. I had written an incredible final book to appropriately complete my career as an author. It was a novel of epic proportion. The only task remaining was the event at the Verizon Center, and I found myself extremely stressed out about the impending attack. I had spent so much time convincing myself that I was prepared for the security in Washington, but I found myself with increasingly cold feet as the event approached. I felt as if I had talked myself into something I wasn't ready for. For all of my previous murders, I had been meticulous in my approach. With the exception of my Cereal kills and the little girl from No Thai, I probably spent a minimum of a month planning every detail of each kill. I was now planning to destroy an entire stadium full of people in a single blast, and there just seemed to be too many potential variables that could go wrong. I could feel my anxiety growing and was uncomfortable with the entire plan. In the end, I looked at the whole thing as being unrealistic. Perhaps I was a bit self-conscious, but I couldn't help but feel as if I was stretching beyond my reach and needed to change my mind. After a long week of contemplation, I decided to cancel my plans and go through with the charity event without killing anyone. In hindsight, I know I made the smart decision. It is always better to be safe than sorry. Even with my knowledge and planning, there were so many potential landmines that could have killed my murder plans.

At first, I felt sad when I decided to cancel the attack. I had written what could easily be considered the next Great American Novel, but I would never be able to publish it because I didn't have a way to catapult my characters into fiction. I wanted to murder the crowds at the youth event because I envisioned a ripple effect in reality that might mirror my novel on a smaller scale. I hoped I could create a reaction from the world that could be admired by all my readers, but I had fallen short of my goal. Fortunately, I learned long ago that, if at first you don't succeed, it doesn't hurt to try again. I took this advice to heart and decided to move forward with my plans for *United We Stand* by lowering my sample size to a more realistic target. At first, I was unsure how to recreate the same group in a smaller setting, but I eventually settled on the one hundred award winners from the event in Washington that would be joining some doctors and other volunteers on a mission trip to South America. The awards and the mission weren't my idea, but, when I heard about them, I thought it was the perfect opportunity to make up for my prior failure. I volunteered to help plan the mission and told them I would even go myself.

When the time finally arrived for my charity event in Washington, it was bigger than ever. I had no idea it would grow so massive, and I was tremendously conflicted over my decision not to kill everyone. I had mixed emotions as I felt sad seeing all the potential lives I could have saved while also feeling relieved when I was given a tour of the overwhelming security the government had provided. During the lead up to the event, my mind bounced back and forth as to whether I could have actually pulled off my original plan, but, once the event was underway, it no longer mattered. I had made a decision that the risk was too high and moved on. Although I had put a lot of effort into organizing the event to kill everyone, my time turned out to still be worthwhile as the gathering at the Verizon Center was remarkable. Although it wasn't the society-shifting event I had initially hoped to achieve, the gathering highlighted the best kids our world had to offer. Not only did the country come together for a brief moment to honor the dreams of our most gifted children, but the outpouring of support led to a massive influx of donations to the charity and allowed us to build twenty more community centers over the following two years. Overall, the event was a success in every way but one.

After the festivities surrounding my charity event in Washington were concluded, I began to focus on the upcoming mission. I was so excited and didn't hide this fact from anyone. About two weeks before the trip, I visited Angela, Jamie, and Derbe in Traverse City and spent the entire time bragging about the importance of my upcoming mission. I must have been convincing because Jamie's eyes lit up, and he tried to convince me to let him come. Jamie was seventeen years old and had the perfect future stretching out in front of him. I loved his eagerness to help and was proud of how much he cared about the people around him. Jamie had all of my compassion without any of my cynicism. He was empathetic to the suffering in the world without knowing the futility of trying to change reality. Jamie was a mirror image of the person I had been when I was his age. His success was unmatched, and his potential was only limited by his imagination. Watching Jamie brought back memories of the best moments of my life. I had worked hard to shape Jamie's world and seeing his perfection gave me the greatest sense of pride imaginable. I smiled at the disappointment in Jamie's face when Angela told him he couldn't come on the mission. Like any successful seventeen-year-old, Jamie's schedule was already completely filled, and there was no way he could join me on the trip. However, I was surprised to hear Derbe say he was interested. It hadn't occurred to me to invite Derbe, but I was thrilled with the idea. It was well known that Derbe was an accomplished detective, but few people knew he was still licensed to practice medicine, and he always relished the chance to work with children when his schedule permitted.

Adding Derbe to the mission only heightened my excitement. I tirelessly worked to iron out the last minute details, and, before I knew it, we had the entire group assembled on our way to South America. We planned to spend four days in three different countries during our two week trip. The first week and a half went smoothly. We spent the majority of our time helping to build, educate, and inspire local communities while Derbe and the other doctors provided much needed medical assistance. I would like to say we saved a lot of lives as was claimed by the rest of the people in attendance, but, unfortunately, we were merely mitigating the physical pain of these people. The amount of suffering I witnessed on the mission made me want to kill everyone I saw. I can handle my own discomfort, but seeing the hopelessness in the eyes of suffering children is too much to bear. As we left the second to last village to go to our final destination, I looked back and wished that it wasn't too late to change the lives we were leaving behind. Although my heart was saddened by what my eyes had recently seen, I knew the purpose of my trip. I did my best to block out the world around me and focus on the upcoming fiction I would soon create.

When we arrived at our final location, I sent the youth volunteers inside to start the evening events while Derbe and I unloaded the final supplies off the truck. There was no lack of appreciation in the eyes of our hosts as they graciously received the food, medicine, and other supplies we brought. I felt my spirits rise and, once again, focused on the real reason I joined the mission. I will never forget our first night in that village. We had a huge feast and then gathered around a large bonfire late into the evening. The night was filled with beautiful music from the native community along with some of our own talented young musicians. The celebration ran late, and it became another one of those nights that no one wanted to end. Finally, we made everyone go to bed. Instead of sleeping in the tents, Derbe and I decided to stay by the fire and sleep under the stars. It was a peaceful night, and I quickly drifted off thinking about the wonderful people I had spent the night with. I was thankful I would never witness a sad ending to their stories.

The next morning, I woke up early and went for a nice run with Derbe. After our run, we took a quick dip in the water to rinse off and then went to the cafeteria for breakfast. Derbe and I were the first ones there but could see the mob from the other building close behind so we quickly got in line. I grabbed a box of cereal from the counter in front of us since that was the only thing being served that morning. Before I could pour the bowl, Derbe grabbed the box out of my hand and asked one of the guys behind the counter if he could make us a couple omelets. I knew Derbe wasn't going to approve of a bowl of cereal, but I always liked listening to him explain his reasoning so I had taken the box mostly just to get his reaction. Derbe went into his usual lecture on how he hadn't had a bowl of cereal since the Cereal Kills had begun and how he wouldn't eat another bowl until the killer was captured. There were numerous times when I had tried to eat cereal around him in the past, and he always included me in his no cereal policy so his speech wasn't anything I hadn't heard before. Fortunately for Derbe, we were in charge of the mission and had been eating much better than the rest of the group so, while everyone else was stuck with cereal, we cut into our omelets.

About a half hour later, everyone in the mission was dead with the exception of Derbe, one of the cooks, and me. People had started collapsing about twenty minutes into the meal which created a massive panic that had lasted about ten minutes while more and more bodies hit the floor. Eventually, it was only Derbe and I remaining on our knees in shock. We immediately tried to call for help, but there was really no one to call. Derbe was in agony as he checked each corpse in hopes of finding someone with a pulse but soon realized none were left alive. As Derbe paced in anger, I sat in the corner leaning on the wall sulking. On the inside I was happy with the manner in which my plan had unfolded, but, outwardly, I was distraught. It didn't take long for Derbe to figure out what had happened and correctly pin the murder on the Cereal Killer. Derbe told me he had known that the Cereal Killer was going to strike again which is why he had continued to work so diligently on the case. Derbe explained that the Cereal Killer must have somehow been aware of his ongoing investigation and tried to kill him because he was getting close. I tried to console my friend and said I was thankful he was alive. I also thanked him for saving my life and told him that, without him, I would have eaten the cereal and been killed. My thanks went in one ear and out the other as Derbe placed the blame for the dead bodies squarely on his own shoulders. Derbe kept torturing himself with the knowledge that the Cereal Killer had wanted to kill him and instead killed so many innocent people as collateral damage. I knew this mass murder actually had nothing to do with

Derbe and did my best to offer my support. Derbe described the tragedy of these murders as being the caliber of lives that were lost. These people were truly the best hope for our world's future and represented the finest our society had to offer. Derbe simply didn't know this was by design. Derbe could clearly see death in front of his eyes but was blind to the resurrection already underway. I had always resented the way in which the Cereal Killer's story had ended, and it was wonderful to see a proper conclusion to that chapter of my life. The Cereal Killer had saved his most important murders for his final act. As I looked down on the lifeless bodies, my mind immediately turned to *United We Stand*, and I was able to find peace in the fact that my final novel was now complete. Although it wasn't a mass murder on the scale I had originally hoped for, the novel made up for the shortcoming. The number of murders was lowered, but I ultimately settled for quality over quantity as these kids were truly the pinnacle of our society. Nothing could provide a better foundation for a perfect world than this young group of altruistic dreamers. I created utopia and was finally content with my life as a writer.

When I returned from the mission, I immediately focused on my family. I quickly published *United We Stand* but didn't do any promotional events because I simply wanted to make sure everyone I loved was taken care of before I left on my final vacation. It was wonderful to spend time with those I loved, and the knowledge that I would soon be gone made every second more precious. I made a point to spend an entire day alone with each person I loved so that I could have a final moment with them and try to determine if there was anything else I could do for them before I left. I had an amazing family and was soon content with the fact that I had done everything in my power to help them. The thought of leaving was bittersweet, but I was comforted by the fact that they would be coming with me in my memory.

Another important part of preparing for retirement was ensuring all the logistics of my future life were taken care of. I had already spent considerable time putting myself in a position to move comfortably around the globe without being noticed. The thought of going off the grid when I retired had been in my mind for a long time, and I had become well practiced in the art of disappearing during my private vacations over the past few years. I knew that, when I left, it would be for good. I would never be seen by the world again which was exactly what I wanted. I would be remembered in the hearts of those I loved, but I didn't need to be part of the world. The important thing was the immortality of my characters whose futures would now be perfect forever. My future life was completely in place. I would say my final goodbyes and retire into the shadows. I was no longer going to live in society. My future would be spent alone, quietly hidden from the view of the world, with only Fantasia to keep me company.

CHAPTER 19

Dream On

No tears in the writer, no tears in the reader.
No surprise in the writer, no surprise in the reader.

-Robert Frost

CHAPTER 19: Dream On

Some dreams are meant to live forever; they are simply too special to let die. The only dream I had left in my life was to quietly drift into my twilight years detached from the world. My literary career was finished, and I had no obligations remaining. For the first time in my life, I was going to be completely free. I no longer would be out at the bar trying to relax while ruminating about what I had to do the next week. My vacations would never again be overshadowed by the weekly planner sitting on my nightstand. My last few years had been less stressful than my college years and early career, but I had never reached the level of freedom I really craved. My retirement would liberate me from the stress of life. I was set to live each moment for the moment without being strangled by future worries. I couldn't wait to leave society and live completely hidden from sight. My dream was nearly a reality.

There was so much I wanted to do before I left. In addition to spending time with members of my family, I gave out a series of extravagant final parting gifts to those I loved. The best part of this gift giving was the lack of surprise in their reactions. I felt proud of the fact that these final gifts didn't seem out of character since I had always lavished the people I loved. Their appreciation gave me a tenfold return on these investments. The hardest part of my final days before retirement was trying to see everyone. I had made so many friends over the years and did my best to travel around the country for a final beer with every one of them. The wonderful thing about real friendships is the fact that time apart has little effect on them. I visited friends that I hadn't seen in years and felt as if no time had passed. I went to see a large number of people, but I left my closest friends for last.

I spent an entire month visiting Dillon in Connecticut which was an absolute pleasure. Every time I would visit, I would wonder why we didn't live closer together. It was the same feeling I got when I visited our other close buddy, Vads, who was another stop on my list. The time I had spent with Peter and Anne in Italy was what my friendships with Dillon and Vads should have been like. Whenever I would visit Dillon, it would be wonderful, but the time constraints always prevented us from delving as deep into our conversations as I would have liked. We both loved the same topics, but yet we could only scratch the surface in the limited time we had. I always wished we had been the type of friends who could meet for coffee every day. My final month with Dillon was an entire month of living the type of friendship I had always wanted us to share.

My time in Connecticut with Dillon was an absolute pleasure but soon came to an end. The next thing I did was schedule a trip to Vegas for my closest friends from college including friends from my time in both Houghton and Ann Arbor. I saw Derbe often but rarely had the chance to spend time with the rest of my college buddies. The trip to Vegas was wild. I knew it would be fun to get my friends back together, but I had no idea that this reunion would cause everyone to revert back to their college behaviors. The trip quickly turned into a massive binge. I was shocked to see how out of control things got, but I guess Vegas can have that effect. I am not going to talk anymore about the trip because I don't want to ruin the reputations of any of the members of this epic vacation. All I will say is that it was great to see so many old friends and have a wonderful weekend that none of them will ever remember.

After I returned from Vegas, I took some time with my family to celebrate what I expected would be my last Fourth of July up north. I have never had a bad weekend at the cabin, and this holiday was no different. I remained awake for nearly the entire four days as I spent the nights watching fireworks, drinking, and dancing at the street dance in Eveleth while spending the days jet skiing, fishing, tubing, wake-boarding, and grilling massive amounts of food. By the time the weekend was over, I was completely worn out. I hated to see everyone leave the cabin, but it felt incredible to fall asleep in my chair on the dock. Staring out over the water put me at peace. I spent a couple days alone at the cabin just soaking in the world around me. I could feel my mood sinking into each moment, and I knew I had to be careful not to get too attached to that relaxation quite yet. It wasn't far off, but I still had a couple more visits to make before I retired. Sitting on the dock at my cabin gave me the feeling of waking up late on a Saturday morning. It was a feeling of being completely rested but yet not wanting to move. I took one last day at the cabin and one final breath of air in my favorite place on earth before I finally got in my car and went back to reality. As I drove away from the cabin, I was reminded of all the cherished times engrained in my memory at that perfect place. I could see the smiles on the faces of those I loved most including many that were no longer alive. I felt the temptation of falling too deep into a sentimental mood, but these were joyful memories. I fought the tendency of turning them into sad reflection simply because they were over with. The memories were from chapters of my life that had long been closed, but that didn't make the story any less enjoyable. I think it is a true shame that we can't go back and reread the best parts of our lives a second time.

After an unforgettable Fourth of July, I went on a visit that I had been looking forward to as much as any. It was a trip to visit JJ in Milwaukee. I had grown up so much during my time in Lincoln with JJ, and it always brought me back to a different place when I would visit him. JJ had moved his family back to Milwaukee and was raising his kids in the gorgeous log cabin that his family had built years earlier. Although I had been looking forward to having a heart to heart talk with JJ, I soon remembered why he was such a fun friend. JJ wasn't the type of person that was going to waste a night on emotional conversation when there was partying to be done. Milwaukee was really the only place for him. Partying with JJ was exactly what I needed. We told old stories, made new stories, and drank a few dozen stones in the hot tub with a group of women from the local bowling alley. It was a classic night, and there didn't need to be anything else said between us. Some of the best parts of a friendship are the things that are never spoken. I never had the opportunity to tell JJ how much I enjoyed our time together, but the open-ended goodbye fit our friendship perfectly. The final thing JJ said to me as I left was his trademark "keep in touch" comment and his usual abrupt ending to the conversation. The friendship never really ended but was just left at its current point ready to resume if our paths would ever cross again. I knew that my retirement meant I was unlikely to ever see JJ again, but I was content with that last night and the final Chipotle burritos we shared.

After visiting Milwaukee, I returned to Minnesota for a final few days with my family. The night I arrived, we had a huge family gathering at my younger sister's house and invited the entire extended family. My good buddy, Tony, also made it to the party which was awesome as he was another person on my list that I would have hated not to have seen a final time. Although my family was unaware of it, this was the last time I planned to see any of them before I left. It was a perfect farewell celebration because no one knew I was leaving. It was just another night of being together which is exactly how I wanted to remember my last moments with the family. I didn't want my final memory to be a tearful goodbye but rather the smiling see you later that it turned out to be.

After I felt confident that my entire family was settled, I was nearly ready to go to Traverse City to spend some final time with Derbe, Angela, and Jamie. I had saved them for last because they held such an important place in my heart, and I figured I might need a considerable amount of time before I would feel comfortable leaving Jamie forever. However, before I returned to Traverse City, I had one final visit to make to see John Vadnais. Vads was one of my best friends, but it was a different type of friendship than I had with my other close friends. In a way, he was a best friend I never had. Unlike my other friends, my relationship with John seemed to be outside of my life. It is strange that I have written so much of my autobiography and my friendship with Vads is just now being introduced, but I guess it is an appropriate reflection of how segregated our friendship was from our normal lives. I had a unique friendship with John in which we would meet for a pizza whenever one of us was passing through town. We would always move directly into discussing the most personal details of our lives and get into the depths of our philosophical outlooks on the world. We would add in a few funny stories from the intervening time and then move back to our respected lives. Unlike my other friendships that often revolved around shared events, my friendship with John revolved around our conversations.

I had first met John when we played hockey together in Lincoln, but our real friendship developed as the years progressed. Although we were different people, our criticism of the world aligned. It is funny to look back on our early conversations and see how far we have come. I have a lot of admiration for many of my close friends but none more so than John. After his hockey career was derailed by injury, John left college and returned to work in his family's plumbing business. Although his life would later catapult into success, this was the period of John's life that was most impressive. It was during this period that his priorities were most evident and his dreams for the future were formed. I enjoyed watching John's success, but not nearly as much as I had enjoyed watching his pursuit. I liked hearing about the life he was living, but I had loved listening to those dreams before they came true infinitely more. Once again, it was the pursuit that was admirable more than the results, and it would have been just as admirable had his grand schemes failed completely. The first thing that was clear when John returned to work as a plumber was the purpose behind his decision. John had massive goals for his own life, but those came secondary to his goal of helping his father retire comfortably. I was in graduate school during most of this period so I didn't get to see Vads as often as I would have liked, but, every time I would visit, it would be clear how hard he was working. John worked over sixty hours a week for the plumbing company doing everything he could to take the stress off his dad's shoulders. It was a noble life choice that required a large amount of sacrifice from a person with numerous more lucrative options available. The sixty hours plumbing were just the beginning of John's work schedule. I have never met a person more driven to succeed. His success story is well established as the model of entrepreneurship, but most people have no appreciation for the struggle he went through before his success was realized. John was an inventor at heart, but it isn't easy for a middle class plumber to turn a good idea into financial success in the era of big business, and John took considerable risk to force his ideas into reality. A lot of my personal accomplishments have brought me pleasure, but I have never enjoyed anything as much as hearing about the success of John's first invention. I was so proud of his achievements and admired his decision to give the money from this first product to his father to give him the comfortable retirement he deserved.

The biggest irony of my friendship with John was the parallel trajectories of our lives. John made his first million the same year I published *Mom in Heaven*. It was interesting how closely the timing of our success aligned. We both developed fame separately, and yet our relationship remained unaltered. Our friendship always consisted of long conversations over a pizza or a couple beers whenever one of us would pass through town. It was awesome having this friendship with John, but it was kind of weird how separate it was from our real worlds. We were both famous for our respective accomplishments, but no one knew we were friends. The best example of this was one of the few times our professional lives collided when we were both booked on the same episode of *Real Time with Bill Maher*. I burst out laughing when I saw John backstage. When Bill asked if we had met, I smiled and proceeded to grab the joint from his hand while we shared a few laughs before the show. I always thought it was funny how we both became famous for our respective lives, but yet our friendship accidentally remained a secret simply because of its dynamic. We had always talked about getting off the grid and rejecting society, but that never seemed to happen as we both moved forward in our success. Although our lives were comfortable, neither of us had gotten completely out of the system. I knew John would be the one person who would truly appreciate my retirement plans, and he was also the only one I planned to tell.

My final visit with John was perfect. We started by entering immediately into our usual deep conversation. We talked about our reactions to things in the news, and then I heard about the three most recent girls John had fallen in love with. After a while, we moved to the subject of my life, and I informed John that I was finally getting off the grid. At first, he thought I was referring to one of my usual vacations where I would disappear for a while, but I corrected him and said I was leaving forever. John was completely overjoyed that I was finally getting away like we had always talked about. I could see he was envious that he wouldn't be joining me, but he was so locked into his empire that he had become a slave to his success. Luckily, that success allowed him to pursue his inventions so it was a somewhat welcome inconvenience. I spared John the details but assured him everything was set so I could never again be found once I was gone. The more I talked about my plans to live alone in complete relaxation, the more excited he got. After Vads listened to my plans and we finished our pizza, he finally stood up with a look of excitement and said, "Well, what the fuck? If you're leaving, this will be the last time I see you so we better have some fun."

Vads and I had enjoyed some good times together over the years, but I would never have guessed where this final visit would go. We had been enjoying a couple afternoon beers, and, before I knew it, we were drinking Blue Label with gorgeous flight attendants on our way to Amsterdam in John's plane. I had previously spent a couple weekends in Amsterdam, but they didn't come close to this trip. In fact, I think it is safe to say the plane ride to Amsterdam was already better than my previous visits as the flight attendants made for quite a party. When John went to the back room for his mile high meeting, I remember thinking that some things never change. Our weekend in Amsterdam was absolutely crazy and would have made Oscar Wilde rethink his position on deviance as we took things far beyond a healthy level. There could not have been a better way to end my final visits with friends than this epic conclusion. I planned to spend the rest of my life on an endless vacation, but I knew I would never to take another trip of this kind so it was nice to have one last wild weekend before I settled down for good. As we flew home, I thanked John for the retirement party, and we enjoyed one last intimate conversation before we parted ways for the final time.

When I returned from my trip, I took more than two weeks to recover from Amsterdam before I finally went to see Derbe and the Wagners in Traverse City. Because I had been spending so much time in Minnesota with my family and visiting other friends around the country, I actually hadn't seen Derbe since we had returned from the mission. I gave him a big hug when I arrived and could tell he hadn't yet recovered from the Cereal Killer's last act. I had been having so much fun that I had actually forgotten about my most recent murders until I saw Derbe's face. Derbe looked like he hadn't slept in months. It felt awful to see him so depressed, and I was thankful to be back to cheer him up. No matter how upset my friend would get with his job, I was always able to make him forget it all when I visited. Derbe and I picked up Angela and Jamie for dinner. On our way to their house, Derbe told me he was focusing all his attention on finding the Cereal Killer and vowed that he would catch him even if it was the last thing he ever did. I have never been as happy as the moment we arrived at the house and saw Jamie shooting pucks in the driveway. It was tough seeing Derbe struggling, but one thing he was incapable of doing was being upset around Jamie. Seeing Jamie immediately changed the mood and brought life back to my friend's face. I was thrilled to see Jamie again as he ran out to give me a big hug. It was amazing to look at that young man. Jamie was a senior in high school and was now bigger than me. He had grown into a man but never lost the gentle smile he had carried his entire life.

That night, we had a fantastic dinner. All four of us were excited to be back together. Jamie asked how long I was staying, and I told him I honestly didn't know. It was fun to have the old Derbe return for that dinner. We talked at length about Jamie's football season that was already underway as well as the upcoming hockey games that would soon be starting. When we finished eating, Angela quieted the table and told us that Jamie had an announcement to make. My ears perked up as I looked over at the shy smile on Jamie's face. Jamie then told us he had made a decision on college and had committed to play hockey and football at Harvard starting the following fall. I erupted with joy when I heard Jamie's decision. He had worked so hard to follow his dreams, and I was thrilled for him. Jamie continued and told us that he had also decided he was going to study medicine and become a doctor like his dad. My merriment turned to sentimental pride as I looked at this wonderful person sitting across the table from me. I raised my glass, and we toasted Jamie's success and the unlimited future he had ahead of him.

After dinner, we brought Jamie and his mom home, and I went for a drink with Derbe. I told him I would treat him to a night out because it was clear he needed to take his mind off the job. Dinner had done wonders for Derbe's mood, and I now had my old friend back. His stress wasn't totally gone, but his normal personality was now dominant. I listened to him speak and was reminded of what an admirable man he was. As I had made my rounds to visit my other friends, I was constantly looking for things I could do to make their lives better, but I knew Derbe could take care of himself. He was such a strong man that there was nothing further I could offer him other than to help catch the Cereal Killer which wasn't realistic. Instead of buying him a new house or giving him a lavish gift, I bought him a beer and simply thanked him for his friendship over the years. One thing that never changed was the pride I felt in having Derbe as my friend. I may have done some things he wouldn't have agreed with, but I cared deeply about him and always appreciated that he was there for Mike's family.

After spending that night with Derbe, my entire focus turned to Jamie. Since I was still in Traverse City, I saw Derbe daily, but our relationship already had the closure it needed so I wasn't concerned about finding a proper ending. The only person I had left to conclude things with was my favorite person in the entire world. It is hard to describe how proud I was of the person Jamie had become. From the moment he was born, I helped shape a world around him that allowed him to develop into a perfect person with a perfect life. I had been more successful in this endeavor than anything else I had ever done. Jamie was perfection personified in every way. My first week back in Traverse City was spent primarily in reflection. I struggled to think about moving forward with my retirement because the mere thought of leaving Jamie crippled me with fear. I spent that entire first week thinking back over his entire life and replaying each precious memory of watching him grow up.

As I looked back on Jamie's life, I had a hard time thinking of him moving into the real world. To me, Jamie would always be that bright eyed little boy who would race across the lawn with a big smile and jump into my arms as soon as I opened my car door on my visits. Jamie was an astonishing young man that had never lost the sweet nature that made me love him so much. In my eyes, he was still the young child that I had told could be anything he wanted when he grew up. Now that he had grown up, I hated the thought of letting him go. When I looked at Jamie now, I could see a mirror image of myself at his age. As much as I have grown as a writer and a philanthropist over the years, I have never been as beautiful of a character as I was at the peak of my dreaming. Jamie was now at the same point in his story, and the only difference between us was that he was a magnification of the things that had made me special. The person Jamie had grown into was a testament to what can be accomplished with enough attention to detail and a complete overdose of love. I had dedicated most of my life to ensuring Jamie's world was specifically shaped in order to give him everything he deserved. I am confident that B.F. Skinner himself would be incapable of matching what I had accomplished with Jamie. In truth, I don't even think there is a writer on earth who could create a character in fiction that matched the glory of Jamie in reality. He was truly a step above the rest of the world, and every moment I spent thinking about him brought me happiness beyond measure.

I had spent my life as an author of inspirational fiction, but the story I was most passionate about was the story I had been writing in real life. I now realized that I had reached the climax of Jamie's story, and he had achieved a greatness I could never have imagined when his story had begun. Jamie's reality had superseded my wildest hopes. He had incomparable character traits and an unmatched potential that casted a shadow over those of us lucky enough to stand in his presence and witness his life. It didn't matter what Jamie decided to do with his future because he was perfect at that moment. I wanted to find closure in my relationship with Jamie before I left for my retirement, but all I could do was sit there and watch his life with pride. It was ironic how much I admired that young man who had looked up to me his entire life. I had been Jamie's idol since he was a young child, and all he would ever talk about was being like me. Jamie wanted his success in life to make me proud. I honestly believe Jamie chose medical school simply because he knew how much it would mean to Derbe and me to see him follow his father's path. I had always been a positive influence on Jamie, but I ultimately hated the fact that he was striving so hard for something I knew from personal experience would never live up to his expectations. The world was simply not worthy of that perfect young man. I was proud of Jamie's accomplishments, but that was nothing compared to how proud I was of his character.

I began to think about Jamie's future and started to get a fearful feeling in my stomach. I knew the world he was about to enter, and it pained me to envision the inadequate routes his future could possibly take. Up until this point, I had looked on Jamie with such delight as I observed his greatness and reflected on my cherished memories with him. I had always focused on Jamie's potential and basked in the beauty of his dreams, but I had ignored the future he would one day encounter. He was the only character whose story I was writing in reality, and I had simply been afraid to address the inevitable climax that I should have been prepared for. I wanted closure on my relationship with Jamie so I could leave my life behind in peace and remember him as he was then. Unfortunately, I had to face the inconvenient truth that, no matter how beautiful it appeared, Jamie's story was written on the backdrop of reality, and it was just a matter of time before the rain clouds moved in. I loved Jamie more than anyone else in the world, and he was perfect. I had been writing Jamie's story for eighteen years, and the writer's block I was now facing represented the greatest adversary of my life. I wanted Jamie to have a happy ending, but I just couldn't see how that was possible in reality.

Years earlier, I had similarly been standing in Jamie's current position. I had the perfect future extending out in front of me and was likewise blinded by the illusion of happy endings. I had been showered with awards and was told I could be whatever I wanted. I found out the hard way that the dreams I had been striving for were nowhere near as incredible as I had hoped. I could see only two options for Jamie and neither was appealing. He could either have his dreams come true or he could have his dreams not come true. Neither one of those options led to the happy ending he deserved. If Jamie's dreams didn't come true, it would be a disaster. He had worked so hard, and any failures would be complete injustice. I saw how much success meant to Jamie as he wanted to live up to the standards set by his role models. What Jamie didn't understand was that his actual worth was within him. He was wonderful just for being himself, and I hated the idea in his mind that he had something to prove to the world. He was already better than anyone I had ever met. Jamie's ambition had the potential to destroy me as I knew the danger it posed to his future. On the other hand, I was even more afraid of the alternative of Jamie's dreams coming true. This was the path I had taken in my own life, and it had disastrous consequences to my character. The idea of Jamie being broken over not reaching his dreams tug at my heart, but the thought of him realizing those dreams were never worthwhile to begin with tore a hole through it. All I wanted to do was find a way to make Jamie the one character to live a happy ending in the real world.

Living in Traverse City during Jamie's senior year was the most emotionally bipolar time of my life. I fluctuated between jubilation and devastation as I enjoyed Jamie's present and feared his future. I was emotionally crippled, and, many days, I simply couldn't move. I cherished every minute of watching Jamie's hockey and just being present in his life, but, during the nights, I was tormented. I thought of every possible option for Jamie's future and simply couldn't find a path leading to happiness. I thought about taking him with me on my one way retreat from society, but even this peaceful life would have fallen short of the future he envisioned in his mind. Spending every day with Jamie allowed my appreciation for his intellect to grow ever greater, and it became clear he was too smart to ever end his life as an optimist. Jamie's beautiful delusions would no doubt be killed by the depth of his curiosity. He was truly happy in his current state as he looked out on the life in front of him. I cursed the fact that the real world guides one inevitably towards disappointment. Happiness is a temporary reality. A happy ending is too cliché to actually exist. All my thoughts were soon consumed with turning Jamie's happiness into his permanent state. I spent a long time living in denial of the truths of the world. Everything I had previously learned was no longer relevant as I thought about Jamie's life. I searched for any possible way to make Jamie's dreams come true, and, for a long time, I simply refused to believe what I knew to be true. Dreams are meant to exist in a person's sleep, not while the person is awake. Dreams are beautiful and fictitious and can overcome most anything but an alarm clock. My dream was to see Jamie happy forever.

The answer was obvious, but I didn't want to acknowledge it. This wasn't a new question; it was simply a new character. The world wasn't going to change just because this time it was Jamie. I loved him too much to acknowledge the only option I had to save his life. I was an emotional rollercoaster as my days were spent in bliss and my nights in distress. I was completely drained of all energy and spent most nights awake staring at the ceiling. Although I wanted it more than anything, I simply couldn't give him a happy ending in real life. Since the moment Jamie was born, I had wanted him to have a life above all others, and I had helped to create the remarkable person he was. My efforts were a major reason Jamie had lived a perfect life up until that point. I was now dumbfounded and helpless against his impending confrontation with reality. I soon became completely lifeless. I didn't want to move forward anymore. All I wanted to do was stop time. I didn't want Jamie's story to end, but I did want it to stop. It is a shame that an author doesn't have the option of stopping a story in the middle. No one wants to read a story without an ending. Unfortunately, a stop sign was the only thing that could have saved Jamie's perfection in the book of real life. I knew there was an obvious option, but I was crushed by the thought before it even entered my mind. Every time I began to comprehend the thought of killing this perfect character, my consciousness would freeze. I could never finish the thought. Both my mind and body were paralyzed by the notion of causing Jamie's timely death. Even as I sit here writing this chapter, I find it difficult to force my fingers to type each word. Writing about Jamie not only causes me to relive that painful period of my life, but it reminds me how repulsive the thought of a world without him truly is. Time has passed, but the fact I even thought about killing Jamie is just as horrific to me today as it was when I was contemplating it then.

I knew the only way to give Jamie happiness was to allow him to graduate into fiction. However, I refused to allow this to happen. I may have conquered my emotions in the past, but the thought of losing Jamie was a fear that I would be incapable of mastering. I justified my decision by arguing to myself that I had already written my final novel and was moving on with a new stage in my life. I was no longer an author so I didn't have to kill Jamie. The only problem with lying to oneself is that it is often hard to get away with. I told myself the same lie every day, but I couldn't avoid the reality of what was the right thing to do. I knew the hypocrisy behind my decision not to protect Jamie from his future, and my fear of watching him live was soon equal to my fear of watching him die. Sparing Jamie from death would be selfish and would destroy his story. I had to kill him, but I couldn't do it. I wished there was a god so that I could curse his name. I was filled with anger but had no outlet to unleash my frustration. My enemy was the harshness of reality, and it was a formidable foe with no weakness. I was at the lowest point in my life and saw no path out of the darkness.

This was the only time in my life that I allowed the rainclouds of tomorrow to block the sunny sky of my current day. I should have been completely focused on the beautiful status of my greatest character, but yet my mind was flipping ahead to chapters that had not yet been written. It was at this low point in my life that Jamie came to my rescue and saved me from the darkness I had fallen into. It was a day like any other. I met Jamie for a sandwich after school, and we talked for a while about the game that night. Jamie's lovable nature was contagious, and my visits with him were the only times I completely forgot my worries. It was a subtle comment that brought me back from the dead. Jamie was telling me about some of the things he wanted to do when he got to college. At one point, he paused in the middle of a sentence, looked across the table, and thanked me for always being there for him. When Jamie told me how lucky he felt to know I would always take care of him, it was truly the pinnacle of my life. At that instant, I felt like a complete coward for abandoning Jamie exactly when he needed me most. I loved Jamie more than words can express. I had taken care of him his entire life, but true love means more than being there when it is convenient. True love requires a willingness to sacrifice everything for the person you love. My conversation that day with Jamie reminded me of this, and I knew I had to give him the ending he deserved. I wasn't ready for the sacrifice I was going to make, but I knew I had to move forward regardless of my own feelings.

As I began thinking of a plan for Jamie's murder, I didn't really believe it was happening. When I had previously thought about the futures of my other characters, I always envisioned their endings in fiction, but I could only see Jamie's story as real. I forced myself to believe in the fantasy world I wanted to create, and I laid out plans for his future that never seemed the slightest bit fake. There was nothing untrue about the fiction I planned to write. I made up my mind, and, every day, I strengthened my resolve to see Jamie's perfect life reach the correct conclusion. I had overcome the hardest part of the process and was once again able to appreciate each moment for the blessing it was. I was living in the story of my greatest character which is a privilege most authors can only dream of. Each week brought new joys to my life as Jamie's success grew steadily. I will always treasure the nights spent watching Jamie's games and will never forget the jubilation as Angela jumped into my arms when Jamie scored the game winning goal in the state championship. There were too many cherished moments in that year to recount them all here, but they have continuously provided the joy in my life ever since.

Of all the highlights that I had the pleasure to witness in Jamie's life, none compared to his high school graduation. I looked to the event with anticipation, and, when the day arrived, I could barely contain myself. We spent the entire graduation day celebrating as we got ready for the ceremony in the afternoon. Jamie went to meet his friends a few hours early while we sat reminiscing about the remarkable young man we had watched grow up. That picture of Mike and Angela holding Jamie on Halloween seemed like a mere moment ago, and yet I was about to see that little baby graduate high school. Time drags on so slowly most days that it makes us forget how quickly it is actually moving. When I had first seen Jamie at the hospital after he was born, I felt as if I could never love someone as much as that baby boy. I could never have imagined the extent to which this love would continue to grow along with that child. Jamie had been a boy I wanted to take care of and had grown into a man I admired. Derbe, Angela, and I were overwhelmed with pride as we sat in the living room talking about Jamie. This was an emotional day for all three of us. Jamie was the most important person in our lives, and the thought of him moving away was bittersweet. We were proud of the person he had become but wanted to freeze the current moment forever. We knew Jamie was capable of doing amazing things, but our own lives had never been better than the present, and we wished to linger there forever. Graduation was a major milestone for Jamie, but it was also an important day in the lives of those who loved him. I had helped shape Jamie's world since he was born, and this was the day I had been helping him towards all these years. Of all the projects I have ever partaken in, Jamie was, without question, my masterpiece. He was perfect.

Walking into the gymnasium for Jamie's graduation gave me chills. We were early as usual so we mingled with a couple of Jamie's teachers and listened to them sing his praises. Everyone who had the pleasure of knowing Jamie couldn't help but be impressed. As I looked at the families of the other students, I felt pride in the fact that we knew the star of the show. The rest of the kids were simply extras in Jamie's story. There was no doubt that he was the main character. After visiting a little while, we found our seats in the crowd. As I waited for the ceremony to begin, the anticipation was almost too much to take. When I finally heard some commotion towards the back of the gym, I could feel my heart beating with an excitement I no longer knew in my own life. The only way my passion could now be aroused to this extent was through Jamie. I smiled as I heard his booming laugh coming from somewhere out of view and couldn't wait to see him walk down with the rest of the graduates. As Jamie and his classmates marched into the gym, his calmness stood out from the rest. The other students seemed nervous with the eyes of the crowd glued to them, but Jamie was right at home in the spotlight. Unlike the other graduating seniors, Jamie was bigger than the event. I was extremely proud as I saw him walking towards our spot in the crowd with a smile on his face. Instead of passing by like the rest of the group, Jamie broke away from the line, gave his mom a big hug, gave me a high five, and then sprinted back to catch up to his place in line. I am sure the class was under strict instructions to stay in formation, but the teachers just smiled when they saw Jamie's detour. This small moment demonstrated so much of Jamie's character and the love he conveyed to the world. If another student had jumped out of line, it would have caused a glance of disapproval from the teachers, but Jamie was held to a different standard. He wasn't looked down upon like the rest of the students in attendance, but, instead, they looked up to him with admiration just as I did.

As the ceremony began, my eyes remained fixed on Jamie sitting in the middle of the stage. I loved watching smiles come to the faces of those sitting next to him as he whispered comments that elicited laughter they struggled to suppress. In the entire time I had known Jamie, I couldn't recall ever seeing him without a smile, and his excitement during the graduation was just an amplified example of his constant character. As different speakers talked about the graduates' accomplishments, I reflected on how true the statements were in Jamie's case. Jamie was the epitome of what a graduation should represent. I was there to celebrate both what he had accomplished over the first eighteen years of his impressive young life as well as the fabulous future he looked out on. In my opinion, there has never been another graduate in the history of graduations that could compete with the quality of that young man. As the speaker talked about the future of the graduates, my mind turned to the hours I had spent listening to Jamie talk about his future plans after graduation. His vision for life was truly inspiring. The only thing greater than Jamie's future was his present. I looked up at him on the stage, and I knew there was nothing more he needed to accomplish to prove his perfection. The power of his ambition could never be matched by any actual accomplishment. He was already ideal in every way, and my love for him was beyond measure.

My mind wandered away from the ceremony as I drifted in thought about Jamie, but my focus soon returned as Jamie was called to receive his award for being Valedictorian. I could feel the tears of pride rolling down my cheeks as he smiled and shook the Principal's hand. Any thoughts I had about killing that perfect baby boy were stopped at that moment as I realized I could never go through with that devastating option. The crowd gave Jamie a standing ovation while I gave Angela a massive embrace and smiled as Derbe screamed with enthusiasm. The ceremony then continued until it was time for the main event. The last speech was to be given by the Valedictorian, and it was the moment I had waited for all day. As Jamie approached the podium, the crowd gave him another round of applause and then sat back awaiting his words. Jamie's speech touched my heart and was as follows.

> Thank you. I'm honored to have the opportunity to represent my fellow graduates and speak to you on this exciting occasion. I would first like to say congratulations to all of my classmates. I have known many of you my entire life, and it is a privilege to stand next to you today. I also would like to take a moment to thank all the family and friends in attendance.

This is as much a testament to your success as our own. Today, I would like to take a moment to talk to you about three things: the past, the present, and the future.

The first thing that comes to mind on a milestone occasion like today is how far we have come. As we stood in the back before the ceremony, I began to think about all the wonderful memories I have made over the last four years. There are far too many to share them all today, but, as I look out at your faces, I can honestly say you will all hold a special place in my heart for as long as I live. Well, maybe not Kyle, but the rest of you for sure. We have had a lot of fun over the past few years whether it was winning championships on the ice rink, drinking a few sodas at a party, or just sitting around complaining about our mean teachers. I won't name names, but you know who you are. Anyway, it has been a pleasure knowing you all, and I will cherish the memories we have made for the rest of my life. Thinking about the past, I would like to take a moment to talk a bit about my own history. I hope you'll forgive me for talking about myself, but I have had the privilege of living an incredible life and would be remiss if I didn't use this opportunity to take a look back and give credence to those who have made this life possible. Many of you simply know me as the resume Mr. Thomson read when I was introduced earlier. Although I am proud of the things I have accomplished, the real value of my past cannot be found within that resume. I have come a long way in my eighteen years, and the true accomplishments of my life have resided in the journey itself and the people who have made that journey possible. I have lived a privileged life that has given me so many advantages, but this nearly didn't occur as my life began with tragedy. When I was less than a year old, my father was brutally murdered and taken from me forever. Although I was too young to realize the tragedy that had befell me, the negative impact on my life was massive. My mother was devastated that the love of her life was gone and could easily have allowed this tragedy to signify the end of her and my life. My father's death was the greatest trial of my life, and I was too young to do anything to defend myself against it. My life could have been destroyed before it even really began.

Fortunately, this tragedy didn't define my life but instead highlighted the love of those left around me and the qualities of the father I lost. At my most vulnerable, I was saved by three people that have loved and looked over me my entire life. These three wonderful people are here with me today. The first person I want to thank is my mother. My mother was faced with the ultimate devastation a person could possibly confront, but she didn't falter. My mother had lost her husband, best friend, and love of her life, but she wouldn't allow her son to lose his mother along with his father. My mother didn't crumble in the face of her nightmare, but, instead, she confronted it head on. There hasn't been a single day in my life in which I haven't appreciated how fortunate I am to have such a strong and loving mother. All that I am has been a result of her dedication. I have received so much from my mother, but nothing has been as valuable as the unconditional love she has empowered me with. In all I do, I strive to make my mom proud with the full knowledge that she would be proud of me regardless. Everything I am I owe to my mother. Mom, I want to thank you for everything. I love you more than you will ever know.

The other major blessings in my life are the two fathers I inherited after my own father was killed. These two men, who are sitting next to my mother today, have been the backbone of my life and have given this fatherless child twice as many dads as his peers. I can't begin to express how much I love you both and how much I appreciate what you have done for my mother and me. Maybe I could find the adequate words to express my appreciation if I was an author like you, E, but I just hope you know my love for you two is never-ending. Not only have you both been father figures in my life, but you were kind enough to return my actual father to me as well. I grew up always wondering what my dad was like, and, thanks to you, I was able to know the man I never met. You gave me back the father that was taken from me, and I will forever be in your debt. Over the course of my life, I have come to find out that I had the greatest father in the world. My life appeared to start as a tragedy, but the ensuing years have taught me that my father was more powerful than death and his memory will never fade. I hope I can someday touch people to the same extent as my father so my impact will likewise outlast my existence. The message I wish to leave you about my past is the impact love can play in the world. There is no tragedy that cannot be overcome with enough love. I consider everything I have accomplished in my life to be a reflection of the amazing love and support I have received. To everyone who has helped me along the way: Thank you and I love you.

I now want to switch gears and talk for a moment about the present. I want you to know how much this moment means to me. I have received many honors in my young life, but the opportunity to speak for my classmates at graduation ranks amongst the greatest. As I look out on you at this moment, I am in awe at what I see. What impresses me most is not the things you have achieved but rather the type of people you are. I hope you can all take a deep breath, appreciate how far you have come, and truly enjoy this moment. On days like today, we so often move from one thing to another in a whirlwind, and, before we know it, we'll be sitting together at our twentieth reunion wondering where the years went. Although it will soon be gone, I want you to know how happy I am right now and how much I admire you all in this current moment. We will all soon be going our separate ways and never be together again, but we are here now, and I can think of nowhere I would rather be. I wish I could linger in this moment with you forever which is no doubt what some of you are thinking this speech is doing already. So I guess I must, as we all must, move on to the future, but, before I do, I just want to end this moment by saying I hope you all take time on this day of looking forward to enjoy the present and extract all possible pleasure out of each moment as it comes. Once a moment is gone, it is gone forever.

And now for the real reason we are gathered here today, the future. Nothing captures the spirit of a graduation ceremony as perfectly as a discussion about the future. As I thought about giving this speech, the first thing I asked myself was what I could possibly tell you about the future. I am barely old enough to vote, and the majority of my experiences have yet to be had so there is no doubt I know a lot less about life than many in attendance today. However, the one thing I do know is that the future belongs to us. We can't freeze time and stop the future from arriving, but we do have the ability to create the future that we are moving into. No matter how helpless the world may appear at times, I have no doubt that each and every one of you has the potential to change the world. One day, years from now, when you are old men and women sitting at home, you will look back and ask yourself if you are proud of the life you lived. You have the potential to do anything, but you also have the potential to do nothing. It is up to you to choose your own path. I hope you all choose the path that leads to making an impact on the world. For better or for worse, I hope you shape the world around you rather than allowing the world to shape you. Don't sit back and be a spectator of life when you were born to be center stage. So many people cower away from life in fear of failure, and they end up living their entire lives in caution. A life guided by caution leads to one merely existing without really living. If you follow your dreams and choose to attack life with your full force, there is nothing that can stop you. My entire life, I have been told that I could be anything I wanted when I grew up. Before today, that statement was meant to inspire our dreams. After today, it is up to us to make those dreams into our reality. I truly believe every one of us has the ability to make our dreams come true. I am confident that I can achieve anything I set my mind to as long as I am willing to work for it. There are no limits to the heights we can soar. I would fly to the gates of heaven itself if it weren't for the perfect world I've already been blessed with on earth. Our dream world doesn't have to be a dream. I hope you all fight to make your dreams come true and never settle for anything less than the ideal. Now is not the time for practicality. We have forever to be realistic. Now is the time to strive for the impossible. The only limitation you will ever face is the limitation of your own imagination. If you can dream it, you can do it. I stare into the face of eternity, and I do not fear the unknown. I look to my future with a smile.

I appreciate the attention you have given me. It has been an honor to stand amongst you today. I wish you all the absolute best in your futures and hope you understand how much I love you. I want to thank you for being the people you are and hope you never lose whatever it is that sets you apart from the rest of the herd. And, with that, I set you free from this speech and send you all off to create that future you have been waiting for your entire life. Thank you.

It is impossible to fully express my reaction to Jamie's speech. As I listened to his words, blood rushed to my heart and tears formed in my eyes. He was such a grounded young man, and I was so proud of him. What stood out above everything else was the vastness of Jamie's optimistic dreams. Hearing Jamie talk about his future was no revelation as I had spent hundreds of hours with him and admired his outlook on the future more than I admired any other single quality in any of my characters. Jamie was a dreamer, and it was these impeccable dreams that had tormented me for so long as I contemplated the dire fate he was bound to encounter in reality. I wanted Jamie's comments in the speech to be true. I wanted him to live his dreams. I wanted his future to be only limited by his imagination. However, I knew the only way this would be true was if I used my own imagination to create a world in which his imagination could reign supreme. As the crowd clapped for Jamie's speech, my body was emotionally overloaded, and I was unable to do anything except give Angela a gentle hug as we wiped the tears from each other's faces. The graduation moved on to the diplomas, but my mind couldn't be removed from Jamie's words and the thought of his dreams coming true. Giving Jamie a happy ending was my primary goal in the world, and I struggled to distract my mind into thinking about anything else.

After the ceremony, I did my best to realign my focus on the present moment. I gave Jamie a massive embrace when he came out of the gym and never wanted to let go. I took a break from worrying about his eternal happiness to enjoy his present happiness. It was a feeling of jubilation as the mood began to change from sentimental to celebratory. Even Angela, who had been an emotional pendulum, began to transition into laughter as the inspirational speeches were replaced with funny stories. It took about an hour outside the gym before all the families were content with the number of pictures they had taken. We then made our way back to Angela's house to get ready for the party. We had scheduled Jamie's graduation party for the night of the ceremony and planned an ambitious celebration. I like to think I was a positive influence on many aspects of Jamie's life, but, if nothing else, I know for sure that it was nice to have a millionaire friend when came time to throw a party.

When we returned to the house, the caterers had everything ready, and all that was left to do was pop the champagne. I poured glasses for Derbe, Angela, Jamie, and a couple of his closest friends who came to have a few drinks before the real party started. I made a toast to Jamie's future and told the boys the only advice I would give them was that, "Life is like a dick: When it's hard you get fucked, but when it's not you can't beat it." The sentimental part of the day was officially completed, and the party had begun. People slowly started showing up, and, before I knew it, the entire backyard was filled with people dancing to Jamie's favorite band that I had hired for the night. I was glad to see the graduates enjoy the party, but the only thing I really cared about was making sure Jamie was having a good time, and his smile left no doubt.

It was an amazing evening. After about an hour, the party was getting really wild and Angela came up to me with a concerned look on her face to ask what we should do about all the underage drinking. I personally didn't care if the kids were drinking since there were plenty of chaperones. As far as I was concerned, they deserved to have a fun night. Instead of responding directly to Angela, I pointed at Derbe who was absolutely plastered on the dance floor. I said we were probably safe since the most respected police officer in the state, and possibly the country, was looking over the party. I told her if anyone gave us any trouble we would leave the explaining to him. At that moment, the band started playing a cover of one of Angela and my favorite songs so I asked her if she wanted to dance. One of my most cherished memories of the night was when we were dancing and Jamie came up to her and said, "Mom, make sure you save the last dance for me." He then ran back into the crowd and continued enjoying the party. That little comment meant so much to his mother, and she was incapable of hiding her joy. Watching her response melted my heart, and, later that evening on my request, the band called Angela and Jamie to the stage for the final dance of the night for which they played, "Save the Last Dance for Me." This final dance was a sweet moment that can never be taken away from Angela and Jamie. I was reminded of the look on Angela's face years earlier when she had danced with Mike on the night he died. It was a different type of love in her eyes, but the amplitude of the emotion was just as strong.

The final song of the evening is the only memory I choose to think about from that wonderful party. I enjoyed the entire night, but no other moment could compare to watching Angela dance with her incredible grown up son. After the band was finished for the evening, we slowly began shutting down the party and getting the kids home safely. Although we didn't have any issues with underage drinking, we did run into one drunken problem when it came time to shut down the party. Derbe, my best friend and the most responsible man I have ever known, was completely uncontrollable. It was nearly impossible to get him to stop screaming at the top of his lungs. He went on and on about how proud he was of Jamie and, the more we tried to convince him to sit down, the more confrontational he became. Jamie loved watching this man he admired stumble around the backyard as a drunken mess, and I kept joking about the fact that the biggest lightweight at a high school party turned out to be the middle aged detective that had once referred to himself as two hundred ten pounds of solid steel sex appeal but was now just two hundred fifty pounds of rusted metal. Derbe chirped me back while Angela did her best to help convince him to call it a night. Finally, I took the one approach that has never failed and tricked him into joining me for a late night meal on our way to his house. As I drove Derbe home, we laughed the whole way. With the help of his third wife, Aimee, I got Derbe upstairs to his room and returned to Angela's house to join Jamie and his best friend by the fire.

I sat with the boys for about two hours before Angela finally came out and told them it was time for bed. We had one of the officers from Derbe's precinct give Kyle a ride home, and Angela went up to tuck Jamie into bed like she had done when he was a little boy. She then returned to the fire, and the two of us reflected on the wonderful day we had just experienced. I have had many intimate conversations with Angela over the years, but this conversation about Jamie and the conversation about Mike during our vacation to Greece were the two that rose to a completely different emotional state. In these moments, the extent of our connection grew into a different dimension. There are very few moments in life in which it feels as if all separation between you and another person have been removed and you are free to communicate completely unobstructed as if you are of one mind. My conversation with Angela on the night of Jamie's graduation was exactly like this. We were both in the mood for this type of conversation after a day filled with sentimental moments. We had listened to Jamie's speech at the graduation, watched him receive his diploma, and then celebrated his success at a party surrounded by pictures of his childhood. I was constantly aware of the large image of Mike and Angela holding Jamie as a baby that was looking over the party the entire night. During my conversation with Angela, we started by talking about how proud Mike would have been but didn't linger long on his absence. We already had closure on that topic, and both of us had come to the realization that Mike was in fact present on that day. Instead, our conversation centered on our pride in Angela's son and the love we shared for him. As our discussion progressed, it became clear that Angela shared the same concerns for Jamie's future as I did. It is a scary thought for a parent to watch a child leave home. Angela loved her son and was proud of the person he had grown into, but she was worried the world could fall short of his expectations or lead to hardships that she didn't want him to bear. There is nothing more helpless than a parent envisioning a child's future. Angela had seen the devastation life could offer firsthand, and the thought of Jamie going through similar hardships was her biggest fear. My conversation with Angela allowed us to share our feelings about Jamie even though she knew there was nothing that could be done to change his fate. As Angela put it towards the end of our talk, "whether we like it or not, he is on his own now."

I hated the thought of Jamie being left to face the harsh world on his own, but I could do nothing to comfort Angela's mind. All I could do was be there as a friend to show her the love and understanding she needed to gain control over her emotions. After this precious conversation was complete, Angela went to bed, and I took a moment by myself under the stars. I sat alone for a while thinking about the amazing day I just experienced. I was in an emotional mood, and it was hard to keep a thought in my head. I have spent many nights in reflection, but this evening was one of the few in which my reflection was more emotional than intellectual. Instead of thinking about Jamie as I had done for the past eighteen years, I allowed myself to only feel for him. There was no questioning the depth of my love for that amazing kid, and I was elated to have watched his perfect day. He deserved everything in his life, and I was thankful to have played a role in helping him achieve that reality. In addition to my feelings about Jamie, I spent some time reflecting on Angela's life. I was moved by our conversation and thankful she had been able to experience this wonderful day. As much as she shared my worry for Jamie's future, she also shared my happiness with his present. I lingered by that fire for a while completely overcome with the love I had for Mike's family before I was finally able to close the chapter of Jamie's graduation and feel completely satisfied with his life.

After about an hour of sitting under the stars alone with my thoughts, I made my way into the house. Before I went to bed, I went into Jamie's room to take a look at that beautiful young character sleeping peacefully in his bed. I looked down at his head resting on the pillow with a slight smile on his face. I had peered in on Jamie sleeping on many nights since he was a baby, and it always brought comfort to my soul. I have never loved anyone more than that young man I watched asleep dreaming in his bed. I walked over to Jamie, gave him a gentle kiss on his forehead, took a deep breath, and murdered him.

Jamie died a peaceful death. He felt no pain and was allowed to drift off into his dreams as he slept. I killed him at the height of his glory and looked down at his peaceful body with love. Jamie was my masterpiece. He lived a perfect life and died right on time. I had been pained by the world that Jamie would have to endure in reality, but that fear would no longer be able to come true. There had been no pain in Jamie's life, and now there never would be. There wasn't even pain in Jamie's death. As far as the world would ever know, his heart simply stopped beating as he passed away comfortably in his sleep. I left no signs of murder, and there was no reason for an investigation. Jamie's death would only be cause for the celebration of a young man whose perfection could never be matched. I had dedicated my life to giving Jamie the story he deserved, and I had finally fulfilled my task. There was no question Jamie was the greatest character I would ever put into fiction. I had searched for the perfect final novel before, but, to my surprise, that final story had been staring at me the entire time. I had always known how the story had to end, but I simply didn't want to write it. Jamie was the perfect counterweight to end my career and balance out the two characters it had begun with. I had known all along what the right course of action was, but I was gripped by the fear of ending Jamie's life and thus unable to come to terms with it until the time arrived and I had no other choice. I could never have allowed Jamie to experience a single ounce of pain that I could prevent. It was for this same reason that he was killed peacefully in his sleep. It was appropriate for Jamie to die dreaming. Jamie died dreaming so that his dreams would never die.

After I killed Jamie, I crumbled to my knees by his bed and held him in my arms one final time. I was overjoyed for Jamie but immediately fell into misery for myself. I had lost the most important person in my life, and the pain was unbearable. It took every ounce of my strength to pull myself off that floor and make my way to my bedroom. I fell onto my bed and wondered if I would ever get up again. I didn't sleep one second that night but just stared depressingly at the ceiling and awaited the terrible news that I would soon be receiving in the morning. The news came sooner than expected as I heard a scream from upstairs around seven. I knew that throbbing voice well and wondered what he was doing at the house so early. Derbe had gone to check on Jamie and found him dead in his bed. I was later thankful fate had spared Angela from this role but was unable to feel any positive emotions when Derbe came into my room and told me Jamie had died. I immediately crumbled into darkness and wouldn't return for a long time.

The day after Jamie's death is a complete fog in my memory. I would have loved to console Angela, but I was overcome by my own depression and simply couldn't function. I was completely lost. This was the only day of my life in which I didn't utter a single word. I suffered in silence as there was nothing I could say to change fate. As I agonized through my despair, I thought about everyone I had killed over the years, but my mind mostly revolved around Mike and Jamie. Killing both of them was the right decision, but yet my reaction to the two kills could not have been in greater contrast. Before I killed Mike, I had been worried about my emotional response. I wondered if I would regret my decision, but, instead, I found myself feeling reinforced afterwards. I was proud of what I had accomplished and was able to see Mike's life for the entirety of the story. Things were different with Jamie. I knew I had done the right thing, but I couldn't take pleasure in the results of my actions. I didn't feel the good vibrations that filled my mind after killing Mike. All I could feel was despair as the image of holding that beautiful little boy in my arms was stuck in my mind. I cried for years after I killed Jamie. Jamie's death ended his life while it was still perfect and would lead to his eternal happiness in fiction, but yet my life had been shattered by the loss. Jamie's death saved his life while destroying the life of his murderer. There was no amount of rational reflection that could overcome the emotion. I was completely incapacitated with grief and struggled to move even an inch in the aftermath of Jamie's death.

Although I would like to say that the first day after Jamie's death was the hardest, I soon found that the sting of this loss would not be lessened by time. As days stretched to weeks, my suffering was not even slightly mitigated. People would try to contact me or comfort me, but I wouldn't acknowledge the presence of anyone else in my life. I sat alone and suffered in a way I didn't know was possible. Jamie was the person I loved above all others from the moment his eyes opened in that delivery room to that final breath I watched him take before he died. Without him in the world, my life no longer seemed worth living. Unfortunately, death no longer seemed worth dying either. There was nothing I wanted in my life and no release from the agony I was experiencing. I was trapped in torment and saw no end to my tragic story. As I think back on this period, it is clear that killing Jamie proved two things. The first thing I proved in killing Jamie was that I still lacked complete intellectual control over my emotions as was evident by the emotional hole I was thrown into after his death. The second thing I proved in killing Jamie was the power of my love for him. My love for Jamie overruled all my other emotions and allowed me to kill him. Unlike my other kills which were rationalized into action, it was my love for Jamie that finally allowed me to end his life. I had already been in agony at the thought of killing him, and this period of tear-filled torture was simply an amplified version of my prior feelings before the murder. I had hoped the knowledge of my impact on Jamie's future would provide consolation to ease my emotions, but this was not the case. My life was destroyed, but at no point did I ever question if I had done the right thing. Jamie's fate meant infinitely more than my own, and I would be willing to sacrifice my own happiness a million more times if it meant he would be sheltered from a tragic ending and able to live his dreams forever.

As I struggled to come to terms with my loss, I began to transition into writing Jamie's story. I knew he deserved to begin his life of fiction as soon as possible so I quickly set out to write his book. Of all the stories I have ever written, Jamie's was the easiest storyline to develop and the hardest story to write. He was the perfect character, and there was no imagination needed to conclude his story, but yet I labored to press each letter on my keyboard. I was writing my magnum opus, and my internal struggle to complete the novel was the hardest task of my life. It took nearly six months after Jamie's death to finish *Dream On*. I had always told Jamie he could be anything he wanted to be when he grew up, and, as it turned out, he instead became everything he wanted to be. The lack of limitations that Jamie described in his final speech provided the foundation for his eternity. *Dream On* was an impeccable novel because there had never been a more perfect life to write about. Jamie's was a story about following one's dreams and making sure they come true. *Dream On* was the novel I had always wanted to write. It was by far my best book. I just never imagined that I would be writing this perfect story in complete sadness.

Once I finished *Dream On*, I sent it to my publisher and then retreated to my solitude. There isn't much to say about this next period in my life other than the fact that I was overcome by devastation. For a long time, I simply didn't know what to do with each moment. The passion I had for living had died along with the purpose in my life. I was completely without direction. Finally, I gave up on myself altogether and instead put my attention back into other people. I came to the conclusion that there was no remedy for my sadness so I simply tried to use each day to stop the sadness in other people. I immersed myself back into my charity and started spending every day helping the kids at my different youth centers. Perhaps I was unconsciously trying to distract myself from my predicament or maybe I was searching for dreams that could remind me of Jamie. Regardless of what drove me to devote so much time to helping kids during this period, it turned out to have an extremely positive effect. It was a long time before I was able to overcome my sadness, but at least I was distracted for those twelve to fourteen hours a day when I was working with the kids. Every one of them would remind me of Jamie, but I would be too busy to linger long on those thoughts before something else would distract my attention. My life stretched on this way for more than three years. It is safe to say this was by far the darkest period of my life, and all the thanks I received for my charity work fell on deaf ears. Nothing could make me feel good about a world without Jamie. There is no doubt I took Jamie's death harder than anyone including his mother and Derbe. They were also devastated, but the darkness of my despair dwarfed any discomfort they could possibly have imagined.

I am thankful that my despair led me to spend more time with my charity, but I didn't actually get closure on Jamie's death until I was finally able to embrace Angela and Derbe again. I had run away from their lives as I cowered under the weight of my own torture. There was nothing any of us could do to comfort the others, and the sight of one another would simply bring us to tears. Finally, we went our separate ways to deal with the loss on our own terms. I was doing my best to regain the composure in my life, but it took years before I was once again comfortable in my emotions. Two events that helped me along this process were the first time I saw Derbe and Angela again after a long time apart.

These first encounters occurred on separate occasions but were similar in nature. The first of these interactions was with Angela. It was about three years after Jamie's death, and I hadn't seen Angela since six months earlier at Christmas. Even then, when we had spent the holiday together, the distance between us had remained. We didn't give gifts, and there was no laughter that year. We simply sat quietly and stared at our food as we ate Christmas dinner. On the night I first saw Angela again, I had just returned from the youth center around seven and was eating some cold left-overs for dinner. I settled into the usual foul mood that filled my evenings during this time as I sat at my kitchen table in silence. When I first heard the knock on the door, I simply ignored it and hoped whoever it was would leave me alone. I didn't want to respond to the world. I only wanted to be left alone. When the knocking continued, I finally sauntered over to answer. I opened the door and saw Angela standing there with tears in her eyes, a smile on her face, and a copy of *Dream On* in her hands. Angela looked at me for a moment and then embraced me with all her strength. Other people may have believed the book was fiction, but Angela could recognize her son anywhere and reading his happy ending was the only thing that kept her heart from stopping. From that day forward, I never saw Angela without a copy of *Dream On* sitting by her side. She clung to Jamie as I clung to Fantasia. Angela and I shared a common bond in that the people we loved most lived only in fiction.

The rest of that evening was spent listening to Angela thank me for writing that beautiful story. It was a nice evening that is better in hindsight than it was at the time. Angela had been moved by the novel so much sooner than me. I wasn't yet ready to accept the beauty of Jamie's story because I hadn't finished my grieving process. However, although Angela's visit didn't change my feelings immediately, it started me down the path towards acceptance that I could only later appreciate. I was still hurt, but I did draw some comfort from knowing that my novel had not only set Jamie free but also acted to ease Angela's suffering as well. I have no doubt in my mind that Angela left happier that day than she had been at any moment since Jamie's death, and it soon became clear that she went to give Derbe a copy of *Dream On* as well.

About a month after Angela's visit, it was Derbe who arrived at my door. Derbe had also been devastated by Jamie's death, and, for the first time in my life, I wasn't there to cheer him up because, this time, I was destroyed more than he was. Just like me, Derbe had been left to suffer alone. It had been a long time since either of us had smiled. When Derbe read my book, hope was returned to his life. Derbe had been the first one to discover Jamie's dead body, and that image was the only thing he had been able to see until he read *Dream On*. Derbe went on at length about how much he loved the notion of Jamie becoming a fairytale and said it had brought him the comfort he needed to move on. I told Derbe that I didn't believe in fairy tails and asked him to leave. In a way, I guess I was glad to see Derbe smiling again, but I was just too bitter to acknowledge that feeling. Derbe and Angela were learning to live again, but I was still completely shattered. I became angry at the fact that it was my noble action that had given Jamie his perfect eternity, but yet I was the one that was unable to enjoy myself. I guess it just goes to show that no good dead goes unpunished.

It took another year after Angela and Derbe's visits before I recovered from Jamie's murder. I spent that time in a state of complete depression while reliving every moment of my time with Jamie. I remembered every single birthday from his first to his last. I must have repeated every conversation between us hundreds of times. It took a long time, but, after four years of tormenting rumination, I was able to once again see Jamie's life for the beautiful story it was. It was a dreadful process, but, at the end of the journey, it was all worth it. If you had told me ahead of time that I would have to be tortured continuously for four years in order to make Jamie's dreams come true, I would have done it in a heartbeat. I would choose eternity in hell to give him even a brief moment in heaven. I had saved the greatest character for my final novel, and my work as an author was finally complete. Thanks to my sacrifice, Jamie would now be able to dream on forever.

CHAPTER 20

To Write a Wrong

Here at the turn, I must leave you.

-The Prestige

CHAPTER 20: To Write a Wrong

Orson Welles once said, "If you want a happy ending that depends, of course, on where you stop your story." After I published *Dream On* and came to grips with the conclusion of my career as a writer, it was time for my story to end. I had a successful career that concluded with my final masterpiece. I was proud of my life's work and thankful that I had found a way to use my talents to make the world a better place. I had lived a remarkable and unexpected life and now found myself at the end of my journey looking back. I would never write another novel, but I decided to write one final book, my autobiography.

As I mentioned at the beginning, I set out with the aim of telling the entire truth behind my novels. I had spent the last few years of my life in complete despair, and, one day, it was simply lifted off my shoulders. I saw a picture of my mom and a letter she had written to me before she died. I had read this letter many times over the years, but, in the aftermath of murdering Jamie, my response had changed. I stared into her face and finally broke down in tears. My spirit was fractured, and I had regressed back to that little boy who was completely at the mercy of his emotions. I felt a mix of guilt and disappointment as I festered in these feelings for a few days, but, mostly, I was just sad. Finally, it went away. Unlike the notable mental breakthroughs one has in life, emotional changes come without explanation. I found myself completely at peace. I had run out of tears, and the torment I had endured seemed to float away without warning. This emotional comfort reminded me so much of my dad's description of the day that he finally got over my mom's death. The loss was never completely gone, but the grief was replaced with cherished memories. Fortunately, I had the added comfort of knowing that those I lost were in a better place. I could feel my spirit improving, and I decided to read *Dream On* for the first time in my life. I had written the story in a single draft and hadn't even looked back to edit it. After the final line was written, I had broken down. I had then sent the book to my publisher and didn't open it again until I finally returned to it when my grieving was coming to a close.

Reading Jamie's story completed my return to happiness in the same way it had done for Angela and Derbe. Jamie's story reminded me how writing can transcend the tragedies of the real world and turn heartbreak into everlasting happiness. During the past few years, I had been living in reality and couldn't pull myself out of the emotional hole I had fallen into. That was now changed as I set out to write the story of my own life. I emerged from that period of internal turmoil with the realization that it was my work as an author that set me apart. I never denied the presence of pain in the world. I just chose to create an alternative world in which my characters wouldn't have to suffer the consequences of nature. The motivation behind my work as both an author and a murderer was always love. I searched for characters I admired and killed them because I wanted to give them a better life. It was not a lack of empathy that caused me to kill people. In fact, it was actually empathy that drove me to commit these murders. Nothing in the world saddens me more than a person with a beautiful face and a sad expression. Pain always has a way of shining through a forced smile. Every time I see a person who fits this description, I am reminded of the value of my writing. There is no plastic surgeon in the world who can take the sadness of time out of a person's face the way I can with my words. I am proud of every character I have written about and wouldn't change a single part of my career. I will love these characters for the rest of my life, and I find comfort in the fact that they will all be alive long after my bones have turned to ash.

Another question that comes to mind when I think about my past is how I arrived at the place I am today. When I was an optimistic young dreamer shooting pucks in my driveway as a child, I never would have thought I would spend my life writing books and murdering people I loved. My naïve dream was to simply play hockey and have a nice family. Instead, I lived an infinitely more valuable life that changed the world for so many people in so many wonderful ways. I could never have predicted the selfishly altruistic person I would become. I spent my youth thinking about my own life, and it wasn't until I started writing that I became completely addicted to helping other people. I hope I have been successful in at least giving an accurate glimpse of the altruistic author who turned his sympathy for those he admired into eternity for those he created. My life was never meant to be remembered. The purpose of my life was for others to be remembered, and, in that sense, I have succeeded beyond measure. The credit for this success lies not with this author but with the quality of my characters themselves. I was simply a vehicle to carry their histories into eternity. The value of the stories was entirely a property of the inspirational characters.

The purpose of this book was to describe the motives behind my novels, but I would be remiss if I didn't at least mention how thrilling it can be to kill a person and the adrenaline rush one gets before, during, and after a murder. The buildup to committing murder is incredible. The volatile cocktail of anticipation and fear creates an extraordinary excitement like a kid awake in bed on Christmas Eve. The feeling of actually killing a person varies from victim to victim but the first time you kill a person is a truly unique exhilaration that I'd advise everyone to experience at least once. Of all the emotional responses I can remember from the first time I committed murder, the one that stands out most was a certain type of poetic feeling as I watched a life vanish from the earth in front of my eyes. The final part of a murder is the chronic thrill that follows forever after. So much of my life was spent on the edge. I knew every knock on my door could potentially be the end of my freedom. The funny thing about this reaction is the fact that it peaks immediately after the murder and then slowly fades as time goes on. Although it never goes away completely, the feeling approaches dormancy with each passing day. Every time I killed a new character, my level of concern would skyrocket before I eventually returned to equilibrium after a few days. Even though I understood the comedy in my temporally activated fear, there was no way to avoid this emotional response, and I actually came to enjoy it as my career progressed.

For those of you who might still doubt the logic that guided of my work, I want you to remember how many dreams I have made come true. Every story I have written has ended in happiness. If any of you think murder is completely wrong regardless of the situation, I urge you to think about the one person you love more than anyone else in the world. Picture that person dead and think about how you would feel. Now picture that same person, but, instead of being dead, they are lying on the floor whimpering in agony. They are crying out for help, but help never comes. The more they struggle, the more their torture increases, and the more helpless they become. They scream for mercy while you helplessly watch them tortured in front of your eyes. When the physical torture couldn't possibly get any worse, their children are dragged in front of them and beaten beyond all recognition. They scream out for help, but no one is listening. I could go on endlessly with this storyline, but you get the point. Perhaps I should go on for another fifty pages to give a better example of true torture. Real torture doesn't last for two minutes like it does in the movies. Actual torture is much more painful and lasts much longer. The description of death only took one painless line to write. To those of you who believe death is the worse of these two options, I can only say I am repulsed by your lack of morality. I have feared the torture of those I love infinitely more than their death. Anyone who lives long enough will inevitably face the torture of reality. It might not be as outwardly graphic as the physical torture just depicted, but the effects are even more brutal. When I saw my characters heading toward these painful conclusions, I chose to intervene. There is no suffering after death. I used death to release them from their future failures. I then used fiction to go a step further and give them the happiness they deserved. It was because I loved the people I killed that I killed the people I loved.

Although murdering people triggered some strong emotions, the true enjoyment in my life has always come from writing. Helping ease someone's suffering would have been useless without a vehicle to replace that pain with pleasure which is exactly what writing allowed me to do. In the past few months, as I have sat writing this autobiography, I have taken the time to look at the stories of all of my victims sitting on my shelf and think about the amazing lives they are now living. My books have given me a large amount of personal wealth and admiration, but my true pleasure has always come from the knowledge that my characters will be flourishing in the minds of readers for years to come. I had the pleasure of meeting many wonderful people in my life and the privilege to control their destinies. I was given a choice for them between an imperfect reality and a perfect fiction, and I made the decision to give them happily ever after. I found it easy to finish off each story with the cliché happy ending that fulfilled their dreams. In reality, nothing repulses me more than an inspirational story. Even my own novels would probably repulse me if they were claimed to be non-fiction. However, the endings in my stories differ from those other happy endings that I deride for their utter impossibility. My happy endings, although taken on face value by the public, were the penance of my actions. The stories I wrote weren't vain attempts to emotionally captivate a reader, but, in reality, they were a final act of mercy towards the characters themselves. If I had simply murdered them, it would have been wrong, but the parting gift was more than adequate compensation for the lives I ended. I always accepted that the world might think what I did was wrong. I just hope my stories show people that, no matter what you do, it is always possible to write a wrong.

So here we are at the end of my story. There is nothing left to say about the life I lived. The only question remaining is how it all will end. I have always said that there is nothing less believable than a happy ending in our world. In my previous books, I have been able to get away with happily ever after because those were books of fiction. Unfortunately for me, this story is real. Although I doubt everyone will be disappointed to see my life end, those of you who care should have seen it coming when you decided to read a non-fiction book. Perhaps some who disagreed with my actions will take comfort in the conclusion. I value poetic justice and have decided this will be my only book without a happy ending. Every character I have written about was killed in real life but lived forever in their story. The only poetic justice would be for their murderer to die at the end of his own story. This will be my only book in which the main character dies. I am not killing myself out of regret but rather to give justice to those I have murdered. I ended their earthly lives and gave them eternity in their books so it is only appropriate that my own book ends in death. I finished my final bowl of cereal at the beginning of this paragraph and will be dead in less than five minutes. I don't fear my own death because I have comfort in knowing the people I love will live forever. Every story must end. This is the end of my story. This is the end of my life.

Made in the USA
Charleston, SC
02 December 2012